A QUANTUM
MURDER

Tor Books by Peter F. Hamilton

Mindstar Rising
A Quantum Murder
*The Nano Flower**

*forthcoming

A QUANTUM MURDER

PETER F. HAMILTON

A Tom Doherty Associates Book
New York

A QUANTUM MURDER

Copyright © 1994 by Peter F. Hamilton

A Tor Book
Published by Tom Doherty Associates, Inc.
175 Fifth Avenue
New York, NY 10010

Tor Books on the World Wide Web:
http://www.tor.com

Tor® is a registered trademark of Tom Doherty Associates, Inc.

Library of Congress Cataloging-in-Publication Data

Hamilton, Peter F.
    A quantum murder / Peter F. Hamilton.—1st Tor ed.
        p.   cm.
    "A Tom Doherty Associates book."
    ISBN 0-312-85954-6 (acid-free paper)
    I. Title.
PR6058.A5536Q36   1997
823'.914—dc21   97-19600
                                                            CIP

First Tor Edition: November 1997

Printed in the United States of America

0 9 8 7 6 5 4 3 2 1

Acknowledgments

ALTHOUGH IT IS MY NAME which appears on the cover of this book, there are a few behind-the-scenes merchants who share the responsibility for placing it there. So my thanks go to Nicholas Blake, co-conspirator extraordinaire, who started the whole ball rolling. Simon Spanton, for finally providing a steadying hand on the shaky tiller of the publishing trade. Jo Fletcher, who placed her great personal experience at my disposal for some critical passages. And my agent, Antony Harwood, for pushing when it was needed most.

A QUANTUM
MURDER

I⟨T WAS THE THIRD⟩ T̲HURSDAY in January, and after a fortnight of daily drizzles, the first real storm of England's monsoon season was due to arrive sometime in the late afternoon. The necklace of Earth Resource platforms that the Event Horizon corporation maintained in low Earth orbit had observed the storm forming out in the Atlantic west of Portugal for the last two days: the clash of air fronts, the favorable combination of temperature and humidity. Multi-spectrum photon amps tracked the tormented streamers of cloud as they streaked toward England, building in power, in velocity. The satellite channels had started issuing the Meteorological Office warnings on the breakfast 'casts. Right across the country, in urban and rural areas alike, people were hurrying to secure their property and homes, lead animals to shelter, and protect the crops and groves.

Had the Earth Resource platforms focused on the county of Rutland as the dawn rose, any observer would have been drawn to the eastern boundary, where the vast Y-shaped reservoir of Rutland Water was reflecting a splendid coronal shimmer of rose-gold sunlight back up into the sky. The Hambleton peninsula protruded from the reservoir like a surfaced whale, four kilometers long, one wide. Hambleton Wood was sprawled across a third of the southern slope, its oak and ash trees killed off by the torrid year-long heat of the Warming that had replaced the old seasons. The rotting trunks were now besieged by a tangled canopy of creepers and ivy, carrion plants feeding off the mulchy bark of the once sturdy giants they choked. Another, smaller, expired copse lay broken on the northern side, adding to the general impression of decay. But a good half of the remaining farmland had been converted to citrus groves, sprouting a vigorous green patina of life. The peninsula was an ideal location to grow fruit; Rutland Water provided unlimited irrigation water during the parched summer months. Hambleton itself, a hamlet of stone houses with a beautiful little church and one pub, nestled on the western side, the whale's tail, above a narrow split of land that linked it with the Vale of Catmose. There was a single road running precariously along the peninsular spine; grass and weeds nibbling away at the edges of the tarmac had reduced it to a barely navigable strip.

At quarter-past nine in the morning, Corry Furness turned off the road a kilometer past Hambleton, freewheeling his mountain bike down the sloping track to the Mandel farmhouse, tires slipping dangerously on the damp moss and loose limestone.

Greg Mandel caught a glimpse of the lad from the corner of his eye, a slash of color skidding down the last twenty meters of the slope into the farmyard, clutching frantically at the brakes. Greg had been out in the field since half-past seven, planting nearly thirty tall saplings of gene-tailored lime trees in the sodden earth, binding them to two-meter-high stakes that he hoped would given them enough anchorage to withstand the storms. When it was finished, the lime grove would cover half a hectare of the ground between the farmhouse and the eastern edge of Hambleton Wood. The planting should have been safely completed a week ago, but the saplings had arrived late from the nursery, and the mechanical digger he was using had developed a hydraulic fault that took him a day to fix. He still had two hundred trees left to put in.

Greg had thought his early start would give him enough time to finish at least fifty before lunch: he was already resigned to carting the rest into the barn until the storm passed. But watching Corry barely miss the side of the barn, then shout urgently at Eleanor, who was painting the ground-floor windows, he knew even that small hope had just vanished. Eleanor pointed at him, and Corry ran over the shaggy grass.

Greg switched off the little digger and climbed out of the cab, Wellingtons squelching in the mud. He was on the last row, just twenty saplings and stakes left to go. They were all laid out ready. Patchy clouds tumbled across the sky, and the reservoir's far shore gleamed from last night's rain, wisps of mist already rising as the day's heat began to build.

"Sir, sir, Dad sent me, sir," Corry shouted. The lad was about ten or twelve, his face ruddy from exertion, fright and exhilaration burning in his eyes. "Please sir, they're going to kill him, sir!" He slithered the last two meters, and Greg caught him.

"Kill who, Corry?"

Corry struggled to gulp down some air. "Mr. Collister, sir. There's everybody up there at his house now. They're saying he used to be a Party Apache."

"*Apparatchik*," Greg corrected grimly.

"Yes, sir. He wasn't, was he?"

Greg started walking toward the farm. "Who knows?"

"I liked Mr. Collister," Corry said insistently.

"Yeah," Greg said. Roy Collister was a solicitor who worked in Oakham, an unobtrusive, pleasant man. He came into the village pub most nights. Someone who moaned about work and the price of beer and inflation. Greg had shared a pint with him often enough. "He's a nice man." And that's always the worst thing about it, Greg thought. Four years after the People's Socialism Party fell, ending ten years of a disastrous near-Marxist-style government, people found it hard to forget, let alone forgive the misery and fear they had endured. Hatred was still simmering strongly below the surface of the nation's psyche. As for Collister, Greg had seen it before: the allegations, the pointed finger. One hint, one whispered suspicion, was all it took: the serpent of guilt never rested after that, gnawing at people's minds. Even the informants working for the People's Constables weren't as bad; at least they had to produce some kind of evidence before they got their blood money.

Eleanor was already backing the powerful four-wheel-drive English Motor Company Ranger out of the barn when he reached the yard. It was a gray-painted farm utility vehicle, with a squat, boxy body on high, toughened suspension coils; the marque was the first of a new generation, powered by Event Horizon giga-conductor cells instead of the old-fashioned high-density polymer batteries.

She gave him a tight-lipped look that said it all. It took a lot to upset Eleanor.

They had been married just over a year. She had been twenty-one years old the day she walked down the aisle of Hambleton's church, seventeen years younger than he, although that had never been an issue. Her face was heart-shaped, liberally splattered with freckles; a petite nose and wide green eyes were framed by a mane of thick red hair that she brushed back from a broad forehead. Physically, she was an all-out assault on his preferences. An adolescence spent on a PSP-subsidized kibbutz where manual labor was emphasized and revered had given her the kind of robust figure a channel starlet would kill for. Eleanor didn't see it quite in those terms, though she had come to accept his unending enthusiasm and compliments with a kind of bemused tolerance. Even now, dressed in a paint-splattered blue boiler suit, she looked superb.

Greg climbed into the Ranger's passenger seat and shut the door. "I want you to walk back into the village," he told Corry. "Will you do that for me?" He didn't want the lad to witness the lynch mob, whatever the outcome was.

"Yes, sir."

"And don't worry."

"I won't, sir."

Eleanor steered the Ranger out of the farmyard and onto the track, moving expertly through the gears as the tires fought for traction on the treacherous surface.

"Did you know about Collister?" she asked.

"No." Which was odd. Not even his intuition had given him an inkling. And it should have. Intuition was one of his two psi faculties that were educed by neurohormones.

It was the English army that had given him a bioware endocrine-gland implant, a sophisticated construct of neurosecretory cells that consumed his blood and extravasated psi-stimulant neurohormones under the control of a cortical processor.

He had been transferred out of his old parachute regiment when the combined services' assessment test graded him ESP positive and shoved straight into the newly formed Mindstar Brigade, along with five hundred other slightly befuddled recruits. Psi-stimulant neurohormones had been demonstrated the year before by the American DARPA office, and Mindstar was the Ministry of Defense's eager response to the potential of psychics providing the perfect intelligence-gathering corps. An idea the tabloid channels swiftly dubbed "Mind Wars." It was a pity nobody paid much attention to the number of qualifiers in the early DARPA press releases.

Based on the assessment test results, Mindstar expected Greg to develop an eldritch sixth sense, a continent-spanning X-ray sight that could locate enemy installations, no matter how well concealed. Instead, he became empathic. It was a useful trait for interrogating captured prisoners, but hardly warranted the million and a half pounds invested in his gland and his training.

He wasn't alone in disappointing the Mindstar brass. The assessment tests only indicated the general area of a recruit's ability; how a brain's actual psychic faculties would develop after a gland was implanted was beyond prediction. The results were extremely mediocre: very few Mindstar recruits produced anything like the performance expected. The brigade had been reluctantly disbanded a few months before the PSP took its ideological knife to the defense budget.

Greg's claims that his intuition had also been enhanced by the gland were discounted by the sounder minds of the general staff as typical squaddie superstition. He shrugged and kept quiet: never volunteer for anything. But intuition had saved him and his tactical raider squad on more than one occasion when he saw action in Turkey.

So why hadn't it given him any forewarning about Ray Collister?

"Nobody expects you to be perfect," Eleanor said quietly.

He nodded shortly. She could plug into his emotions with the same efficiency as his espersense rooted around in other people's minds.

"I'll bet Douglas Kellam is leading the pack," he said. Douglas Kellam, who fancied himself in the role of local squire, the village's loudest anti-PSP Momus. Now it was safe to speak out.

"From the rear, yes," she agreed.

He grunted wryly. "Who would have thought it, you and I rushing to rescue an *apparatchik.*"

"But we are though, aren't we? Instinctively. It's not so much what Collister was, but what Kellam's mob will do. There'll be hell to pay the morning after, there always is."

"Yeah."

"But?"

"What if he turns out to be one of the high grades?"

"He won't," she said firmly. "You would have known if he was anything important."

"Now there's confidence." He hoped to God she was right.

The EMC Ranger lurched out onto the road. Eleanor gunned the

accelerator, wheels tearing gashes in the tarmac's thin moss covering.
Fans of white spray fountained up as they shot through the long pud-
dles that lay along the ruts.

Greg looked out of the window. On the other side of the reservoir's broad southern prong he could see the Berrybut Spinney timeshare estate sitting on the slope directly opposite the farmhouse. It
was set in a rectangular clearing above the shoreline, a horseshoe of
wooden chalets with a big stone clubhouse and hotel at the apex. The
spinney was a mix of dead trunks festooned with creepers and new
trees, tanbark oaks, Californian laurels, Chinese yews, and other va-
rieties imported from tropical and subtropical zones as the year-
round heat killed off native vegetation. Their shapes and colors were
strange in comparison to the glorious old deciduous forests that occupied so many of his childhood memories.

The hurriedly enacted One Home Law had enabled the local council to commandeer the chalets and hotel to provide emergency accommodation for people displaced from low-lying coastal lands by
rising seas. He had spent the PSP decade living in one of the chalets,
telling people he was a private detective, a perfect cover occupation
for someone with his ability. He even managed to attract a few paying cases to add authenticity. Then a couple of years after the PSP's
demise, Eleanor came into his life, and at the same time the gigantic
Event Horizon Company hired him to clear up a security violation
problem. The case had turned out to be far more complex and involved than anyone had realized at the start, and the bonuses and fa-
vors he and Eleanor were given by its extremely grateful owner, Julia
Evans, were enough to retire on—enough for their grandchildren to
retire on, come to that. Multi-billionairesses, especially teenage ones,
he reflected, had no concept of gracious restraint, certainly not when
it came to money.

It left him and Eleanor with the problem of what to do next.
Lotus-eating was fine, they both agreed, providing it was in the context of a break from real life. They had sunk some (a fraction) of their
money into the rundown farmhouse with its neglected fields and
moved in after their honeymoon, both of them eager for the kind of
quiet yet busy life the citrus groves would give them.

He could see a pile of ash just below the chalets, a pink glow still
visible. The residents lit a bonfire each night, using it to bake food

and as a focal point for company. An undemanding style of life; not quite the archetypical poor but happy existence, but damn close. Geography wasn't all the move across the water entailed.

A horse-drawn cart, piled high with bales of hay, was clumping slowly down Hambleton's main street as they drove in. Eleanor swerved round it smoothly, drawing a frightened whinny from the mud-caked shire horse and a shaken fist from the driver. If it wasn't for the glossy-black solar panels clipped over the slate roofs and a clump of well-established coconut trees in the churchyard, the hamlet could have passed as a rural scene from the nineteen-hundreds. Gardens seemed to merge lazily into the verges. Tall stumps of copper beech and sycamore trees lined the road, festooned in vines that dangled colorful flower clusters; a frost of greenery that brought a semblance of life to the dead trunks. But only from a distance; wind, entropy, and vigorous insects had already pruned away the twigs and smaller branches, leaving frayed ends of pale-gray, sun-bleached wood jutting out of the shaggy hide.

Roy Collister's home was one of the smaller cottages a couple of hundred meters from the Finch's Arms. It personified the retirement-cottage dream: gentrified during the end of the last century, yellow-gray stonework pointed up, windows double-glazed, brick chimney-stacks repaired. More recently it had acquired a row of solar panels above the guttering to provide power after the gas and electricity grids were shut down at the start of the PSP years. Three bulky air conditioners had been mounted on the side wall to cope with the stifling air that invariably saturated the interior of pre-Warming buildings. The front garden was given over to vegetable plots, and the fence had disappeared under a long mound of gene-tailored brambles, with clumps of ripe blackberries as large as crab apples hanging loosely.

Greg was already opening his door as Eleanor drew up outside. He was vaguely aware of pale faces in the windows of the houses opposite, interested and no doubt appalled by what was going on, but not doing anything about it. The English way, Greg reflected. People had learned to keep their heads down during the PSP decade; avoiding attention was a healthy survival trait while the Constables were on the prowl. A habit like that was hard to snuff.

The wooden gate through the dune of brambles was swinging slowly to and fro on its hinges, and two of the ground-floor bay windows had been smashed. When he reached the front door, he saw the wood around the lock was splintered; judging by the marks on the paintwork, someone had taken a sledgehammer to it. There was the sound of angry voices inside.

Greg walked into the hall and ordered a low-level secretion from his gland. As always, he pictured a lozenge of liver-like flesh nestled tumor-fashion at the heart of his brain, squirting out cold, milky liquids into surrounding synapses. In fact, neither gland nor neurohormones looked anything like the mental mirage, but he'd never quite managed to throw off the idiosyncrasy—Mindstar psychologists had told him not to worry, a lot of psychics developed quirks of a much higher order. His perception shifted subtly, making the universe just that fraction lighter, more translucent. Auras seemed to prevail, even in inert matter, their misty planes corresponding to the physical structures around him. Living creatures glowed. A world comprising colored shadows.

There were twelve people in the lounge, making the small room seem oppressively crowded and stuffy. Greg recognized most of them. Villagers, that same quiet, friendly bunch in the pub each night. Frankie Owen, the local professional dole-dependent and fish poacher, leaning on his sledgehammer, resting after a bout of singularly mindless destruction. He had set about the furniture, smashing up the Queen Anne coffee table and oak-veneered secretaire and dresser; the three-meter flatscreen on the wall had a big frost star dead center. Expressing himself the only way he knew how. Mark Sutton and Andrew Foster, powerful men who worked as laborers in the groves, were sitting on Roy Collister behind the overturned settee. The slightly built solicitor's clothes were torn, his face had been reduced to pulped flesh, cuts weeping blood onto the beige carpet.

Clare Collister was being held by Les Hepburn and Ronnie Kay. Greg hadn't seen much of her since he moved into the farm, she didn't venture out very often; an ordinarily prim thirty-five-year-old with rusty brown hair and a long face. She had obviously been struggling hard, one eye was bruised, swelling badly, her blouse was torn, revealing her left breast. Les Hepburn had a vicious grip on the back of her head, knuckles white with the strain of forcing her to watch her husband being beaten.

And of course Douglas Kellam, chief cheerleader, standing in the tight circle of onlookers, a forty-five-year-old with a round face, slender mustache and fading brown hair, dressed in blue trousers and white shirt, thin green tie. Smart and respectable even now, although his face was flushed from the kind of exhilaration Greg was wearily familiar with: the thrill of the illicit. Douglas was the descendant of the original Victorian toff, a master of duplicity. Perfectly suited to attending a charity dinner, then going on to a pit-bull fight, watching Globecast's Euroblue channel at night, condemning it by day.

The jeering and shouting cut off dead as Greg stepped into the lounge. Andrew Sutton froze with a fist cocked in midair, his knuckles wet with Collister's blood, looking up at Greg, suddenly pathetic with guilt.

With his espersense expanded, the group's emotions impinged directly into Greg's synapses, a clamor of blood-lust and anger and secret guilt. They were feeding off each other, building up a collective nerve for the finale. It would end with a shotgun blast, the cottage set on fire, consuming bodies and direct evidence. And the police would turn a blind eye; overstretched, undermanned, and still trying to regain public trust, to shake off the association with the People's Constables. They couldn't afford to be seen taking sides with PSP relics.

"What the fuck do you think you're doing?" Greg asked, and there was no need to force a tired tone into his voice, it came all too easily.

"The bastard's Party, Greg," someone called.

"No messing? Have you seen his card? Was it signed by President Armstrong himself?" He was aware of Eleanor coming to stand behind him. Her presence sparked off a ripple of severe agitation in the minds around him.

"He's guilty, Greg. The Inquisitors said he was an *apparatchik* over in Market Harborough."

"Ah . . ." he said. The Inquisitors (actually, the Inappropriate Appointee Investigation Bureau) had been set up by the New Conservative government to purge PSP appointees from Civil Service posts, where it was feared they would deliberately misuse their positions to stir up trouble in their own interest. Identifying them had turned out to be an almost impossible task; a lot of records had been lost or destroyed when the PSP fell. Nearly all the old Party's premier grades had been routed out, they were notorious enough in their own areas for the Inquisitor teams not to need official datawork; but the small fry, the invisible Party hacks who did the committees' groundwork, they were hard to pin down. A lot of suspect names had been leaking from the Inquisitors' office lately. Rough justice eradicated the tricky problem of no verifiable evidence.

"An official charge has been brought against him, has it?" Greg asked.

"No," Douglas Kellam said. "But we've heard. Bytes that came straight from the top." His voice changed to a slicker, more appealing tone. In his mind there was still the hope that he could win through, a refusal to admit defeat. And nervousness that was beginning to churn up through his subconscious, like all of them, all disquieted by Greg and the infamous gland.

Sometimes, Greg reflected, an unending diet of tabloid crap could be useful. He smiled humorlessly. "Sure they did. Your cousin's friend's sister, was it?"

"Come on, Greg. He's Red trash, for Christ's sake. You don't want him around Hambleton. You of all people."

"Me of all people?"

Kellam squirmed, searching round for support, finding none. "Christ, Greg, yes! What you are, what you did. You know, the Trinities."

"Oh. That." No one in Hambleton had actually mentioned it out loud before. They all knew he had been a member of the Trinities, Peterborough's urban predator gang, fighting the People's Constables out on the city's sweltering streets; the stories, fragmented and distorted, had followed him over the water from the Berrybut estate. But the New Conservatives, as a legitimate democratically elected government, could not officially sanction the massive campaign of hardline violence that had helped rout the PSP. So Greg's involvement had earned him a kind of silent reverence, a wink and a nudge, the only gratitude he was ever shown. As if what he had done wasn't quite seemly.

"Yeah, me of all people," he said deliberately, looking round the troubled faces. "I would have known if Roy was Party. Wouldn't I?" They began to shuffle round, desperately avoiding his eye. The high-voltage mob tension shorting out.

"Well, is he?" Kellam asked urgently.

Greg moved forward. Collister was groaning softly on the floor, fresh blood oozing out of the gashes that Foster's heavy rings had torn. Foster and Sutton exchanged one edgy glance, and hurriedly scrambled to their feet.

"Do you really want to know?" Greg asked.

"What if he is?" Kellam said.

"Then you can call the police and the Inquisitors, and I will testify in court what I can see in his mind."

Kellam gave a mental flinch, stains of guilt blossoming among his thought currents. Panic at Greg's almost casual reminder that he could prize his way into minds, triggering a cascade of associated memories.

"Yes, sure thing, Greg, that's fine by me."

There was a fast round of mumbled agreement.

Greg pursed his lips thoughtfully, and squatted down beside Roy Collister. He focused his espersense on the solicitor's mind. The thoughts were leaden with pain, sharp stings of superficial cuts, heavier dull aches of bruised, probably cracked, ribs, nausea like a hot rock in his belly, warmth of urine between his legs, the terror and its twin, the knowledge that he would do anything, say anything, to make them stop, a bitter tang of utter humiliation. His mind was weeping quietly to itself. There was little rationality left, the beating had emptied him of all but animal instinct.

"Can you hear me, Roy?" Greg asked clearly.

Saliva and blood burped out from between battered lips. Greg located a small flare of understanding amid the wretched thoughts.

"They say you were an *apparatchik*, Roy. Are they right?"

He hissed something incomprehensible.

"What did he say?" Mark Sutton asked.

Greg held up a hand, silencing him. "What were you doing in the PSP decade? Don't try and speak, just picture it. I'll see." Which wasn't true, not at all. But only Eleanor knew that.

He counted to thirty, trying to recall the various conversations he and Roy had had in the Finch's Arms, and rose to his feet. The lynch mob stood with bowed heads, as sheepish as schoolboys caught smoking. Even if he said Collister was guilty, there would be no vigilante violence now. The anger and nerve had been torn out of them, sucked into the black vacuum of shame. Which was all he had set out to do.

"Roy wasn't an *apparatchik*," Greg said. "He used to work in a legal office, handling defense cases. Did you hear that? Defense work. Roy was supporting the poor sods that the People's Constables brought into court on trumped-up charges. That's how he was tied in to the government by your bollock-brained Inquisitors, his name is on the Market Harborough legal affairs committee pay-slip package. The Treasury paid him for providing his counseling services."

The silence that followed was broken by Clare Collister's anguished wail. She ran over to her husband, sinking to her knees, shoulders quaking. Her fingers dabbed at his ruined face, slowly, disbelievingly, tracing the damage; she started to sob uncontrollably.

Douglas Kellam had paled. "We didn't know."

Greg increased the level of his gland secretion, and thought of a griffin's claw, rigged with powerful stringy muscles and tendons, talons black and savagely sharp. Eidolonics took a lot out of him, he had learned that back in his Mindstar days: his mind wasn't wired for it, which meant he had to push to make it work. On top of that, he hated domination stunts. But for Kellam he'd overlook scruples this once. He visualized the talon tips closing around Kellam's balls. "Goodbye," he said, it was a dismissal order. Black needles touched the delicate scrotum.

Kellam's eyes widened in silent fright. He turned and virtually ran for the door. The others filed out after him, one or two bobbing their heads nervously at Eleanor.

"Oh sweet Jesus, look what they've done to him," Clare groaned. Her hands were covered in blood. She looked up at Greg and Eleanor, tears sticky on her cheeks. "They're animals. Animals!"

Greg fished round in his overall pockets for his cybofax. He pulled the rectangular palm-sized 'ware block out, and flipped it open. "Phone function," he ordered, then told Clare: "I'll call for an ambulance. Some of those ribs are badly damaged. Tell the doctors to check for internal hemorrhaging."

She wiped some of her tears with the back of a hand, leaving a tiny red streak above her right eye. "I want them locked up," she said, fighting for breath. "All of them. Locked up for a thousand years."

Greg sighed. "No, they didn't do anything wrong."

Eleanor flashed him a startled glance. Then understanding dawned, she looked back down at Clare.

"Nothing wrong!" Clare howled.

"I only said Roy was innocent," Greg said quietly.

She stared at him in horror.

"When the ambulance comes, you will leave with it. Pack a bag, some clothes, anything really valuable. And don't come back, not for anything. If I ever see you again, I will tell Douglas and his friends exactly whose mind is rotten with guilt."

"I never hurt anybody," she said. "I was in Food Allocation."

Greg put his arm round Eleanor, urging her out of the lounge. The sound of Clare Collister's miserable weeping followed him all the way down the hall.

Eleanor kissed him lightly when they reached the EMC Ranger. There was no sign of the lynch mob. Nor the watching faces, Greg noted. The only sound was the birdsong, humidity gave the air an almost viscid quality.

"Are you all right?" she asked. Her lips were pressed together in concern.

His head had begun to ache with the neurohormone hangover that was the legacy of using the gland. He blinked against the sunlight glaring round the shredded clouds, combing his hand back through sweaty hair. "Yeah, I'll live."

"That bloody Collister woman."

"Tell you, she's probably right. Food Allocation was a little different from the Constables and the Public Order Ministry."

"They took away enough of the kibbutz's crops," Eleanor said sharply. "Fair and even distribution, like hell."

"Hey, wildcat." He patted her rump.

"Behave, Gregory." She skipped away and climbed up into the Ranger, but her smile had returned.

Greg slumped into the passenger seat, and remembered to pull his safety belt across. "I suppose I ought to sniff around the rest of the village," he said reluctantly. "Make sure there aren't any premier-grade *apparatchiks* lurking around in dark corners."

"That is one of the things we came here to get away from." She swung the EMC Ranger round the triangular junction outside the church, and headed back the way they came. "You and I, we've done our bit for this country."

"So now we leave it to the Inquisitors?"

Eleanor grunted in disgust.

They met Corry Furness on the edge of the village. Eleanor stopped the Ranger and lowered her window to tell him it was all right to use his bike again.

"Mr. Collister wasn't one of them, was he?" Corry asked.

"No," Greg said.

Corry's face lit with a smile. "I told you." He pedaled off down the avenue of dead trees with their lacework of vines and harlequin flowers.

Greg watched him in the mud-splattered wing mirror, envying the lad's world view. Everything black and white, truth or lie. So simple.

Eleanor drove toward the farm at half the speed she'd used on the way in, suspension rocking them lightly as the wheels juddered over the skewed surface. The clouds on the southern horizon were starting to thicken.

"You'll have to give me a hand to get the lime saplings into the barn when we get back," Greg said. He was watching the way the loose vine tendrils at the top of the trees were stirring. "I'll never get them planted before the storm now."

"Sure. I've nearly got the undercoat finished on all the first-floor windows."

"That's something. It's going to be Monday before I'm through with the saplings. After this downpour it'll be too wet to get into the field for the next couple of days, and then we'll have to spend Sunday clearing up, no doubt."

"Better make that Tuesday. We've got Julia's roll-out ceremony on Monday," Eleanor said. "That'll cheer you up."

"Oh, bugger. I'd forgotten."

"Don't be so grumpy. There are thousands of people who would kill for an invitation."

"Couldn't we just sort of skip the ceremony?"

"Fine by me, if you want to explain our absence to Julia," she said slyly.

Greg thought about it. Julia Evans didn't have many genuine friends. He was rather pleased to be counted amongst them, despite the disadvantages.

Julia had inherited Event Horizon from her grandfather, Philip Evans, a company larger even than a kombinate, manufacturing everything from domestic music decks to orbital microgee-factory modules. Two years ago she had been a very lonely seventeen-year-old girl; wealth and a drug-addict father had left her terribly isolated. Greg had got to know her quite well during the security-violation case. Well enough for her to be chief bridesmaid at his wedding. Julia, of course, had been thrilled at the notion of adding a little touch of normality to her lofty plutocrat existence. The mistake of asking her had only become apparent when he and Eleanor had left for their honeymoon.

Every tabloid gossipcast in the world had broadcast the pictures. Greg Mandel: a man important enough to have the richest girl in the world as his bridesmaid. More millionaires than he knew existed wanted to be friends with the newlyweds; buy them drinks, buy them meals, buy them houses, have them as non-executive directors.

Julia had also developed a mild crush on him for a while. A hard-line ex-urban predator and gland psychic, the classic romantic mysterious stranger. Of course, he had done the decent thing and ignored it. Hell of a thing, decency.

Greg found he was grinning wanly. "I don't want to try explaining to Julia."

NICHOLAS BESWICK LOOKED OUT OF his mullioned window, watching a near-solid front of thick woolly clouds slide over the secluded Chater valley. It was midafternoon, and the storm was arriving more or less on time. The warm rain began to fall, a heavy gray nebula constricting oppressively around the ancient Abbey.

His room faced west, giving him a good view out over the long gentle slope of grassy parkland that made up that side of the valley. But the brow was no longer visible; in fact, he was hard pressed to see the road slicing through the park outside the front of the building, beyond the deep U-shaped loop of the drive. Mist was struggling to rise up from the grass, only to be torn apart by the deluge of hoary water.

There would be no swimming in the fish lakes this evening, he realized ruefully, no opportunity of seeing Isabel in her swimsuit. The daily swim had become an iron-cast habit for the six students; Launde Abbey didn't have any outdoor sport pitches or indoor games courts, so they clung to whatever activity they could make for themselves with a grim tenacity.

The lack of facilities had never bothered him. He had been at the Abbey since October, and he still found it hard to believe he had been admitted. Launde Abbey was looked upon as a kind of semi-mythical grail by every university physics student in England: the chance to study under Dr. Edward Kitchener.

Kitchener was regarded by most of his peers as the Newton of the age, a double Nobel Laureate for his work in cosmology and solid-state physics; his now-classic molecular interaction equations had defined a whole range of new crystals and semiconductors that could be produced in orbiting microgee factories. The royalty payments from the latter work had made him independently wealthy before he reached forty, which also kicked up the embers of envy among his colleagues whose work tended more to the intellectual. Nor did it help that he was slightly unconventional in the way he approached his subject matter; at his level of theorizing, physics verged on philosophy. He considered he had a perfect right to intrude on the country of the mind, to develop new aspects of thought processes. It had led to some fierce disagreements with the psychology establishment, and he didn't always confine his arguments to the pages of respected journals—critics were often subjected to an open tirade of abuse and scorn at scientific conferences. Then twenty-two years ago, after nearly twenty years of ill-tempered confrontation with his fellow theorists, he had, with characteristic abruptness, resigned from his position at Cambridge and retreated to Launde Abbey to pursue his theories without carping interference from lesser minds, his brilliance and loud vocal intolerance of the dry, crusty world endemic to academia creating a media legend of bohemian eccentricity in the process.

When psi-stimulant neurohormones were developed seventeen years ago, he awarded them an unqualified welcome, saying they gave the human mind direct access to the cosmos at large, presenting physicists with the opportunity to perceive firsthand the particles and waveforms they had only seen on paper and in projection cubes. Even after it became clear that neurohormones couldn't produce anything like the initial over-optimistic results predicted, he never lost his conviction. Psi, he contended, was the greatest event in psychics since relativity, exposing hitherto unquantifiable phenomena. Simply defining the mechanism of psi in conventional terms was enough to fascinate him, a rationale that would tie up nature and supernature, something beyond even the elusive Grand Unification theory.

This tenuous goal was one to which more and more of his time was devoted. But every year he invited three degree students into his home for an intensive two-year session of lectures, research, and intellectual meditation.

And childish tantrums, Nicholas had discovered, at first to his embarrassed surprise, and then with secret amusement. Even the most brilliant of men had character flaws.

Launde Abbey wasn't just about profound reasoning and scaling new heights of metaphysics. The human dynamics of six young people cooped up with an increasingly crotchety sixty-seven-year-old was weird. Fun, but weird.

Nicholas could now see a tributary network of steely rivulets coalescing on the grassland, trickling across the road and running down the slope into the first of the three little lakes to the north. The rain was incredibly heavy, and Globecast's news channel said it would last for six or seven hours. The River Chater at the bottom of the valley would flood again; it was probably up to the rickety little bridge already.

There was some sort of vehicle crawling along the road, heading down toward the river. He frowned and peered forward, nose touching the chilly glass. It was a rugged four-wheel-drive Suzuki jeep. Probably the farmer who leased the park's grazing rights checking to make sure he'd rounded up all the sheep and llamas.

Lightning burst across the valley, ragged sheets of plasma ripping the gloom apart. It revealed the small powder-blue composite geodesic dome sitting like some baroque technological sentry on the brow of the valley. Nicholas could see a couple of the hexagonal panels were missing. The gravity wave detector that it housed was now long abandoned. In the height of summer, sheep used the dome for shade.

Another bout of lightning erupted overhead, vivid blue-white forks lashing down, giving him the impression that the sky itself was fracturing. One of the flashes was bright enough to dazzle him and he jerked back from the window, fists rubbing the blotchy purple afterimages from his eyes.

Thunder rattled the glass. The farmer's vehicle had gone. Humidity was steaming up the windows.

Nicholas abandoned the monsoon with a reluctance rooted in a perennial child-awe of the elements. He turned on the air conditioner to cope with the rampant humidity, punched up some Bil Yi Somanzer from his music deck, then retreated back to his desk. His room was on the top floor of the Abbey, a large L-shape, with old but expensive furniture. It had a small private bathroom at one end. The bed was a large circular affair, easily big enough for two, which often made him think of Isabel on sleepless nights. There was an array of large globular cacti in red clay pots on a copper-topped table below the window; he was mildly worried that he wasn't watering them properly, there had been no sign of the flowers Kitchener told him to watch out for.

He hadn't brought much to the room himself, a couple of big rock-band holoprints, his music deck, reproduction starcharts, some reference books (paper ones); his clothes didn't take up half of the drawer space in the solid oak chest, and the wardrobe was almost empty. He had been too nervous back when he arrived to bring much in the way of personal possessions, unsure what liberties Kitchener would tolerate—after all, the Abbey was nothing like student digs. Of course, now he knew the old boy didn't care what the students did in their rooms, or at least claimed he didn't.

Bil Yi's *Angel High* thumped out of the speakers, drowning the sound of the storm in howling guitar riffs. Nicholas activated his desktop terminal; it was a beautiful piece of gear, a top-of-the-range Hitachi model with twin studio-quality holographic projection cubes. He used the keyboard to access the CNES mission-control memory core in Toulouse and requested the latest batch of results from the *Antomine 12* astronomy satellite platform. A map of gamma-ray sources began to fill one of the cubes, and he called up his frequency analysis program. It was a marvelous sensation, being able to punch a data request into any public-access memory core on the planet without having to worry about departmental budgets. Back at the university, a request like this one would need to be referred almost back up to the dean. Kitchener's data costs must be phenomenal, but all his students had to pay for were their own clothes and incidentals.

His subroutines jumped into the second cube and he started to integrate them. Kitchener might or might not ask how his gravity-lens research project was progressing at supper but he wanted to be ready with some kind of report. The old boy simply didn't tolerate fools at all, let alone gladly. That fact alone did wonders for Nicholas's self-esteem. He knew he was bright, his effortless formal first at Cambridge proved that: but the downside was the trouble he had trying to fit into the university's social scene; he had always preferred his studies to the politics and culture-vulturing of his fellow students. Bookish eremitism was all right at university, you could get lost in the crowd and nobody would notice, but it wasn't possible at Launde. Yet Kitchener had agreed after a mere ten-minute interview, during which Nicholas had mumbled virtually every answer to the old boy's questions.

"We can sort you out here," Kitchener had said wryly, and winked. "There's more than one type of education to be had at Launde."

Nicholas had experienced the unsettling notion that Kitchener had perceived the sense of destitute isolation that had clung to him for as long as he could remember.

After he got into Launde Abbey, money ceased to be a problem for the first time in his life. His parents had always been proud of his university scholarship, but they hadn't been able to contribute much to his grant; they were smallholders, barely able to feed themselves and his sister. He went to Cambridge a month after the People's Socialism Party fell; the country was in complete turmoil, jobs and money were scarce. He scraped through the first year working as a fast-food cook grilling burgers in the furnace heat of a cramped McDonald's kitchen for six nights a week. It wasn't until halfway through his second year that the economy stabilized and the New Conservative government began to prioritize the education department. But after he graduated and then received that golden invitation, sponsorship for the two-year sojourn had been ridiculously easy to find. Eight medium-sized companies and three giant kombinates had made him an offer. In the end, he settled for accepting the money of Randon, a French-based 'ware and energy-systems manufacturer, mainly because it was coupled with the promise of a guaranteed research position afterward.

All of Launde's graduates tended to enjoy a privileged position later in life; Kitchener did seem to have a knack for spotting genuine potential: they formed one of the most elitist old-boy networks in the world. It was all part of the price of spending two years isolated in the middle of nowhere. Nicholas didn't mind that at all; after his appalling first year at Cambridge, he thought it was quite a bargain.

Supper at Launde Abbey was held at half-past seven prompt each night. Everybody attended, no matter how engrossed they were with their work. It was one of the Kitchener's house rules. He didn't lay down many, but God help the student who broke one of them.

Nicholas had a quick shower, then put on a clean pale-blue T-shirt before he left his room at quarter-past seven. It was dark outside, the wind soughing plaintively as it slithered around the chimney-stacks.

Uri Pabari and Liz Foxton were coming out of Uri's room, a couple of doors down from Nicholas's. They were talking in low, heated voices as they emerged into the corridor, some sort of argument. Both of them looked belligerent, faces hard and unyielding.

An awkward grin flickered over Nicholas's lips. He hated it when people argued in the Abbey; cramped together as they were, everyone else always seemed to get dragged in. It was doubly excruciating when the argument was a personal one. And he had enough experience to recognize a personal argument between Liz and Uri. It didn't happen often, but when it did . . .

They caught sight of him, and the sibilant words stopped. There was a moment's hesitation during which they held some invisible negotiation, then Uri's arm was around her shoulder and they walked toward him. He waited, trying to hide his trepidation. They were both older than he; Uri was twenty-four, Liz twenty-two, in their final year at Launde.

Out of all the students at Launde, Nicholas felt closest to Liz. She wasn't quite as stilted as he when it came to other people, but she was one of the quietest, always giving the impression of thoughtful reserve. She was half a head shorter than he, with a pleasant round face, hazel eyes, and shoulder-length raven hair. Tonight she wore a simple fuchsia one-piece dress, its skirt coming just below her knees, something indefinably American about its cut.

By contrast, Uri was perpetually easygoing. The ex-Israeli had a dark complexion and a thick mass of curly jet-black hair that reached his shoulders. His build was stocky, yet he was the same one-meter-eighty height as Nicholas, a combination that made his varsity rugby team welcome him to their ranks with open arms. Recently he had piled a couple of kilos on around his waist, which Liz had started to nag him about during meals. He was in jeans and a bright-green rugby shirt.

"Missed your swim?" Liz asked as the three of them walked down the stairs.

Nicholas nodded. "Yes, but I managed to catch up on some of my datawork."

"No formal graduation exams, no last-month sweat and panic . . . that's the thing about this place." She grinned, mimicking Kitchener's waspy tone. "You know whether or not your mind can work, it's not up to me to tell you."

The Abbey's rooms were divided into two distinct groups: the formal ones, which had been maintained in a reasonable degree of the original style despite the privation of the PSP decade that followed the physical and economic chaos of the Warming; and the rest, which were turned over to Kitchener's lifelong pursuit of quantifying the entire universe: the two laboratories, a compact heavily cybernated engineering shop, the computer center, Kitchener's study, a small lecture theater, and a library with hundreds of paper books. The dining room was definitely one of the former; its gold-brown wooden paneling had been immaculately preserved, and the Jacobean fireplace never failed to impress Nicholas. It had been furnished with a long Edwardian mahogany table, polished to a gleam; the fragile-looking chairs around it were upholstered with dull rouge leather, covered with a web of ochre cracks. Nicholas was always terrified he would split one of the antique masterpieces when he sat on it. Above the table, two biolum chandeliers emitted a bright, slightly pink, light.

Cecil Cameron was lounging in one of the chairs, the last of the second-year students. A rangy twenty-four-year-old with frizzy blond hair, cut short. He was using his kinaware left hand to open a bottle of white Sussex wine, chrome-black metalloceramic nails shining dully every time he twisted the corkscrew. The hand's leathery skin had a silver sheen, which Cecil said he had chosen in preference to flesh-tone. "Why bother going through life being boring? If you're enhanced, then flaunt it." He claimed he'd lost his forearm in an anti-PSP riot. True or not, and Nicholas wasn't entirely convinced, Cecil exploited his hand and the interest it earned him quite shamelessly to his own advantage.

Kinaware was still rare—and expensive—enough to draw attention wherever he went. Not that the six students got out much: a weekly trip to the Old Plough in Braunston, the nearest village; an occasional foray into Oakham. Cecil was forever bitching about the confines of the Abbey and worked a little too hard on projecting his boisterous image. But Nicholas had to admit he was a first-rate solid-state physicist.

"Don't look so eager, proles," Cecil drawled. "The storm means Mrs. Mayberry isn't here. Our lord and master sent her home after lunch. So it's cook-it-yourself-night tonight."

Nicholas and Uri let out a groan.

"So why aren't you cooking it?" Liz asked.

Cecil flashed her a smile. "I always find the female of the species is so much better at that kind of thing."

"Pighead!"

"Go on, admit it, did you really want to taste my cooking? Besides, I looked in a minute ago; little Isabel is coping just fine."

"Isabel's cooking supper?" Nicholas asked. He hoped it had come out sounding like an innocent inquiry.

Cecil's smile broadened. "Yes. All by herself. Say, Nick, why don't you go and see if she wants a hand, or anything else?"

Nicholas could hear what sounded like a chuckle coming from Uri. He refused to turn and find out for sure. "Yes, all right," he said.

Liz was giggling by the time he reached the door into the kitchen. Well, let them, he thought; he didn't mind the steady joshing the others gave him now, it was all part of a day at Launde Abbey. Funny what you could get used to if it went on long enough.

Isabel Spalvas had arrived at the same time as he, a mathematician from Cardiff University. At first he didn't even have the nerve to meet her eyes when they were talking—not that they talked much, he could never think of anything to say. But mortification at his own pathetic shyness eventually bullied him out of his shell. They were going to be under the same roof for two years; if nothing else, he could talk to her as if she was just one of the boys, it was often the simplest approach. That way, at least they'd be friends, then maybe, just maybe . . .

The kitchen had a long matte-black cast-iron range running along one whitewashed plaster wall, with a set of copper pots and even an antique bedwarmer hanging above it. A wicker basket stood at the end, piled high with logs, but for once the fire was out. The big square wooden table in the middle of the room was covered in dishes and trays; there was a mound of wet lettuce leaves drying out in a colander next to a collection of sliced tomatoes, cucumbers, radishes, and chives.

Isabel was busy carving a joint of ham. She was the same age as Nicholas, twenty-one, about a head shorter, with sandy-blonde hair that was arranged in a mass of tiny curls just brushing her shoulders. The way she was bent over the table meant the strands obscured her face, but he could visualize her features perfectly at any time. Almost invisible lashes framed enchantingly clear ice-blue eyes, pale freckles decorated the top half of her cheeks, the lips were narrow. Nicholas was fascinated by the dainty features, how expressive they could be: fearsomely intent when she was listening to Kitchener, beaming sunlight smiles when she was happy, when the students got together for their evening meetings in one of the rooms. She laughed most at Cecil's jokes of course, and Rosette's acid gossip; Nicholas never had been able to master the art of perfectly timed one-liners, or even rugby club-style stories.

He paused for a second, content just to look at her, for once without all the others nudging and pointing. She was wearing tight, faded jeans, and a sleeveless white blouse, with Mrs. Mayberry's brown apron tied around her waist. One day he'd have the courage to come out and say what he felt to her face, say that she was gorgeous, say that she made the whole world worth living in. And after that he'd lean forward for a kiss. One day.

"Hello, Isabel," he blurted. Damn, that had come out too loud and gushy.

She glanced up from the joint. "Hi, Nick. It's going to be salad tonight, I'm afraid."

"You haven't done all this yourself, have you? You should have said, I would have helped. I did some cooking when I was at Cambridge. I got quite good at it."

"It's all right, Mrs. Mayberry prepared most of it after lunch. You didn't think she'd trust us with it, did you? I'm just finishing off. Do you think this'll be enough?" She wagged the knife at the plate of meat she had cut.

"Yes, fine. If they want any more, Cecil can cut it."

"Hmm, that'll be the day."

"Is there anything I can do?"

"Take the trays through, would you?"

"Right." He grabbed the one nearest to him, piled high with plates and dishes.

"Not that one!"

Nicholas put it down with a guilty lurch. The plates threatened to keel over. Isabel put her hand out hurriedly to stop them.

"Those are the plates from lunch, Nick," she said with a tinge of reproach.

"Sorry." How stupid, he raged silently. He knew the heat he could feel on his face was a crimson blush.

"Try this one," she said in a gentler voice.

He picked up the one she indicated and turned for the door, feeling totally worthless.

"Nick. Thank you for offering to help. None of the others did."

She was giving him a soft smile and there was something in her expression that said she understood.

"That's okay, any time."

Nicholas and Uri were setting the places when Edward Kitchener and Rosette Harding-Clarke came in at twenty-nine minutes past seven. He saw the old boy was in his usual clothes: baggy white trousers, white cotton shirt, cream-yellow jacket with a blue silk handkerchief tucked into his breast pocket, and a tiny red bow tie, which always made Nicholas think a butterfly had landed on his collar. There was still an air of the tiger left in Kitchener, age was not a gift he accepted gracefully. He was reasonably slim, carrying himself with undiminished vigor; his face was a long one, with skin stretched thinly around his jaw, scratchy with stubble; a crew cut of silver hair looked almost like a cap.

Rosette Harding-Clarke walked beside him, taller by ten centimeters, an athletic-looking twenty-three-year-old, with soft auburn hair styled so that long, wavy strands licked her back well below her shoulder blades. Her presence alone intimidated Nicholas. She had arrived along with him and Isabel, with a degree in quantum mechanics from Oxford, but her aristocratic background gave her a self-confidence that he found daunting. He had suffered too many casual put-downs from her social clique at Cambridge not to flinch each time that steel-edged Knightsbridge voice sliced through the air. She was wearing dark-gray tweedy trousers and a scarlet waistcoat with shiny brass buttons, the top two undone. And nothing underneath, Nicholas soon realized. He prayed he wasn't blushing again, but Rosette could be overpoweringly sexy when she wanted to be.

Kitchener and Rosette were arm in arm. Like lovers, Nicholas thought, which he privately suspected was true. It wasn't only Kitchener's attitude toward his fellow physicists that caused conflict in his earlier years. Tabloid channel 'casts were always sniping with rumors of him and female students. And how Kitchener had lapped that up, relishing his media-appointed role as the notorious roué! There had even been a statement, shortly after he bought Launde Abbey, that he was only going to invite female students to become his tyros, providing himself with a harem of muses. He never had, of course; it was always a fifty-fifty split, but which member of the general public made the effort to discover that? The legend remained solidly intact.

"Anybody been watching the newscasts?" Kitchener asked after he sat in the carver's chair at the head of the table.

"I've been correlating the gamma-ray data from *Antomine 12*," Nicholas said.

"Well done, lad. Glad somebody's doing something in this slackers' paradise. Now what about that little problem I set you on magnetosphere induction generators, hey, have you solved that yet?"

"No, sorry, the gravity lens idea was fascinating, and nobody else has been tabulating the data the way I am," Nicholas offered by way of compensation. He ducked his head, unsure how it would be received. The topics for research were always set by Kitchener, but sometimes the old boy displayed a complete lack of interest in the answers. You could never work out what he was going to press you on, which could get disconcerting. That aside, Nicholas reckoned he'd learned more about the methodology of analyzing problems in the three months he'd been at Launde Abbey than in his three years at university. Kitchener did have the most extraordinary insights at times.

"Bloody typical," Kitchener groused. "How many times do I have to tell you delinquents, the abstract is all very well, but it makes piddle-all difference to the human condition. There's no bloody point in me teaching you to think properly if you can't use those thoughts of yours to some benefit. The way this clapped-out world is limping along, a clean source of fresh energy would be like manna from heaven right now. A wealthier world will be better able to support eggheads chasing metaphantoms. It's to your own advantage. God, take me, unless I'd come up with those molecular interaction equations—"

"You could never have bought Launde," Uri and Cecil chorused, laughing.

"Little buggers!" Kitchener grunted. He glanced down at the plate Isabel put in front of him and started to poke around distrustfully with a fork. "And don't giggle, lad," he said without looking up. "Only bloody women giggle."

Nicholas clamped his mouth shut and concentrated on his plate. From the corner of his eye he could see Isabel laughing silently.

"I was watching the newscasts this afternoon," Kitchener said. "It looks like the Scottish PSP is about to fall."

"It's always on the verge of collapse," Cecil protested loudly. "They said it wouldn't last six months after our lot got kicked out."

"Yes, but Zurich has cut off their credit now."

"About time," Liz muttered.

Nicholas knew she had lost her mother when the PSP was in power in England. She always blamed the People's Constables, but thankfully never went into details. His own memories of President Armstrong's brutish regime were more or less limited to the constant struggle to survive on too little food. The PSP never had much authority in rural areas; they had had enough trouble maintaining control in the urban districts.

"I hope they don't want to link up with us again," Cecil said.

"Why ever not?" Rosette asked. "I think it would be nice being the United Kingdom again, although having the Irish back would be pushing the point."

"We can't afford it," Cecil said. "Christ, we're only just getting back on our own feet."

"A bigger country means greater security in the long run, darling."

"You might as well try Eurofederalism again."

"We'll have to help them," Isabel said. "They're desperately short of food."

"Let them grow their own," Cecil said. "They're not short of land, and they've got all those fishing rights."

"How can you say that? There are children suffering."

"I think Isabel's right," Nicholas said boldly. "Some sort of aid's in order, even if we can't afford a Marshall Plan."

"Now that will make a nice little complication for the New Conservatives during the election," Kitchener said gleefully. "Trapped whichever way they turn. Serves 'em right. Always good fun watching politicians squirming."

Conversation meandered, as it always did, from politics to art, from music to England's current surge of industrial redevelopment, from channel-star gossip (which Kitchener always pretended not to follow) to the latest crop of scientific papers. Cecil walked around the table pouring the wine for everyone.

Isabel mentioned the increasing number of people using bioware processor implants, the fact that the New Conservatives had finally legalized them in England, and Kitchener declared: "Sheer folly."

"I thought you would have approved," she said. "You're always going on about enhancing cerebral capacity."

"Rubbish, girl, having processors in your head doesn't make you any brighter. Intellect is half instinct. Always has been. I haven't got one and I've managed pretty well."

"But you might have achieved more with one," Uri said.

"That's the kind of bloody stupid comment I'd expect from you. Totally devoid of logic. Wishful thinking is sloppy thinking."

Uri gave Kitchener a cool stare. "You have few qualms about using other enhancements to get results."

Nicholas didn't like the tone, it was far too polite. He shifted about in the chair, bleakly waiting for the explosion. No one was eating, Cecil had stopped filling Rosette's glass.

But Kitchener's voice was surprisingly mild when he answered. "I'll use whatever I need to expand my perception, thank you, lad. I've been a consenting adult since before you were shitting in your nappies. Being able to discern the whole universe is the key to understanding it. If neurohormones help me in that, then that makes them no different than a particle accelerator, or any other form of research tool, in my book."

"Neat answer. Pity you don't stick to neurohormones, pity you have to expand your consciousness with shit."

"Nothing I take affects my intellect. Only a fool would think otherwise. Expanded consciousness is total crap, there's no such thing, only recreational intoxication; it's a diversion, stepping outside your problems for a few hours."

"Well, it's certainly helped you overcome a few problems, hasn't it?" Uri's face was blank civility.

"I always thought bioware nodes would be terrifically useful if you want to access data quickly," Rosette said brightly.

Cecil's hand came down on Uri's shoulder, squeezing softly. He started pouring some wine into Uri's glass.

Kitchener turned to Rosette. "Use a bloody terminal, girl, don't be so damn lazy. That's all implants are, convenience laziness. It's precisely the kind of attitude that got us into our present state. People never listen to common sense. We shouted about the greenhouse gases till we were blue in the face. Bloody hopeless. They just went on burning petrol and coal."

"What kind of car did you use?" Liz asked slyly.

"There weren't any electric cars then. I had to use petrol."

"Or a bicycle," Rosette said.

"A horse," Nicholas suggested.

"A rickshaw," Isabel giggled.

"Perhaps you could even have walked," Cecil chipped in.

"Leave off, you little buggers," Kitchener grunted. "No bloody respect. Cecil, at least fill my glass, lad; it's wine, not perfume, you don't spray it on."

Nicholas managed to catch Isabel's eye and he smiled. "The salad's lovely."

"Thank you," she said.

Rosette held her cut-crystal wineglass up to the light, turning it slowly. Fragments of refracted light drifted across her face, stipples of gold and violet. "You never compliment Mrs. Mayberry when she cooks supper, why is that, Nicky, darling?"

"You never complimented Mrs. Mayberry or Isabel," he answered. "I was just being polite, it was considered important where I was brought up."

Rosette wrinkled her nose at him and sipped some wine.

"Well done, lad," Kitchener called out. "You stick up for yourself, don't let the little vixen get on top of you."

Nicholas and Isabel exchanged a furtive grin. He was elated, actually answering back to Rosette and having Isabel approve.

Rosette gave Kitchener a roguish glance. "You've never complained before," she murmured in a husky tone.

Kitchener laughed wickedly. "What's for dessert, Isabel?" he asked.

The storm began to abate after midnight. Nicholas was back in his room, watching a vermiform pattern of sparkling blue stars dance through his terminal's cube like a demented will-o'-the-wisp. The program was trying to detect the distinctive interference pattern caused by large dark-mass concentrations; if there was one directly between the emission point and Earth (a remote chance, but possible), the gamma rays should bend around it. Kitchener was always interested in the kind of localized spatial distortions such objects generated. His program was using up a good third of the Abbey's lightware cruncher capacity. The kind of interference he was looking for was incredibly hard to identify.

Nicholas had thought about making a start on the magnetosphere induction problem, but the dark-mass project was *much* more interesting. It was worth enduring another of Kitchener's tongue-lashings to be able to see the results as they came in from orbit. Dark-mass detection was well down the priority list of CNES's in-house astronomers; it was exciting to think he might actually be ahead of them, up there at the cutting edge. Nicholas Beswick, science pioneer.

He had been in Uri's room for most of the evening after supper, along with Liz and Isabel. It had been a good evening, he reflected; they'd chatted, and the flatscreen had been tuned to Globecast's twenty-four-hour news channel with the sound muted. And it really did look like the Scottish PSP was going to be overthrown at last. There was rioting in Glasgow and Edinburgh, and the assembly building had been firebombed, the flames soaring impressively into the night despite the heavy rain. They had watched the text streamers running along the bottom of the flatscreen and talked, drinking another bottle of Sussex wine. The others never seemed to mind that he didn't say as much as they; he was under no pressure to venture an opinion on everything.

They had packed up around midnight, or at least he and Isabel had left Uri and Liz alone.

He shut Uri's door, thinking that for once he might find the nerve to ask Isabel into his room.

She stood on the gloomy landing glancing at him expectantly.

"It was a nice evening, thanks," he said. Pathetic.

Her lips pressed together. It was her solemn expression, the one that made her look half-tragic.

"Yes, I enjoyed it," she said. "Let's hope there's a new government in Scotland tomorrow. Liz will be over the moon."

"Yes." Now, he thought, now say it. "Goodnight," he said meekly.

"Goodnight, Nick."

And she'd walked off to her room.

Surely if a girl liked a boy she was supposed to show it: some small word or deed of encouragement? But she hadn't actually discouraged him. He clung to that. If it hadn't been for the fact that he could never keep his mouth shut, Nicholas might have asked Cecil for advice. Cecil never had any trouble chatting up girls when they visited the Old Plough.

The clouds above the valley were disintegrating; pale beams of moonlight probed down through the tattered gaps. Nicholas looked up from the cube, watching them shiver across the undulating parkland. After the uniform darkness of the storm, they seemed preternaturally bright. Trees and bushes imprinted on his retinas, ragged platinum silhouettes that vanished almost as soon as they were revealed.

A face looked back at him through the glass. It was a woman, probably not much older than he; her features were slightly indistinct, misted somehow, but she was certainly attractive, with thick red hair combed back from her forehead.

All he did was gawk for a second, his thoughts shocked into stasis, a gelid fingertip stroking his spine. Then he realized her spectral image must be a reflection. She was standing behind him! He yelped in panic and jerked around in the chair, a thousand-volt current replacing his normal nervous impulses.

There was nobody there.

He twisted back to stare at the window. There was no face.

Slowly, his shoulders trembling faintly, he let out a long sigh. Idiot! He must have been dozing, dreaming. The clock on the bedside cabinet read quarter past one.

Too late, Nicholas, he told himself wanly. Besides, since when did beautiful women ever come stealing into your bedroom in the middle of the night?

He canceled the gamma-ray search program. That was when he heard somebody talking on the landing outside, two people, voices murmuring softly. The chilly breath of static washed down his back again, but he was wide awake now. He frowned, concentrating, filtering out the intermittent patter of residual rain on the window. He knew one of them was Isabel, by now he could have plucked her voice out of hell's bedlam.

Curiosity warred with dread, he wanted to know what she was doing, he was terrified of making a fool out of himself. But if he didn't go to the door quickly, the chance to do either would be lost. In the end, it was the thought of having to live with not knowing, spending days wondering while his over-active imagination summoned up grotesque scenarios, that propelled him up out of the chair.

He turned the brass door handle, already trying to think of an excuse. I was just going to fetch something from the library, my toilet's blocked . . . feeble.

There was only a single biolum globe illuminating the landing, its weak pink-white lambency disfiguring the familiar corridors and twisting the proportions of the stark wooden chairs outside each door. Long serpentine shadows dappled the walls, veiling the vague figures depicted in the dusty hanging tapestries behind a crepuscular fog.

The two girls had their backs to him, walking with a measured companionable pace toward the stairs. They stopped as soon as the bright fan of light from his room splashed out into the landing, and slowly turned toward him. Rosette was wrapped in a jade-green silk kimono, embellished with fantastic topaz griffins. She was obviously riding some kind of high; he'd seen enough of that at Cambridge to tell: black sun pupils, dawdling movements. Probably Naiad, a sophisticated derivative of street-syntho, guaranteed no bad trips, no cold turkey. The vat in the lab downstairs was elaborate enough to produce it.

Isabel was still in her jeans, held up by a braided leather belt she'd fastened with a big loop tucked back into her waistband. She had taken off her blouse, leaving just a plain black bra to cup her high, exquisitely shaped breasts.

Nicholas stared at her with lightheaded dismay, the kind of sensation he got whenever his father butchered spring lambs. The scene and all it implied was too macabre, too lascivious to take in. In the gloom behind the girls he could see the redheaded woman again, all of her this time. She was tall and broad-shouldered, wearing some kind of jacket with a long skirt. He blinked, dizziness forcing him to grip the door to stop himself falling. His skin was ice-cold, needled with hot beads of sweat. He thought he was about to be sick. The world buckled alarmingly, sight and sound dissolving under a suffocating wave of heat. He was hallucinating, he was sure of it, the only explanation, trapped in a terrifying loop of nightmare. When his vision shimmered back into focus, the phantom woman had gone. But Isabel and Rosette were still solidly, undeniably present.

A corner of Rosette's mouth lifted in a lazy chaffing smile, as if she was glad he'd interrupted them. "Adults only, Nicky darling," she said in a throaty voice. "Sorry."

He looked at Isabel, a long, anguished appeal that this wasn't happening. All she did was give a minute shrug, a gesture of almost total indifference. It was a blow that hit him harder than the first shock of discovery.

He stared in abject misery as they continued silently down the landing, Rosette's feet unseen inside the kimono, giving the impression she was gliding above the carpet. Isabel had her shoulders square, lean bands of muscle shifting pliantly below the flawless skin of her tapering back.

They walked all the way past the stairs, along to the north wing, swallowed up in the gloaming. Then orange light shone out of the door Rosette opened. Kitchener's suite of rooms.

Isabel didn't even glance back to see if he was watching before she closed the door behind them.

Why? He couldn't understand it. She wasn't on drugs. She wasn't suffering from delusions. She was always so level-headed. Not like him, having fantasy women and the agony of sexual treachery running loose in his brain, twisting his mind until he could barely think.

Nicholas clawed at his sheets, petrified the redheaded woman would materialize again, hoping in some perverse way that she would. Nothing made sense anymore.

Why? Was it a price the female students had to pay for admission? But he would have heard, the ones who refused would have run screaming to the tabloid channels.

The moon had set now, leaving cold starlight to kiss the valley. He could hear lost gusts of wind swirling around the eaves, gurgles of water from the overflowing lakes.

Why? She didn't have to do it. Not with Kitchener. Not with Rosette. So she must want to. Why? Why? *Why?*

Nicholas snapped awake, his head rising off the pillow in a reflex jolt. What had woken him? He was still in his T-shirt and jeans, waist button undone. The duvet was a crumpled mess below him.

It was like every nerve fiber was shooting distilled trepidation into his brain. He knew it was going to be bad, very bad.

The scream assaulted his ears. Female. Powerful and utterly wretched. Dragging on and on, enough to leave a throat raw and withered.

He rolled off the bed fast. There was just enough pre-dawn light leaking through the window to see by. The scream stopped as he reached the door, then started up again as he pulled it open.

He looked about wildly. Orange light was shining down at the far end of the north wing. He could see Rosette kneeling brokenly in the doorway to Kitchener's suite, clinging desperately to the wooden frame.

Getting to her was a confused blur. His feet pounding. The other doors opening. Pale, anxious faces. That unending, spine-grating scream.

Tears were streaming down Rosette's face. She was shaking violently.

He rushed past her and saw the bedroom for the first time. The curtains were still shut, and tinted biolum globes shone from the middle of bulbous paper-moon shades that hung from the ceiling. The furniture was supremely tasteful: a dark antique dresser, matching wardrobe, Chinese carpet, full-length mirror, a porcelain-topped table below the window, brass ornaments on the mantelpiece, monk chest. The centerpiece was a large four-poster bed with an amber canopy.

Edward Kitchener was lying on the snow-white silk sheets, at the middle of a deep scarlet bloodstain spreading to the edge of the mattress. Nicholas felt the intolerable pressure of his own scream building in his chest.

Kitchener's head was intact, showing an almost serene peacefulness. But the body . . . ripped. Torn. Squashed. The ribcage had been clawed open, pulped organs spread across the bed.

Nicholas's scream burst out of his mouth. The roaring in his ears meant he couldn't even hear it. He was vaguely aware of the other students crowding in behind him.

His leg muscles pitched him onto the floor and he vomited helplessly onto Kitchener's superb Chinese carpet.

THE NINETEEN-FIFTIES VINTAGE ROLLS-ROYCE Silver Shadow glided along at eighty kilometers an hour, its white-walled tires soaking up all the punishment the gritty ruts of the decrepit M11 could inflict without a hint of exertion. Julia Evans adored the old car; it was the absolute last word in style and its rugged old-fashioned engineering was easily equal to the strengthened suspension and broad silicone rubber tires of any modern car. Apart from a closed-loop recombiner cell that allowed it to continue burning petrol without leaking fumes into the atmosphere, and the installation of various security systems, it hadn't needed any modifications to cope with England's decaying-road network.

Outside the darkened glass she could see the rug of grass, weeds, and lush emerald moss that had swamped the hard shoulder; even the crash barriers along the central reservation had been swallowed up by bindweed, snow-white trumpet-shaped flowers pushing out from between the cloak of broad leaves. The original tarmac surface was still in use, scored by deep tire ruts along each carriageway; this afternoon it was solid because of the weekend's cooling rains, but for nine months of the year the sun reduced the roads to swaths of mushy black treacle.

The New Conservative government agreed in principle that nationwide road refurbishment should be given priority, coating the millions of kilometers of tarmac with a layer of tough thermo-cured cellulose, but they were hanging back until giga-conductor-powered vehicles became widespread before starting.

The Rolls approached junction ten, and the lead car in their four-strong police escort switched on its blue strobe lights. There seemed to be a lot of people lining the slip road.

"Who are they?" Julia asked.

Rachel Griffith, one of her two permanent bodyguards, was sitting in the jump seat opposite. A twenty-five-year-old security division hardliner, wearing a smart blue two-piece suit. She turned around, scanning the road ahead. Her lean face flashed Julia a quick, reassuring smile. "Just some protesters," she said. "You and the Prime Minister at the same event is a publicity opportunity they can't ignore."

Julia nodded. Rachel had been with her for five years, tough, smart, and loyal. She liked to think of her as a friend as well. If Rachel wasn't worried, there was nothing to be worried about.

"This is as near to the Institute as they can get," said Morgan Walshaw, Event Horizon's security chief, from the second jump seat. Even sitting, he couldn't appear relaxed, spine stiff, shoulders squared, wearing an immaculate charcoal-gray suit. He fit her conception of a crusty old retired Home Counties general perfectly. Except Morgan was far shrewder than any general. Thank God.

He was sixty-two years old, silver-gray hair clipped down to a centimeter from his skull, the thick, tanned skin of his face heavily crossed with narrow lines, hard-set light-blue eyes that always made her feel incredibly guilty whenever he stared at her. Everything she did eventually filtered back to him: nights out with her girlfriends in Peterborough's clubs, holiday adventures, party antics, boys. Morgan had been with the company for years, protecting her grandfather, and now her, a job he performed with superb efficiency and complete devotion. His approval was always tremendously important to her, mainly because he would never make a gratuitous compliment. She had to *earn* it, something that never happened with most of the people in her life. And words of praise had indeed been awarded, albeit grudgingly, with more frequency in recent years. She often caught herself wishing he was her real father. The knowledge that he would be retiring in a few years was something she always tried to bury right at the back of her mind; it was a horrifying thought.

Access RollSpeech, Julia told her bioware processor node silently. Colorless words flowed from one of the three memory nodes buried at the back of her skull, forming a ghostly script behind her eyes. She reviewed it for what must have been the tenth time since breakfast. Event Horizon's PR department had written it for her, but she'd made a few alterations. It had sounded terribly stilted before. She couldn't forget it of course, not with the nodes reinforcing her memory, but they couldn't help her out if she stumbled over pronunciation.

The roll out was going to be the technological event of the year; she couldn't afford to make a mistake. There were going to be too many people, too many channel cameras. It felt as though a squadron of butterflies were performing dynamic aerobatic routines in her stomach.

The four-thousand-pound Sabareni suit she had chosen to wear for the ceremony was sheer silk, a bright coral pink. The tailored jacket had a broad collar and large white buttons, its skirt was straight, hem five centimeters above her knees. Sabareni was one of her favorite designers; the suit made her feel wonderfully elegant. She had decided against ostentatious jewelry, settling for her usual gold St. Christopher and a Cartier diamond brooch. Her maid had straightened her chestnut hair so that it fell down her back almost to her hips; it was a lot of trouble to condition, but after growing it for a decade, she was damned if she was going to have it cut now. Besides, a lot of girls were copying the "Julia" hairstyle. She had a media profile that rock stars and channel celebrities could only fantasize about.

Exit RollSpeech. If she didn't know it now, she never would.

She could hear the faint shouts of the protesters through the thick glass. "They look too well-fed to be dole dependents," she observed as the Rolls left the motorway, cruising past a big green-and-gold sign that read:

Duxford
Event Horizon Astronautics Institute

A rank of police, wearing bulky navy-blue riot uniforms, stood along the side of the slip road, arms linked, forming a human barricade to keep the protesters back from the little convoy. The protesters Julia could see seemed to be in their early twenties, dressed in T-shirts and jeans, most of them male. They were clean, healthy. Probably students.

"Most of them come from colleges at Cambridge," Morgan said.

Julia awarded herself a mental point.

"Rent-a-mob fodder," he continued. "They were bussed out here this morning by a couple of radical groups, Human Frontier and the Christian Luddites; they actually get paid attendance money. Nobody would come otherwise."

Access Company Security File: Christian Luddites, Radical Group. She had never heard of them before, the names conjured up all sorts of amusing images. Their file squirted into her mind, illusive datastacks she could run or hold on a whim, not quite sight, not quite sound. Raw neural information. The Christian Luddites claimed to be a back-to-the-earth movement, rejecting technology in all forms except for medical purposes. Security said there were possible links with ex-*apparatchiks*, as yet unproven. They had fifteen chapters, spread around the major cities, a couple more in Europe. A detailed membership list had been compiled. She scanned the hierarchy, most of whom were involved in other small, intense activist groups. Today's radicals were a nepotistic, incestuous lot, she thought.

Cancel File.

"It must cost a lot of money to mount protests if you're paying attendance fees," she said. "Where did it all come from originally?"

"We're looking into it," Morgan said.

"Shouldn't be allowed," said Patrick Browning, who was sitting next to her. "They're just gaining publicity at your expense." He gave her his positive smile, the one that said he would champion her against the whole world if need be.

Patrick was twenty-one, with golden-blond hair coming down to his collar, a very handsome angular face, deep hazel eyes that held just a hint of wickedness, and a body that any Greek god would envy. His family was wealthy, a typical European finance dynasty, with interests in shipping, construction, and medium-scale engineering, operating through anonymous Zurich and Austrian offices. So money wasn't quite so much an issue as it had been with previous boyfriends. He had just earned a business administration degree at Oxford, which gave him a nice air of self-confidence; coming on top of his debonair mannerisms and beautifully realized sense of fun, it made him virtually irresistible.

Five weeks ago she had been at a party when she overheard his previous girlfriend, Angela Molloy, boasting that he had the rutting stamina of a bull in springtime. Throughout the following fortnight it seemed as though Patrick couldn't go to a party or club without bumping into Julia. It was uncanny; one might almost suspect fate was pushing them together. After he realized how many mutual interests they had, asking her for a date was only logical.

And Angela had been quite right.

"They have a perfect right to be there," Julia said neutrally. "This country paid the most appalling price so that individuals had the right to express opinions again, however extreme or unwelcome. Only PSP *apparatchiks* try to oppress people for saying what they think." She met Rachel's eye levelly, reading the meticulously contained amusement in the hardliner's composed expression.

Patrick paled slightly at the rebuke, for an instant looking like a five-year-old who had just had his chocolate bar confiscated. "Yes," he said carefully. "But I don't like it when it's you they're expressing about."

Julia nodded fractionally. There were substantial dividends to be collected by keeping boys on their toes, unsure precisely where they stood. That way, they always knew exactly who was in charge.

She leaned over Patrick to get a closer look at the placards being waved. It wasn't strictly necessary, the protesters were on both sides of the slip road, but the angle would give Patrick a good view down her cleavage. She held back on a smile when she caught his eyes straying down to her neckline. Mr. Suave was no different than any of the others. Mr. Hormones in masquerade. Easy meat.

She read some of the placards, the usual obscenities and crude caricatures printed in yellow and pink fluorocolors, then started to giggle.

"What is it?" Morgan asked. He was peering out of the window.

"That one." She pointed.

A red-haired youth in a blue sweatshirt held up a kelpboard placard that said:

> *Julia already owns the Earth,*
> *don't let her have the stars as well.*

Company security guards in immaculate gray-blue uniforms saluted sharply as they passed through the first of the Astronautics Institute's ten gates. The police escort peeled away, leaving the Rolls to drive on to Building One alone. The circular structure was made up from an outer ring of offices, laboratories, design bureaus, computer centers, cybernetic integration bays, and test facilities; five stories high, eight hundred meters in diameter, presenting a polished cliff-face of green-silver glass to the outside world. A jet-black dome of solar collector panels roofed a central space hardware assembly hall.

In the distance she could see Building Two, a twin of One, as yet unoccupied; contractors were busy dismantling the scaffolding. A week late, they were going to pay a hefty penalty clause for that. Architectural data constructs of Building Three were already well advanced, big enough to put One and Two inside, then rattle them around.

Julia always got a kick out of the Institute; its sheer size, sprawled over the old Imperial War Museum site and now beginning to creep out toward Thriplow, was a spectacular statement of intent. Event Horizon was staking out its claim on the future for everyone to see, rekindling the old High Frontier dream. There was something fundamentally exciting about commanding such a grandiose venture.

Philip Evans, her grandfather, had started to build the Institute a month after the PSP fell. He believed passionately that space industry would be the catalyst in reinvigorating the country's post-Warming economy. His aim was to develop a center of excellence where every discipline of space industry could be cultivated and refined, ensuring the company had complete technological independence.

Microgee material-processing had already established itself as a hugely profitable enterprise. The number of low-Earth-orbit factory modules churning out 'ware chips, crystals, exotic compounds, and super-strength monolattice filament had grown steadily even during the worst of the global recession that followed the Warming. But the raw materials the factories needed had to be lifted from Earth, battling against gravity throughout the whole ascent. Philip Evans's vision had the giga-conductor revolution reducing launch costs to a fraction of the chemically powered boosters', increasing profits by orders of magnitude. After that, he predicted, the exploitation of extraterrestrial resources would become economically feasible, and he was determined that as the solar system opened up, England would be the trail-blazer, with Event Horizon at the forefront. Julia had inherited that faith along with the material reality.

She had continued to pour money and resources into the Institute and its ambitious programs in the two years since he died, despite all the pressure and criticism from the company's financial backing consortium. Now the first phase of her plan was coming to fruition, after Heaven alone knew how many minor setbacks and delays.

Today was the day she would shut those whining know-nothings up for good. She wanted to sing and shout for the sheer joy of it. If nothing else, Patrick was in for the night of his life tonight.

Building One's vast car park was full to capacity with company minibuses and rank after rank of scooters—private cars were still a rarity. The Rolls drove past it and out onto the concrete desert on the other side of the building. Two long temporary seating stands had been erected on the apron, covered from possible showers by red-and-white-striped canvas awnings; they formed a broad avenue, leading away from Building One's huge multi-segment sliding doors. There were seven thousand invited guests waiting for her: Institute personnel and their families, premier-grade executives from most of the kombinates, channel celebrities, politicians, the Prime Minister, Prince Harry, even a few friends.

A press stand had been built at the far end of the avenue. Every place was taken, which gave her a final heart-flutter of nerves. She had secretly hoped the reporters would all still be up in Scotland after the momentous weekend.

Over a hundred cameras swiveled around as the Rolls drew up beside the VIP podium at the side of Building One's doors. Julia took a breath as the Institute's general manager scuttled forward to open the door, then climbed out with a professional smile in place.

Julia was thankful that the usual January heat was tempered by scrappy clouds and a full breeze. If it was up to her, there wouldn't even be a ceremony, but politics dictated otherwise, and the work-force needed some kind of recognition for their efforts. So she sat patiently while the bunting flapped noisily overhead and overdressed women kept a surreptitious hand on wide hats.

The Prime Minister, David Marchant, made the first speech; he was a dignified fifty-two-year-old in a blue-gray suit, the embodiment of calm competence. He praised Philip Evans and Julia for their fore-sight and optimism, then moved on to the workforce and compli-mented their professionalism, followed by a couple of political points against the three main parliamentary opposition groups. Julia found herself envying his delivery; he avoided rhetoric and theatrical emphasis, the words just flowed. When it was her turn, she accessed the speech and let her words glide straight from the node to her vocal cords, promising that her commitment to funding the space program remained unchanged, giving a brief outline of projects that would be initiated over the next three years—the larger low-Earth-orbit dormitory station, expanded science program, constructing a manned asteroid-survey craft—and managed to get in a joke about one of the engineering apprentices who had been strung up from a hoist by his mates a couple of months ago. She had been on an inspection tour of Building One at the time. It brought an appreciative cheer from the section of the stands where the workers and their families were sitting.

She handed over to Prince Harry for the actual roll out. He got more applause than she had. But then, royalty always did. Since the Second Restoration, people saw them as a continuity jump-lead to the past; they were a symbol of good times, when there was no Warming and no PSP. Now they were back, and life was picking up again.

Building One's doors slid open ponderously when Prince Harry pressed the button on the pedestal; somewhat predictably a band struck up the "Zarathustra" theme, and the *Clarke*-class spaceplane emerged into the afternoon sunlight, escorted by a troop of engineers in spotless white overalls. It had a swept-delta planform with a fifty-meter span, sixty meters long; the metalloceramic hull was an all-over frost-white, except for the scarlet Dragonflight escutcheons on the fin. Two streamlined cylindrical nacelles blended seamlessly with the underbelly, air-scoop ramps closed; reaction-control thruster clusters on the nose and around the wedge-shaped clamshell doors at the rear were masked by protective covers, *"Remove before flight"* tags dangling.

Julia clapped along with everyone else, impressed despite herself. The spaceplane was giga-conductor powered, the first of its kind, capable of lifting fifty tons into orbit without burning a single hydrocarbon molecule to injure the diseased atmosphere any further. Event Horizon already had orders for two hundred and twenty-seven, with options on another three hundred.

It was an icon to the new age that the giga-conductor was ushering in. The power-storage system was the ideal cheap, easy-to-manufacture Green solution to the energy problems of the post-Warming world, where hostility to petrol and coal was a tangible, occasionally fatal, aspect of life. And Event Horizon held the world-wide patent; every kombinate, company, and state factory on the planet paid her for the privilege of manufacturing it. The royalty revenue was already over two billion Eurofrancs a year, and it had been available for only twenty-three months. Every nation was racing to restructure its transport system around it.

She had seen artists' impressions of the commercial hypersonic jets that kombinate aerospace divisions were developing, long arrow-finned needles that looked like scaled-up missiles, cutting the transit time between continents to less than an hour. Car companies, those that had survived, were eager to bring out new vehicles, retooling factories that had lain idle for nearly fifteen years. Scooter sales were already booming.

Julia walked down the VIP podium's steps, accompanying the Prime Minister and Prince Harry, lesser dignitaries trailing after them. She kept a beautifully straight face as she showed them around the spaceplane, pointing out features of interest; for once grateful for the steely discipline she had learned at her Swiss boarding school. But it was hard—this is the air scoop, these are the wheels.

They posed under the flattened bullet nose as the press gathered for a video-bite opportunity.

"I would just like to say how immensely proud I am to be here today," David Marchant told the gaggle of reporters and channel crews. A forest of arms thrust AV recorders toward him. "This spaceplane is a quite tremendous achievement by the Event Horizon Company. A clear sign that our social market policies are the right ones to put England back on its feet again. And my New Conservative government wishes to demonstrate its firm commitment to the space industry by awarding Dragonflight the contract to dispose of eleven thousand tons of radioactive waste. This waste is made up of the cores and ancillary equipment of redundant nuclear reactors, currently being stored at great public expense around the country. And we hope that ultimately all the old reactors in this country will be broken up and disposed of in a similar fashion."

His aide stepped forward and handed him a sheaf of papers. He smiled and passed it to Julia. The contract's datawork had been completed a week ago, but they had both decided to give it a high profile. The roll out was a golden opportunity. With the elections due in two months, it would be a valuable campaign issue for the New Conservatives, supporting industry without direct PSP-style subsidies and showing a practical commitment to the environment.

"Thank you very much, Prime Minister," she said as the reporters shouted questions. "I'll just give you a brief clarification of what the contract entails. First, Event Horizon will be vitrifying the waste into ten-ton blocks in our Sunderland plant. Dragonflight will then lift them into orbit, where they will be assembled into clusters of five and attached to a solid rocket booster that will launch them into the Sun. This way, we shall be getting rid of the waste once and for all. Something I'm sure we all have cause to celebrate."

"How much is the contract worth, Julia?" someone shouted. Too loud to pretend she hadn't heard.

"As it says quite clearly in your information kit, operating costs for the *Clarke*-class spaceplane work out at four hundred pounds New Sterling per ton lifted into low Earth orbit. If you know anyone who can offer a cheaper price, I'm sure the Prime Minister would be interested to hear from them." She took a pace back and turned sharp right as soon as she finished speaking, gesturing to Prince Harry and David Marchant toward Building One. A posse of aides and management staff instinctively clustered around, isolating her. Nobody else got a chance to shout any more questions.

Access GeneralBusiness. She loaded a note to postpone the announcement about the new cyber factories for a couple of weeks. There were eighteen of them, due to be built under stage twelve of Event Horizon's expansion program, ranging from a precision-machinery shop to a large-scale composite structures plant, employing nearly thirty-five thousand people when they were complete.

Exit GeneralBusiness. It would never do for people to draw any unwarranted connections between the waste-disposal contract and the siting of all eighteen factories in marginal constituencies.

The VIP reception was held in Building One, a spacious rectangular lounge on the second floor. Chairs had been pushed back against one wall, leaving room for the caterers to set up their table opposite. The

seafood buffet was proving popular with the guests. Waiters circu-
lated with glasses of Moët champagne on silver trays. A loud purr
of conversation was drowning out the pianist.

Julia stood by the window wall sipping some of the champagne,
watching the crowd of spectators traipsing around the spaceplane
below. It was mainly family groups, parents leading eager children,
stopping to take pictures under the nose. Five different channel news
teams were recording, their reporters using the spaceplane as a backdrop.

Patrick left the buffet table and came over. "You should eat something," he said around a mouthful of shrimp and lettuce.

"I didn't think you liked fat girls," she retorted.

"I don't." There was a gleam in his eye she knew well enough.
"How long have we got to stay here?"

"Another hour, at least. Be patient. It could be rewarding."

"Could be?"

"Yah," she drawled.

"All right." He gave her a hungry look.

She grinned back. It would have been exciting to sneak off into
one of the disused offices upstairs. But there were security cameras
everywhere, and experience had taught her that Rachel would never
let her get out of the lounge alone.

"I suppose I'd better do my eager-hostess act," she said in resignation. Most of the people in the lounge were so much older than
she, which meant she'd have to stick with small talk, or business. So
boring. She had seen Katerina and Antonia and Laura milling about
earlier, along with their boys. But they would all be chatting to the
channel celebs. She didn't fancy that either; the silver-screen magic
tarnished rapidly in real life, she found. Greg and Eleanor were over
on the other side of the lounge, talking to Morgan Walshaw and
Gabriel Thompson, the woman he lived with. Greg looked uncomfortable and serious, but then he hated having to wear a suit and tie.
She started toward them; at least she could tease Greg.

"Miss Evans."

The urgency in the voice surprised her. It clashed with the day's
mood. She turned.

It was Dr. Ranasfari. Julia sighed inwardly, very careful not to show any disappointment. She couldn't even make small talk with Dr. Ranasfari. The tall, wiry physicist was forty-five years old, neatly turned out, as always, in a light-gray suit, white shirt, and a pink tie that matched her own suit's color. His dark face looked strained, brown eyes blinking incessantly, glossed raven-black hair shining a spectral blue under the lounge's bright biolum panels.

Dr. Ranasfari was another of those people Julia always felt she had to impress. Though she doubted many people could impress Ranasfari. He was the genius in charge of the research team that had produced the giga-conductor for Event Horizon. It had taken him ten years, but her grandfather had never doubted he could do it.

"The man's dedicated," Philip Evans had told her once. "Bloody boring, mind, Juliet, but dedicated. That's what makes him special. He'll spend his life on a project if need be. We're lucky to have him."

After the giga-conductor was unveiled to the world and the need for total security was abolished, she had built Ranasfari a laboratory complex in Cambridge, and gave him a budget of twenty million pounds New Sterling a year to spend on whatever projects he wanted. He was currently working on a direct thermocouple, a solid-state fiber that would convert thermal energy straight into electricity, eliminating any need for conventional turbines and generators. The potential applications for geothermal power extraction alone were colossal. If he asked for fifty million a year, she would grant it.

"No drink, Cormac?" she asked lightly. He never actually objected to her using his first name, although she was always Miss Evans to him. "You really ought to have one glass at least, this is as much your day as it is mine."

His lips twisted nervously, showing a flash of snow-white teeth. "Thank you, no. Miss Evans, I really must speak with you."

She had never seen him so agitated before. Her humor spiraled down. "Of course." She signaled to Rachel.

Julia supposed she ought to be grateful Ranasfari had come directly to her, it was a silent acknowledgment of her authority. There were dozens of premier-grade executives who supervised Event Horizon's innumerable divisions, but ultimately they all answered to her. The company wasn't just hers in name; she took sole responsibility for its management, to the amazement and increasing fascination of the world at large. Responsibility, but not the burden of organization; that was shared, quietly, unobtrusively.

The Neural Network bioware core was the final gamble of a dying billionaire, a bid for immortality of the mind. It had to be a billionaire, nobody else could afford the cost. Philip Evans had spliced his sequencing RNA into the bioware, replicating his own neuronic structure. When the NN core had grown to its full size, his memories had been squirted out of his dying brain and into their new titanium-cased protein circuitry.

And it had worked. His memories operated in a perfect duplicate of his neural pathways, providing a continuation of personality. Julia had never heard the NN core utter a single out-of-character remark. It was Grandpa.

He had plugged himself into Event Horizon's datanet, orchestrating the company's expansion with an efficiency far in excess of any ordinary managerial system. Seventy years of experience, knowledge, and business guile put into practice by a mind with more spare processing capacity than a lightware number cruncher. No detail was too small to escape his scrutiny, every operational aspect could be overseen with one-hundred-percent attention. With him to guide her faltering steps, it was no surprise that Event Horizon had flourished the way it had. Poor old Patrick with his dusty academic degree could never hope to match her when it came to business tactics. In tandem with her grandfather, she made more commercial and financial decisions in a day than he would make in the next ten years working for his family organization.

And at the end of the day, she could confide in Grandpa totally. He always understood. The invisible friend of childhood imagination, upgraded for the rigors of adult life, infallible and virtually omnipotent. It was wonderfully reassuring.

The empty office Julia and Ranasfari wound up commandeering overlooked Building One's giant central assembly hall. Even today, with half of the hall's staff attending the roll-out ceremony, there was a lot of activity on the floor. Integration bays around the inner wall were brightly lit, showing white-coated technicians maneuvering large sections of machinery into place or crowded around terminal display cubes. Little flat-top cyber trucks followed color-coded guidance strips along alleyways formed by bungalow-sized blocks of equipment. The spaceplane production line dominated the center of the hall. The way the craft in various stages of construction were pressed nose to tail along its length was reminiscent of some biological growth process, Julia thought, a cyber-queen's birth passage, straight out of one of those big-budget channel horror shows. At the far end were skeletal outlines, triangles of naked ribs and spars that caged spherical tanks and contoured systems modules coated in crinkled gold foil. As the spaceplanes progressed down the line, sections of the metalloceramic hulls had been fitted, the wheel bogies added, engines installed. Three almost complete craft were parked in the test bays right in front of the doors, people walking over their wings, big ribbed hoses and power cables plugged into open inspection hatches, polythene taped over various vents and inlets.

Julia sat in the swivel chair behind the desk, a black imitation-wood affair with an Olivetti terminal linked into a complicated CAD drafting board. The office belonged to a middle-manager in the microgee module power systems bureau. Rachel checked it out, then closed the door behind her, standing sentry duty. Dr. Ranasfari sank into the cheap, thickly padded chair in front of the desk.

"What is it, Cormac?" Julia asked.

He gave another nervous grimace. "Perhaps I should have gone to Mr. Walshaw, but I really feel this must be taken up at the highest level. And the Prime Minister is here, he will listen to you."

Julia moved from studious interest to outright fascination. Ranasfari never showed the slightest concern for anything outside his work.

Open Channel To NN Core.

Hello, Juliet, what's the problem? I thought you'd be enjoying yourself today, Philip Evans said soundlessly into her mind.

It's Ranasfari, she told him. *I'd like you to listen in on this. I might want your opinion.*

"That sounds very drastic, Cormac," she said out loud. "But you know I'll help in whatever way I can."

He nodded, squeezing the knuckles of his left hand. "Thank you. It concerns Dr. Edward Kitchener. You know I used to be one of his students?"

"I didn't know that, no. But I've heard of Edward Kitchener." Even as she said it, she remembered: Kitchener's gruesome murder had dominated the newscasts three days ago, even managing to nudge Scotland off the premier bulletins on Friday night. She couldn't remember seeing much else about it since, although there had been an update this morning, some poor detective in the hot seat, unable to satisfy the incessant questions that reporters were flinging at him.

Grandpa, have they caught the killer yet?

No.

Ah. I think I see where we're leading.

"His death was a tragedy," she said hurriedly.

"Yes. And the culprit still has not been brought to justice. That is what I want, Miss Evans, justice. Kitchener was a brilliant man. Brilliant. He had flaws, weaknesses, we all do. But his genius is undeniable. Simple dignity demands that his murderer is caught. I'm not asking for vengeance. I do not want the return of the death penalty. Nor do I want this barbarian quietly eliminated. But I do want him caught and tried, Miss Evans. Please. The police . . . they've had three days. I'm sure they're doing their best, but after all, Oakham is just a provincial station. You must impress the Prime Minister, and through him, the Home Secretary, on the absolute urgency of this case."

Tricky one, Juliet. According to finance-division records, we were paying Dr. Edward Kitchener for research work.

What? I don't remember that.

It was a contract issued by Ranasfari.

Bloody hell.

Damn right, girl. You start pushing Marchant for action now and people will accuse you of meddling in police affairs. There's enough allegations about you and Event Horizon having undue influence over the New Conservatives as it is.

"What project was Dr. Kitchener working on for us?" she asked Ranasfari.

He stopped playing with his hands. "I didn't think it was worth bringing to your attention," he said evasively.

She decided to go all out on the friendship routine. "Cormac, you know you have my full confidence. That's why your budget doesn't have to be cleared through the finance division first; I don't want you having to justify yourself to accountants. I genuinely do appreciate the value of pure research."

Seductress! Mental laughter echoed faintly.

"Well, thank you." Ranasfari ducked his head. "I asked Edward to look into wormholes for me. It corresponds with his field of interest. He was quite intrigued by the prospect. We discussed a fee, but he was more interested in the specialist programs our software division could provide for his lightware processor than in actual money. He agreed to take the contract, and I would channel his software requests through my laboratory. The money was just a token."

Access General Encyclopedia. Query: Wormholes, Category Physics.

A neat little précis emerged from the processor.

"When you say wormholes, you mean the instantaneous connections through space-time, I take it?" she asked.

"Yes. Wormholes are quite permissible under Einsteinian relativity."

"I know it's off the point, but what exactly is your interest in these wormholes?"

"I thought, Miss Evans," he said stiffly, "I thought that there might be a possible application in interstellar transit."

"A stardrive?" she said in a surprised whisper.

He nodded, thoroughly miserable.

"Faster-than-light travel?"

Another brief nod.

"Bloody hell," said Julia. She summoned up a logic matrix from the processor node, feeding in the relevant bytes. The combination of irrational brain and coldly precise nodes gave her an ability to dissect problems from oblique angles, fusing intuition and syllogism in a way no pure computer could match. Data packages flowed and merged through the mental construct, budding into ideas. Most she rejected, the remainder opened up interesting options.

"Who else would know that Kitchener was working for us?" she asked.

"Secrecy was not something I would wish to impose on Edward. But he was not naturally communicative, certainly not to the media. His students would know, of course, probably several high-level theoretical cosmologists. He maintained contacts throughout the physics community, in fact, academia in general. The free exchange of ideas is vital in such a field."

She ignored the defensive tone.

How about it, Grandpa? Could Event Horizon be tied in?

You mean, was he killed to prevent us from obtaining a stardrive?

Yes.

It's a probability, Juliet, you know it is. But I can't see anyone getting so worked up about it that they'd butcher the old boy, not for something that hypothetical. Besides, if it is possible to build an FTL stardrive, then ultimately it will be built. Kitchener might have been a wild card, but plodders have their place too. I expect Ranasfari could crack it if he put enough time in.

Lord, I hope he doesn't. I rather wanted that direct thermocouple.

What are you going to do, Juliet?

Well, we can't ignore Kitchener's murder now. If there is someone that paranoid about Event Horizon walking around loose, then I want him behind bars pronto.

Attagirl.

She put her elbows on the desk and pressed her palms together. "I will have Morgan Walshaw contact the Home Office directly," she said. "I think I can see how we can get this terrible crime solved quickly."

"How?" Ranasfari asked.

"The Home Office can authorize local police stations to hire specialist advisers when the circumstances warrant it."

"What sort of specialist?"

She smiled. "I was thinking a psychic might be appropriate."

4

GREG STOOD BEHIND THE MOSS-COVERED stone wall of his farmyard and watched a swarm of bilious clouds buffet the southern sky, blocking out the clean gold and orange colors of the low morning sun. Fast, cool gusts of air chased random wave-patterns in the shaggy grass around the lime saplings, twitching the slate-gray water of the reservoir into small peaks.

In the long thistle-mottled field running between the groves and Hambleton Wood he could see the rabbits venturing out of their huge warrens hidden below the dead trees. Small, tawny mounds sloping through the nettle clumps and spindly mildewed forget-me-nots that flourished around the rank of perished hawthorn bushes marking the boundary of the wood. There must have been over eighty of them. He and Eleanor went out on regular shoots two nights each week, infrared laser hunting-rifles picking off fifty at a time. It never seemed to make the slightest difference to their numbers the next morning.

The hot climate had expanded their breeding season to ten months of the year, and the impenetrable tangle of lush undergrowth in the wood meant he couldn't reach their warrens to cull them properly. A Forestry Commission logging team was scheduled to fell the dead trunks in a couple of years, replanting with Chinese pines; otherwise he would probably have torched the wood at the height of summer and to hell with the owner. The rest of the peninsula's citrus farmers certainly wouldn't object.

Rabbits were a countrywide problem; despite the massive shooting and trapping campaigns that had turned them into a cheap staple meat, they were making serious inroads into England's food crops. The Ministry of Agriculture was holding discussions with the Farmers' Union about releasing a new virulent strain of myxomatosis. It was a nasty virus, but Greg couldn't see an alternative.

He shrugged his black leather jacket over a dark-blue short-sleeved cotton sports shirt. His olive-green trousers had a tropical weave, which should keep him from sweating. He would have preferred shorts, but that was pushing it. At least he could wear comfortable suede ankle boots today, the Armani suit and shiny black leather shoes Eleanor had made him put on for the roll-out ceremony had been a torture. Too stiff, too hot. It reminded him of the dress uniforms he had had to wear for regimental dinners. But at least they had been introduced to Prince Harry at the VIP reception, which made up for a lot. Then Julia waylaid him with her oh-so-reasonable favor.

He shook his head at the memory. He was irritated, more by the fact that she had automatically assumed he would help the police than by being dragged back into that kind of work, but he couldn't honestly say there was any real anger. In any case, the idea of a killer as psychotic as Kitchener's stalking the district wasn't a particularly welcome one. Just so long as this wasn't going to set a precedent. The citrus groves were his life now, and hopefully children before too long.

Eleanor came out of the front door and blipped the lock. She was wearing a navy-blue waiter-cut jacket over an embroidered Indian cotton blouse, deep-purple culottes. Her gaze ran over the windows she had been painting before the weekend; the frames were coated in a dull-pink undercoat, waiting for the white gloss finish. She crinkled her nose.

"Maybe I should stay," she said, sounding unconvinced.

"Not a chance; if I have to go, so do you. I've still got those limes to plant. And our neighboring army of killer bunnies is waiting for a chance to eat the ones I did put in, look."

She glared at the mounds of brown fur bopping about through the undergrowth. "Perhaps we ought to torch the wood after all."

He opened the EMC Ranger's door and climbed in behind the wheel. "It's too near Hambleton, and it's not the real solution anyway."

"I suppose." She sat in the passenger seat. "I hate the idea of myxamatosis."

He drove up the slope and into the village. The broken windows on the Collister's cottage had already been boarded up with clean sheets of plywood, and a heavy padlock held the front door shut. Someone had picked all the ripe brambles from the hedge.

Eleanor gave it a somber look as they went past, but didn't say anything.

The EMC Ranger's fat, deep-tread tires made short work of the slushy vegetation matting the peninsular link road. Monday night's rains had left the flat fields beside the road looking like rice paddies. They were planted with gene-tailored barley, a design that utilized the increased level of atmospheric carbon dioxide to produce high yields. Long lines of verdant green shoots as thick as his thumb were poking up through silver pools of water; flocks of gulls waded up and down the ranks, pecking up the bounty of worms that had risen to the surface.

When they reached the roundabout on the Oakham bypass, Greg steered straight around and headed down the A606. The fields of gene-tailored barley gave way to cacao plantations for the last kilometer into town. Over the last few years Oakham had gradually been encircled by the bushes, and more ground was being prepared, expanding the plantations outward like a vigorous mushroom ring. They were a valuable addition to the town's economy. The price of the seed was rising all the time as processed-food factories came back on stream, bringing chocolate back into the shops; and the gene-tailored variety flowered twice a year. Their cultivation also soaked up a fair fraction of the unemployed refugees who had been billeted in the town when the Lincolnshire Fens were flooded by the rising sea.

The expanse of small amber flowers was just starting to bloom, but Greg ignored it. In his mind he was still running through yesterday afternoon's conversation with Julia.

"It'll just be half a day's work for you," she'd said. "It's *really* important to me. Please, Greg."

All he could see was a pretty young oval face and big tawny eyes looking up at him entreatingly. That kind of sly appeal, the not-quite-innocent adolescent adoration, was really below the belt. Typical Julia. The number of boys with broken hearts left in her wake could populate a small city.

"I'm a psychic," he said out loud.

Eleanor turned and gave him an expectant glance. "Yes?"

"So how come I can never win an argument with Julia?"

"Because you want to lose. You know the way she feels about you."

"Why didn't you object? This Kitchener thing, it's exactly why we moved out to the farm, to get away from it."

She flashed him a dry, knowing smile. "I didn't object because you were interested. Julia was right when she said you could clear it up in an afternoon. And once she mentioned it, you were hooked. Admit it."

"Yeah," he said. Immensely grateful that she understood once again. Though right at the back of his mind was a tiny smack of disquiet, a subliminal certainty that something didn't quite gel. His intuition playing up again, although he hadn't used his gland since leaving the Collisters' cottage. It had started as soon as Julia mentioned Kitchener's murder at Launde Abbey. And the more he tried to resolve it, to find the reason, the more elusive it became. It would come eventually of course, and then he'd kick himself for missing the obvious.

Inside Oakham, the road surface improved noticeably; thistles and twitch grass still burrowed up through the tarmac near the curbs, but the streets were open to two-way traffic. Scooters and bicycles clogged the middle of the town, forcing Greg to reduce speed; horse-and-cart rigs queued up patiently behind pre-Warming juggernauts. The big lorries had been converted to burning methane, true dinosaurs now, paintwork scarred and fading, drive mechanisms cannibalized from a dozen different wrecks.

The ramshackle stalls that used to run the length of High Street during the PSP years had recently been evicted and the tarmac sealed over with thermo-stabilized cellulose. Greg used to enjoy the souk-like atmosphere of the town center, but the economic upswing was steadily squeezing street-traders and spivs out of national life. Die-hard stall-holders had moved back to the market square, but it wasn't the same. Shops were in vogue again. Almost two-thirds had reopened, and he could see another three being refurbished; although they mainly sold consumer products and clothes, the market retained its hold over supplying fresh food. He wondered sourly how long it would take for the supermarket chains to reestablish themselves. Back to sanitized, mass-produced packets of tasteless pap. A sure sign of prosperity.

The way the country was right now was just about perfect, he reckoned. Emerging from the nightmare past and looking forward to a future rich with promises—most of them made by Julia.

They turned off High Street and drove down Church Street, past Cutts Close, the central park. It was bounded by earth ramparts and terribly overgrown; dead oak trees lying where they had fallen, waist-high grass choking the ancient swings. The affluence of High Street didn't extend far.

A cluster of thirty-odd sleek white and silver trailers and caravans was drawn up in the middle of Cutts Close, looking like some kind of futuristic Gypsy convoy. Greg saw the corporate logos of channel newscast companies splashed on them, a thicket of tripod-mounted satellite uplink dishes pointing up into the southern sky.

His fingers tightened around the steering wheel in reflex dismay. Of course! How stupid, he should have realized. A groan escaped from his lips.

"What is it?" Eleanor asked.

"Them!" He nodded ahead.

The police station was sited just past the bottom of the park, backing on to what had once been the famous public school's playing fields. The rugby pitches and cricket squares had long since been dug up to provide allotments for the Fens refugees displaced by the rising seas; over two hundred families had been crammed into the school buildings by the PSP Residential Allocation Bureau. It was only a temporary accommodation, they were promised. Now, twelve years on, they were still waiting for proper housing.

The main part of the station was a broad two-story building built out of drab rusty-colored brick, roofed by steel-gray tiles. A single-story wing jutted out of the front, almost like an afterthought, long, narrow windows facing the road. It dated from the tail-end of the last century, and despite the architect's use of curves and split levels to reduce its starkness, it had a fortress-like appearance. The image wasn't helped by the relics of the People's Constables' tenure. Metal grilles had been fitted over the long ground-floor windows, black security-camera globes hung from the eaves, and the entrance to the rear car park was guarded by a high fence of thin monolattice slice-wire with skull-and-crossbones warning signs on each post. The brickwork facing the street was covered in ghostly remnants of paint-bomb impacts and fluorospray graffiti; an ineffectual solvent wash had left several anti-PSP slogans visible. Tapering soot scars, like frozen black flames, showed where the Molotovs had hit.

The rioters and celebrants who had laid siege to the station the day the PSP fell had now been replaced by the media army.

"Good God," Eleanor murmured when they reached the end of Church Street.

Greg guessed there must have been over two hundred of them; and it was like an army, rank denoted by the uniform: reporters in smooth suits, broadcast crews in T-shirts and shorts, production staff in designer casuals. The majority had taken over the broad pavement opposite the station, although some camera operators had staked out positions on the park's earth embankment, giving them a good view of the station. Several fast-food caravans had set up shop in front of the Catholic church a hundred meters farther down the road. They were doing a good trade with production PAs.

Greg sounded the horn as he indicated to turn into the station. A knot of twelve people were just standing in the middle of the road, channel logos on their jackets.

"Well, I suppose the local pubs will be happy," Eleanor said.

There was a lone bobby standing outside the gate in the slice-wire fence. He was about twenty-five, wearing dress whites, shorts, and half-sleeve shirt, with a peaked cap, and looking very fed up.

"Oh, bugger," Greg muttered as he lowered the window. The rearview mirror showed him the reporters converging *en masse* on the EMC Ranger.

"Yes, sir?" the bobby asked.

"I'm here to see Detective Inspector Langley," Greg said. He held up his general ident card, pressing his thumb on the activation patch.

The bobby pulled out his police-issue cybofax, and the two exchanged polarized photons in a blink of dim ruby light. Reporters were clustering around the bobby, jostling to see what was going on. Two camera operators had shoved their lenses up against Eleanor's window.

"Go straight in, sir," the bobby said after his cybofax had confirmed Greg's identity. He blipped the gate lock. It started to swing open.

The action triggered off a barrage of questions from the reporters.

"Who are you, mate?"

"What have you come here for?"

"Are you a relative of Kitchener?"

"Smile for us, luv!"

Greg toed the accelerator as soon as the gate started to open, nudging the EMC Ranger toward the gap in short jerks. The bobby was trying to shove the crush of reporters to one side.

Greg switched to a broad Lincolnshire accent and bellowed out of the open window: "I'm here to see about me bleedin' sheep, ain't I? Some bastard's been pinching 'em right out o' the field. What's it got to do with you buggers? Get out the bleeding way!"

The EMC Ranger must have added authenticity, a mud-caked farm vehicle, even though it was new and expensive. A chorus of groans went up. The reporters gave each other annoyed shrugs and gave up.

The gate closed behind them.

Eleanor was smiling broadly. "Very good. I give it less than twenty minutes before they discover you are the Greg Mandel who had Julia Evans as a bridesmaid at his wedding."

"I expect you're right."

There were five police vehicles parked in the yard, four old EMC electric hatchbacks, powered by high-density polymer batteries, and a rust-spotted Black Maria with ten-year-old license plates. Greg parked the EMC Ranger next to a line of scooters.

There was a woman officer waiting for them. She introduced herself as Detective Sergeant Amanda Paterson, a pleasant-faced thirty-year-old with mouse-brown hair, wearing a white blouse and fawn skirt. She shook hands with a surprisingly strong grip, but her manner was fairly reserved.

"I'll take you to see Inspector Langley," she told them briskly. "He's heading the inquiry."

"Are you working on the case?" Greg asked.

"Yes, sir." There was no elaboration. She opened the door and ushered them into the station. The air inside was cool and stale, there were no fans or air conditioners to circulate it. Biolum strips screwed onto the ceiling cast a weary light along the corridor. The original electric tubes had been left in place, their pearl glass covers gray with dust.

It was all very basic, Greg thought as she led them to the central stairwell. The gray-green ribbed carpet was badly worn, walls were scarred with rubber shoe marks above the skirting-board, cream-colored paint had darkened, doors were scuffed and scratched and didn't even have 'ware locks.

The police didn't enjoy much public confidence right now, he knew. But starving them of money and resources was hardly going to help their morale and efficiency, certainly not at a time when the New Conservatives were trying to claim the credit for resurrecting an honest and impartial judicial system.

They passed a mess room, and three uniformed constables glanced out. Their faces hardened as soon as they saw Greg and he began to wonder just what sort of stories were orbiting the station.

The CID office was on the second floor. Amanda Paterson knocked once on the door and walked in. Greg followed her into the noise of shrilling phones and murmuring voices. There were six imitation-wood desks inside, three of them occupied by men, detectives in shirt sleeves typing away at their terminal keyboards, one with an old-fashioned phone handset jammed between his shoulder and jaw. They all stared at Greg and Eleanor. Metal filing cabinets were lined up along the wall next to the door, kelpboard boxes piled on top. A big flatscreen covered the rear wall, displaying a large-scale map, with half of Oakham showing as a red and brown crescent along the right-hand side. The air was warm despite two of the windows being open; a single air conditioner thrummed loudly.

Detective Inspector Vernon Langley was in his late forties. He was almost a head shorter than Greg, and his dark hair had nearly van-ished, leaving a shiny brown pate. He was sitting behind a desk at the head of the room, jacket draped over the back of his chair, mauve tie loosened, buttons on his white shirt straining slightly, looking about seven kilos overweight.

The desk was littered in printouts, folders, thumb-sized cylindri-cal memox crystals, and sheets of handwritten notes. Langley was typ-ing on an English Electric terminal. The model was a decade out of date, and pretty inferior even when it was new. English Electric had been a nationalized conglomerate formed by the PSP, a shotgun mar-riage between a dozen disparate 'ware companies. Only government offices used to buy their equipment; everyone else went to black-market spivs for up-to-date foreign gear.

He stood up to greet them, wincing slightly, one hand rubbing the stiffness from his back as he rose. He had obviously been working close to his limit on the Kitchener case: his face was lined, there was a five o'clock shadow on his chin. Greg felt exhausted just looking at him.

"I wasn't informed that there would be two of you," he said as he shook hands with Eleanor.

"I act as Greg's assistant," Eleanor said levelly. "I am also his wife."

Vernon Langley nodded reluctantly as he sat back down again. "All right, I'm certainly not going to make an issue of it. Find yourself a seat, please."

Greg drew up a couple of plain wooden chairs. At a second nod from Vernon, Amanda Paterson left them to go sit at a desk next to the other three detectives. The four of them put their heads together, talking in low tones.

Greg was tempted to use his gland there and then, but he guessed the only emotion in the room would be resentment. They had all been working hard on an important case, under an immense, and very public, burden to produce quick results; now some civilian glamor-merchant had been brought in over their heads because of political pressure. He knew the feeling of frustration well enough; army brass had worked according to no known principles of logic.

"The Home Office called me at home this morning," Langley said. "Apparently you have been drafted in to act as my special adviser on this case. Officially, that is. Unofficially, it was made fucking clear you are now in charge. Would you mind telling me why that is, Mandel?" The lack of any inflection was far more telling than any bitterness or anger.

"I am ex-Mindstar," Greg said deferentially. "My gland gives me an empathic ability, I know when people are lying. Somebody once described me as a truthfinder."

"A truthfinder? Is that so? I've heard you spent a lot of time in Peterborough after Mindstar was demobbed."

"Yeah."

"They say you killed fifty People's Constables."

"Oh, no."

Langley's eyes narrowed in suspicion.

Greg couldn't resist it. "More like eighty."

The detective grunted. "Had a lot of experience solving murders, have you, Mandel?"

"No. None at all."

"Twenty-three years I've been in the force now. I even stuck it out in the PSP years." He waved a hand airily as Eleanor shifted uncomfortably. "Oh, don't worry, Mrs. Mandel, the Inquisitors cleared me of any complicity with the Party. That's why I was posted here from Grantham; a lot of Oakham's officers failed that particular test. Not politically sound, you see. Well, not as far as this government is concerned."

"I wonder if Edward Kitchener cares what political color the investigating officers are," Eleanor said.

Langley gave her a long look, then sighed in defeat. "You're quite right, of course, Mrs. Mandel. Please excuse me. I have spent the last four days and nights trying to find this maniac. And for all my efforts, I have got exactly nowhere. So tempers in this office are likely to be a little frayed this morning. I apologize in advance for any sharp answers you may receive. Nothing personal."

"I didn't know the Home Office had told you I was in charge," Greg said. "As far as I'm concerned, it's still your investigation. I really am just a specialist."

"Sure, thanks," said Langley.

Greg decided to press on. It was obvious there wouldn't be the usual small talk, the getting-to-know-you session. He'd just have to do what he could. "The press reports said Kitchener was butchered, is that true?"

"Yes. If I didn't know better, I'd say it was a ritualistic killing. Satan worship, a pagan sacrifice, something like that. It was utter barbarism. His chest was split open, lungs spread out on either side of his head. We have holograms if you want an *in situ* review."

"Not at the moment," Greg said. "Why would anybody go to that much trouble?"

Langley gestured emptily. "Who knows? I meet some evil bastards in this job. But Kitchener's murderer is beyond me, that kind of mind is in a class of its own. Nobody knows what makes someone like that tick. To be honest, it frightens me, the fact that they can walk around pretending to be human for ninety-nine percent of the time. I suppose you can spot one straight off?"

"Maybe," Greg said. "If I knew what to look for."

"Whoever he is, he's not entirely original. It was a copy-cat method."

"Copy cat?"

"This spreading-the-lungs gimmick; Liam Bursken used to do it." Greg frowned, the name was familiar.

"He was a serial killer, wasn't he?" Eleanor said.

"That's right, he roamed Newark picking people at random off the streets, then butchering them. The press called him the Viking. He murdered eleven victims in five months. But that was six years ago. Now he really was psychopathic, a total loon. Newark was like a city under siege until he was caught. People refused to go out after dusk. There were vigilante groups patroling the streets, fighting with People's Constables. Nasty business."

"Where is he now?" Greg asked.

"HMP Stocken Hall, the Clinical Detention Center where they keep the really dangerous cases. Locked away in the maximum-security wing for the rest of time."

"That's close," Greg murmured. He conjured up a mental map of the area. Stocken Hall was only about fifteen kilometers from Launde Abbey as the crow flies.

"Give me some credit. I did check, Mandel. Bursken was there four nights ago. They won't even take him out of the Center if he gets ill; the doctors have to visit him."

"There is no such thing as coincidence." Greg smiled apologetically. "Okay. It wasn't Bursken. You say you haven't got a suspect yet? Surely you must have some idea."

"None at all." The detective slumped farther back into his chair. "Embarrassing for us, really. Considering there are only six possible culprits. A neat solution, somebody we could charge quickly, would have been the best thing that could have happened to this station. Not the town's favorite sons, we are." He flicked a finger at Amanda Paterson. "And daughters, of course. As it is, I can't even go outside to that pack of jackals and say I hope to make an arrest in the near future."

"Who are the six possibles?"

"Kitchener's students. And a bigger bunch of wallies you've never seen; bright kids, but they're plugged into some other universe the whole time. Typical student types, naïve and fashionably rebellious. They were the only ones in Launde Abbey at the time. The Abbey's security-system memory showed no one else sneaked in, and it's all top-grade gear. But I'm not just relying on that as evidence. It was a nasty storm the night Kitchener was murdered, remember?"

"Yeah," Greg said. He remembered the day of Roy Collister's lynch mob.

Langley climbed to his feet and went over to the big flatscreen on the rear wall. "Jon Nevin will show you what I mean. He's been checking out all the possible access routes to the Abbey."

One of the other detectives stood up; in his late twenties, thinning black hair shaved close, a narrow face with a long nose that had been broken at some time. He made an effort to rein back on his hostility as Greg and Eleanor trailed after Langley.

The map was centered on Launde Park, an irregular patch colored a phosphorescent pink. A tall column of seven-digit numbers had been superimposed alongside. From the scale, Greg judged the park had an area of about a square kilometer; he hadn't quite realized how remote it was, situated halfway up the side of the Chater valley. A lone road bisecting the valley was its only link with the outside world.

Nevin tapped a finger on the little black rectangle that represented the Abbey. His face registered total uninterest. If he'd still been in the army, Greg would have called it dumb insolence.

"Because of its isolated position, we don't believe anyone could have got to Launde Abbey at any time after six o'clock last Thursday afternoon," Nevin recited in a dull tone.

"What time was Kitchener killed?" Greg asked.

"Approximately four-thirty on Friday morning," Langley said. "Give or take fifteen minutes. Certainly not before four."

"The storm arrived at Launde Abbey at about five p.m. on Thursday," Nevin said. His hand traced northward along the road outside the Abbey. "We estimate the bridge over the River Chater was submerged by six, completely unpassable. The rainfall was very heavy around here, fifteen centimeters according to the meteorological office at RAF Cottesmore. Basically, that bridge is just a couple of big concrete-pipe sections with earth and stone shoveled on top; it's a very minor road, even by the last century's standards.

"That leaves us just the route to the south. The road goes up over the brow of the valley and into Loddington; but there is a fork just outside Loddington that leads away to Belton. So in order to get onto the road to Launde, you have to go through either Loddington or Belton."

Greg studied the villages; they were tiny, smaller than Hambleton. Long columns of code numbers were strung out beside them. He could see where Nevin was leading. They were small, insular farming communities, and anything out of the ordinary—strangers, unknown vehicles—would become a talking-point for weeks. He pointed to the thin roads that led to Launde Park. "What sort of condition are these roads in?" he asked.

"The map is deceptive," Nevin admitted. He swept his hand over the web of yellow lines covering the land to the west of Oakham; it was a bleak stretch of countryside, furrowed with twisting valleys and steeply rounded hills. A few lonely farmhouses were dotted about, snug in the lee of depressions. "All these minor roads are down to farm tracks in most places. Some stretches are completely overgrown, you have to be a local to know where to drive."

"And you're saying nobody went through Loddington or Belton after six o'clock on Thursday?" Eleanor asked.

"That's right, there wasn't even any local traffic," Jon Nevin said. "Everybody was battened down before the storm began. We did a house-to-house inquiry in both Loddington and Belton." He pointed at the columns of numbers. "These are our file codes for the statements; you can review them if you want, we interviewed everybody. You see, the streets in both villages are very narrow and if any vehicle had gone through, the residents would have known."

Eleanor shrugged acceptance and gave him a warm smile. The detective couldn't maintain his air of indifference under those circumstances. Greg pretended not to notice.

Langley went and sat behind the nearest desk, hooking an arm over the back of the chair. "In any case, the important thing is, we know for a fact that nobody came out of the valley between six o'clock Thursday evening and six o'clock Friday morning. The murderer was there when we arrived."

"How do you figure that?" Greg asked.

"The Chater bridge was still under water until midday Friday. That leaves just the south road again. If you were coming out of the valley, you had to use it. The students called us from the Abbey at five-forty on Friday morning. It was Jon here and a couple of uniforms who responded. They took a car down to the Abbey just after six."

"We were the first to use that road after the storm finished," Nevin said, "and we had a lot of trouble. It was covered in fresh mud from the rains, and it was absolutely pristine. No tire tracks. I was very careful to check. And you couldn't cut across country, not with the ground in that state, it was saturated; even your EMC Ranger would sink in up to the hubcaps. The only people in that valley when Kitchener was killed were his students."

Greg checked the map again and decided they were probably right about the roads. He thought about how he would go about killing Kitchener. There had been enough similar missions in Turkey. Covert penetrations, tracking down enemy officers, eliminating them without fuss, stealing away afterward, leaving the Legion troops unnerved by their blatant vulnerability. An old man confined in a verified location would be an easy target.

"What about aircraft?" he asked.

Langley let out a soft snort. "I checked with the CAA and the RAF. There was nothing flying around the Chater valley early Friday morning, nor Thursday evening for that matter."

"Can we shift this focus to show the rest of the Chater valley?" Greg asked.

"Yes," Langley said. He waved permission to Nevin. The detective started to tap out instructions on a desk terminal. After a minute the map blinked out altogether and he cursed. Amanda Paterson joined him at the terminal.

"This is how it goes here," Langley said, half to himself. "I don't suppose your Home Office contact considered allocating us a decent equipment budget as well?"

"I doubt it."

He curled up a corner of his mouth in resignation.

The map reappeared, flickering for a moment, then steadied and slowly traversed east to west until Launde Park touched the left-hand edge of the flatscreen.

"Is that all right?" Paterson asked.

"Yeah, thanks," Greg said. He tracked the River Chater out of

Launde Park toward the east. It was almost a straight course. Farther down from Launde, the floor of the valley was crossed by a few minor roads, but essentially it was empty until it reached Ketton, twenty kilometers away. "If it was me," Greg said, his eyes still on the map, "I would use a military microlight to fly in. You could launch anywhere west of Ketton and cruise up the river, keeping your altitude below the top of the valley to avoid radar."

The detectives glanced about uncertainly.

"A microlight?" Langley said. His mind tone betrayed a strong skepticism.

"No messing. The Westland ghost wing was the best ever made, by my reckoning anyway. They had a high reliability, a minute radar return, and they maneuvered like a dream. Nobody could hear it from the ground once you were above a hundred meters; and you glided down to a landing." His fingernail made a light *click* as he touched the screen above Launde Park. "The gradient of the slopes around the Abbey would be ideal for an unpowered launch afterward."

They were all staring at him, humor and contempt leached away.

"The winds," Eleanor said matter-of-factly into the silence.

"Yeah. They could be a problem, certainly right after that storm. We'd have to check with RAF Cottesmore, see what speeds they were around here."

"This is somewhat fanciful, isn't it?" Langley asked mildly.

"Somebody killed him, and you say it wasn't any of the people who were there."

"We haven't proved any of them did it," Nevin countered. "But we're still interviewing them."

"Even if someone did fly in like you say," Paterson said, "he still had to get past the Abbey's security system."

"If a hardline tekmerc had been contracted to snuff Kitchener, he would go in loaded with enough 'ware to burn through the security system without leaving a trace."

"A tekmerc?" Langley asked. Disbelief was thick in his voice.

"Yeah. I take it you have drawn up a list of people who disliked Kitchener? From what I remember, he was a prickly character."

"There are a few academics who have clashed with him publicly,"

Nevin said cautiously. "But I don't think a grudge over different physics theories would extend to this. Everyone acknowledged he was a genius, they made allowances for his behavior."

Greg looked around at the stony faces circling him. He had entertained the notion, absurdly guileless now, he realized, that he would be welcomed by a team who would be delighted to have his psi faculty at their disposal. He wasn't expecting to be taken out for beers and a meal afterward, but at least that way he could have approached the case with some enthusiasm. All Langley's dispirited squad could offer was a long uphill yomp.

"Did any of you know that Kitchener was working on a research project for Event Horizon?" he asked.

The reaction was more or less what he expected: flashes of disgust, quickly hidden, tight faces, hard eyes. Langley dropped his head into his hands, fingertips massaging his temple.

"Oh, shit," he said thickly. "Greg and Eleanor Mandel, who had Julia Evans as their bridesmaid. How stupid of me. She had you sent here. And there I was thinking that it was just the Home Office panicking for a quick arrest."

"Did you know about the contract?" Eleanor asked waspishly. Her face had reddened under her tan.

"No, we didn't," Langley replied, equally truculent.

Greg touched her shoulder, trying to reassure her. She flashed him a grateful smile. "Well, I suggest that corporate rivalry is now a motive for you to consider," he said. "Does that make any of the students a likely candidate?"

"No, of course not." Langley was struggling to come to terms with Event Horizon's involvement. Greg guessed he was trying to work out how this would affect his career prospects. Maybe a quiet word when the rest of the CID wasn't looking on would help smooth the way. It certainly couldn't make the situation any worse.

"Does Event Horizon have any idea who might have murdered Kitchener? Which rival would benefit from having him snuffed by a tekmerc?" Langley asked.

"No. No idea."

"They don't know? Or they don't want us to know?" Paterson asked.

"That'll do," Langley said quickly.

She gave Greg and Eleanor a sullen glare, then turned and went back to her desk.

"What sort of research was Kitchener doing for Event Horizon?" Jon Nevin asked.

"Something to do with spatial interstices," Greg said. Julia hadn't managed to explain much about it to him. He didn't think she entirely understood it herself.

"What are they?"

"I'm not entirely sure. Small black holes, from what I gather. It all goes a long way over my head."

"Are they worth much?" Langley asked.

"They might be eventually. Apparently you can use them to travel to other stars."

This time the silence stretched out painfully. The detectives clearly didn't know what to make of the idea.

Join the club, Greg thought.

"All right, Mandel," Langley said. "What is it you wish to *advise* me to do now? Because I'm buggered if I know where to go from here."

Greg paused, attempting to put his thoughts in some kind of logical sequence. Most of the training he'd received in preparation for Mindstar had been data-correlation exercises. "First, I want to visit Launde Abbey, have a look around. Then I want to interview the students. Where are they?"

"We're still holding them."

"After four days?"

"Their lawyers advised them to cooperate. For the moment, anyway. It wouldn't look good if they start throwing their legal rights around too much. But we had to agree that six days is the maximum limit; after that we'll either have to apply to a magistrate for them to be taken into police custody or let them go."

"Okay. I want to see their statements before I meet them. And the forensic and pathology reports as well, please."

"All right, we'll assign you an authority code so you can access the files on this case. And I'll take you out to Launde myself."

THREE MORE UNIFORMED BOBBIES HAD been drafted in to help keep the channel crews back from the police-station gate. Ribbons of sweat stained the spines of their white shirts as they shouted and pushed at the incursive horde. Eleanor drove out into the road and turned hard right, heading down toward the railway station. The way to do it, she discovered, was to imagine the road to be empty and just *go*. Reporters and camera operators nipped out of the way quickly.

She had been right about them tracking down Greg's personal-data profile, though.

"Mr. Mandel, is it true you're helping the police with the Kitchener murder?"

"You don't farm sheep, Greg, what are you here for?"

"Did Julia Evans send you?"

"Is it true you used to serve in Mindstar?"

"Eleanor, where are you going?"

"Come on, Greg, say something."

"Can we have a statement?"

She passed the last of them level with the fast-food caravans and pressed her foot down. The hectic shouts faded away. A smell of fried onions and spicy meat blew into the EMC Ranger through the dashboard vents.

"Christ," she murmured. When she lived on the kibbutz, she had often accompanied her father and the other men when they took the hounds out hunting. She had seen what happened to foxes, wild cats, and even other dogs when the hounds ran them down. They would keep on worrying the bloody carcass until there was nothing left but shreds. The press, she reflected sagely, had an identical behavior pattern. For the first time, she began to feel sorry for Langley, having to conduct his inquiry with them braying relentlessly on his heels.

If she had known about them as well as the way the police would treat her and Greg, she might well have played the part of shrewish wife and told him no. Too late now.

A quick check in the rearview mirror showed her the police Panda car carrying Vernon Langley and Jon Nevin was following them. Langley had assigned Amanda Paterson to accompany her and Greg in the EMC Ranger. Eleanor wasn't quite sure who was supposed to be chastised by the arrangement. Amanda was sitting in the rear of the big car, hands folded across her lap, a sullen expression on her face as she watched the detached houses of Station Road whiz past.

So defensive, Eleanor thought, as if the Kitchener inquiry was some shabby secret she was guarding. And now the barbarians were hammering on the gate, demanding access.

"You okay?" Greg asked.

"Sure."

He held her gaze for a moment. "How about you, Amanda?" he asked.

Startled, the woman looked up. "Yes, fine, thank you."

"Have they been like that the whole time?" Eleanor asked her.

"Yes." She paused. "It hasn't helped when we went around the villages collecting statements. They often got the residents' stories before we did." Her mouth tightened. "They shouldn't have done that."

Eleanor drove over the level crossing and took the Braunston road. The clouds were darkening overhead, a uniform neutral veil. It would rain soon, she knew, a thunderstorm. Weather sense was something everybody cultivated these days.

Greg inclined his head fractionally toward her, then flipped open his cybofax and started to run through the statements he'd loaded into the memory. Gray-green data trundled down the small LCD screen, rearranging itself each time he muttered an instruction.

Devious man, she thought, holding back a smile. Among his other qualities. She could read him so easily, something she'd been able to do right from the start; and vice versa, of course, him with his gland. Greg always said she had psychic traits, although he didn't want her to take the psi-assessment tests. Not putting his foot down, they didn't have that kind of relationship, but heavily opposed to her having a gland. He was more protective about it than anything else, wanting to spare her the ordeal. Several Mindstar veterans had proved incapable of making the psychological adjustment necessary to cope with their expanded psi ability.

There were so few people who saw that aspect of Greg: his concern, the oh so human failings. Gland prejudice was too strong, an undiluted paranoia virus; nobody saw past the warlock power, they were dazzled by it.

Countless times she had watched people flinch when they were introduced to him, and she could never decide quite why. Perhaps it was all the time he'd spent in the army and the Trinities. He had the air of someone terribly intimate with violence; not an obvious bruiser type, like those idiots Andrew Foster and Frankie Owen, more like the calm reserve martial-arts experts possessed.

The first time they met, the day she ran away from the kibbutz, her father had come looking for her. He backed down so fast when Greg intervened; it was the first time she had *ever* seen her father give way over anything. He always had God's righteousness on his side, so he claimed. More like incurable peasant obstinacy, she thought, the cantankerous old Bible-thumper. The whole of her life until then, or so it seemed, had been filled with his impassioned skeletal face craning out of the pulpit in the wooden chapel, broken purple capillaries on his rough cheeks showing up tobacco-brown in the pale light that filtered through the turquoise-glass window behind the altar. That face would harangue and cajole even in her dreams, promising God's justice would pursue her always.

But all it had taken was a few quiet-spoken resolute words from Greg and he had retreated, walking out of her life for good. Him, the kibbutz's spiritual leader, abandoning his only daughter to one of Satan's technological corruptions.

She had moved into Greg's chalet that night. The two of them had been together ever since. The other residents at the Berrybut timeshare estate warned her that Greg could be moody, but it never manifested with her. She could sense when he was down, when he needed sympathy, when he needed to be left alone. Those long anarchistic years in the Trinities, the cheapness of life on Peterborough's streets, were bound to affect him. He needed time to recover, that was all. Couldn't people see that?

She always felt sorry for couples who were unable to plug into each other's basic emotions. They didn't know what they were missing; she'd never trusted anyone quite like she did Greg. That and the sex, of course.

"Kitchener was fairly rich, wasn't he?" she asked Amanda.

"Yes. He had several patents bringing in royalties. His molecular interaction equations all had commercial applications, crystals and 'ware chips, that kind of thing. It was mostly kombinates who took out licenses; they paid him a couple of million New Sterling a year."

Eleanor let out an impressed whistle. "Who stands to inherit?"

Amanda's features were briefly illuminated with a recalcitrant grin when she realized how smoothly they had breached her guard. "We examined that angle. No one person benefits. Kitchener had no immediate family, the closest are a couple of younger cousins, twice removed. He left a million New Sterling to their children; there are seven of them, so split between them, it doesn't come to that much. The money goes into a trust fund anyway, and it's limited to how much can be withdrawn each year. But the bulk of the estate goes to Cambridge University. It will be used for science scholarships to enable underprivileged students to go to the university; and funding two of the physics faculties, with the proviso that it's only to be spent on laboratory equipment. He didn't want the dons to feather their nests with it."

"What about Launde Abbey, who gets that?"

"The university. It's to be a holiday retreat for the most promising physics students. He wanted them to have somewhere they could go to escape the pressure of exams and college life, and just sit and think. It's all in his will."

"That doesn't sound like the Edward Kitchener we hear about," Eleanor observed.

"That was his public image," Amanda said. "Once you've talked to the students, you'll find out that it really was mostly image. They all worshiped him."

The EMC Ranger started up the hill which led out of town. A new housing estate was under construction on both sides of the road, the first in Oakham for fifteen years. The houses had a pre-Warming Mediterranean look, thick white-painted walls to keep out the heat, silvered windows, solar-cell panel roofs made to look like red clay tiles, broad overhanging eaves. And garages, she noted; the architects must share a confidence about the future.

She had been relieved when the council passed the planning application. Considering all they'd been through when they lost their homes, and the cramped conditions of the school campus, the Fens refugees deserved somewhere for themselves. After the economy started to pick up, she had worried that they would develop into a permanent underclass, resentful and resented. A lot of them had actually been employed to build the houses, but despite that and the cacao plantations the numbers of unemployed in the Oakham district was still too large. The town urgently needed more factories to bring jobs into the area. The transport network wasn't up to supporting commuters yet, allowing people to work in the cities like they used to. She often wondered if she should ask Julia to establish an Event Horizon division in the industrial estate. Would that be an abuse of privilege? Julia could be overbearingly generous to her friends. And there were a lot of towns which needed jobs just as badly as Oakham. Of course, if the Event Horizon factory had to be built anyway, why not use what influence she had? At the moment she was just waiting to see if the council development officers could do what they were paid to, and attract industrial investment. If they hadn't interested a kombinate after another six months or so, she probably would have a word.

A favor for a favor, she thought, because God knows this Kitchener case is tougher than either of us expected. Julia would have to site a whole cyber precinct next to the town to be quits.

She took the west road out of Braunston. It was a long straight stretch up to the recently replanted Cheseldyne Spinney. The turning down to Launde Park was five hundred meters past the end of the tanbark oak saplings. There was a row of yellow police cones blocking it off, tire-deflation spikes jutting out of their bases like chrome-plated rhino horns. One of Oakham's Panda cars, with two uniformed constables inside, was on duty in front of them. Eleanor counted ten reporters camped opposite, their cars parked on the thistle-tangled verge.

As soon as the EMC Ranger stopped by the Panda car, the reporters were up and running. Cybofaxes, switched to AV record, were pressed against the glass like rectangular slate-gray leeches.

Amanda pulled out her police-issue cybofax and used its secure link to talk to the bobbies in the Panda car.

Eleanor saw one of them nod his head languidly, then they both climbed out and walked toward the cones.

"Are you taking over the case from the police, Mr. Mandel?"

"Is it true the Prime Minister appointed you to the investigation?"

"Are you Julia Evans's lover, Greg?"

Eleanor refused to snap the retort which had formed so temptingly in her mind. Instead she forced a contemptuous smile, thinking how good it would feel to stuff that tabloid channel reporter's cybofax where the sun didn't shine.

The bobbies finished clearing away the cones and waved Eleanor on. They could have cleared them away before we arrived, she thought; perhaps it's part of the needling, making us run the press gauntlet.

The Chater valley was a lush all-over green, the steep walls bulging in and out to form irregular glens and hummocks. Dead hawthorn hedges acted as trellises for ivy-leaf pelargoniums, heavy with hemispherical clusters of cerise-pink flowers. The fields were all given over the grazing land, although there was no sign of any animals; the permanent grass cover helped to prevent soil erosion in the monsoon season. As they moved over the brow on the northern side, she began to appreciate how secluded the valley was; there had been no clue of its existence from the road out of Braunston.

They started to go down a slope with a vicious incline. The road was reduced to two strips of tarmac just wide enough for the EMC Ranger's tires, speedwells forming a spongy strip between them, tiny blue-and-white flowers closed against the darkening sky. Trickles of water were running out of the verges, filling the tarmac ruts. Eleanor slowed down to a crawl.

"Mr. Mandel," Amanda said. There was such a sheepish tone to her voice Eleanor actually risked glancing from the road to check her in the mirror.

Greg looked back over his shoulder. "What is it?"

"There was something else we didn't release to the press," Amanda said. "Kitchener had a lightware number cruncher at the Abbey, he used it for numerical simulation work. Its memory core was wiped. I didn't think about it until you mentioned Event Horizon's involvement. Whatever Kitchener was working on, it's lost for good now."

"No messing?" Greg said. He sounded almost cheerful.

"We weren't sure if the 'ware had been knocked out by the storm or something. We didn't really connect the two events. But if you take commercial sabotage as a motive for the murder, then it was probably deliberate."

"Do you know when the core was wiped?" Greg asked. "Before Kitchener was murdered? After? During?"

"No. I've no idea."

"What did the students say?"

"I don't know. I can't remember if they were asked."

Greg thought for a moment, then started defining a search program that would run through the statements stored in his cybofax. Eleanor heard Amanda doing the same thing. That was when they reached a really steep part of the road, just above the Chater itself. She put the EMC Ranger into bottom gear and kept her foot on the brake pedal. The water channeled by the ruts was running a couple of centimeters deep around the tires.

"Are you sure about the bridge?" she asked Amanda.

"It should be passable by now. There was only a five-centimeter fall last night."

"You mean you don't know?" There was a bend at the foot of the slope. Eleanor nudged the EMC Ranger around it, dreading what she'd see. Turning around here would be difficult. Right at the bottom of the valley the river had worn a cramped narrow gully in the earth. The scarp had been scoured of grass and weeds by the recent monsoon floods, leaving a pockmarked face of raw red-brown earth. Ahead of the EMC Ranger the road had miraculously reappeared in full, grass, moss, nettles, and speedwells swept away by the water.

The Panda car was holding back; she caught a glimpse of it on top of the final slope.

Waiting for us to find out what the river is like, she thought. Bastards.

"We're waterproof, remember," Greg said. He winked.

She grinned savagely and urged the EMC Ranger along the last ten meters to the bridge. The Chater was a turbulent slash of fast-flowing brown water, boiling over the bridge. Eleanor used the white handrail as a guide as she gingerly steered over it. Water churned around the wheels. She estimated it was about fifteen centimeters deep, not even up to the axle.

Once they were over the river, the road turned right. Greg pulled at his lower lip, looking back thoughtfully. The smaller Panda car was edging out over the bridge, water up to the base of its doors.

"Tell you, Jon Nevin was right; nothing would have got over that on Thursday night and Friday morning," Greg said.

There was a lake ahead of them, a rectangle fifty meters long, draining into the Chater through a crumbling concrete channel. A small earth bank rose up behind it, sprouting dead horse-chestnut trees that were leaning at precarious angles.

They started to climb up the slope, a dreary expanse of scrimpy, slightly yellowed grass. The road surface on this side of the Chater was even worse than the northern side. Past the end of the first lake, and ten meters higher, was a second, a triangular shape, a hundred meters along each side. It was being fed by a waterfall at the head. A decrepit wooden fence slimed with yellow-green lichen ran around it.

"Stop here," Greg said.

Eleanor pulled up level with the end of the lake. She guessed there was another above them.

Greg opened the door and got out, standing in front of the bonnet, staring at the lake. His eyes had that distant look, the gland neurohormones unplugging him from the physical universe. *A world sculpted from shadows*, he'd said once when he tried to describe the way neurohormones altered his perception, *similar to a photon amp image, everything dusty and grainy. But translucent; you could see right through the planet if you had enough strength. The shadows are analogous to the fabric of the real world—houses, machinery, furniture, the ground, people. But not always. There are . . . differences. Additions. Memories of objects, phantasms, I suppose.*

And I can perceive minds, too. Separate from the body. Minds glow, like nebulas with a supergiant star hidden at the core.

The remoteness faded from his face. He gave the lake a last look, fingers stroking his chin, a faintly puzzled expression pulling at his features.

"What did you see?" she asked as he got back into the passenger seat. His intuition was almost as strong as his empathy. When they first looked around the farmhouse on the Hambleton peninsula, he had suddenly grabbed hold of her as she walked into one of the small upstairs bedrooms. He couldn't give a reason, just that she shouldn't go in. When they gave it a thorough examination, they found that a whole section of the floorboards in front of the door was riddled with woodworm. If she had just marched in, she would have fallen straight through.

"Not sure," Greg said.

The Panda car was lumbering up the road behind them. Eleanor started off toward the third lake. The first tiny spots of drizzle began to graze the windshield.

"A microlight landing spot?" she asked.

"No."

Amanda was giving them a slightly bemused look from the back seat.

The third lake was a slightly larger version of the second. Eleanor could see the ruin of a small brick building situated halfway up the earth bank on the far side. She thought it might be an ancient ice-house. A flock of Canada geese was grazing around the thick tufts of reedy grass that flourished around the shore.

"I'm sure I remember reading something else about Launde Abbey," Greg said. "Or maybe it was on a channel newscast."

"I can't remember anything," Eleanor said.

"It was a few years ago. I think. Seven or eight, maybe more." He didn't sound very convinced. "What about you, Amanda? Have there been any other incidents up here?"

"No, not that I can recall."

"What sort of incident?" Eleanor asked.

He gave her an abashed grin. "Can't remember. Definitely something newsworthy, though."

"And it's connected to the Kitchener murder?" she asked.

"Lord knows. I doubt it, not that long ago."

Launde Abbey was another hundred and fifty meters past the third lake, set in a broad, curving basin that seemed to have been chiseled into the side of the valley. A wooden fence marked the boundary of the parkland. The EMC Ranger rattled over a cattle grid, and the grass magically reverted to a shaggy, verdant green. Large black tree stumps were scattered about, each one accompanied by a new sapling—kauri pines, giant chinquapins, torreyas—healthy replacements that relished the heat, turning the park back to its original rural splendor. Tarmac reappeared under the tires. Eleanor turned off the road, which disappeared over the brow of the basin, and drove down the loop of drive to the Abbey.

She was somewhat disappointed with what she saw. She'd been expecting some great medieval monastery, all turrets and flying buttresses; reality was a three-story Elizabethan manor house, built from ochre stone, with a broad frontage and projecting wings. The roof of gray-blue slate was broken by five gables, a row of solar panels capping the apex. There were two sets of chimney-stacks, one on each wing; three cream-white globes were perched amid the southern wing's stacks, weather coverings for the satellite dishes. Climbing roses scrambled over the stonework around the porch, scarlet and yellow blooms drooping from the weight of water they had absorbed, petals moldering.

It backed on to a copse of high, straggly pines, most of which had survived the Warming, their depleted ranks supplemented by some new banyan trees.

Two unmarked white vans and a Panda car were parked outside, belonging to the police crime-scene team that had been combing the Abbey for clues since Friday. Eleanor drew up behind them. It was raining steadily and they made a dash for the porch.

A constable was waiting just inside; he saw Amanda and waved them all through. The interior was vaguely shabby, putting Eleanor in mind of a grand family fallen on hard times. The elegance still existed, in the furnishings, and decor—the staircase looked exquisite— but it had been almost neglected. Clean, but not polished.

Vernon Langley and Jon Nevin came in, shaking the rain from their jackets.

Langley took a breath. "I forgot to mention it before, Mandel," he said, "but the Abbey's lightware memory core has been wiped."

"So Amanda told me," Greg said dryly.

Eleanor kept her grin to herself. One to the good guys.

"I see." He straightened his jacket. "Well, we've set up shop in the dining room, if you'd like to come through."

There was very little of the dining room table left visible. At one end, the forensic team had set out their equipment, a couple of Philips laptop terminals and various boxy 'ware modules that Eleanor guessed were analyzers of some kind, although one looked remarkably like a microwave oven. The rest of the table, about three-quarters, was covered in sealed polythene sample bags. She could see clothes, shoes, books, hologram cubes, a lot of kitchen knives, glasses, memox crystals, small porcelain dishes, candlesticks, even an old wind-up-type clock. Some of them looked completely empty. Dust, or hair, she thought.

She was still puzzling over why they'd want to seal up a potted cactus when Vernon Langley introduced Nicolette Hutchins and Denzil Osborne, a pair of forensic investigators who had stayed on to continue the *in situ* examination. They had been drafted in from Leicestershire, part of a ten-strong team that the Home Office had ordered to the Abbey. Both of them were wearing standard blue police one-piece overalls. Nicolette Hutchins was in her forties, a small woman with a narrow, slightly worn face, her dark hair wrapped in a tight bun. She glanced up from one of the modules she was engrossed with and held out her hands. "Excuse me for not shaking." She was wearing surgeon's gloves.

Denzil Osborne had the kind of build Eleanor associated with ex-professional sportsmen, muscle bulk that was starting to round out and sag. He must have been in his late fifties, with a flat, craggy face, and receding blond hair tied into a neat pony-tail. He had a near-permanent smile, showing off three gold teeth, a flashy anachronism.

He shook Greg's hand warmly. Then his smile broadened even wider when he took Eleanor's.

"And I'm *very* pleased to meet you."

The play-acting made her grin. His genuine welcome was a refreshing change from the rest of the investigating team.

"So, you were in the Mindstar Brigade, were you?" Denzil asked Greg.

"Yeah."

"I was in Turkey, Royal Engineers; worked with a Mindstar Lieutenant called Roger Hales."

Greg smiled. "Springer!"

"That's right."

"We called him Springer because it didn't matter what kind of booby trap the Legion left behind, Roger could always spot it and trip it," Greg explained to Eleanor. "He had one of the best bloody short-range perceptive faculties in the outfit."

"Saved my arse enough times," Denzil said. "Those mullahs were getting plenty tricky toward the end of that campaign."

"No messing," Greg said.

"I was chuffed when I heard they were bringing you in. Our Nicolette here doesn't believe what you blokes can do."

"I do believe," she said, not looking up from the analyzer module. "I just get bored with hearing about it day in, day out. You'd think Turkey lasted for a decade, the number of stories you tell."

"Well, don't worry, Greg won't bore you today," Denzil said. "Far from it. Today is the day when this investigation gets moving again. Right, Greg?"

"Do my best."

"You need something to fixate on?"

"No. I need data."

Denzil's eyebrows went up appreciatively. "Intuitionist?"

"Yeah."

"Okay, what do you want to start with?"

"The security system," Eleanor said.

"No problems with that," Denzil answered. "It's all top-grade gear. Fully functional."

"Could an intruder melt through it and then back out again without leaving a trace?" Greg asked.

"Hell, no, it's built by Event Horizon; a customized job. Low-light photon amps, windows wired, internal-motion sensors, IR, plus UV laserscan. Unless your identity and three-dimensional image are loaded in the memory core, you couldn't move a millimeter inside the building without the alarm screaming for help. And it's got a secure independent uplink to Event Horizon's private communication satellite network as well as the English Telecom West Europe geosync platform. Why? You think somebody got in here?"

"Possibly," said Greg. He explained his theory about the microlight, then went on to the contract Kitchener had been given with Event Horizon.

When he had finished, even Nicolette Hutchins had abandoned her analyzer module to listen. "That adds some unusual angles to our problem," she said with morbid interest. "Nobody was thinking along those lines when we arrived; we all thought it was a murder, not an assassination. And it's too late to look for signs of a microlight landing now. There have been three heavyish rainfalls since Thursday night's storm. They would have washed the valley clean."

"Ever the optimist," Denzil retorted.

She shrugged and returned to her LCD display.

"Hell, Greg, I don't know about a tekmerc penetration," Denzil said. "If it happened that way, then the software they used against the security core must have been premier grade. I wouldn't even know how to start writing it."

Eleanor exchanged a knowing glance with Greg. "Let me have what details you have on the system," she said. "We know someone who can tell us if it's possible to burn in."

Vernon Langley would clearly have liked to ask who. But she just gave him her best enigmatic smile as Denzil typed an access request on his Philips laptop.

"Here we are," he said. "Complete schematics, right down to individual 'ware chips, plus the layout."

Eleanor held up her cybofax and let him squirt the data package over.

"I think the murder scene next," Greg said.

Eleanor didn't know about Greg, but she was picking up bad vibes from the minute they walked in to Kitchener's bedroom. Apart from the furniture and Chinese carpet, it had been stripped clean: there were no ornaments or clothes; the occupier's stamp of personality had been voided. There were some funny patches on the carpet close to the door, as though someone had spilled a weak bleach on it, discoloring the weave; adhesive tags with printed bar codes labeled each one. More tags were stuck over the table and the dresser; the tall, freestanding mirror was completely swathed in polythene.

The curtains had been taken down. Rain was beating on the window, unnaturally loud to her ears. And it was warm. She saw the air conditioner had been dismantled, its components scattered over a thick polythene sheet in one corner.

"We wanted the dust filter," Denzil said absently. "Surprising what they accumulate."

Langley and Nevin had followed her in. Amanda had stayed with Nicolette in the dining room. "I've seen it enough times," she'd muttered tightly.

Eleanor looked at the four-poster bed and grimaced. The sheets had been removed. There was a big dark-brown stain on the mattress. Three holographic projectors had been rigged up around the bed, chrome-silver posts two meters high, each with a crystal bulb on top. Optical cable snaked over the floor between them.

The player was lying on the carpet at the foot of the bed. Denzil picked it up and gave her an anxious glance. There was no sign of his smile. "Standard speech, but it really isn't pretty."

"I'll manage," she said.

"All right. But if you're going to vomit, do it out in the corridor, please. We've cleaned enough of it off this carpet already."

She realized he wasn't joking.

An egg-shaped patch of air above the bed sparkled, then the haze spread out silently; runnels dripped down the sides of the mattress onto the floor, serpents twisting up the carved posts. Edward Kitchener materialized on white silk sheets.

The remains of Edward Kitchener.

Eleanor grunted in shock and jammed her eyes shut. She took a couple of breaths. Come on, girl; you see far worse on any schlock horror channel show.

But that wasn't real.

The second time it wasn't quite so bad. She was incredulous rather than revolted. What sort of person could calmly do this to another? And it had to be a deliberate, planned action; there was no frenzied hacking, it had been performed with clinical precision. A necromantic operation. Hadn't the Victorian police suspected that Jack the Ripper was some kind of medical student?

She glanced around. Greg had wrinkled his face up in extreme distaste, forcing himself to study the hologram in detail. Jon Nevin was looking at the floor, the window, the dresser, anywhere but the bed.

"Yeah, okay," Greg said. "That's enough."

The faint aural glow cast by the projection faded from the walls. When she looked back at the bed, Kitchener had gone. Air hissed out through her teeth, muscles loosening. Edward Kitchener had looked like such a chirpy old man, a sort of idealized grandfather. A gruff tongue, and a loving nature.

"How was he actually killed?" Greg asked.

"We think he was smothered by a pillow," Vernon said. "One of them had traces of saliva in a pattern consisten with it being held over his head."

"So what did all the damage?"

"Pathology says a heavy knife," said Denzil. "Straight blade, thirty to forty centimeters long."

"One of the kitchen knives?"

"We don't know. There are drawers full of them downstairs, some of them are virtually antiques. We cataloged eighteen, and none of those had any traces of blood. But the housekeeper can't say for sure if one is missing. And then there's all the lab equipment, plus the engineering shop, plenty of cutting implements in those two. Blimey, you could make a knife in the engineering shop, then grind it up afterward. Who knows?"

Greg led them all back out into the corridor. "Did the murderer leave any traces?"

"The only hair and skin particles we have found anywhere in the bedroom belong to either Kitchener, the students, or the housekeeper and her two helpers."

"What about when the murderer left?" Greg asked. "Do you know the route he took? There must have been some of Kitchener's blood or body fluid smeared somewhere."

"No, there wasn't," Denzil said, vaguely despondent. "We've spent the whole of the last two days in this corridor going over the walls and carpet with a photon amp plugged into a lightware number cruncher running a spectrographic analysis program—had to get a special Home Office budget allocation for that. This carpet we're standing on has blotches of wine, gin, whiskey, cleaning detergent, hair, dandruff, skin flakes, shoe rubber, shoe plastic, a lot of cotton thread from jeans. You name it. But no blood, no fluid, not from Kitchener. Whoever it was, he took a great deal of care not to leave any traces."

"Was Liam Bursken that fastidious?" Greg asked Vernon.

"I'm not sure," the detective said. "I can check."

"Please," Greg said.

He loaded a note into his cybofax.

"What does that matter?" Nevin asked.

"It helps with elimination. I want to know if someone that deranged would bother with being careful. A tekmerc would at least make an effort not to leave any marks."

"We do think the murderer wore an apron while he murdered Kitchener," Denzil said. "One of the housekeeper's was burned in the kitchen stove on Friday morning. The students had a salad on Thursday night. So the stove was lit purposely, it was still warm when we arrived. But there are only a few ash flakes left. We know there was blood on the apron, but the residue is so small we couldn't even tell you if it was human blood. It could have come from beef, or rabbit, or sheep."

"The point being, why go to all the trouble of lighting a fire to destroy an apron if it wasn't the one used in the murder," Vernon said. "You and I know it was the one the murderer used. But in court, all it could be is supposition. Any halfway decent brief would tear that argument apart."

"If it was a tekmerc, why bother at all?" Eleanor asked. "Why spend all that time fiddling about lighting a fire, when he could simply have taken the apron with him? In fact, why use one in the first place?"

"Good point," said Greg. He seemed troubled.

"Well?" Vernon asked.

"Haven't got a clue."

"Sorry," Eleanor said.

They shared a smile.

Greg looked at the carpet in the corridor, scratching the back of his neck. "So we do know that the murderer didn't leave by Kitchener's bedroom window," he said. "He went straight down to the kitchen, burned the apron, then left."

"If he or she left," Vernon said.

"If it was one of the students, then he would have to make very certain no traces of Kitchener left the bedroom, or he would be incriminated," Jon Nevin said. There was a touch of malicious enjoyment in his tone. "That would fit this cleanliness obsession, the need to avoid contamination."

"Contamination." Greg mulled the word over. "Yeah. You gave the students a head-to-toe scan, I take it?"

"As soon as they were back in Oakham station," Vernon said.

"Three of them had touched Kitchener of course, but only in the presence of the others."

"Figures," said Greg. "Which three?"

"Harding-Clarke, Beswick, and Cameron. But it was only a few stains on their fingertips, entirely consistent with brushing against the body and the sheets."

"Okay," Greg said. "I'd like to see the lightware cruncher that's been wiped. Is there anything else our murderer tampered with?"

"Yes," Denzil said. "Some of the laboratory equipment. We found it this morning."

The computer center was at the rear of the Abbey, a small, windowless room with a bronze-colored metal door. It slid open as soon as Denzil showed his police identity card to the lock. Biolum rings came on automatically. Walls and ceiling were all-white tiles; the floor had a slick cream-colored plastic matting. A waist-high desk bench ran all the way around the walls, broken only by the door. There were three elaborate Hitachi terminals sitting on top of it, along with racks of large memox datastore crystals and five reader modules.

The Bendix lightware number cruncher was in the center of the room, a steel-blue globe one meter in diameter, sitting on a pedestal at chest height.

"Completely wiped," Denzil said. He crossed to one of the terminals and touched the power stud. The flatscreen lit with the words: DATA LOAD ERROR. Above the keyboard, a few weak green sparks wriggled through the cube. "Kitchener used to store everything in here, all his files, the students' work. He didn't need to make a copy; the holographic memory is supposed to be failsafe. Even without power, the bytes would remain stable until the actual crystal structure began to break down—five, ten thousand years. Probably longer. Who knows?"

Eleanor looked around the room. There was one air-conditioning grille set high on a wall; the air was clean but dead. She couldn't see a blemish anywhere; the tiles and floor were spotless, as were the terminals.

"Could the storm have knocked it out?" she asked.

Denzil gave her a surprised look. "Absolutely not. This room is perfectly insulated; and even if the solar panels were struck by lightning, there is a triplicated surge-protection system. Besides, a voltage surge wouldn't cause this."

"So what would?" Greg asked.

"There are two things. One, a very sophisticated virus. An internecine, one that wipes itself after it's erased all the files, because there's no trace of it now. Second, someone who knew the core management codes could have ordered a wipe."

"Who knew the codes?"

"I don't know," Vernon said apologetically.

"All right, we'll ask the students when I interview them. What about access to this room, who is allowed in?"

"Kitchener and the students," said Denzil. "But there are terminals dotted all over the Abbey. You could use any of them to load a virus or order a wipe."

"What about someone outside plugging in?"

"You can only plug into the lightware cruncher through one of the terminals in the Abbey," Denzil said. "But all the terminals are plugged into English Telecom's datanet. So you have to be inside the Abbey to establish a datalink between the Bendix and an external 'ware system."

"And to get inside the Abbey, you have to be cleared by the security system," Greg murmured. "Neat." He turned to Vernon Langley. "English Telecom should be able to provide you with an itemized log for the datanet. Check through it and see if there were any unexplained datalinks established on Thursday night or Friday morning."

"If it was a tekmerc operation, it was the best," Denzil said soberly. "The very best."

The laboratory was virtually a caricature, Eleanor thought. Either that, or set designers on channel science fiction shows did more research than she had ever given them credit for. But it was a chemistry lab, not a physics lab.

The room was spacious, with a high ceiling and the usual ornate mullioned windows, which helped to give it the *Frankenstein* feel. Tall glass-fronted cabinets were lined up along the walls. Three long wooden benches were spaced down the center of the room. Each of them had a vast array of glassware on top, immensely complicated crystalline intestines of some adventuresome beast, plastic hardware units clamped around tubes and flasks, a spaghetti tangle of wiring and optical cable winding through it all. Small Ericsson terminals, augmented with customized control modules, were regulating each of the set-ups.

Denzil led them to the middle bench. "Take a look at this." He was indicating one section of the glassware, spiral tubing and retorts surrounding what reminded Eleanor of an incubator. "We found it yesterday when we started classifying the equipment." He shot a wily look at Vernon Langley. "Recognize it?"

The detective shook his head.

"It's a syntho vat. High-quality stuff, too. Well above what you find on the street; this formula is similar to Naiad."

"Were the students on it?" Greg asked.

"Three of them were using it on Thursday night," Vernon said. "We took blood samples as soon as they came into the station. Harding-Clarke, Spalvas, and Cameron. But the count was low, they're not addicts." He sighed. "Students experiencing life; it's a thrill for them, a little taste of adventure. I imagine bright sparks of that age could get bored very easily with this place."

Eleanor thought he pronounced *students* with well-emphasized contempt.

"And the other three?" Greg prompted.

"Clean as newborns," Jon Nevin said. "Of course, all six of them had been drinking. They had wine at their evening meal, and then some more in their rooms later on."

"But not enough to unhinge them?"

"No."

"Kitchener was taking the syntho as well," Vernon said. "It was in the pathology report. Expanding his mind, no doubt. Some such nonsense. He was always on about that, his New Thought ideology."

Greg exhaled loudly. "At his age. Christ."

"And he encouraged the students," Jon Nevin said disapprovingly.

"Yeah."

"And this," Denzil said theatrically, "is something we found this morning." He rapped at another chunk of the glassware on the third bench. It had more hardware units than the rest. "You ought to know what this is, Greg; there's a smaller version in your head."

"Neurohormone synthesizer."

"Well done. Themed neurohormones, to be precise. Makes your blanket educement look old-fashioned."

"Kitchener was using neurohormones?" Greg asked in surprise. "Psi stimulants?"

"Yes," said Vernon. "Quite heavily, as far as we can determine. It's all in the pathology report."

"What sort of psi themes?" Eleanor asked.

"Ah, can't be as helpful there as I'd like," Denzil said. "There is a low-temperature storage vault full of themed ESP-educer ampoules. But those are a standard commercial type from ICI; he was a regular customer, apparently. However, there's also a small batch of un-marked ampoules that I'll send off for analysis, although we may have problems with identifying it, especially if it's something experimen-tal. We don't have a large database on the stuff. As far as I know, this is the first time it's ever cropped up in a police investigation."

"We may be able to help you there," Greg said. "I'll find out if Event Horizon has any information on neurohormones."

"Fine."

"Do you know what he was using the ESP theme neurohor-mone for?"

"Apparently it was part of his research, according to the students," Vernon said. "He wanted to perceive electrons and protons directly."

"Get a meeting with Ranasfari set up," Greg told Eleanor. "I want to know if there's any connection between these neurohormones and the research work Kitchener was doing for Event Horizon."

"Right." She flipped open her cybofax.

"You will inform us, won't you?" Vernon said.

"Yeah," Greg growled back.

He tried not to flinch at the stab of animosity. Eleanor diplomat-ically busied herself with the cybofax file. That good old Mindstar reputation again.

Greg ran a forefinger along a module on the top of the neurohor-mone synthesizer. "Is this the stuff in the unmarked ampoules?"

"No idea," Denzil replied. "It would be the obvious conclusion, but the control 'ware has been wiped clean just like the Bendix. There's no record of the formula they were producing." He pointed at the dark gray plastic casing of the hardware modules that were integrated into the refining structure. "These units contained endocrine bioware. Very complex, very delicate. They are dead now."

"How?"

"Somebody poisoned them. They infused a dose of syntho into the cells. It was all quite deliberate."

"The murder was tied in with his work," Greg said quietly.

"If this was his work, then yes."

6

THE SILVER-WHITE DORNIER EXECUTIVE TILT-FAN dropped through the cloud layer above the imposing condominiums and exclusive shopping arcades of Peterborough's New Eastfield district and banked to starboard, heading out over the Fens basin. Julia ordered her nodes to cancel the company's last quarter financial summaries that they were displaying behind her eyes. They would be landing soon.

Another bloody ceremony. Wheel me on, point me at the cameras, and wheel me off again. Might as well use a cyborg.

But it was important, a crux in company development, so she had to go.

When isn't it important, vital?

She was sitting on a white leather settee in the lounge at the rear of the little plane. Alone for once. Her staff was in the forward cabin. She imagined them swapping gossip, laughing; it would have been easy to go forward and join them, or to invite them back. They weren't that inhibited around her. But it didn't fit her mood.

Being alone was becoming a precious commodity these days.

It might have been her mood, the broodiness that came from anticipating the meeting later in the day, that had prompted her rather drastic image overhaul this morning. She had dressed up in full Goth costume, improvising with a three-thousand-pound velvet Deveraux skirt, a scarlet one, sweeping round her ankles, then black-suede boots from Paris, five gold Aztec pendants hanging on thin leather straps around her neck, and a black weblike jacket from Toska's. Her maid had darkened her hair and given it a tangled arrangement. They had argued about make-up; eye wings of black mascara on her complexion would have been criminal, so in the end they settled for some strategic highlighting. She was quite pleased with the effect; it was far less stuffy and lots more fun than yesterday's outfit at the spaceplane roll out. It would certainly make people take notice.

She looked out of the window. All she could see ahead was mud:

dun-brown supersaturated peat tinged with an elusive gray-green hue from the algae blooms. It came right up to the city's eastern boundary, slopping around the ruins of the Newark district; long, regular silt dunes freckled with bricks and fractured timbers marked the outline of drowned streets. Newark had lacked that crucial extra meter when the tide of sludge came oozing and gurgling across the Fens.

Two parallel green lines stabbed out from the southern end of the city, the Nene's new course, stretching into the gloomy heat haze that occluded the eastern horizon. It had been dredged deep enough to allow cargo ships to sail right into the heart of the city, where a flourishing deep-water port had been built. The banks were gene-tailored coral, covered with thick reeds, intended to prevent the mud from dribbling back in, although two dredgers were on permanent duty sailing up and down the channel, scooping out the sludge that did build up and flinging it back over the banks.

The Nene would have to be widened soon, she knew; the volume of traffic it could carry was approaching its limit. Just like everything else in Peterborough these days. The city's own success was turning against it, stalling further development.

Ninety percent of the Fens refugees had retreated to Peterborough, establishing a vast shantytown along the high ground of the western perimeter. They'd found dry, high land and a working civil administration; it was enough, they were through with running, they sat there and refused to budge.

The PSP was faced with a nightmare of relief work at the worst possible time, when every resource in the country was being deployed against the ecological destruction and economic collapse. The refugees needed work and housing. The Treasury certainly couldn't fund the kind of massive schemes necessary, so the Party was forced into making an exception to its ideological golden rule of repudiating any form of foreign investment, the bogeyman of economic imperialism.

Peterborough was declared a special economic zone, and huge concessions were granted to any investors; planning regulations became virtually nonexistent. Money began to pour in and new housing estates rose up to replace the shacks of plastic and corrugated iron. They served as dormitory villages for the fast-growing industrial estates occupied by kombinate subdivisions and the supply companies that sprang up to provide them with specialist services. Their products were exported, duty free, all over the globe, helping to pay off the loans for the housing. A self-contained micro-economy, free from the decay and chaos rampant throughout the rest of the country. Peterborough was unique in the PSP decade, prospering while every other English city declined. After the PSP fell, Philip Evans selected it as his headquarters when he moved Event Horizon back to England. With its plethora of modern industries to supply the company's cyber-factories with components, it was an ideal location.

But now, four years later, Event Horizon was suffering from space restrictions inside the city boundaries. New cyber-factories were being parceled out around the rest of the country, easing the load. But they were subsidiaries, non-critical; what Julia wanted was a nucleus, a focal point for administration, research, finance, security, and the strategically important giga-conductor manufacture. The data age notwithstanding, distance brought control problems, exacerbated by England's shoddy transport links. It all added up to reductions in efficiency that even her grandfather's NN core couldn't compensate for. They needed the major installations in one area, under their collective thumb.

She sighed lightly, shifting in her seat. Management problems were like a fission reaction, each one triggering a dozen more. And if they weren't dealt with swiftly and correctly, they would soon multiply beyond her ability to solve.

Still, at least she'd circumvented the expansion problem. For a price.

The communication console bleeped for attention. The call was tagged as personal, Eleanor's code. Julia leaned over the leather settee's armrest, pecked the keyboard to let it through, and Eleanor's face appeared on the bulkhead flatscreen. She was sitting at some kind of table, scratched wooden surface piled with printouts. Her forehead was damp with perspiration, she looked irked.

"That bad?" Julia said quickly. Get in fast, and be disarming. Eleanor was more big sister than a friend, she could tell her anything without ever having to worry about it being splashed by the tabloid channels. But at the same time, she could be a trifle formidable. And not just physically; Eleanor was only three years older, but her adversarial background had given her self-determination in abundance.

"No messing," Eleanor said.

"Where are you?"

"Oakham police station. We've just arrived back from taking a look around Launde Abbey." Eleanor shivered. "God, I hope we catch the killer soon."

"Did Greg find anything out there?"

"Several ambiguities."

"So it wasn't one of the students?"

"Can't say for sure; he's interviewing them now. We should know in an hour or so. But assuming none of them did it, I have some requests."

"Sure, shoot."

"First, we want to talk to Ranasfari about these wormhole theories he had Kitchener working on. Tomorrow afternoon; we're both busy in the morning."

Julia loaded a memo into her node's general business file. "He'll be at Wilholm waiting for you."

"Fine. Second, I take it Event Horizon has a biochemical research division?"

"Yes, of course."

"Anyone there conversant with neurohormones?"

Access Biochemical Division Files, Research Facility Departments: Current Projects and Specializations. The list slipped through her mind, a cool jejune stream of bytes.

"Yes," she said. "We have two projects running. After Greg's last case for us, Morgan decided it would be a good idea to introduce psychics into the security division. I thought it best that we weren't dependent on external sources."

"Good. There were some ampoules of themed neurohormones at Launde. I want them analyzed. The police forensic lab is good, but this is somewhat out of their league. No doubt that is going to bruise some pride . . ." Stress lines appeared at the corners of Eleanor's mouth as she tightened her jaw muscles. Julia remained prudently silent. "Well, the hell with them," Eleanor said. "We need to know what the theme is as soon as possible, please."

"Weren't they labeled?"

"No. The endocrine bioware that produced them was deliberately killed, and its control 'ware was wiped. There are no records. It was one of Kitchener's private projects. But it's obviously an important one for the murderer to single it out like this. Nothing else in the lab was touched."

"I see. No problem. I'll have a courier at Oakham within the hour."

"Which brings us to the final point," Eleanor said with a baleful relish that had Julia squirming. "Greg and I have just become media megastars again. Julia, there are hundreds of bloody reporters here! They've already connected us with you; God knows what conspiracy theories they'll be producing by the evening bulletins."

Julia closed her eyes and let out a groan. "Oh, dear Lord." She should have foreseen it. Hindsight was so bloody wonderful.

"A bit of intervention on your part wouldn't hurt," Eleanor said. "We're not circus performers, you know."

"I'm sorry. I didn't know about the reporters. I'll do whatever I can, I promise."

Eleanor gave her a quizzical look. "All right. But for God's sake, no strong-arm tactics, don't make it any worse."

"I won't," she said meekly.

"Sure. See you tomorrow."

"Yah, unless one of the students did it," Julia said.

"Don't hold your breath. Bye, Julia."

"Bye."

Eleanor's image blanked out.

"Bugger!" Julia yelped. Why could nothing ever be *simple?*

A pre-Warming map superimposed over the quagmire would have told Julia the Dornier was descending over Prior's Fen, six kilometers due east of Peterborough. Below the extended undercarriage bogies, thick concrete groyne walls were holding back the mud from a hexagonal patch of land three hundred meters in diameter. Five large Hawker Siddeley cargo hovercraft were docked to raftlike floating quays outside; and a couple of saucer-shaped McDonnell Douglas helistats were drifting high overhead, their big rotors spinning idly as they waited for the ceremony to finish so they could start unloading.

I wonder how much it's costing to keep them up there, she thought. The nodes would tell her, but somehow she didn't want to know.

Everything to do with PR seemed such a folly. Yet all the experts swore by it, the God of good publicity, of customer relations, being—and being seen to be—a good corporate citizen.

Fan nacelles on the Dornier's canards and wings rotated to the vertical, and the plane touched down on one of the floating quays. There were only Rachel Griffith, Ben Taylor, her second bodyguard, and Caroline Rothman, her PA, in the cabin forward of the lounge. For once, Morgan had stayed in his office. It must mean he trusts me, she thought, or more likely, Rachel.

She wished Patrick was there as she stepped out of the plane and into the most appalling humidity. Just someone who could hold her hand, in both senses; she always hated the way the crowds stared at her during these events. But Patrick was busy in Peterborough, helping to establish an office for his family company.

Steeling herself against the incursive eyes, she smiled as her boots reached the rough metal grid of the floating quay. She put on a very foppish wide-brimmed hat of black suede, grateful for the scant relief it offered from the sun. There was a strong whiff of sulfur coming off the quagmire, mingling with brine.

Stephen Marano, the project engineer, trotted up to greet her. He was in his mid-forties, stuffed into a light-gray suit that didn't really fit. He was a perfect choice to boss the labor crews, but completely out of his depth talking to her. His smile flickered on and off, words got tangled in his throat, he seemed taken aback by her Goth get-up.

She wanted to tell him not to say anything, ease his suffering a bit, but he would only interpret that as a rebuke, so she let him struggle on and introduce her to the fifteen-strong management team of architects and site engineers. A long exercise in tedium and discomfort.

Three channel camera crews followed the procedure from a distance. She recognized one of the teams from the Globecast logo on their jackets.

After the introductions they all trooped down a long ramp to the foot of the excavation. Julia realized they were actually below the level of the mud outside. Yellow JCB diggers were parked on the black peat, crews standing around them. They whistled and cheered as she went past. She didn't actually hear any jeers, but there were plenty of wolf-whistles. Stephen Marano winced at each of them.

It was wet underfoot; mercifully her skirt hem hovered five centimeters above the ground, but her boots received a liberal splattering. The site had been crisscrossed by drainage trenches, their pumps whirring noisily in the background.

They stopped by a wood-lined square hole close to the sheer groyne wall. A big cement-mixer lorry stood beside it, its rumbling dying away as the operator pressed a button on its side.

One of the managers handed her a microphone.

Access FootingSpeech.

She cleared her throat, the sound echoing loudly around the groyne walls. The camera crews focused on her. Rachel and Ben stood unobtrusively on either side, heads moving slowly back and forth as they scanned the assembled crew.

"I don't suppose you want a long speech," Julia said, suddenly very self-conscious about her finishing-school accent. "And you're not going to get one, not while you're on my time." She saw smiles appearing under the colored hard hats. "I would simply like to say that although the company space program draws most of the media attention, you people slogging through the mud out here are just as important. Space isn't the only direction the future lies in. Out here we have got a vast wasteland that everyone despises and resents, while back on shore there are too many people living too close together. This tower that we are starting today is going to lead the way in alleviating some of the pressure on population density, as well as the demands that industry is placing on the green belt. Land is becoming a very precious resource, and I am extremely proud that Event Horizon is setting this example, showing that expansion is possible without coming into conflict with the environment. In the scramble to rebuild our economy, we must never forget the reasons for the Warming. We cannot afford to ignore the painful lessons of the past if we are to prevent the repetition of our grotesque mistakes in the future."

Exit FootingSpeech.

She handed the microphone back as the management group applauded loudly.

"This way, Miss Evans," Stephen Marano said. He gestured at the cement mixer.

The operator was a stocky man in a yellow T-shirt, grubby jeans, and an orange hard hat. He grinned broadly and pointed to the small control panel on the back of the lorry. It had five chrome-ringed buttons running down the center. The green button had a new sticker above it that said: PRESS ME.

"Even I can't make a mess of that," Julia told him. Lord, what a dumb thing to say.

"No, miss." He bobbed about, delighted at being the center of attention.

Julia pressed the button.

The mixer started up again, concrete sliding down the chute into the footings.

It looks like elephant crap, she thought.

The management team started clapping again.

She clamped down on a laugh that threatened to escape. Didn't they realize how stupid they looked?

But of course they did. They were less worried about appearing foolish than they were about annoying her.

She sobered sadly and offered Stephen Marano her hand to shake. "I didn't appreciate what the conditions were like out here before today, Stephen. You really have done a terrific job getting this phase completed, and on time too. Thank you."

He nodded in gratitude. "Thanks, Miss Evans. It's been tough, but they're a good bunch of lads. It should be easier next time, now we know what we're doing."

She guessed that was about as subtle as he would get. It made a nice change; sometimes she was ten minutes into a conversation with a kombinate director or a bank finance officer before she realized everything said was a veiled question. Business talk was conducted in its own special code of ambiguities.

They started to walk back toward the ramp.

"The next two times," she told him. "I want to bring a couple of complete cyber-precincts out here next and link them to the city with a train line. Of course we'll have to build a service tributary from the Nene as well."

He gave her a genuine grin. "I wish you'd been around before the Warming, Miss Evans. A few more people with your kind of vision and we'd never have wound up in this damn great mess."

"Thank you, Stephen."

Access GeneralBusiness: Review Stephen Marano, Civil Engineer. Invite to Next Middle-Management Dinner Evening.

As they reached the base of the ramp, a group of about ten workers moved toward her. Rachel and Ben closed in smoothly. Nothing provocative, but *there,* ready.

Julia gave the group an expectant look as they stopped short. One of them was nudged forward by his mates. He looked about seventeen, not quite needing to shave every day, wearing the regulation jeans and T-shirt, shaggy dark hair sticking out below his scuffed light-blue hard hat. He was clutching a bouquet of red roses with a blue ribbon done up in a bow. She suspected he'd been chosen for his age; there couldn't have been many younger than he working out here. And he clearly wanted to be anywhere right now but standing in front of her.

"M-M-Miss Evans?" he stammered.

She gave him a gentle, encouraging smile.

"Er, I, that is, all of us. Well, we really appreciate what you do, like. Investing so much in England, and everything. And giving us all jobs as well, 'cos we wouldn't be any use in no office or a cyber-factory. So, like, we got you these." The bouquet was jerked up nervously. "Sorry it's only flowers, like, but you've got everything . . ." He trailed off in embarrassment.

Julia accepted the bouquet as though she was taking a baby from him. She prayed the cameras weren't recording this, for the boy's sake.

"What's your name?" she asked.

"Lewis, Miss. Lewis Walker."

"Did they bully you into this, Lewis?"

"Yeah. Well, no. I wanted to anyway, like."

She deliberately took her time sniffing the roses. The humidity stifled most of the scent. "What a lovely smell." She put one hand on her hat and leaned forward before the boy could dodge away, brushing her lips against his cheek. "Thank you, Lewis."

A rowdy cheer went up from the onlookers. Lewis blushed crimson, eyes shining.

The Dornier lifted from the floating quay, cabin deck tilting up at a ten-degree angle as it climbed, nose lining up on Peterborough.

Julia thought about the incident with Lewis as the hexagonal site dropped away below the fuselage. It couldn't possibly have been one of the "spontaneous" demonstrations the PR division was forever dreaming up. They would have plumped for something far more elaborate. The sheer crudity had made it incredibly touching.

She had given the bouquet to Caroline Rothman as soon as they were back in the tilt-fan. "Put them in water. And I want them on the dining room table this evening." Pride of place.

She couldn't get rid of the image of Lewis Walker being joshed and having his back slapped by his mates as he returned to them. As she was returning to the Dornier, her world.

That poor, poor boy, there was something utterly irresistible about someone looking so lost. And his T-shirt had been tight enough to show a hard flat belly. Real muscle, not Patrick's designer gym tone.

She allowed herself exactly one lewd grin.

It couldn't happen, not with Lewis Walker, but fantasies existed to be enjoyed.

Funny how different they were; yet only a couple of years apart. He stammering, elated and terrified at being thrust into the limelight; she simply breezing through every public appearance on automatic, bored and resentful.

She could monitor him from afar to make sure he did all right, a modern-day fairy godmother, pushing opportunities his way. Event Horizon ran dozens of scholarship schemes for workers who wanted to advance themselves. And she was on the board of two charities promoting further education.

Of course he wouldn't dare refuse if a place was offered. Nobody in the company ever did refuse her gifts. She saw the site-management team clapping conscientiously—obediently. But would he be happy plucked from what he was doing now and shoved into night schools and polytechnic training courses?

Should I interfere?

That's what it boiled down to.

No. The only possible answer. Not unasked. Not in individual lives. People had to be responsible for themselves.

She activated the phone and placed a call to Horace Jepson. Uncle Horace, though he wasn't really, just a friend of her grandpa's, and now hers. A solid rock of support when she took over Event Horizon. He was the chairman of Globecast, the largest satellite channel company in the world.

His ruddy face appeared on the bulkhead flatscreen. He was in his early sixties, but *plastique* had reversed entropy and returned him to his late forties. A rather chubby late forties, she thought disapprovingly.

"Julia! How's my favorite billionairess?"

"Soldiering on, Uncle Horace."

"You don't look like you're suffering. You look gorgeous. Damn, but you grew up pretty. I wish I was twenty years younger."

She put on her most innocent expression and batted her eyelashes for him. "Uncle Horace, why ever do you want to go back down to being sixty again?"

"Julia!" He looked crestfallen.

"Have you been skipping your diet again?" she asked sternly.

"Terrific. I don't hear a word for three weeks and she phones me up to nag."

"You have. Well, stop it. You know what your doctor said. You should get out of the office and down to the executive gym."

"Sure thing, Julia. I'll start tomorrow."

She sucked on her lower lip, a bashfulness that wasn't entirely artificial. "Uncle Horace."

"Oh, my God. How much is this going to cost?"

"Nothing. Um, I need a sort of favor."

"You owe me fifteen."

"Can we go for sixteen?"

He rolled his eyes dramatically. "You don't want to meet another actor, do you? Some of my guests still ain't talking to me after that party."

There was a warm tingling in her cheeks at the memory. She was sure she hadn't been as tipsy as everyone said. "No, Uncle Horace," she said firmly. "Definitely no more actors. Do you remember Greg and Eleanor Mandel?"

"Sure, who could forget Eleanor? Greg seemed like a nice guy, on the level. Psychic, right?"

"Yes. I've asked him to assist the police working on the Edward Kitchener murder case."

He frowned, fleshy wrinkles deepening around his eyes. "You're involved with that?"

"Event Horizon had a research contract with Kitchener. Right now

I'm praying that isn't the reason behind his death. Greg will find out for me."

"I see."

"But the press is giving him a hard time."

"Now come on, Julia."

"I don't want them to stop reporting the case," she said hurriedly. "If they could just lay off badgering Greg. He didn't want to take the case in the first place. And you know he doesn't play the political game, he's too honest. The last thing he needs is the press jumping all over him just for doing his job."

Horace Jepson sighed resignedly. "All right, Julia. I'll tell the editors to go easy."

"Uncle Horace, you're an angel."

"And I'd like you to come to a program launch party next month." He started typing on a keyboard out of the camera's field of view. "*Dreamland Nights*, it's called, a ten-part fantasy drama. It's gonna be big, Julia. This summer's ratings winner."

"I'll be there. Promise."

"Cliff is gonna be organizing it," he said hopefully.

Her contented expression never wavered. She was proud of that self-control. "That'll be nice. I haven't seen him for ages." Clifford Jepson was Horace's son from the first of his four marriages. Julia couldn't stand the sight of him, he had his father's drive without any of his father's charm. It made him come over as brattishly domineering. The trouble was, Uncle Horace had them down as the perfect match, with himself as Cupid.

"Okay, Julia, my staff will squirt the details to your office."

"Fine. I'll look forward to it. And thank you again, Uncle Horace."

He signed off smiling happily.

Julia pursed her lips in antipathy. She'd solved Eleanor's grouse, but there was no way she could get out of that bloody launch party now.

7

THE INTERVIEWS WERE THE ONE part of the case Greg had been dreading. The word-association game, watching the way minds reacted to key phrases, was chained too tightly to his army days. It intimated funereal dug-out bunkers; sweating, defiant prisoners in torn, bloody fatigues; the smell of gun oil and vomit; the high-voltage emotions of hatred and terror, perceptible even to non-psychics. The seemingly limitless brutality that men were capable of.

Even the interview room at Oakham police station was a party to the anamnesis: somber fawn-colored walls, a lead-gray desk, acutely curved plastic chairs, scuffed black door. A rectangular air-conditioning grille emitted an annoying buzzing sound just on the threshold of audibility. Steely light shining through a high window was complemented by a harsh glow from two biolum panels set in the old fluorescent-tube recesses in the ceiling. A wide-angle camera was mounted on the wall above the desk, optical cable running down to a twin-crystal AV recording deck.

Greg sat on one side of the desk, Langley and Nevin flanking him. He took out his cybofax and summoned up the list of questions he wanted to ask, then placed it on the desk.

Rosette Harding-Clarke came in, accompanied by her lawyer, Matthew Slater. Since the New Conservatives had been elected, anyone being interviewed by the police was entitled to legal advice, irrespective of whether they were being charged or not. The measure was intended to allay public mistrust of the dodgy practices that the People's Constables had included in police procedure.

There were three lawyers, out of Oakham's pool of five, representing the six students. They had objected when he said he wanted to interview the students.

"You aren't an official investigating officer," Lisa Collier, a matronly fifty-five-year-old, had told him pompously. "You have no authority to conduct an interview, certainly not with cooperating witnesses, which is all the students are at this point. And I'm not having my clients subjected to a psychic privacy invasion. They have a right to silence so they don't incriminate themselves."

Greg had simply turned to Vernon Langley. "Arrange for a magistrate's hearing this afternoon. Charge all six students with suspected manslaughter." He gave Lisa Collier a thin smile. "As a specialist assigned to the investigation, I am entitled to sit in on any subsequent questioning of legally detained suspects. And any evidence acquired psychically during those interviews is admissible in court."

The three lawyers had gone into a huddle and decided not to call his bluff.

Matthew Slater slotted a matte-black memox crystal into the recording deck and sat down beside Rosette. She was wearing a black singlet of some glossy fabric, a cropped black jacket with thin white curlicues embroidered on the shoulders, and a short black leather skirt. Her auburn hair was worn in a neat bun.

She gave Greg a fleeting glance of acknowledgment, completely ignoring the detectives behind him. The whole act informed them that she wasn't going to be intimidated.

He had to admit she was an impressive girl physically. Nor was there any hint of weakness in her emotional makeup.

Langley pushed a memox crystal in the recorder's free slot and touched the power stud. "Interview with Rosette Harding-Clarke," he said formally. "Conducted by CID advisory specialist Greg Mandel in the presence of officers Langley and Nevin."

Matthew Slater leaned forward. "For the record, Miss Harding-Clarke's participation in this interview is entirely voluntary. She is here because of her wish to help apprehend the killer of Edward Kitchener. And therefore she reserves the right to refuse to answer any question that is not directly applicable to this topic."

Rosette Harding-Clarke stared straight at Greg and gave him a lopsided, knowing smile. "Silence wouldn't do me any good, would it?" she said. "Not with you. You could strip anything you wanted from me."

He ordered a low-level secretion from his gland. Her amusement began to impinge on his perceptions; it bordered on contempt. Rosette looked down on everybody from her own private Olympus.

"The reaction of your mind to questions cannot be disguised," he said.

"I can run, but I can't hide."

"Yeah. Something like that."

"If you begin to ask Miss Harding-Clarke irrelevant questions, we shall be forced to terminate the interview," Matthew Slater warned.

"No, I won't," she said. "I'm glad you are here. This case is obviously well beyond the ability of these bumbling Mr. Plods. And I want the bastard caught. Too bad we haven't got the death penalty anymore. So ask away. Did I do it? No. You can confirm that, can't you?" Her eyebrows arched challengingly.

"Unfortunately, it's not that simple. I need to know what happened that night at Launde, to build up a complete picture, so I have several questions."

"Yes, all right, get on with it then."

"Did you make any external calls that day, or establish a datalink to an outside 'ware system?"

"I made a few phone calls, sure. Just friends. I'd go bananas if the only people I had to talk to were the other students. And I was doing some work that morning; Edward had me trying to produce a more accurate figure for the age of the universe. I plugged into the Oxford University astronomy department mainframe for reference data."

"Now, that Friday morning, you were the first to find the body. Is that right?"

"Yes."

"What time was that?"

"God. It's in the statement, I must have told these oafs a hundred times."

"What time?"

"God, all right. About half-past five on Friday morning, give or take five minutes."

"And you didn't see anyone else in the corridor when you went to Kitchener's room?"

"No."

Greg tightened the focus of his espersense. "How about a presence you weren't sure about? A shadow? A noise? Something you didn't want to mention to the police because you couldn't prove it, or you thought it would sound stupid."

"No. Nothing. Nobody."

"Where were you before you discovered the body?"

"In my room."

"Was anybody with you?"

"No."

"Half-past five is a funny time to be visiting Kitchener. Was there a reason?"

She rubbed an index finger along the bottom of her nose. "So I would be there when he woke up. Edward didn't like to be alone."

"Nicholas Beswick said you went into Kitchener's room at quarter-past one that morning. Is that true?"

"Poor old Nicky. Yes, it's true. You want to know something else? I was having sex with Edward, I had been for three months. And to save you the trouble of working it out, he was forty-four years older than I."

"You had sex with him at quarter-past one?"

"Yes."

"When did you leave?"

"Isabel and I packed in about half-past two. Edward was nearly asleep by then anyway."

"Why not stay?"

"Edward snores. Silly, isn't it? But I'm a light sleeper, as well as being a virtual insomniac. I need only two or three hours' sleep each night. So out I creep after he's nodded off; then I get my head down for a while, and I'm back snuggled up beside him when he wakes. He probably knew, but—"

"So everybody would know that you left him alone for a few hours each night?"

"Every Peeping Tom, yes."

"Which of the other students knew about you and Kitchener?"

"I would say all of them. Even Nicky, though he would never dare talk about it outright."

"So it was common knowledge?"

"Yes."

"What about the housekeeper and her staff?"

"Oh, yes, Mrs. Mayberry knew. You can't keep secrets from the person who collects your sheets."

"Did you wash after you left Kitchener?"

Rosette sat up straighter. "Pardon me?"

"Did you wash, take a shower, bathe?"

"Yes. I had a shower afterward. I always do."

"How long had Isabel Spalvas been having an affair with Kitchener?"

Rosette gave him a derisive grin and started to laugh. "I'm sorry. The way you said it. 'An affair.' Like some Victorian aunt. Rutland really is the back of beyond, isn't it? Are you married until death do us part, Mr. Mandel? Or may I call you Greg? Eleanor seems like quite a spectacular girl, physique-wise, that is. I saw the two of you on the channel newscasts at lunchtime."

"I'm happily married, thank you."

"And Julia Evans, no less, was at the ceremony. Your bridesmaid."

"Is that a problem for you?"

"No, an observation."

"Careful, your lawyer might stop this line of questioning."

Matthew Slater shot Greg a look of undiluted malice. Rosette burst out laughing again.

"Oh, yes," she said. "I can see why they sent for you. Nobody gets off the hook when you're on their case, do they, Greg?"

"No. Now, Isabel Spalvas?"

"She wasn't having an affair, or whatever else you want to call it, with Edward."

"You said she was in his room for sex."

"She was there for pleasure, for interest, for self-exploration. I'm not saying they didn't have sex. They did. She also took some syntho. Perhaps it made it easier for her."

"Made what easier?"

"Sex with Edward. Oh, he was still reasonably capable. But he was sixty-seven, after all. You couldn't ignore it; not, lie back and think of England. She found it difficult with me as well, to start with."

"You and Isabel made love?"

"I'm not sure about love, Greg darling. But sex, yes. Edward enjoyed watching. She enjoyed it too, eventually, when the syntho was really boosting her. Am I turning you on, Greg?"

"No."

"Really? You surprise me. The first time I made this statement, all the boys in the office found an excuse to listen in." She cocked her head at Nevin. "Didn't you, Jonnie darling?"

Greg caught his mind clogging with fierce embarrassment.

"Was there any pressure placed on female students to sleep with Kitchener?" he asked.

"Not if you mean blackmail. Come to bed with me or I kick you out of the Abbey. Edward doesn't need to, he is . . . intriguing. Girl students are almost a double bluff. You understand? He tells the world he does. He tells us he wouldn't dream of it. And there he is, one of the geniuses of the age, complete with wicked reputation. Always there, day in, day out. He had this mockery for convention. He was so very clever at ridiculing any stricture society placed on his life. He makes you examine and challenge your own beliefs. That's why Isabel had joined us; she was probing her own limits, finding out where they lie. You can do that with Edward there to guide you. He made us feel safe, we trusted him. He'd never let us hurt ourselves, not with drugs or sex, or radical politics, come to that. He knew what we were capable of and showed us how to achieve it, intellectually, emotionally, physically. Launde was an incredible experience, spiritual more than anything else." She shook her head softly, re-emerging from the vortex of reminiscence.

Greg could perceive how sincere she was when she talked about Kitchener. Fondness for the old guru acted as a subtle reinforcement for the philosophies the old man had spun out. He was suddenly very curious about Edward Kitchener. How much of this professional dissident ideology had he believed in, all or none?

"How long had Isabel been taking part in these sessions with you and Kitchener?"

"Sessions! You have no soul, Greg darling, no poetry. About a fortnight, I think. As soon as we came back from the New Year break."

"Did Nicholas Beswick know that Isabel was becoming involved with Kitchener?"

Rosette pursed her lips, contrite for once. Her thought currents were subdued. "Oh, dear little Nicky. No, he didn't know a thing about us until that night. Caught us sneaking down the corridor to Edward, he did. Such a shame. He is quite infatuated with Isabel, did you know that? Now that is authentic love, Romeo and Juliet revisited. Teasing him was such fun, it's so dreadfully easy. Nicky lacks that cosmopolitan touch necessary to survive adult life, he's just a country boy at heart. He makes me seem terribly jaded and old by comparison. Edward was delighted with him, of course."

"Why 'of course'?"

"Because people like Nicky are the reason he founded Launde in the first place. Nicky is very intelligent, he's far smarter than I am. And if the four of you in this room were to add up your IQs, the figure would be less than half of mine. That gives you some idea of what he's like. But he's flawed; emotionally retarded, if you like. Edward called it perpetual adolescence. Whatever, Nicky has this terrible trouble relating to other people. And that is what Launde is for, to cure us of our adolescence, realign our thought patterns into sensible maturity. Edward plays the tyrant king to great effect, and the students bond together for mutual protection. You can't do anything else, survival depends on it. And for all its crudity, the technique works. Even with Nicky, although it was pretty slow-going in his case, but there was definitely some progress. When he arrived, Nicky would sooner starve than ask someone to pass him a knife and fork. Then the evening before Edward was killed, Nicky actually answered me back at supper. Me! Edward didn't stop talking about it for the rest of the evening, he was simply over the moon. Then I went and ballsed it up by getting caught when I went and fetched Isabel out to play. Naughty me."

"So Nicholas Beswick would have been on an emotional roller-coaster that night?"

Rosette's eyes narrowed. "Oh no you don't, Greg darling. You're not pinning that perverted atrocity on Nicky. He wouldn't do that. Besides, I was there when he came into the room and saw what had been done to Edward. He was in hysterics, worse than me. Go away and harass someone else, Greg. Not Nicky."

"And how about you? Were you at all jealous that Kitchener was becoming involved with Isabel?"

"My, my," she cooed. "And I thought I was a prime bitch. No, Greg darling. I wasn't jealous. But I am disappointed. In you, darling. I thought you would be able to see why not. You should. If you're any good, that is. Or is Mindstar like a rock star's codpiece, pumped up with hot air?"

It was the tone that keyed him in. Greg concentrated on the shimmering thought currents in front of him, congealed with hauteur and smug complacency. Something was helping her to recover from the anguish of Kitchener's death; the shock scars of the psyche were healing too rapidly. When he went deeper, he found her cherishing a brittle triumph. Intuition kicked in. He refocused his espersense, moving it down through her body, feeling the grainy texture of warm cells, a fast surge of blood through the veins like velvet pipes; obtuse chemical reactions flared and died all around, nerves flashed like lightning conductors. He left her brain behind, slipping past her throat, neck, breasts, chest, farther down.

"Oh, shit," he said. "You're pregnant." The embryo hung in the center of black and scarlet shadows, a delicate white-porcelain sculpture, beautiful, tiny, and tragically fragile.

"What?" Langley jerked upright.

"This interview is now over!" Slater cried.

Rosette slapped her hand against the desk as the detective and the lawyer started to shout at each other. "Not yet!" she yelled. "We haven't finished yet."

Slater bent over her urgently, plucking at the arm of her black jacket. "Miss Harding-Clarke, I must insist you do not continue."

"No." She waved him away. "You are afraid the child gives me a motive. That I can contest Edward's will on behalf of the baby. That's right, isn't it?"

Slater glanced around at the detectives, his lips pressed together. "That is a likely argument for the prosecution, yes."

"My family is richer than Edward. Money is irrelevant to me."

"Please!" he implored her.

"Are we still being recorded?" she asked.

"Yes," Nevin said.

Greg sat perfectly still. He could guess what was coming next. Like she said, she had an IQ well above average.

"Excellent. Now I've been sitting patiently in this squalid, filthy little room and opened my soul to one of the most experienced and highly trained psychics in the country. I haven't held anything back, and I've answered every question put to me. Now, Greg darling, would you please tell everyone here whether I've been telling the truth."

"You have," he said, awash with the sense of inevitability.

"Did I kill Edward?"

"No."

"Thank you!" She stood up. A grinning Slater rose behind her.

"Rosette?" Greg said.

She turned, exasperation on her face. "Now what?"

He pointed casually at the camera. "For the record, could you tell us which of the other students at Launde you slept with, please?"

Her fists clenched and unclenched, long red nails leaving white imprints on the flesh of her palms. "Cecil," she said woodenly. "That's all."

"Thank you, Rosette. No more questions."

"You used to be Rosette's lover," Greg said.

Cecil Cameron inclined his head reluctantly. "Yes. When she first came to Launde, last October. Talk about impact; we started screwing the day after she arrived."

"How long did it last?"

"About a month."

"Why did it end?"

He shrugged expansively. "You've met Rosette. How long could you put up with her?"

Greg heard Vernon chuckling softly behind him. Lisa Collier, who was acting as Cecil's adviser, tapped on his arm, giving him a disapproving frown. "No opinions," she murmured.

"I didn't even get on with her to start with," Greg said. "You obviously did."

"For a while. I mean, don't get me wrong. Rosette and I are still good friends. But she's difficult to please. She thrives on variety, everything has to be fresh for her. Her tolerance threshold is nonexistent. We burned out. I knew it would right from the beginning. It was good while it lasted, mind. I mean, let's face it, she can take her pick."

"Did she pick Kitchener?"

"No. That was mutual attraction."

"What were you doing on Thursday night after supper?"

"Working on a project of Kitchener's; I was studying theoretical perturbations in electron orbits."

"Were you interfacing with the Abbey's Bendix lightware cruncher?"

"Yes. Why, you think I can do that kind of thing in my head?"

"What time did you stop using the Bendix?"

"About eleven o'clock."

"Could you be more precise, please?"

"Five past, ten past, something like that."

"Was it functioning normally when you were interfacing with it?"   •

"Yes."

"Did you use the English Telecom datalink to access any 'ware cores outside the Abbey that night?"

"No."

"Did you use the datanet for anything that night?"

"No."

"What did you do after you stopped work?"

"Rosette came in, that's why I stopped. We had a drink and a talk. The other four were in Uri's room. She doesn't get on terribly well with Liz, and Nick isn't exactly enthralling conversation at the best of times."

"Do you like him?"

"Who, Nick? Yeah, I don't mind him. He's a bit shy, but he's a sodding genius when it comes to physics. We all knew that."

"How long was Rosette with you?"

"Until after midnight—quarter-past, half-past maybe. She went off to see Kitchener then." He pulled an indignant face. "What a waste. Old man like that. Her choice, mind."

"What about the other three students, how did you get on with them?"

"Fine. Uri and Liz had been involved for a year. Uri's great, one of the lads. Liz too, come to that."

"And what about Isabel?" Greg watched the conflicting emotional surges corrupt Cecil's thought currents, the twinges of guilt coupled with an almost paternal urge of protectiveness. Cecil was being pulled apart by indecision.

"Nice girl. Bit disoriented by Abbey life, but she was coping."

"Did you sleep with her?"

"Hey! I said we were friends."

"Your relationship is something more than an ordinary friendship, though."

Cecil looked around at Lisa Collier for guidance.

"It's a legitimate question," she said sourly.

"You can tell that from my mind?" Cecil asked apprehensively.

"Yeah."

"Okay. Well, I meant what I said, mind. We weren't screwing each other. Wish we had been, she's got a terrific body. I asked her often enough, but she wasn't keen. She said that it couldn't last, not with me leaving at the end of the year, so it would be pointless, she'd only wind up getting hurt. I might have managed to change her mind in the end. Still . . . I was happy enough playing big brother to her. There weren't many others she could turn to. I mean, all that New Age crap Kitchener spouted about liberating your mind. Christ. The longest chat-up routine ever written. He said anything that would get them into bed with him, and they did as well, two by two. Isabel was confused by it. So we talked, that's all. Nick would have burst into tears if she'd told him what she was up to with Kitchener. As for Liz and Uri, hell, it's a miracle if they get out of bed for a meal! And Rosette, well, she was with Kitchener."

"Did Isabel come and talk with you that night?"

"No."

"You were taking syntho. Why was that?"

Cecil drummed his kinaware fingers on the desk, black nails producing a tiny click on the smooth surface. "Because it was available. I never took much."

"You infused some that night." Greg found himself staring at the silver-hued hand. Powerful enough to make the butchery easy?

"Yes."

"When?"

"Rosette brought some in. I was bored. I'd been in the Abbey all day. We didn't even get out for a swim."

"A swim?"

"Yes, we usually went for a dip in the top lake in the afternoon. Mornings as well, if it was fine. We're all reasonable swimmers, even Nick."

Greg hesitated; that ambiguous notion returned at the mention of the lake. What was it about those three lakes? He hadn't been able to explain, not even to Eleanor. It was more than intuition, there was memory involved as well. Something had happened at Launde, quite a while ago. For the life of him, he couldn't think what. It was bloody annoying.

"Was there ever anything unusual about those lakes?" he asked.

"No, not as far as I know." Cecil gave Lisa Collier another mistrustful glance. She maintained her cantankerous expression, eyes not leaving Greg.

"Okay." Greg gave up. He touched a key on his cybofax, bringing up another page of questions. "Did you ever take any syntho with Isabel?"

"Once or twice, yes. She was always timid about narcotics. Her background is very middle class."

"Could anybody help themselves to Kitchener's stash?"

"It wasn't kept under lock and key. I always asked him, or Rosette. He would have known if someone had been taking it. The only thing he was concerned about was that we didn't OD."

"Tell me what happened when the body was discovered."

"Christ. The screams woke me up. That was Rosette. By the time I got into the corridor, Nick and Uri had already got there. I . . . went in to Kitchener's bedroom . . . wish to God I hadn't. That was one sick fucker who did that, Mr. Mandel. I mean seriously fucked."

"I know."

"Yes. Well. Nick was puking his guts up. Uri was in shock; he just stood there, like he wasn't seeing it. What do they call it? Thousand-meter stare. I think Rosette had fainted by then. Passed out, swooned, something. She'd stopped screaming, anyway. I got in one look and tried to stop Liz and Isabel from going in."

"When did they arrive?"

"Right after me."

"Both together?"

"God, I don't know. Yes, more or less."

"Did you see any movement in the corridor before you got to Kitchener?"

"The murderer, you mean? No. If I had, I would have killed him."

Lisa Collier gave a censorious cough.

Cecil looked around at her. "I would have killed him," he repeated firmly.

"When did you wash that night?" Greg asked.

"When did I wash?"

"Yeah."

"About eleven o'clock. I had a shower. My air conditioner couldn't cope with the storm. My room was like a sauna. I couldn't open the window, not with the rain we had that night."

"Okay, thanks, Cecil."

"That's it?"

"Yeah."

"Aren't you going to ask me if I did it? I thought that's why they brought you here."

"There's no need, not a direct question. It wasn't you."

Greg stood up and flexed his arms while they waited for Uri Pabari, shrugging off the stiffness that came from sitting in a chair designed for Martians. The air in the interview room was growing stuffy.

"Vernon, do you remember anything else ever happening at Launde?" he asked. He just couldn't ignore the presage—if that's what it was.

"Such as?"

"I don't know. Something important enough to be newsworthy, or gossipworthy." Where did I hear it? Or did I see it? Bugger.

"Kitchener was in the news once or twice each year with his lectures," Langley said reasonably. "Universities and societies used to invite him to make addresses. He was famous, after all."

"No, not Kitchener, not something he said. An event. Or an incident." He was annoyed at the amount of petulance creeping into his voice.

"Kitchener and a girl student?" Nevin suggested. "I mean, he's had two out of the three staying with him this year. Maybe one of them objected."

"Could be," Greg said. But he knew it wasn't.

They both looked at him expectantly.

"Buggered if I can remember. Can you run a check through your files for me?"

"Yes." Langley loaded a note into his cybofax. He had been laying off the dudgeon since Greg started the interviews. More impressed, or unnerved, by his espersense than he was willing to admit. Even

Nevin had stopped looking for flaws in everything he said, taking opportunities to underline the obvious.

Progress. Of sorts.

Edwin Lancaster was representing Uri Pabari. The first of the three defense counselors who actually looked like a lawyer, to Greg's mind. A sixty-year-old in a suit and silk waistcoat, pressed white shirt, small neat bow tie. He sat behind Uri, stiffly attentive. Instead of using a cybofax, a paper notebook was balanced on his leg, the tip of his gold-plated Parker Biro flicking constantly, producing a minute shorthand.

Uri gave Greg a curious stare as he settled into the chair, not nearly as apprehensive as Cecil.

The student had a powerful build. Greg called up the police-data profile on the flatscreen. Uri had played rugby for his university; he was also a karate second dan.

"You were the third into Kitchener's bedroom, is that right?" Greg asked.

"Yes. I got there on Nick's heels."

"And prior to that, you were with Liz Foxton all evening?"

"Yes."

Greg caught the tension budding in Uri's mind. "Pleasant evening, was it?"

Uri tried to smile. "God, that gland of yours is quite something, isn't it?"

"So what happened?"

"We had a row. Early on, before supper. Stupid really."

"What was it about?"

"Kitchener. His syntho habit. Except Liz didn't think it was a habit. She said . . . well, she kind of drinks up that dogma of his. Everything he says is right because he's the one that says it. Me, I'm a bit more skeptical." He grinned reflectively. "Kitchener taught me that. And that evening things got said that shouldn't have been, you know how it is."

"Do you and Liz quarrel often?"

"No. That's what makes it worse when we do. And Liz was already wound up tight over Scotland. She can get a bit political at times, she had a rough ride in the PSP decade."

"Didn't we all," Greg murmured under his breath. "Is that why there was a scene at supper between you and Kitchener?"

Uri laughed. "There's a scene at every meal. God, he was an obstinate old sod."

"And afterward? You made up, you and Liz?"

"Yes. We're in love." He looked at Greg, trying to gauge the reaction he was getting. "Hopefully, we'll get engaged. I was going to do it during the summer, I thought it would be a nice way to leave Launde."

"Okay, back to Thursday. What happened after supper?"

"Nick and Isabel came up to my room and we sat around talking and watching the newscasts. They left around midnight."

"When did you wash?"

Uri's forehead formed narrow creases as he frowned. "Just before we went to bed. Liz and I had a shower. It was hot that night."

"What time did you go to bed?"

"About half twelve."

Greg couldn't help a small smile. "And what time did you go to sleep?"

"Just after one. Liz was still watching the newscasts, though. I don't know what time she fell asleep. But we were both awake at three again."

"Who woke who?"

"Dunno. It just happened, you know."

"Was your flatscreen still showing the newscasts?"

"Er, yeah, I think so. Couldn't swear to it in court. Wasn't paying much attention, see?"

"Were you aware that Rosette was having an affair with Kitchener?"

Uri gave a mental flinch at Rosette's name. He wasn't afraid of her, Greg decided, more like demoralized.

"Yes," Uri said. "It was bound to happen, those two."

"Oh?"

"Two of a kind. Intellectually, you know. Didn't give a stuff for convention."

"And did you know about Isabel?"

Uri scratched his stubble. "The old nocturnal visiting? Yes. Shame, that. I blame Rosette more than Kitchener."

"Why is that?"

"She'd enjoy seducing Isabel. It would be a challenge to her."

"You liked Kitchener, didn't you?"

"He was bloody amazing. I don't just mean his work. When I came to Launde, I was almost as bad as Nick, all meek and tongue-tied. It's trite, but he really was like a father to me. He brings people out of themselves. God, the stories he told us! That reputation of his was one-hundred-percent earned. He was wicked, disgraceful, terrible. And absolutely beautiful. Totally unique. The only thing I disagreed about was the syntho, but it didn't seem to affect his serious thinking. And he's still pushing at frontiers even now—" The lively smile on Uri's face died a tormented death. "Was pushing . . ." he whispered.

"Did you notice anything out of the ordinary about the Abbey that night?"

"Like what?"

"A visitor."

"No—God, I would have told the police if I had!"

"Yeah. There was no trace of syntho in your blood when the police took a sample."

"Well, there wouldn't be," Uri said cautiously.

"Have you ever taken it at Launde?"

Edwin Lancaster's gold Biro halted, its tip poised a couple of millimeters in the air. "You are asking my client to incriminate himself," he said. "I'm sorry, but that wasn't part of the basis for this interview."

"We are not interested in bringing charges against anybody concerning past narcotic infusion," Langley promised. "Providing it is external to this case."

"As a police officer, you have a duty to investigate illegal narcotics abuse."

"We know the source of syntho at Launde. Kitchener's vat is in police custody; it cannot be used to supply anyone in the future. And we have no desire to prosecute past victims."

"Your client has infused syntho at some time," Greg said.

"Hey!" Uri protested.

"I simply wish to know how familiar you are with the narcotics availability at Launde, that's all," Greg said. "It's going to help me a lot."

"Okay. All right," Uri held up his hands in placation. "No big deal. Yes, I tried it. Once, okay? One time. Like I told you, it's not my scene. I don't like that kind of loss of control, not in myself or other people. Infusing it just confirmed my view. It's stupid, self-destructive."

"You know where it was grown?"

"Yes. The vat in the lab. Everybody knew that."

"Thank you. Did you use the Bendix that night?"

"No."

"Do you know its management-program codes?"

"No, not offhand, but they're stored in the operations file. We all have access to that. Kitchener trusted us not to do anything stupid; we're all 'ware literate."

"What about the datanet; did you use it on Thursday, plug into a 'ware system outside the Abbey?"

"No."

Liz Foxton, Greg decided, was the kind of girl who was always open to other people's problems. To say that she was motherly would be unfair; she had a steely reserve, a no-nonsense practicality, but in addition there was a definite aura of reassurance about her. Even he felt less disquieted about this interview.

"I've been told you don't get on well with Rosette Harding-Clarke; is that true?" he asked.

"I don't dislike her," Liz said defensively. "There is no percentage in grudges, not when you have to spend a whole year cooped up in the same house together. I understand her perfectly; I'm just unhappy with her, that's all."

"Why?"

"She made a pass at Uri. More than one, actually. He turned her down each time."

"I see. What time did you get to sleep last Thursday night?"

"About two o'clock. I was watching the Globecast news channel. I was so happy about Scotland. Now this."

"I understand you were, um, active at three o'clock Friday morning. Did you hear or see anything unusual at that time?"

"No. There was just us."

"Was the flatscreen showing the newscasts at that time?"

"Yes. I'd fallen asleep watching it."

"What about after three o'clock, did it stay on?"

"Yes. I watched it for a while. I don't know for how long, I dozed off again."

"And you were woken by Rosette's screams?"

"Yes," she said in a tiny voice.

"Then you went straight to Kitchener's bedroom?"

"Yes."

"Was Uri in the bedroom when you woke up?"

"Yes! He was out of the door before me, but only by a few seconds."

"Do you remember if you arrived at Kitchener's bedroom before or after Isabel Spalvas?"

"Before, I think. She was standing behind me. She caught me. My legs went, you see." Her eyes filled with liquid. She blinked furiously, dabbing at them with a handkerchief.

"I understand," said Greg. "Just a couple more questions." He gave Lancaster an admonitory look. "Did you ever take syntho at the Abbey?"

She sniffed. "Yes, a few times. Three, I think. That was last year, about a month after I arrived. Just to try it. Edward was there to make sure I'd be all right. But that was the last time, Uri has a real bug about it."

"And you argued about it?"

"Yes. So silly." She gave him a fast, plaintive grimace. "You remember the old song? The best part of breaking up is making up. That's us."

"Right. So you must have known that syntho was being cooked up at the Abbey, that there was a vat in the lab?"

"Yes."

"Were you using the Bendix on Thursday?"

"No, I should have been, but Scotland seemed so much more important. I was watching the newscasts for most of the day."

"So you didn't use the datanet either, then?"

"No."

"Did you ever sleep with Edward Kitchener?"

He perceived the answer in her mind, in amidst all the turmoil of guilt, adoration, remorse, and grief. She took a long time to speak. The answer in her earlier statements to the police had been a resolute no.

"I did once," she said. "When I first went to Launde. I was lonely. He was kind, sympathetic."

"Was that one of the times when you infused syntho?"

"Yes," she whispered.

"Does Uri know?"

"No." Her head was bowed. "You won't tell him, will you?"

"These interviews are strictly confidential," Greg said. "There's no need for him to know."

She rose slowly from her chair, gratefully accepting the hand Lancaster offered. "Do you know who it was?" she asked.

"Not yet, no."

Isabel Spalvas looked as tired as Greg felt. She was wearing jeans and a baggy mauve sweatshirt, her light fuzzy hair tied back in a ponytail. Her face had wonderfully dainty features. She would have been very attractive under ordinary circumstances, he guessed, but today her skin was sallow, almost gray; there were red rings around her eyes from crying, slim lips were turned down mournfully. She moved listlessly when she came in, sitting down, showing no real interest in the proceedings. Matthew Slater sat behind her, looking appropriately concerned.

Greg could sense just how grave her depression was, a bleak distress interwound with every thought. Out of all the students so far, she was easily the most affected by the murder. He would go so far as to say traumatized.

"I understand you were seeing Edward Kitchener," Greg said delicately after Langley had started the AV recording.

She nodded apathetically.

"You were with him that night?"

Another nod.

"What time did you go to him?"

"Quarter-past one."

"Until when?"

"Half-past two."

"So you left Uri's room about midnight and stayed in your own room until Rosette arrived, is that right?"

"Yes."

"What time did she arrive?"

"Half-past twelve, I think. She'd been in Cecil's room. We talked for a while, then we got changed, ready for Edward. Rosette is quite fun when she's relaxed, when she's not trying to prove something. Don't get the wrong impression about her, most of that attitude is put on. She can't help it."

"When you left Kitchener's room, did you see anyone else in the Abbey?"

"No."

"Did you hear anything strange?"

"No."

"What about lights—shining under someone's door, or downstairs, outside even?"

"No. Oh, there was a bit of light in Uri's room. Bluish. I think the flatscreen might have been on. We were watching it in there earlier."

"You were taking syntho that night. Had it worn off by then?"

"Not quite, I was just starting to come down. I don't—" She took a breath, then looked resolutely at the floor. "I don't like being in there after the boost has gone."

"In Kitchener's bedroom?"

"Yes."

"Why not?"

"I get cold. Not physically cold, but it's hard to face them afterward. We get so high together, you see; when it comes to sex, Edward and Rosette have lifetimes more experience than me, they made me feel completely free with them. The way a child trusts an adult. His bedroom contained our own private universe, we were safe inside, nothing mattered apart from ourselves and what we wanted. But then when it was over, the illusion vanished so quickly. And this shabby old world with all its inbuilt guilt comes flooding back in." She tugged at a strand of hair, twisting it nervously around and around her index finger. "You must think I'm horrible."

"I'm not a judge, Isabel. Your sex life is entirely your own. But I'd like to know why you started going, please?"

"Rosette started—well, it was just hints at first. Joking. Then . . .

I don't know. Somehow it wasn't a joke anymore. And then I went home for Christmas. There was nothing wrong with that, with my family. Except it was sort of pale, lacking substance; I was going through the motions. The Abbey, Edward—we were learning so much there, learning how to think, how to question. It was so much more real. Color, that's what Launde had. I was glad to get back. I wanted more of it, more of the adventure. They offered me that."

"Cecil said you were unhappy."

"Not really. It's peculiar, what I was doing, so far outside my norm. Edward called it walking the boundaries of the mind. I had trouble adapting to the affair at first; when I was with Edward and Rosette, it didn't matter at all; it was just outside, afterward, when it seemed wrong, or stupid, or both. I was going to them more frequently, and staying longer, too. But that wasn't the answer, not shutting myself away with them. Talking about it to someone who understood helped me. Cecil was the only one I could really go to. Cecil is worldly wise, or so he claims. He sympathized in a funny sort of way, and he didn't criticize. That meant a lot to me."

"Did you know Rosette was pregnant?"

Isabel's head came up, her blue eyes full of melancholy. There was no resentment in her mind, which was what he actually wanted to know. No grudge. He didn't think a gentle soul like Isabel *could* hold a grudge.

"Yes," Isabel said. "She never said. But I knew. I'm glad in a way, certainly now. It means there will be something of Edward left. I almost wish it was me."

"How about Kitchener, what sort of mood was he in that night?"

"Edward? Happy. Rosette and me . . . I . . . it was good that night."

"No, apart from that. His general mood that night, over the last few days. Was he preoccupied at all? Worried about something? Agitated?"

"No." She gave him a brave little smile. "You don't know Edward or you wouldn't even have asked. He pretended to be this awful old monster. But it was all a sham. Oh, he'd shout at us if we were blatantly stupid. And politicians infuriated him. Apart from that, he didn't have any worries. That was part of the attraction, I've never met anyone so carefree. He'd done so much in his lifetime, won so many battles. I don't think anything could upset him anymore."

"I have to ask this, Isabel: how do you feel about Nicholas Beswick?"

"Oh, God!" She buried her face in her hands. "Why did he have to come out and see us? He's so sweet. I didn't want to hurt him. Really. Why did any of this happen? What did we do?"

Slater patted her gently, but she shrugged him off. He shot a silent appeal at Greg.

Greg waited until she finished wiping tears from her eyes with damp knuckles.

"Were you the last to reach Kitchener's bedroom after Rosette discovered the body?" he asked, feeling a prize lout for pressing the anguished girl.

"Yes. I think so. They were all ahead of me. I don't remember much. I'm sorry."

"No matter. Before then, after Nicholas had found you and Rosette together in the corridor, did you tell Kitchener he had seen you?"

"No. God, I couldn't. I didn't know what to do about that. Even Rosette was upset. Edward had a real soft spot for Nick, he had such high hopes for him. Nick has a very high IQ, and he wants to learn, I mean really wants. The whole universe is a glorious puzzle to Nick. That's the only time he ever comes out of his shell; when we're talking about the everyday things like the channels or politics, he sits quietly in the corner; but say anything about Grand Unification or quantum mechanics and you can't shut him up. He's lovely like that, so animated. I'm rambling, sorry."

"Did you and Rosette discuss what to do about Nicholas seeing you?"

"Not much. It was a sort of mutual silence. I made up my mind to go see Nick in the morning. Really I was. I would have tried to explain. He was about the one person I would have given Edward up for. I looked after I left Edward, but Nick's light was out. And anyway, it wouldn't have been right, not going in straight afterward. That would have seemed like Edward had total priority on me. But then . . . ."

"Nicholas Beswick's light was off at two-thirty? You're sure of that?"

"Yes."

"When did you wash that night?"

"I had a shower before I started getting our supper ready, then I had another after I left Edward."

"Were you using the Bendix at all on Thursday?"

"Yes, most of the afternoon."

"Did you access any external 'ware systems?"

"No."

The last question slid from his cybofax's little screen. He couldn't think of any more. Isabel already looked like he'd physically wrung the answers from her.

It was raining outside again, big warm drops beating incessantly on the high window.

"Okay," he told Vernon. "Let's have Nicholas Beswick in."

I<small>T WAS RAINING OVER</small> P<small>ETERBOROUGH</small> again. Sheet lightning sizzled through the covering of low cloud, highlighting the new tower blocks that stood on the high ground to the west, austere monoliths looking down on the organic clutter of the smaller buildings in the city's original districts.

Julia hated flying in thunderstorms. Her Dornier tilt-fan might have every safety system in existence built in, but it seemed so insignificant compared to the power outside.

Another flash burst over the city. Glossy rooftop solar panels bounced some of the light back up at her, leaving tiny purple dazzle spots on her retinas. She had seen the Event Horizon headquarters building dead ahead, a seventeen-story cube of glass, steel, and composite panels. There was nothing elegant about it, thrown up in twenty-six frantic months so that it could accommodate the droves of head-office data shufflers necessary to manage a company of Event Horizon's size, as well as Morgan's security staff. A monument to haste and functionalism. Its replacement out at Prior's Fen would be far more aesthetic; the architects had come up with a white-and-gold cylinder which, with its panoply of pillars and arches, resembled the Leaning Tower of Pisa. Only straight this time, of course. Event Horizon didn't build crooked.

She poured herself a chilled mineral water from the bar and switched the bulkhead flatscreen on, flicking through the channels until she came to the Northwest Europe Broadcast Company. Jakki Coleman was on, a middle-aged woman with iron-cast gold-blonde hair, wearing a stylish mint-green satin jacket. She was sitting behind a Florentine desk in the luxurious study of some mansion.

Julia grinned gamely as she sprawled back on the white-leather settee, propping her feet up on the chair opposite. Jakki Coleman was the queen of the gossipcasts; rock stars, channel celebrities, aristocrats, sports personalities, politicians, she shafted them all.

"Pauline Harrington, the devoutly Catholic songstress, seems to have mislaid her religious scruples," Jakki said, her French accent rich and purring. "At least for this weekend. For whom should I see but the delightful Pauline, who is at number five with 'My Real Man' in this week's white soul chart, with none other than Keran Bennion, number one driver for the Porsche team."

The image cut to a picture of Pauline and Keran walking through the grounds of a country hotel, somewhere where the sun was shining. They were hand in hand, oblivious to the fountains playing in stone-lined ponds around them; in the background, bushes blazed with big tangerine blooms. The recording had obviously been made with a telephoto lens, the outlines were slightly fuzzy.

"Perhaps Keran's wife sent him for singing lessons," Jakki suggested smugly. "The three days they spent together should certainly have got his voice in trim."

A swarthy young male in a purple-and-black Versace suit walked into the office and put a sheet of paper in front of Jakki. She read it and "Ohooed" delightedly. "Well, fancy that," she said.

The item was about a Swiss minister and her toyboy. After that was one about a music-biz payola racket.

Julia took a sip of the mineral water, then noticed her boots. They were crusted with mud from the tower site. She tried rubbing at them with a tissue as Jakki stage-whispered that certain pointed questions were being asked about a countess's newborn son; apparently the count was absent the night of the conception.

Julia chortled to herself. It was the set she moved in that featured in the 'cast, Europe's financial, political, and glamor elite; snobbish, pretentious, corrupt, yet forever projecting the image of angels. And she had to deal with them on that level, the great pretense, all part of the grand game. So it was a joy to watch Jakki spotlighting their failings, taking a machete to their egos; a kind of secondhand revenge for all the false courtesies she had to extend, the interminable flatteries.

"The *big* event in England yesterday was the Event Horizon spaceplane roll out," Jakki said. "Simply anybody who is anybody was there, including little *moi*."

Julia held her breath. Surely Jakki wasn't going to lampoon the Prince's haircut? Not again?

"And I can tell you several self-proclaimed *celebrities* were left outside explaining rather tiresomely that their invitations had been squirted to their holiday houses by mistake," Jakki gushed maliciously. "But leaving behind the nonentities, we enter the *interesting* zone. Appropriately for an event so large, and *très* prestigious, it boasted the greatest laugh of the day." Oh, dear Lord, it was going to be the Prince: "Mega, mega-wealthy Julia Evans has spent a rumored three and a quarter billion pounds New Sterling on developing the sleek machine intended to spearhead England's economic reconstruction."

Julia scowled. Where had Jakki got that estimate from? It was alarmingly close to the real one. Not another leak in the finance division, please!

The flatscreen image switched to the roll-out ceremony, showing her escorting the Prince and the Prime Minister around the spaceplane.

"Unfortunately," Jakki continued, "these daunting design costs must have left poor dear Julia's cupboard quite bare. Because, as you can see, her otherwise enviably slim figure was clad in what looks to me like a big Valentine's Day chocolate-box wrapper."

The Dornier landed on the raised pad at the center of the headquarters' roof. Caroline Rothman held a broad golfing umbrella over Julia as they made their way to the stairwell door. Rachel and Ben marched alongside. Nobody was looking at her. It could have been coincidence. But then they had all been incredibly busy when she came out of the tilt-fan's rear lounge as well.

Be honest, girl, she told herself, stomping out of the lounge. That *bitchsluthussy!*

Sean Francis, her management-division assistant, was waiting for her inside the building. She actually quite liked Sean, although he annoyed a lot of people with his perfectionistic efficiency. She had appointed him to her personal staff soon after inheriting the company.

He was thirty-four, a tall, dark-haired man with a degree in engineering administration who had joined Event Horizon right after graduation. It said a lot for his capability that he had risen so far so fast. Greg had checked him out for her once; his loyalty was beyond reproach.

He was wearing the same conservative style of suit as every other data shuffler in the building. Sometimes she wondered what would happen if she let it be known she preferred employees to wear tank-tops and Bermuda shorts. Knowing the way people jumped around her, they probably would all turn up in them.

Might be worth doing.

"Did you have a nice flight, ma'am?" Sean asked pleasantly.

Julia put her hands on her hips. "Sean, it's pissing down with rain and the bloody plane nearly got skewered by lightning bolts. What do you think?"

His jaw opened, then closed. "Yes, ma'am," he said humbly. "Sorry."

She caught a tiny flickering motion from the corner of her eye and thought Caroline was making a hand signal. But when she turned, her PA was rolling up the umbrella, a guileless expression in place.

It's a conspiracy.

She took a grip on her nerves. I am not affected by what that senile whore Jakki Coleman said. I'm not.

"My fault, Sean." She gave him one of her heartbreaker smiles. "Those thunderbolts are frightening when you're so close to them."

"That's all right, ma'am. I'm scared of them, too."

The conference room was on the corner of the headquarters building; two walls were made from reinforced glass with a brown tint, giving a view over the rain-dulled streets of Westwood. It was decorated in the kind of forced grandeur that was endemic among corporate designers the world over: deep-piled sapphire-blue carpet, two Picassos and a Van Gogh hanging between big aluminum-framed prints of the Fens before the Warming, huge oval oak table, thickly padded black-leather chairs, pot plants taller than people. Everything was shameless ostentation.

Julia was all too aware that her boots were leaving muddy footprints as she walked to her chair at the head of the table. There were several startled glances among the delegates when they saw her Goth clothes. Damp hair hanging in flaccid strings didn't help.

Eight of her own staff were sitting along one side, premier executives from each of the company's divisions. Lined up against them were Valyn Szajowski, Argon Hulmes, Sir Michael Torrance, Karl

Hildebrandt, and Sok Yem, the representatives from Event Horizon's financial backing consortium. There were over a hundred and fifty banks and finance houses in the consortium, making it one of the largest in the world. In the first two years after the fall of the PSP they had extended seventy percent of the money that Philip Evans had needed to reestablish the company in England. Event Horizon under his guidance had proved to be an ultra-solid investment; even though there had been some nervousness about his enthusiasm for the company's space program, he had never missed a payment. With the global economy at that time still extremely shaky, membership in the consortium was highly prized and jealously guarded.

But then two years ago, after Julia inherited the company lock, stock, and barrel, the once eagerly proffered loans became suddenly hard to obtain and those that were available had inordinately high interest rates. The conservative financial establishment had zero faith in teenage girls as corporate owner-directors. They wanted more say in the way Event Horizon was run, a position on the management board, possibly even the directorship. Just until she was older, they explained, until she understood the mechanism of corporate management—say, in about twenty years. Their reluctant but firm insistence had turned into the biggest tactical error in modern financial history. Respected financecast commentators were already calling it the Great Loan Shark Massacre.

Armed with the giga-conductor royalties and (unknown to the consortium) her grandfather's NN core, she stuck up a grand two-fingered salute and carried on, expanding the company at an even faster rate. Existing loan repayments came in ahead of schedule, with corresponding loss of interest payments, and fewer loans were applied for. The consortium's income began to fall off while Event Horizon's cash flow and profits grew; their golden egg was tarnishing rapidly.

Sean pulled her chair out and she sat down, glowering at the artificial smiles directed toward her. Sean and Caroline sat on either side.

Open Channel To NN Core.

Well, hello there, Miss Grumpy Guts. And what's today's temper tantrum all about?

I am not in a temper, Grandpa.

Ha! I'm plugged into the conference room's security cameras. If looks could kill, my girl, you'd be in a room of corpses.

Did you see . . . never mind. No. Did you see Jakki Coleman's 'cast this morning?

Bloody hell, girl, I haven't got time for crap like that, not even with my capacity.

She was going on about what I wore yesterday. I had three fittings for that outfit, you know. Three.

Really.

Sabareni is one of the best haute couture houses in Europe. It's not like I'm going to Oxfam.

That's a great relief to hear.

Seven thousand pounds it cost.

I wouldn't want you stinting, Julia.

Don't be so bloody sarcastic. Seven thousand pounds! Well, I can't possibly wear it again. Not now.

Juliet, could we possibly start the meeting, please.

Yah, all right. I bet they all saw the 'cast. Seven thousand pounds!

Oh, Gawd. The silent voice carried a definite air of pique.

The management team and consortium representatives sat down, their earlier *bonhomie* fractured by her black mood.

Good. They might cut short the usual smarmy attempts to ingratiate themselves.

The terminal flatscreen recessed into the table in front of her lit up with the meeting's agenda.

"I am happy to report that, as I'm sure you all saw yesterday, the *Clarke* spaceplane project is on schedule," Julia said. "First flight is due in a month, first orbital test flight should take place ten weeks later. Assuming no catastrophic design flaw, deliveries will start in a year."

"That's excellent news, Julia," Argon Hulmes said. "Your Duxford team is to be congratulated."

"Thank you," she replied equably.

The consortium representatives had all been changed over the last two years until not one of the original members remained. This new batch were all younger, a not very subtle attempt to make her feel more comfortable. Although even now the banks still couldn't quite bring themselves to appoint anyone under thirty-eight; Sok Yem from the Hong Kong Oceanic Bank was the youngest at thirty-nine. Rumor said that Argon Hulmes's superiors had ordered him to have *plastique* before he got his seat, bringing his appearance down from forty-three to thirtyish.

Thirty and then something, Julia thought. He was always trying to talk to her about groups and albums and raves; his Christmas present had been a bootleg AV recording of a Bil Yi Somanzer concert. She imagined him dutifully plugging into the MTV channel each evening, updating himself on current releases, who's hot and who's flopped. A fine occupation for a middle-aged banker.

"We will break even on three hundred spaceplanes," she said. "That should come in about three years' time. My space-line, Dragonflight, has just placed firm orders for another fifteen, and options on thirty-five, to cope with the nuclear waste-disposal contract we were awarded yesterday. We are expecting additional disposal contracts from five or six more European governments to be signed over the next few months, and of course national aerospace lines will want to get in on the act."

Sean Francis took his cue flawlessly. "Nuclear waste disposal has enabled us to upgrade our estimates on space-related industry turnover by forty-five percent over the next four years," he said. "It is a completely untapped revenue source. Should it be exploited fully, its potential is staggering. No government on the planet will be able to refuse its electorate a safe and final solution to disposing of radioactive material. And there are currently forty-three redundant nuclear power stations in Europe alone, with a further seventeen scheduled to be decommissioned over the next decade."

"Such a pity the consortium didn't consider my Sunderland vitrification plant a worthwhile investment," Julia said. "You could have shared in the profits. The margin is considerable, given that I now have a virtual monopoly on the technology."

Sir Michael leaned forward earnestly. "We would be very happy to fund any expansion to the vitrification plant, Julia. Now that the requirement has been proved, and very ably proved if I might say so. The nuclear waste-disposal contract is a marvelous development, we're all very pleased."

No, Juliet, absolutely not, cut them out of the vitrification. Squeeze the bastards.

She gave Sir Michael a smile that withered his sudden display of enthusiasm. "The vitrification plant was a five-hundred-million-pound risk," she said in her lecturer's voice. "And having taken that risk all by myself, I intend to benefit all by myself. The profits generated by this new venture will be more than sufficient to fund its own expansion. Thank you."

"Julia, I think we are all agreed that your handling of the company is impeccable," Sir Michael said. "And in view of this, we would like to offer to set up a floating credit arrangement of three billion New Sterling that you can call upon at any time to fund new ventures. This way, we could avoid the delays and queries inherent with having to process loan requests through the consortium's standing review committee."

The other representatives murmured their approval, all of them watching her, willing her to accept.

We've got 'em, Juliet. They don't offer anyone a blank check unless they're under a lot of pressure. Now, remember what we agreed, girl?

Hit them with the wind-up scenario. Then the Prior's Fen scheme.

That's my girl.

She tented her fingers and gave them an apologetic look. "Oh dear, how embarrassing. I believe my finance director has a summary he wanted to present. Alex, if you would, please."

Alex Barnes stood up, a fifty-three-year-old Afro-Caribbean with a receding cap of grizzled hair. His suit with velvet lapels did at least lift him above the level of corporate clone. He began to recite a stream of accounts; figures, dates, and percentages merging together in a wearisome drone of statistics.

The representatives were looking very itchy by the time he finished.

"What it means," Julia said sweetly, "is that the loans that the consortium has so far extended to Event Horizon will be repaid in seven years. After that, the company will be totally self-financing. Now, as the company's expansion plans have already been finalized for that period, with the exception of Prior's Fen, I really can see no reason to extend my period of indebtedness. Certainly not at the level of your floating credit proposal, which I have to say is disappointingly paltry, given Event Horizon's size."

There was a moment of silence as the representatives exchanged a comprehensive catalog of facial expressions. Interestingly, only Argon Hulmes allowed any ire to show. So much for solidarity amongst fellow youth-culture subscribers.

Some clandestine and invisible voting system elected Sir Michael as their spokesman. "Exactly what were you proposing to do out at Prior's Fen?" he inquired in a wary tone.

Karl Hildebrandt remained behind after the meeting. The request for a talk—"Not business, I assure you"—from the wily old German was intriguing enough for Julia to humor him.

Sean remained seated at her side, while Caroline helped shepherd the others from the room. Eventually there were only the three of them left at the table, plus Rachel, sitting quietly on a chair by the window.

Diessenburg Mercantile, the Zurich bank that Karl represented, was one of the larger members of the consortium, accounting for six percent of the investment total. Karl himself was in his late forties, and putting on weight almost as fast as Uncle Horace; a fold of pink flesh was overlapping his collar (she could count about four chins), his blond hair was veering into silver. His suit came from Paris, a narrow lapel helping to de-emphasize his barrel chest; steel-rimmed glasses were worn for effect, bestowing an air of dependability.

She approved of him for the one reason that he didn't try to pretend, like Argon Hulmes.

"I know it has been said before, Julia," he said, "but you are quite a remarkable young girl." There was hardly any German accent. Perhaps one of the reasons he'd been selected as a representative.

"Thank you, Karl. You're not going to come on to me like Argon, are you?"

He laughed softly and closed up his cybofax, slipping it into his inside jacket pocket. "Certainly not. But to squeeze a fixed-interest twelve-billion-pound investment loan out of banks and finance houses is an achievement beyond some kombinates."

"Prior's Fen is a viable project. No risk."

"The cyber-precincts, maybe. But to make us pay for a rail link before we can invest in them. That's cruel, Julia."

"You get your interest payments, I get my cyber-precincts. Point to a victim, Karl."

"None, of course. That is why you triumph all the time."

"So you think the review committee will approve the loan?"

"Yes," he said simply.

"I thought this wasn't going to be business."

"I apologize. But everything has its roots in politics."

She couldn't ever remember seeing Karl in such an ambivalent mood before. It was as if he wanted to talk about some important topic but didn't quite know how to broach the subject. A parent explaining sex to a giggly teenager. "You want to talk about politics? I wasn't old enough to vote at the election even if I had been in the country. I will in the next, though."

"You certainly play politics like a master, Julia. That's why I was not surprised when you were given the nuclear waste-disposal contract. Admiring, but not surprised."

"Thank you, it took some arranging, but I'd like to think I am flexible when it comes to cooperating with the English Ministry of Industry."

"Yes. However, there are questions being asked in some quarters about the closeness of Event Horizon and the Ministry. It might almost be referred to as a partnership."

"I have never offered cash to an MP," she said. "And I never will."

"No. But the relationship, imaginary though it is, can be seized upon by opposition parties. The Big Lie, Julia; say something loud enough for long enough, and people will begin to believe. Ultimately that will affect Event Horizon; artificial constraints will be placed on you. Your bids will be refused simply because they are yours; politicians publicly demonstrating that they are not showing any favoritism. And that cannot be allowed." He smiled crookedly. "It's bad for profits, if nothing else. Bad for us."

Julia began to wonder which "us" he was talking about. "I will just have to shout louder. And I can shout, very loud indeed."

"An official denial is like an Oscar to a rumor."

"Are we going to sit here all afternoon and quote *bons mots* at each other, Karl?"

"I would hope not."

"Well, what would you like to see me do?"

"Some circumspection wouldn't hurt, Julia. I know you are reasonably adroit; that's why I find your latest action somewhat puzzling."

She sneaked a questioning look to Sean. But he just shrugged minutely.

"What action?"

"Imposing that Mindstar veteran, Greg Mandel, on the Kitchener inquiry. It was terribly public, Julia. You were his bridesmaid. Really! It leaves you wide open to the rabble-rousers and conspiracy theorists."

She regarded him thoughtfully. "How did you know about Greg?"

"It was all over the channel newscasts."

"Oh." Even so, it was odd that he should know so quickly. She had spent most of the morning poring over datawork for the meeting, and that was with nodes augmenting her brain. Did he really have each news item concerning Event Horizon brought to his attention? Then she remembered Jakki bitch Coleman. It hadn't been every minute, after all. "I take your point, Karl. Actually, I've already started damage limitation."

"Mandel has been taken off the case?"

"No, I need to know who killed Kitchener. But you won't be hearing about the link between Greg and myself anymore, not on the channels."

"Ah. I'm glad to hear it."

9

NICHOLAS WASN'T REALLY INTERESTED IN his surroundings anymore, so the pokey interview room didn't lodge in his mind until Greg Mandel looked at him. Looked inside him, more like, right through his skull into his brain.

The lawyer, Lisa Collier, had explained about the psychic being assigned to the investigation. She had seemed very irate about it, going on about how his rights were being violated, procedural irregularities, hearsay being taken as evidence. Nicholas didn't mind a psychic being appointed; anything, anything at all that would bring the killer a step nearer to justice was totally justified. That was simple logic, obvious. Why couldn't the Collier woman see that?

He had been staying in one of the cells at the Oakham police station since Friday, although the door was always left unlocked. "You aren't being held on remand," the police kept explaining. "You're just here to help us." He nodded at their anxious faces and answered every question the detectives asked. They seemed surprised that his answers were so consistent. As if he could forget anything that had happened on that night.

It was the last night of his life. Nothing had happened to him since. There were only the mechanics of the body, eating, going to the toilet, sleeping. That was all he had done since then, slept and answered questions. He was allowed to mix with the other students, but they never expected him to say anything anyway. They had moaned about the accommodation, about not being allowed out, the food, the bathroom.

The one person he wanted to talk to, Isabel, was farther away from him now than she had ever been at Launde. She would sit in one corner of the community room they had been assigned, her legs tucked up against her chest, peering vacantly out of the window, and he would sit in the corner opposite, just gazing at her. He was too afraid even to say good morning, because if they did talk, he would have to hear about her and Kitchener and Rosette. What happened in that bedroom, how many times it happened. Even why it had happened. He couldn't possibly stand that.

Kitchener had been the architect of his mind. For the first time in his life, he had really begun to think straight. Kitchener, with his own love of knowledge, had been the one who nurtured his talent, who made him realize his ability was nothing to be ashamed of, wasn't freakish like people said. Kitchener was the one who encouraged him to join in the Abbey's camaraderie.

Kitchener had taken Isabel from him.

Kitchener was dead.

The world, which had been so close to becoming accessible, had eluded him once again. Which was why he said he didn't mind the psychic asking questions; after all, Kitchener had used neurohormones. They couldn't be bad.

Except that now he was faced with the prospect of actually going through with the interview, it didn't seem quite so easy.

There was a very unforgiving quality about Greg Mandel as he sat patiently behind the desk, some weary tolerance that even Nicholas, with all his social inadequacy, could recognize. The man had the appearance of having been everywhere, witnessed every human state. Excuses would not work, not on him. Yet at the same time, he could see how receptive Greg was. It was confusing, the two almost contrasting aspects of character existing side by side.

Nicholas dropped into the chair, not in the least reassured by the formality of the proceedings as Vernon Langley and Lisa Collier made their stiff lead-in statements for the AV recorder. There was something unnaturally creepy about someone rooting round in his mind; for a start, there were so many pathetic secrets about himself, all those hundreds of failings and disasters littering his life.

"I can't plug into your memories," Greg said in a palliative tone. "So you can stop worrying about the time you pinched your little brother's chocolate bar."

"I haven't got a brother," Nicholas blurted. "Only a sister. And I've never stolen anything from her."

"There you are then, I can't tell."

"Oh, right." He felt such a fool. "How did you know I was worried about you reading my memories?"

"Because everybody does that when they meet me. Vernon and Jon here are worried about the cash they lifted from the station's Christmas-party box, Mrs. Collier is extremely worried about her dark past. But the only thing I can sense inside a brain is the emotional content. So the sooner you relax and all that worry vanishes, the sooner I can ask the questions, and the sooner you can be out of here. Okay?"

Nicholas nodded vigorously, secretly cheered by the way Lisa Collier's disapprobation had darkened still further at the gibe. "Yes. Of course. I do want to help."

"Yeah, I can see that. You really liked Kitchener, didn't you?"

Lisa Collier had warned him never to lie to the psychic; no matter how painful any admission, he would see it, and it would be entered against him. "I did. I do. But . . ."

"Isabel," Greg said sympathetically.

"I didn't know about her and Kitchener. Not before that night."

"What time did you see her and Rosette going into Kitchener's room?"

"About a quarter past one."

"And then what did you do?"

"Went to bed."

"Did you sleep?"

"Suppose so. I was thinking a lot at first. But I was asleep when I heard Rosette screaming."

"Before you went to sleep, did you hear anything?"

"No!" Nicholas said hotly.

"I meant, Nicholas, anybody walking about in the Abbey?"

He knew he would be blushing again. Why couldn't he ever understand what people meant straight off? Why did they always have to use baby talk to get through to him? "Oh. Sorry. No, nobody was moving around."

"So you didn't hear Isabel and Rosette leaving Kitchener's room?"

"No."

"What were you doing in the time between leaving Uri's room and seeing Rosette and Isabel?"

"Running the *Antomine 12* data through a detection program. I was looking for dark-mass concentrations."

"Dark mass?" Greg sounded privately amused.

"Yes. In space. Kitchener was interested in them. He thought they might act as wormhole termini. You see, if you move a wormhole in a specific fashion, it may be possible to generate a CTC directly. A non-paradoxical temporal loop would . . ." Nicholas forced himself to stop, chastened. He'd done it again. There was that dreadfully familiar expression of polite incomprehension on Greg's face. "Sorry," he mumbled.

"Don't be ashamed of a gift, Nicholas."

He looked up, startled. But Greg was serious.

"I go on, sometimes," he said limply. "I don't realize. Cosmology is *interesting,* Mr. Mandel."

"I know what it's like. My wife tells me I talk about Turkey too much."

"Turkey?"

"The war."

It took a moment before Nicholas remembered the Jihad Legion. He had been eight or nine at the time the Islamic forces had invaded Turkey, so it was classed alongside all the other terrible incidents that childhood jumbled together. "Oh, yes."

"About the detection program," Greg prompted. "Were you running it on the Abbey's Bendix?"

"Yes."

"Until when?"

"When I saw Isabel and Rosette, quarter past one. I couldn't work after that."

"Did you use the English Telecom datanet that night?"

"Yes."

"Why?"

"I had to, the *Antomine* data comes direct from its mission control in Toulouse. There's no other way of accessing it."

"So you used only the one datalink?"

"Yes."

"Okay." Greg typed something into his cybofax. "Did you know Rosette was mildly insomniac?"

Funny question. He couldn't think why Greg should want to know. "No. But she was never tired at the end of an evening when we were in a room or if we went to the Old Plough. And she was usually first up. So I suppose, thinking about it, I knew she didn't sleep much."

"Have you ever taken syntho, Nicholas?"

"No," he said, because it was true, so he could say it without any guilt showing. But he dropped his gaze in shame. There was an achingly long moment of silence.

When he risked looking up, Greg was giving him a calculating stare. All his doubts about the psychic searching freely through his memories returned in a flood.

"Let's see," Greg said. "You took another kind of narcotic?"

"No," Nicholas said miserably.

"Somebody offered you syntho?"

"Yes."

"Rosette?"

"Yes."

"And you refused?"

"Yes. I know Kitchener says there's nothing wrong with it. But I didn't want to."

"I can see the incident has a lot of connotations for you; what else happened?"

Nicholas decided the best thing to do was just say it fast. Greg might move on to another subject. He stared unblinkingly at his Nike trainers. The lace on the left foot was fraying. "She wanted me to go to bed with her."

"When was this?"

"November the third."

"Did you?"

"No! She thought . . . she thought it was funny."

"Yeah; I can imagine, I've been introduced to Rosette. So you knew syntho was available at the Abbey?"

"Yes."

"Did you know where the vat was?"

"In the chemistry lab."

"You were the first person to arrive at the bedroom after Rosette screamed, is that right?"

"Yes."

"Did you see anybody else in the Abbey, apart from the other students?"

"No. Well . . ." Nicholas tugged at the front of his sweatshirt. It seemed to be constricting around him; his skin was very warm. Both detectives were studying him keenly. This was all going to sound so incredibly stupid, they really would think he was backward now. "There was a girl," he said reluctantly.

Greg's eyes had closed, his face crinkled with the effort of concentration. "Go on."

"It was earlier. When I saw Isabel and Rosette. She was a ghost."

Nevin let out an exasperated groan, leaning back in his chair. "For Christ's sake!"

Greg held up a hand, clicking his fingers irritably to silence him. "You said: girl. How old?"

"About my age. She was tall, very pretty, red hair."

"How do you know she was a ghost?"

"Because I saw her outside first. Then she was in the corridor behind Isabel and Rosette."

"You mean she was out in the park?"

"No. Right outside my window. I thought it was a reflection in the glass at first."

"Your room is on the second floor, isn't it?"

"Yes. That's why she couldn't be real. I think I imagined her. I was very tired."

"Have you ever seen the combat leathers that army squaddies wear?" Greg asked. "They are a bit like biker suits, only not so restrictive, matte-black, broad equipment belts, and there's normally a skull helmet as well."

"Yes, I think I know what you mean."

"Was this girl wearing anything like that?"

"Oh, no. She had a jacket on that was quite dark, but it was just an ordinary one; I think she was wearing a long skirt, too."

Greg opened his eyes and reached up to scratch the back of his neck. "Interesting," he said guardedly.

Nicholas studiously avoided eye contact with the two detectives.

"Hardly relevant, Mandel," Langley said.

Greg ignored him. "Have you ever seen her before?" he asked Nicholas.

"No."

"What about other ghosts, or visions?"

He hung his head. "No."

"What time did you get up that morning, Nicholas?"

"Half-past seven."

"Okay. It probably was just fatigue." He sounded satisfied. "A lot of squaddies used to suffer from it in Turkey; amazing what they thought they saw after two or three days without sleep. There; told you I talked too much about my old campaigns."

Nicholas smiled tentatively, it didn't seem as though he was mocking.

Greg yawned and squinted at his cybofax. "When was the last time you washed?"

"Lunchtime, just after the lawyers finished briefing us about you conducting our interviews."

Nevin's face split into a huge grin.

"No, Nicholas." Greg was laboring against a similar grin. "I meant last Thursday. When was the last time you washed prior to the murder?"

Blood heated his cheeks and ears. "Just after seven o'clock. Before I went down to supper."

Nevin frowned and pulled out his cybofax. He muttered an order into it and scanned the screen.

Greg had turned to watch him.

"Must have been later than that," he said in a low tone.

Langley took the cybofax and looked at the data on display. Greg joined them; the three of them put their heads together, talking quietly.

Nicholas squirmed unhappily. He wasn't sure what he'd done wrong this time. At least Greg hadn't accused him of lying.

"What sort of wash?" Nevin asked.

"A shower. We've all got showers."

Nevin pointed at the cybofax screen. "There, see? The back of his hands are as clean as his legs."

"Yeah, but the particle accumulation on both is quite well established," Greg said.

"That doesn't mean . . ."

Nicholas stopped listening. He remembered the body scan they gave him when he arrived at the station. It was in a white-composite cubicle, similar to a shower. A sensor, like a brown bulb the size of his fist, had telescoped down from the ceiling on the end of a waldo arm and slowly spiraled around his naked body. He had imagined it sniffing like a dog. Then there had been the blood tests, the urine sample, his clothes taken away for examination, finger- and palm-prints recorded.

"Did you wash later on?" Greg asked. "After supper?"

"Yes. My hands, a few times. I went to the toilet; we were eating peanuts in Uri's room, they leave your hands sticky."

"The time is wrong," Nevin insisted.

"It's not tremendously reliable," Langley said grudgingly. "We can't contest anything with those results."

"What is it?" Nicholas asked, pleased that he had found the courage from somewhere.

"The amount of dirt you were carrying on Friday morning is rather low, that's all," Greg said. He closed his eyes. "Tell me again, what time did you have a shower?"

"After seven, about quarter-past. We have to be down for supper at half-past, you see."

"And you didn't have another shower later?"

"No."

"He's telling the truth."

"Is there a point of contention?" Lisa Collier asked.

Greg and Langley both looked at Jon Nevin. The detective gave the cybofax screen one last scan, then snapped the unit shut. "No."

10

Maybe it was the rain, a relentless heavy downpour, that had cleared the reporters from the pavement outside the police station, or maybe the prospect of incurring Julia's wrath had put the fear of God into them. Whatever the reason, when Greg drove out of the station gates late on Tuesday afternoon, there was only a handful of camera operators in plastic slickers left to watch him go.

"Thank heavens for that," Eleanor muttered beside him. "I thought they'd put down roots."

He turned up Church Street and flicked on the headlights. The sun hadn't quite set, but the solid clouds had smothered Oakham in a gray penumbra. Raindrops emitted a wan yellow twinkle as they slashed through the beams.

"Yeah," he agreed. "You had a word with Julia, then?"

"Absolutely. You know, it's still hard to associate the girl we know with this demon-machinator billionairess all the channels carp on about. I mean, the Prime Minister couldn't call off reporters like this. They'd all race up to the top of the nearest hill and start screaming about oppression and press freedom."

"No messing. But then, Marchant doesn't own the launch facilities that boost the broadcast satellite platforms into geosync orbit."

"There is that."

Greg glanced over at Cutts Close; lights were shining in all the caravans, dark figures shuffled across the grass. They hadn't actually retreated then, just regrouped ready for tomorrow.

He nudged the EMC Ranger up to thirty-five kilometers an hour. The rain had driven most of the traffic off the roads, leaving a few cyclists pedaling home, faces screwed up against the spray. His neurohormone hangover was ebbing; it wasn't as if he had to strain for the interviews. The Launde students had been cooperative, a welcome change from the hideously antagonistic mullahs in Turkey.

"What did Julia say about analyzing the themed neurohormones?" he asked.

"No problem, we should have the answer sometime tomorrow. The courier came and picked up the ampoules while you were doing the interviews." Eleanor gazed blankly at the deserted stalls in the market square. It was the empty expression she used whenever she was more irritated than she wanted to admit. "I had to threaten to call the Home Office for clearance before he authorized their release."

"Who, Denzil?"

"No, one of the detectives in the CID office."

"Oh. Tell you, I think Vernon is softening, and Jon Nevin isn't far behind."

"Great." The tone was biting.

"Nothing pleasant in life ever comes cheap."

She let her head loll back on the support cushioning. "No. As you always tell me. So how did you get on with the students? Are they all innocent?"

He grinned at the double meaning. "I'm pretty certain none of them killed Kitchener. Although God knows, enough of them had the motive. He's actually slept with all of the girls."

Eleanor gave him a sideways look. "All of them?"

"Yeah. Sixty-seven years old; now that's the way I'd like to go."

"Humm." Her lips pouted disapprovingly. "Which of the students had a motive?"

"Isabel Spalvas. She wasn't actually sleeping with Kitchener against her will, but it's bloody close. Nicholas Beswick. I feel kind of sorry for him. Nice kid, but a bit naïve, head-in-the-clouds type; you know, bright and stupid at the same time. He's head over heels in love with Isabel, although I doubt he's even kissed her yet; they're certainly not lovers. Finding her with Kitchener that night was a monumental shock, but he adored the old man too. Uri Pabari might have had a motive if he'd known Liz Foxton had slept with Kitchener."

"But he didn't know?"

"I didn't ask him; I'll have to check." Greg sagged mentally at the prospect. "And if he didn't know, he will after that kind of leading question. Bugger."

"I thought you said none of the students did it. What's the point of asking Uri about that?"

"Psi isn't an exact science. I can't get up in court and give absolutes, you know that, and I'm bloody sure the lawyers do. All I can ever say is that I haven't perceived them giving me false answers. But suppose somebody had an overwhelming motive to kill Kitchener; they might just be able to conceal their guilt from me, because they don't feel any. Certainly not if I ask them directly. So I creep up on the fact, by checking the peripheries. They can't lie about everything and get away with it, I'll catch them eventually."

"Okay, so are there any other students who have a plausible motive?"

He kept his eyes firmly on the road. "One. It's a possible money motive. That belongs to our Miss Rosette Harding-Clarke. Although if anyone at Launde Abbey was due to be murdered, I would have put money on it being her."

Eleanor perked up. "This sounds interesting, especially with the way you're trying to crush the steering wheel."

"Yeah, well, maybe I'm imagining it's her neck. Jesus, Eleanor, you've got to meet her to disbelieve her. Tell you, how she survived life this long with that attitude of hers is a bloody mystery to me. I felt like giving her a damn good smack, but she'd probably only enjoy it." He tried to halt that line of thought. No personal involvement: the first law. Although how anybody could view Rosette dispassionately was beyond him.

"But I thought Rosette Harding-Clarke was the rich one," Eleanor said.

"Yeah, so she claims. She is also the pregnant one."

"Pregnant?"

He smiled at the surprise in her voice. "That's right. And the kid is Kitchener's, or at least she claims it is. And she believes it too, which makes me inclined to believe her. So the first thing I want you to check out tomorrow morning is whether Rosette is really as rich as she says she is. A lot of these so-called aristocrats are worse off than people drawing the dole. And we'll need a legal opinion as well: will the kid stand to inherit anything even though it's not mentioned in the will? Rosette says she won't contest it, but I would have thought the executors have some sort of obligation to provide for the child."

"Right." Eleanor pulled her cybofax out and loaded the order into it.

*　*　*

After living in a two-room chalet for over a decade, the interior of the farmhouse always seemed vast. Furniture rattled around, nothing was ever conveniently near to hand.

The builders had renovated most of it before they moved in, fixing up the roof tiles, replacing the rotten floorboards, stripping out the damp plaster, installing new plumbing and air conditioning, rewiring. They were lucky to get the work done at all. England's industrial regeneration meant the building trade was in the middle of a boom; old factories were being restored, new ones constructed, housing estates were springing up across the country. There was very little spare capacity right now, certainly not for refurbishment jobs in out-of-the-way villages. But Julia's name ensured they were given top priority with the firm they hired, although even her clout didn't extend all the way down into the shady levels of subcontracting. There were still three rooms waiting to be plastered, and the conservatory was a stack of cut and primed wood sitting on the lawn, ready to be joined together.

Eleanor had already suggested that he could put it up. As if the groves didn't occupy all his time.

But the farmhouse had definitely acquired that indefinable sense of being home, the animal refuge against a howling world. Returning to it caused a tangible wash of relief. He had half expected some reporters to be standing at the entrance to the drive.

The interior had been decorated by a London firm, their designer working in tandem with Eleanor, to give an early twentieth-century theme: the country house of Victorian nobility. Everything was light and somehow rustic, curtains and carpets in pastel shades, the furniture in delicately stained pine. Neoteric domestic systems were all built in to reproduction units. The only modern setting was the gym, filled with black and silver chromed equipment.

When they arrived back from the police station, Greg slumped down on a settee in the lounge and pointed the remote at the long mock-painting of an eighteenth-century harvest scene that disguised the inert flatscreen. The picture shivered away into a game show where contestants were hanging upside down from the studio ceiling on long bungee cords; they were bouncing in and out of large barrels filled with water, trying to bob apples with their teeth.

He stared at it incredulously for a minute, then shook his head in weary dismay. Mr. Domesticity, back home after a hard day at the office, with the wife bustling around in the kitchen.

Except, as usual, his mind was full with little scraps of information from the case, all of them swirling around in a chaotic vortex, stirred by the witching fingers of inquisitiveness and intuition in the hope they would settle into some kind of recognizable pattern. His army mates had called him obsessive. Maybe it could be deemed a character flaw, but he could never let go of a problem. He had almost forgotten how involved he could become in a case. The worrying thing was, it felt good. On the chase again. That bastard who had chopped up Kitchener *needed* to be put away.

Eleanor came in with a couple of lagers in tall Scandinavian glasses. She took one look at the game show and switched the flatscreen off. Merry peasants and bales of hay snoozing under a sky of golden cloud reappeared.

"You weren't watching it," she said when he protested. "You were thinking about Kitchener."

He snagged one of the lagers. "Yeah."

"You said Rosette was a real bitch," Eleanor said as she sat down on the settee, wriggling her shoulders until she was nestled snugly against him. "Do you really think she would kill the father of her own baby just for money?"

"No. Now you put it like that, I don't. Tell you though, the one thing those students did have in common was the way they idolized Kitchener. That came through loud and clear; a couple of them actually called him a second father. Instinct says it isn't any of them. But . . . it's funny. There are a lot of things that don't add up, certainly not if it was a tekmerc snuff operation." He put his arm round her, enjoying the warm weight pressing into his side.

"The apron," she said. "Now that is really strange."

"That's right. Like you said, why bother with it at all? I can't believe our hypothetical tekmerc used it simply to incriminate the students. First off, we actually can't implicate one of them with it. If they were going to plant evidence, why not the knife, some bloodstains?"

"Too obvious."

"Maybe. But the apron isn't obvious enough. And why spend precious time starting a fire? I know covert penetration operations, Christ, I've been on enough in my time; the cardinal rule is to get *out* once you've finished, don't loiter."

"Whoever it was, they must have been there a while, though. First they had to wait until Kitchener was alone, then the Bendix was burned, as well as the neurohormone bioware. It all adds up to a lot of time spent in the Abbey."

"Which gives them an even stronger reason to leave straight after the murder," he countered. "Every extra minute in the Abbey is one more minute when they could be discovered. And why use syntho to kill the bioware in the first place?"

"Because it's there, saves carrying a poison in with them."

"Exactly, but how did they know that? It must have been someone totally familiar with the lab set-up, and even then they couldn't have known for sure that there was any syntho available that particular night. Suppose Kitchener and good old Rosette had been infusing heavily? A tekmerc would have brought a poison, or more likely used a maser. Whatever the method, it would never have been left to chance."

"There are all sorts of other chemicals in the lab, as well as the acids, and the heaters," she said. "There was bound to be something that could kill the bioware. Pure chance they used the syntho."

"Yeah. Could be." But the junked-up thought fragments refused to quiet down; he kept seeing flashes of Launde Park, the Abbey, those bloody lakes, Denzil's data-rich tour, the students' broken, shocked faces. None of them connected in any way.

He took a gulp of the lager; it was cold enough to numb the back of his throat. "But that still doesn't explain the time they were in the Abbey before the murder," he said.

Eleanor gave a tiny groan.

"Sorry," he said quickly. "We can drop it for the night."

"And put up with moody silences while you're thinking about it? No thanks. But next time, Julia can definitely go find someone else. This is Mandel Investigations' last case, Gregory."

He flashed her a smile, squeezing her tighter. "No messing."

"So what about the time?" She sipped at her own lager.

"Why wait until Rosette and Isabel left Kitchener? A tekmerc wouldn't care about snuffing them as well; in fact, it would even be beneficial from the mission's point of view. Two less people to spot him leaving, raise the alarm."

"But they were a complication, Greg. Killing three people in one room would be risky. Certainly one of them would manage to shout."

"Maybe. But it would mean he had to wait somewhere inside the Abbey for hours. No tekmerc would do that, the exposure risk is too great. And in any case, it implies he knew Rosette would leave Kitchener alone for a while."

"Everyone knew she was an insomniac."

"Her friends, yes. But how would anyone else know?"

"Good question." She leaned forward and rescued her cybofax from the coffee table. "There's a couple of other points. Amanda Paterson and I spent the afternoon chasing up English Telecom." She started reading the data on the cybofax screen. "The only datalinks from the Abbey on Thursday were the three we've accounted for: Nicholas and CNES, Rosette and Oxford University, and Kitchener himself; he was plugged into Caltech, over in America. On top of that, there were twenty-one phone calls made from cybofaxes; two of them were Mrs. Mayberry's, the housekeeper, one of her helpers made another, then Rosette made nine, Cecil made a couple, so did Liz; Nicholas and Isabel both made one each, the other three were all Kitchener's. Amanda and another detective are calling the numbers and confirming the calls were vocal. We thought someone could have plugged a cybofax into one of the Abbey's terminals, the bit rate would be substantially lower, but you could still use it to squirt a virus into the Bendix."

"Yeah, assuming it was done on Thursday. There's nothing to prevent you from loading the virus a month ago and putting it on a time-delay activation."

She gave him a disappointed look. "We had to start somewhere."

"Yeah, sure. Sorry. But nobody's going to remember a phone call from a month or half a year ago."

"I know, but what else can we do?"

"Nothing, it was only a very long shot, closing off options. I can't see anyone wanting to wipe the Bendix until after Kitchener was dead, not if the object was to destroy his work. To wipe it when he was alive would be counterproductive; he would be able to recreate his equations or whatever, and you'd alert him to the security problem. And if it was loaded a month ago, how did they know the timing, or when the students would stop accessing it? No, I'm sure it must have been done from within the Abbey after he was killed; that's the only scenario that makes sense."

"You're probably right. Anyway, while Amanda was running down the phone calls, I checked with RAF Cottesmore about the weather conditions on Thursday. There were winds up to a hundred kilometers an hour locally that night, some gusts reached a hundred and twenty. Here is their squirt."

"Bugger." He put down the lager and looked at the meteorological data that the cybofax was displaying. The purple and blue cloudforms of the weather radar image were superimposed over a map of Rutland; pressure and wind velocity/direction captions flashed across it.

"Can you fly a microlight in that?" Eleanor asked.

"Not a chance. Even high level would be risky; low level with the microbursts you'd get in the Chater valley, impossible."

She rubbed his arm. "Couldn't they just hike in and out?"

"It's four kilometers to Launde from the A47 by the straightest possible route, eight there and back. The trip there would be in the middle of a hurricane, with a diversion around Loddington to be sure they weren't sighted, and carrying enough gear to melt through the security system. You wouldn't catch me trying to do it."

"But it could be done?" she persisted.

"Theoretically, yeah, an inertial guido would place you within a couple of centimeters. But that terrain, well, you saw it."

"Yes." She gave him back the glass of lager and curled her legs up, resting her head on his shoulder.

He felt the kiss on the bottom of his jaw; then she was rubbing her cheek against his. Up and down, slowly. "You're all tensed up," she murmured in his ear. "You won't solve anything like that."

For a moment, he thought of pulling away. But only for a moment. Besides, she was right, he wouldn't settle it tonight.

*　*　*

The bedroom overlooked the reservoir's southern prong, a long, dark stretch of water with its wavelets and gently writhing curlicues of mist. Walls and furniture were silky white; vases, picture frames, curtains, sheets, and the bedposts were all colored in shades of blue; the oaken floorboards were smoothed down and waxed until they resembled a ballroom floor.

None of that really mattered, not the surroundings, just the bed, with Eleanor. Clad in black silk and lace, naked, provocative, sensual, demanding, submissive, thick red hair foaming down over her shoulders. She possessed a myriad sexual traits, combinations ever-changing, making each time different, unique.

The only light came from the bonfire on the opposite shore, a distant orange glimmer, barely enough to show him her outline. He undid the bows and buttons of her nightdress, licking at the flesh that was exposed, tasting the salt tang of damp skin, the heat of arousal.

Embraced by the warmth and folds of shadow, he had learned to cast off reticence, taking his lead from her. Eleanor didn't care, wasn't ashamed. Maybe rampancy was a gift of youth, or just part of her nature. So he was free to lose himself in the feast of sensuality, the feel of her body. Long, powerful legs wrapped round him, big breasts weighted down his hands. He sucked on an erect nipple, caressed her belly. A tiny neurohormone secretion showed him her body's reactions, which action brought the greatest rapture. The material world faded to dream silhouettes, revealing Eleanor's nerve strands alive with neon-blue light, her naked excitement. He slid inside her, a drawn-out penetration accompanied by her fervid groan, and joined her at the center of that blazing animal euphoria.

But afterward, intuition, or possibly plain confusion, played hell inside his skull and he couldn't let go of the case. He lay back on the crumpled sheeting, hands behind his head, staring up at the shivers of firelight on the ceiling. Snapshots of Launde, the students, Kitchener, police reports, they all chased across his consciousness in endless procession, sharp-edged and insistent.

"So much for my prowess," Eleanor grumbled softly.

"I thought you were asleep."

"No."

"Sorry."

"This really has you bothered, hasn't it?" She sounded more concerned than annoyed. "You were never so intense about a case before, at least not since I've known you."

He rolled on to his side, his face centimeters from hers. Warm breath gusted over his cheeks. "Tell you, what I don't understand, what's really got me beaten, is why bother?"

"What do you mean?"

"What is the point of murdering an old man in such a grotesque fashion? Even if one of the students had murdered Kitchener, it wouldn't be like that. You've read the statements, what happened when they found him. They were having fits. And I don't blame them, that hologram was bad enough. I'm bloody sure I couldn't do it, not like that. A maser beam through the brain, quick and clean, yes. But who could do that to someone else? Like Cecil Cameron said, it was one sick fucker."

"Sick enough for you to perceive with your espersense?"

"I would have thought so. That's one of the reasons I want to visit Liam Bursken tomorrow, so I know what mental characteristics to look out for."

"Ugh." She shivered slightly. "You're welcome to him. Even in the kibbutz we heard about him."

"Yeah, he was notorious enough. But he was mad. He didn't have a reason for killing. Somebody had a reason for killing Kitchener. And a lot of preparation went into it. But I just don't understand why the tekmerc used that method. It can't be an attempt to throw us off the scent, because even the police were convinced it wasn't one of the students. And that was before my interviews backed up their alibis. So why bother? Why not just send a sniper into Launde Park on a clear night? It doesn't make any sense!"

Her forefinger traced a line from the corner of his eye to his mouth. He sucked the tip gently.

"Like you said, this tekmerc is good," Eleanor said. "The snuff was done this way for a purpose. We don't have all the facts yet, that's why it seems so weird."

"Yeah. Paradox alley, and no messing." He frowned, trying to remember some scrap of conversation; word association was involved. "Hey, do you know what CTCs are?"

"Aren't they the things that helped to screw up the ozone?"

"I don't think that's what he meant."

Eleanor's finger had reached his chin, she tickled his stubble. "Who?"

"Nicholas Beswick."

"The wimpy one?"

"He's not wimpy, just very innocent. You'd probably like him. Trigger your maternal instinct."

She made a fist and rapped on his sternum. "Chauvinist!"

"Parental instinct, then. I went easy on him; anything else would have seemed like bullying. It was like coaxing answers out of a ten-year-old."

"But you were hard enough to be sure it wasn't him."

"Oh yeah, no room for ambiguity . . . except, the sensor data was questionable."

"In what way?"

"He said he had a shower about quarter past seven Thursday evening. And the police gave him a scan at nine o'clock the next morning. He was still quite clean. His body ought to have picked up more dirt than it did in that period."

"How reliable is that kind of scan?"

"It's not the scan, that's perfect; if the body has any contaminants, the sensor will detect them. Vernon told me afterward they could never take the dirt accumulation record into court, because no one could say how much dirt he would have picked up in that time, not with any degree of certainty. There are far too many variables: where he was, how active he was, how dirty his sheets are, even if his clothes picked up a static charge. They are all contributory factors. But as a general rule of thumb, it should have been more."

"Did he lie about the time of the shower?"

"No."

"So he didn't wash off the bloodstains?"

"No. Actually, he was one of the students who did touch Kitchener. But Cecil Cameron confirms that, it's in his statement. So that's not in question."

"Humm." She placed her hand palm-down on his chest and began to stroke him, moving in an expanding circle. "What does your intuition say?"

He leaned closer and kissed the end of her nose. "Nothing. Not a bloody thing. You were right. We need more information."

"In the morning."

He slipped his hands around her hips, squeezing the taut curve of her buttocks. "No messing."

THE NEXT MORNING BEGAN WITH a break in the rainclouds. Only a few immobile strips of cirrus were left crouched over the eastern horizon, fluoresced a pale saffron by the rising sun. According to the channel weathercasts, the next stormfront would arrive by teatime.

The A47 into Peterborough was even more snarled up than usual. Scooters were in the majority: the city's morning shifts on their way to work, riding up to four abreast in the spaces between juggernauts, vans, and company buses. They were used to the traffic, Eleanor wasn't. By the time she reached the section of road that ran alongside the Ferry Meadows estuary, she was shouting at the three riders keeping station two meters ahead of their bonnet. The glittery red-and-blue metallic helmets with their black visors remained unmoved by her diatribe, easily anticipating the surges of the methane-powered van in front of them, braking smoothly. In comparison, she seemed to be hopping forward like a kangaroo. A steady stream of cyclists zipped by on the inside. Infuriating.

Thirteen years ago, the raised land to the north of the estuary had been a mix of open countryside and pleasant woodland. Twelve years ago, it had been swamped by a slum zone of shanty housing the like of which Europeans had seen only in 'casts from the Third World. Now it was a solid cliff of whitewashed apartment blocks, long balconies dribbling fronds of colorful vegetation from clay pots, washing hanging on lines between support arches. Solar-cell roofs glinted brightly in the morning sun.

Below the concrete embankment, the tide was going out, leaving long stains of milk-chocolate mud visible above the sluggish water. A line of artificial stone islands was strung out across the two-kilometer width of the estuary, the eddy turbine barrage, creating vast, slow-moving whirlpools in each gap.

The first time she had ever come to Peterborough—the first time she had ever been to any city—she had accompanied Greg along the same route, visiting the same person. Even two years later, the difference was pronounced. More traffic, more people, more urgency, less tolerance. It was all due to Julia. Event Horizon's arrival had tweaked the city's dynamic economy into overdrive. After ten years of copious growth and financial exuberance, Peterborough still hadn't lost its Frontiersville verve. Everybody was on overtime, chasing impossible dreams. And they seemed to thrive on the compulsive *achiever* atmosphere.

My God, is this what regeneration is bringing us back to? Traffic jams and yuppies?

At least none of the vehicles was burning petrol. Not even Julia could take that short cut. Energy generation and supply was becoming a problem again, countrywide. Worldwide, from what the 'casts said. Solar cells simply couldn't meet industrial demands; coal was out of the question. Hydro dams were one possibility for England, given the increased rainfall, but the country's chronic land shortage all but ruled them out. Tidal barrages were a viable option, but they were big, their construction time could be anything up to a decade. England needed the electricity *now*. Peterborough had its eddy turbines in addition to its quota from the beleaguered National Commerce Grid, but even that fell well below the level demanded by Event Horizon, the kombinates, and the plethora of smaller light-engineering companies nesting in the suburbs.

Eleanor couldn't think how Julia intended to power the tower and cyber-precincts she was beginning out at Prior's Fen. It couldn't be fusion; the JET5 reactor at Cullham had passed the break-even point a year ago, but commercial applications were still seven or eight years away, and looked like being at least as expensive as fission. Perhaps Julia was planning to ship it in using old oil tankers converted to carry giga-conductor cells. They could be charged up in equatorial ports; the power would be there if she spread a few hundred square kilometers of solar cells over the new deserts in Africa and Asia. Her Prior's Fen project was certainly pitched at that sort of macro-scale.

The channel breakfast newscasts had devoted a lot of time to reports of Julia pouring the first footings of her new headquarters building. Eleanor and Greg had watched it from bed, eating toast and sipping tea, enjoying the quiet period of togetherness. Because she damn well knew it would be the only one they'd get today.

The traffic began to quicken, her three helmeted outriders opening some distance. She drove past the entrance to the Milton Park estate. Normally she used it as a short cut into Bretton, but at this time of day she would have to fight her way through the traffic in the Park Farm industrial precinct. Quicker to stick to the trunk road.

A comet's tail of red brake lights flared up ahead.

Bretton was a hive of construction activity. Neglected through the PSP decade as the vivacious new developments flourished in what had once been the green belt, it was now back in demand with property developers despite its strategically disadvantaged position, sitting between Mucklands Wood and Walton. Housing and industrial units tussled for space in old parklands, streets were parking yards for the lorries of various building contractors.

Eleanor parked behind a low-loader carrying a pair of factory-new dumper carts. The first thing she missed were the children. Bretton used to be swarming with them.

Rounded up and carted off to school, most likely. And a good thing, too. There was so much catching up to do. The one thing she always regretted was not having a formal education; all the kibbutz had given her were the basic reading, writing, arithmetic, and databasing lessons; then they put her straight into animal husbandry courses. She had enjoyed them at the time, because it meant that for three nights a week she went into Oakham to the sixth-form college. Two hours just sitting down and not having to work. Heaven.

The adult courses, or at least getting out of the kibbutz and seeing there were alternative ways to live, had planted the seeds of rebellion that ultimately resulted in meeting Greg that night two years ago. She knew all she needed to run the groves with Greg, although she still toyed with the idea of going back and picking up some more qualifications. One of those warm misty daydreams that helped life slip down a little easier, a *what if* that was slightly more than idle fantasy.

Now, of course, education for children was a New Conservative priority, and a real one, not just a manifesto declaration. One of the reasons for the current bout of inflation was the amount of money the Treasury had to print to pay for repairing schools and providing them with up-to-date equipment. So Julia always said. But then, it was Julia who was so insistent that total education be implemented as soon as possible.

Only because she needs computer literates to work in her cyber-factories. And what Julia wanted, Marchant granted, so went the op-position chant. *And why am I being so cynical this morning?*

"You were dead ten paces ago," a gravelly female voice said in her ear.

Eleanor turned. It was Suzi.

The Trinities girl only came up to the base of Eleanor's neck; she was slim to the point of androgyny, with spiked purple hair and a bony face. She wore a pair of tight black jeans and a brown singlet under a new leather biker jacket that had the Trinities symbol stamped on the right breast—a fist closed around a thorn cross, drops of blood falling. Her age was impossible to pin down, though Greg said she was in her mid-twenties. In a girlie summer frock, she could have passed for fifteen.

She was grinning up at Eleanor.

"I saw you skulking about as soon as I got out of the Ranger," Eleanor said, making it as condescending as possible. "I just didn't want to hurt your ego, that's all."

"Bollocks!"

Eleanor laughed and scrupulously refrained from ruffling Suzi's hair. For all her butch swagger, Suzi could get very touchy about her lack of centimeters.

She had met the Trinities girl back when Greg took his first Event Horizon case. It was her first, and please God, last experience of hardlining. Both of them had been hurt during the mission, although Suzi had suffered by far the worst injuries.

Eleanor still wasn't quite sure if they were friends; Suzi had a very frugal social behavior pattern. *Relationship* wasn't a word or concept that featured heavily in an urban predator's mental lexicon. But there was certainly a degree of respect, which was a big step; non-urban predators were universally regarded with complete contempt.

"What have you come for?" Suzi asked as they walked up the slope toward the Mucklands Wood estate.

"I need to have a rap with Royan."

"Yeah?"

Eleanor grinned at the blatant curiosity. "Greg's working on a case again."

"No shit. I thought you weren't going to let him do that anymore."

"I wasn't. But Julia asked him to."

Suzi chuckled delightedly. "Christ, that girl bypasses their brains and plugs directly into their balls. What's she got that I haven't?"

"Ten trillion pounds and a medieval virgin-princess's hairstyle."

They laughed together.

As they approached the housing estate, Suzi drew a large Luger maser pistol from a shoulder holster, carrying it quite openly.

Mucklands Wood always reminded Eleanor of old Soviet-style cities in the last century. It was a cultural and architectural throwback to prudent realism: low-cost council housing, the PSP's contribution to the refugee crisis, a magnet for the underclass who couldn't hope to get into one of the overseas-funded projects. Rich with the nutrients that bred resentment, the starkness and dejection of lives condemned to the dole.

Fifteen identical tower-blocks, twenty stories high, sheer concrete walls hidden beneath a scale of cheap, low-efficiency solar panels. Crushed limestone covered the ground around them, sticky with a tar of mud; weeds and needles grew in defiant clumps, the only vegetation. A few small, single-story workshops had been built by the council, earmarked for PSP skill-training projects. But they were all empty shells, burned out, breeze-block walls already alarmingly concave; another couple of years would see entropy and vandalism reduce them to rubble.

Eleanor always hated coming to Mucklands. It infected aspirations and dignity like a cancer. You could never rise out of Mucklands, you could only fight. The Trinities exploited that ruthlessly.

She caught glimpses of people lurking among the workshops, walking between the towers. All urban predator types: leather jeans, camouflage jackets, and AK carbines. Even though she had a Trinities card, she always called in advance, waited until there was someone to escort her in.

"Do the kids here go to school?" she asked Suzi.

"Yeah. Father makes sure they do. It's a pain, some of 'em make good scouts. Who's gonna suspect a nine-year-old?"

"You'll cope."

Suzi gave her a glum look. "I know what you're thinking. Get 'em out, fill 'em with smarts, break the poverty cycle."

"That's right."

"Brilliant. Then who's going to carry on the fight?"

The fight against their nemesis the Blackshirts was everything for the Trinities, the reason for their existence. Blackshirts were the remnants of the People's Constables, with whom they had fought a running war for nearly a decade along Peterborough's cluttered, frantic streets. And the two were still fighting as if nothing had changed, as if the PSP was still in power. There were too many dead, too many old scores to settle.

"You can't fight forever," Eleanor said, knowing it was a waste of time. Trinities lived for combat, lived for death. It was sequenced into their genes now, unbreakable.

"Try me," Suzi growled dangerously.

Two guards stood outside the tower's door, saluting sharply as Suzi walked through. Eleanor didn't even feel a reflex laugh coming on, it was too sad. The inside of the tower was kept meticulously clean, a sharp contrast to the external atrophy.

Suzi knocked once on the door of the old warden's flat and went straight in. The far end of the room was lined with dilapidated metal desks supporting a range of communication gear; six Trinities, all girls, were operating the systems. Seven flatscreens were fixed to the wall above them, showing images fed from cameras that had to be perched on the top of the towers. Five of them displayed a panoramic view of Mucklands Wood, scanning slowly; while the remaining two were zoomed in on Walton, two kilometers away on the other side of the A15, a dense conurbation of rooftops and chimneys, interspaced with the tapering tops of evergreen pines. The quagmire of the Fens basin was just visible in the background, a grubby brown plain vanishing into the distorted haze line that occluded the horizon.

Walton was to the Blackshirts what Mucklands was to the Trinities: headquarters, barracks, recruiting ground, armory, police and public no-go zone. Both areas were resented by the rest of the city. Even the reserve of gratitude people felt for the Trinities, in their role as focal point for local opposition to the PSP, had withered to nothing over the last four years. Peterborough's residents wanted the guerrilla war stopped, wanted to be rid of the urban predators, wanted to get on with their lives without the constant threat of violence and anarchy hovering in the background. The city council was already talking of implementing a clampdown, maybe even sending in the army to flush Mucklands and Walton clean of undesirables.

Eleanor knew it would never end that way. You couldn't drive the Trinities and Blackshirts any farther underground. Long before any clean-out operation finished the bureaucracy-stultified preparation phase, the two of them would have it out, head to head, straight on, putting everything they'd got into one final hardline strike.

The communication-gear operatives were emitting a constant murmur as they talked into their throat mikes, occasionally switching the flatscreens to different cameras. It looked like a very professional operation.

The instigator of it all sat at a desk behind the operators, command position. Teddy La Croix, an ex-English army sergeant whom the Trinities had named Father, swiveled around in his chair and grinned broadly. He seemed to get bigger each time she met him, easily two meters tall, with at least two-thirds of his bodyweight made up from muscle, probably more; she couldn't imagine anything as soft and vulnerable as human organs being a part of Teddy's makeup. Biolum light glinted dully on the dark ebony skin of his bald scalp. He was dressed in his usual combat fatigues, cleaned and ironed as though they had been out of the laundry for only an hour.

Boa-constrictor arms circled around her and he gave her a hug, kissing her cheek. "Goddamn, gal, you finally did it, you left him and ran away to me."

"Stop it," she giggled and slapped at his shoulder. "I'm legally hitched to him till death do us part, you were at the wedding. So behave yourself."

He gave a theatrical sigh and put her down. "You're looking good, Eleanor."

"Thanks."

They stood and looked at each other for a long moment. Teddy was one of Greg's oldest friends; they had served together back in Turkey. She had been secretly thrilled at gaining Teddy's trust; approval like that came hard, but it brought her orbit just that fraction closer to Greg's.

"What's that?" She pointed to his left hand. It was covered in a thin, flexible foam of blue dermal seal.

"Bit of extra-parliamentary action couple o' days back. Nothing bad."

Eleanor heard Suzi's soft snort. She could guess just how fierce it had been.

"Oh, Teddy."

He rolled his eyes. "Yeah, yeah, I know. I'll be careful."

"That'll be the day."

He put his arm around her shoulder and walked to the back of the room, away from the communications operators. "Tell me something. You're here to see Royan, right?"

"Yes."

"Special visit, coming by yourself. This some sort o' deal Greg's working on?" He sat on the edge of a wooden table covered in maps and thick folders, resting his buttocks on the edge. The table legs let out little creaks of stress.

"Yes."

Teddy's expression turned serious, forbidding. "He's outta that, gal. He's got the farm, he's got you. You got a job now, you gotta keep him out. He's made it, clean free. Outta all this shit."

She put a hand on his forearm. "No hardlining, Teddy. I wouldn't let him do that again, you know I wouldn't. This is just a case for Julia. It's puzzling, and it's ever so slightly bloody weird, but it's nothing physical. Okay?"

Teddy worried at his front teeth with a fingernail. "Julia?" The tone was indecisive.

"Yes. She needs his espersense."

"There's other psychics. This themed shit they's shoveling out these days."

"Name one as good as Greg."

"Yeah," he growled. "Well, you tell that rich bitch from me, it's her ass if anything happens to Greg." His eyebrows lifted in emphasis. "Or you."

She stood on tiptoes and planted a kiss on his forehead. "You're gorgeous."

"Jesus, shit."

Was he actually blushing?

"What is this fucking case, anyway? Gotta be heavy-duty shit for her to ask in the first place. Last time we rapped, she's as hot as me for Greg to quit."

"Edward Kitchener. She needs to know who killed him."

"The physics guy? Why?"

"He was working on something for her." She put her hands up in surrender. "Don't ask me what. I don't understand a word of it."

"Yeah, well, I can see why you need to rap with Son. Crap like that, right up his alley. Now don't you go tie up all his capacity, we need him too, more'n ever right now."

Her lips turned down. "Teddy . . ."

"No choice, gal." He waved at the two screens covering Walton. "Fucking Party's crawling like ants down there. Someone gotta stomp on 'em. Don't see no police doing it. Or this new fucking wonder government we got lumbered with. You ask Julia, you don't believe me. Three o' her factories hit by thermal bombs this month, not five klicks from here."

She nodded weakly. Trinities and Blackshirts; it was all a far more deadly version of the *apparatchiks* and Inquisitors game, a game with no rules, nor time limit, nor physical boundary. She knew from bitter experience that it wasn't something that could be solved by police, the due process of law; Greg's last Event Horizon case had shown her that. In that respect, the world terrified her, there was too much subterranean activity, too much hidden from public view. Dark circuitry wiring subliminal power shifts. Ignorance could be a blissful thing, almost enviable.

He patted her gently. "Don't you fret so, gal. You ain't got the face for it. Now then, been too long, you gotta stop by more often."

"You know where the farm is, Teddy. I'd like you to come see it sometime. Stay over for a few nights. You know how much Greg would love that."

"Turtle out of its shell, gal." He glanced about the room, taking his time, as if he hadn't seen it for a while, checking to see that everything was in its proper place. " 'Sides, won't be here much longer." His voice dropped to a doleful whisper. "Not long now. I can feel it coming, gal, like summer heat. Ain't nobody got no respect for the Trinities no more. Time was, you could walk down any street in this town and you'd get treated like a superhero. Well, that time's over now. But we know what we gotta do 'fore we go. Bibles in hand, AKs primed, yessir. We ain't gonna turn tail now. Gonna *finish* what we started. Gonna finish those card-carrying sons of bitches, gonna finish them but good."

"I'll give this a miss," Suzi said when the lift opened on the tower's top floor.

"There's nothing that ultra-hush about it," Eleanor protested.

"Nah, 'sall right. I'll be downstairs when you want out." She pressed the button for the ground floor, forcing Eleanor to hop out. The lift doors slid shut, cutting off Suzi's wave and wolfish grin, and any chance to argue.

Eleanor thought she knew the real reason. Julia's Austrian clinic had been good, repairing all the physical damage both of them had suffered. But the memories of its infliction were hard to suppress. Royan could act as an all-too-potent reminder.

The corridor was narrow, windowless. A long ceiling-mounted biolum strip, with an emission decaying into the green edge of the spectrum, lit her way. She stopped outside 206 and knocked.

Qoi opened the door, a fifteen-year-old Oriental girl in a blue-silk robe. She bowed deeply. "Pleasure to see you again, Miss Eleanor." Her voice was high-pitched and scratchy.

Eleanor followed her into the tiny hall, as always slightly uncomfortable at Royan's combination nurse and guardian angel. The door to the lounge slid open and Qoi ushered her through, doll-like face smiling politely.

The air was hot, saturated with a smell of vegetation that was almost fungal, a dozen braids of flower perfume clotted together. Long plant troughs were laid out on the floor, hosting a fabulous collection of flowers, vivid primary colors shining under the glare of the ceiling's Solaris spots. Little wheeled robots roamed among them; they looked as if they had been cobbled together out of a dozen different cybertoy kits by someone working from a very distant memory of a cartoon-channel mechanoid. Forks, copper watering roses, and secateurs protruded with no sense of rationale.

One wall was completely obscured by the glass bricks of ancient television screens, removed from their cases and bolted into a grid of metal struts. They were all switched on, showing a multitude of channel 'casts and datasheets. A broad workbench was piled high with gear modules, parts of gear modules, individual components, circuit boards, pieces of mechanical junk; two big waldo arms stood silent sentry duty at each end.

A camera on an aluminum tripod followed her cautious steps around the troughs. It acted as Royan's eyes, fiber-optic cable plugged into the black modem balls in his eye sockets. He was sitting on a metallic-green nineteen-fifties dentist's chair in the center of the room. Sitting wasn't quite the right word: propped up, wedged in by cushions. Royan had no legs or arms; plastic cups covered the end of each stump, axon splices, trailing more fiber-optic cables to banks of 'ware cabinets next to the bench. His torso was covered by a white T-shirt spotted with food stains down the front.

Greg had told her Royan was a victim of the People's Constables, a street riot years ago. He'd been there the night it happened, although he never went into details. Despite his youth and agility, Royan just hadn't been fast enough to escape the bullwhips of the Constables as they charged the protesters. He had been badly burned, too, in the cascade of Molotovs that followed.

Every time she came, she thought she'd be immune to the sight of him, exposure building up a protective crust around her emotions. Every time, he affected her just as badly as the first. Coldness flickered through her, dendritic frost fingers twisting up her stomach.

The images and datasheets on the old television tubes vanished, replaced by meter-high green letters that moved right to left across the wall, delineation frequently interrupted by the individual screen rims.

HI, ELEANOR, YOU LOOK LOVELY LOVELY LOVELY TODAY.

"Hello, flatterer. What have you been up to?" She spoke fairly loud, trying not to make it obvious; slow, clear words always made her think of the way people addressed the retarded. Royan was anything but. His audio nerves were about the only genuine sensory input he retained; everything else was electronic, enhanced by the modules he had gradually cocooned himself in. Gear had become his interest, his obsession, his speciality. His comprehension of 'ware systems was probably equivalent to a degree, Greg reckoned, maybe even better. His hands-on experience was total; he had to learn simply to survive, and he had nothing else to do but learn, sit passively and absorb the bytes flowing through the country's datanets, day after day after day. And once he had mastered his art, he returned to the fray with a vengeance, fueled by a cold, malevolent hatred whose compulsive power only Greg could fully perceive. He became Son to the other Trinities, their digital oracle, a passive presence backing up each campaign with the smartest intelligence data, tracing Blackshirt positions and strength through every memory core in the city and beyond, exposing them wherever they were hiding.

BEEN OUT DANCING, SURFBOARDING, CYCLING. THE USUAL.

"I brought you these," she said and pulled the envelope of seeds out of her jeans pocket. "They're orchids, *Ludisia discolor*; they've got red leaves and a white flower. I think you'll like them."

His lips parted to reveal a few bucked yellow teeth. *THANKS THANKS THANKS.*

Qoi stepped forward and took the envelope, bowing slightly.

Greg always brought bits and pieces of gear for him, but she preferred cuttings or seeds. He went to a lot of trouble nurturing his little garden, there wasn't an unhealthy plant anywhere.

After Qoi disappeared into the kitchen, Eleanor ducked 'round a hanging basket of pink begonias and sat herself in a plain oak admiral's chair.

COFFEE?

"Please." It was part of the visit's ritual.

One of the robots trundled over, a pot of coffee resting on its flat top. She poured herself a cup. It tasted perfect.

YOU LOOK TIRED.

"I've been working." More disapproval slipped into her tone than she intended.

ON THE FARM?

"No. Mandel Investigations got hauled out on a case."

JULIA JULIA JULIA. HAS TO BE. GREG WOULDN'T DO IT FOR ANYONE ELSE.

"You've been peeping."

NO. I KNOW YOU ALL TOO WELL, MY FRIENDS. I WATCHED JULIA ON THE CHANNELS THIS MORNING. A BILLIONAIRESS POURING CONCRETE, FUNNY FUNNY FUNNY. I WATCH HER EVERY DAY, YOU KNOW. SHE'S NEVER OFF.

"I know. She could make another fortune if she charged the news-cast program an appearance fee."

SHE'S PRETTY PRETTY PRETTY. JUST LIKE YOU. LUCKY LUCKY LUCKY ME. TWO PRETTIEST GIRLS IN THE COUNTRY ARE MY FRIENDS.

She took another sip, surprised to find herself relaxing. "Aren't you going to ask me why I'm here?" she asked slyly.

I KNOW WHY. HE WANTS SOMETHING, SO HE SENT YOU. HE KNOWS I'M A SUCKER SUCKER SUCKER FOR A BEAUTIFUL GIRL. I AM, TOO.

"We had to split up, actually. There's a lot of ground to cover today."

WHAT'S THE CASE?

"The Kitchener murder." She started giving him a review of the data they'd amassed. As far as she could tell, he was listening atten-tively; the vaguely eerie lettering faded from the screens, a sure sign of contemplation. The session wasn't turning out as emotionally ar-duous as she had been expecting. The trick was to block out the rest of his life, the daily horror of eating, crapping, peeing, the pain spasms that convulsed him every few hours. Pretend everything stopped when she wasn't there, that all he did was meet visitors who brought him gossip, and problems he could gain a measure of satis-faction from solving. It was weak of her to think like that, craven, but it was the only way she could cope. The suffering he went through was a tragedy on an epic scale.

IF IT WASN'T THE STUDENTS, AND IT WASN'T A TEKMERC SNUFF DEAL, THEN WHO WHO WHO DUNNNNNIT?

"Good question. I didn't say a tekmerc definitely wasn't involved; but they certainly didn't drive in, and they didn't fly in either. Of course we're not ruling out the possibility that someone yomped in, but Greg says he doesn't think it's likely."

IF HE SAYS IT DIDN'T HAPPEN, IT DIDN'T DIDN'T DIDN'T.

"He says he's not sure."

Royan's rucked smile appeared again. *WHAT DO YOU THINK?*

"I think it would have been absolutely impossible for anyone to walk in and out of the Chater valley that evening. It was bad enough driving our EMC Ranger in yesterday. Launde Abbey is very iso-lated."

I BELIEVE YOU. WHAT DO YOU WANT ME TO DO?

She put down the empty coffee cup and held up her cybofax. "I've brought the schematics for the Abbey's security system. I need to know if it is possible for someone to burn through, enter the Abbey and then get out again afterward without raising the alarm. The police forensic team says it was completely undisturbed."

One of the 'ware modules on the top of the bench let out a small bleep. When she turned, blue-and-green LEDs were winking on the front of the scuffed gray-plastic casing.

SQUIRT THE BYTES OVER. NO NO NO PROBLEM FOR ME.

She pointed the cybofax at the module and keyed a squirt.

GOT IT. I'LL START LOOKING FOR A WAY THROUGH. SHOULD HAVE AN ANSWER BY THIS AFTERNOON.

"Fine." Eleanor slipped the cybofax into her back pocket. "Can you also find out if any hotrod was contracted to supply this hypothetical burn virus?"

I'LL ASK. MIGHT NOT GET A HUNDRED %%%%% ACCURATE ANSWER. IF IT WAS DONE, THE WRITER WON'T BE ADVERTISING.

"Have you heard of anyone asking for a virus like this?"

NO NO NO. CROSS HEART.

"Okay, final point; Greg thinks it would be useful to know what sort of rumors are floating about. Ask around the circuit, find out what people think Kitchener was working on for Julia, whether they even knew he was working for Julia; and also, did Kitchener owe money to anyone?"

HE WAS A MILLIONAIRE. MULTI MULTI MULTI.

"He was a regular syntho user, and so were some of the students. He had his own vat at Launde, but the basic compounds still cost money. So it probably wouldn't be banks we're talking about."

GOTCHA. KITCHENER USED SYNTHO?

"Yes."

MAN LIKE THAT. WOW WOW WOW.

She gave him a sad smile. "Yes, a man like that. Funny old world, isn't it? You wouldn't think he'd need it, a brain like his."

MAYBE BECAUSE HE HAD A BRAIN LIKE THAT. NOBODY ON THIS PLANET WAS HIS EQUAL. MAYBE HE WAS LONELY LONELY LONELY.

"Oh, no, not Kitchener, not lonely. One of the girl students is having his child."

There was no answer for a moment; the last *LONELY* remained splashed across the three right-hand screens. Then the word evaporated like morning dew. She heard the lens on the camera whirring softly, zooming in on her face.

HE WAS OLD.

"Sixty-seven, I think."

ALL THAT TIME. SO MANY YEARS.

"He accomplished an awful lot," she said, uncertain where Royan was leading. Not true; at the back of her mind, she knew exactly. She just didn't want to acknowledge it.

DO YOU LIKE ME, ELEANOR?

That grin didn't have to be forced. "I keep coming back, don't I?"

YES YES YES. THANK YOU.

She stood up, straightening the creases out of her sweatshirt. "Now don't spend all your time working on the Abbey's security system. Teddy says he needs you for Trinities work."

BUGGER HIM . . . PARDON MY FRENCH. I DECIDE MY OWN PRIORITIES. ME ME ME.

"You'll get me into trouble."

NEVER. SAY HI TO GREG. TELL HIM HE HAD BETTER SHOW UP HIMSELF NEXT TIME.

"I will."

AND YOU. COME BACK. SEE ME.

"Yes." She gave him a last glance, shamed by the fact that she could never in a million years show so much bravery. There was no point in even asking him to come out to the farm. It could be done physically, with stretchers and vans and plenty of advance planning. But his inheritance tied him to Mucklands far tighter than the web of fiber-optic cables ever did. He and Teddy, neither of them would leave; there was no point, they were Mucklands, it went with them wherever they were.

Qoi popped up out of the kitchen without being summoned and showed her to the door.

12

"AS ALWAYS, THE SYLPHLIKE JULIA Evans remains resolutely wedded to her fallal dress sense," Jakki Coleman said. She was at her Mediterranean villa, lounging on a sunbed at the side of a kidney-shaped pool. On the far side was a white stone balustrade, guarding the steep drop down to a muzzy blue sea. Tall palm trees were growing out of stone barrels, fronds stirring in a gentle breeze.

"Considering the perennial obsession that the Gothic cult has for the afterworld, this particular selection of garments worn for the Prior's Fen footings ceremony is highly appropriate. Because, let's face it, our poor dear Julia looks as if she's been exhumed after a few weeks residing in a grave."

"BITCH!" Julia shrieked.

Her teacup hit the flatscreen in the center, smashing into crescent fragments; it was the first object her searching hand could find, a big yellow-and-blue breakfast cup from the bedside tray. Sugary dregs began to trickle down the flatscreen, smearing the dark-haired young man who climbed out of the pool and began toweling himself off.

Patrick raised his head from the mounds of pillows that had accumulated on his side of the bed, blinking sleep from his eyes. "What?" he grunted blearily.

"Oh, go back to sleep." Julia fired the remote at the flatscreen, imagining it was a laser pistol, beam scorching a hole through Jakki Coleman's head, her *middle-aged* head, and the shiny blue swimsuit showed her thighs were getting flabby too. She folded her arms below her breasts and glared at the blank rectangle.

Her bedroom was decorated in a soothing montage of pink-and-white tones, extremely feminine, with exquisite lacy frills on all the furniture, subdued lighting, a huge four-poster bed with a Romany canopy, ankle-deep pile carpet. It was the third redesign in four years; each time she edged closer to her ideal, the romantic French-château image she secretly treasured.

And what would Jakki Coleman have to say about it? Bitch!

"You're upset about something," Patrick said.

"Oh, ten out of ten, give it a banana."

"Was it me?"

"No," she said tightly.

"Ah, right." He subsided back into the pillows.

Well, that ruined the morning mood, Julia thought; there would be no sex now.

She pointed the remote at the windows. The thick imperial-purple velour curtains swept aside to show her the balcony. Wistaria vines, gene-tailored against the heat of the new seasons, were wrapped round the wrought-iron railings, producing a solid wall of delicate mauve flower clusters. Wilholm's rear lawns formed a splendid backdrop with their English country-house formality; she could just see the long trout lake at the bottom, its fairytale waterfall tinged brown from the silt washed down the stream by the heavy rains.

Not even the garden's naturalistic perfection could break her ire. Bugger Jakki Coleman anyway. Who cared what she said?

Although that wasn't the half of it. She still felt guilty about asking Greg to look into the Kitchener murder. And the murder itself was a complication she could do without. Right now Morgan's security division was stretched pretty thinly defending the company from conventional threats—industrial sabotage, industiral espionage, crooked accountants, hotrod hackers infiltrating the datanet. Why would anybody feel strongly about something as weirdly abstract as superphysics wormholes? Surely it couldn't be an anti-Evans gesture? Not slaughtering a defenseless old man? She couldn't believe anyone was that sick and warped; besides, there had been no announcement. If any operational PSP remnants had killed Kitchener, they would have been crowing about it all across the media by now.

At least there hadn't been much mention of Greg on the newscasts she had caught before flicking over to the Coleman trollop. Some jerky pictures taken from a shoulder-mounted camera, the operator running after the EMC Ranger as it drove out of the police station, Eleanor's tight-lipped anger, Greg impassive as always.

Patrick touched her shoulder. "You're very tense." His fingers slid down her arm to the elbow, then stroked her breast, circling the nipple.

She tilted her head back and sighed through clenched teeth. "No, Patrick."

His tongue nuzzled her ear, stubble scratching her collarbone. "I can massage all that tension away. You know I can."

It was very, very tempting. There wasn't a chime in her head Patrick couldn't ring whenever he chose. But for all that ecstasy, he was a mechanical lover. She had begun to suspect a great deal of his excitement came from the way he controlled her body, almost a voyeur of his own performance.

"No," she said abruptly, and shoved her feet out of the bed. "Sorry, I've got a busy morning." She picked up her negligé from the floor where he'd thrown it last night and went into the bathroom.

She sat on the side of the circular marble bath and dropped her head in her hands, staring glumly at the swan mosaic on the wall opposite. There were just so many issues clamoring insistently for her attention right now: the petty, the important, and the personal.

She made an effort to blank them out, as if her whole mind was one giant processor node she could shut down when she wanted. It didn't work; Patrick was easy to ignore, a feat that raised its own slightly disquieting question, but she found herself returning to yesterday's strange conversation with Karl Hildebrandt. Greg was always telling her to trust her native instinct; it's a variant on precognition, he explained, not quite rational, but ninety percent reliable. And right now her instincts said that conversation was desperately wrong.

The bad PR she had been picking up from leftish organizations and pressure groups had been more or less constant for two years, ever since the giga-conductor was announced to the public. In that context, Greg and the Kitchener case was just one more incident. Nothing special. The way she was siting factories in marginal constituencies was far more blatant, provocative.

The PR angle was a blind, then; it had to be. Karl had wanted Greg off the case, plain and simple. From what she had heard about the strange circumstances out at the Abbey, Oakham's CID would be very unlikely to find the murderer without Greg and Event Horizon's resources behind them. How would Karl benefit from that?

Wrong tack, she realized; Karl was the bank's mouthpiece, the perfect corporate cyborg. How would Diessenburg Mercantile benefit from allowing Kitchener's murderer to go free?

Open Channel to NN Core.

Morning, Juliet.

A wan smile crept onto her face. Good old Grandpa, he was so indefatigable.

Morning, Grandpa. Anything important happen last night?

Someone tried to break into our Leicester music deck factory warehouse; it was a local gang, they'd even brought a lorry with them to cart away their loot. Security suspects someone on the inside was feeding them information on the shipments. There was an attempt to snatch data out of the genetics research-division memory core; we think they were after the land-coral splices. The guardian programs prevented any data loss, and security is working with English Telecom to see if they can backtrack the hackers. Hopeless, of course. The pound closed three cents up on the dollar, and the FTcast index was up eight points. Market confidence is high after the spaceplane roll out. There was a lot of data traffic between our backing consortium partners right into the wee small hours. Got 'em on the run, we have, Juliet.

Did you break any of their squirts?

No, they're using a high-order encryption code. It could be done, but it would tie up a lot of processing capacity. Not cost-effective. They'll agree to Prior's Fen.

Hope so.

Everything all right, Juliet?

Yes. No.

Executive material if ever I saw it. So bloody decisive you are, my girl.

What do you think of Patrick, Grandpa?

Handsome, rich, cultured, quite clever, well-mannered. Picked yourself a good one again, Juliet.

There was a shade too much emphasis on *again* for her mind. She glanced up at the mirror above the basin. And boy-oh-boy, did she look melancholy. Her hair was a complete mess as well. Patrick did so enjoy seeing it tossed about. His husky voice in the dark, encouraging her, whispering how wild she was. It never seemed to matter in bed, excitement overriding everything.

Yah, she replied. *So how come they never last?*

I said good, I never said flawless.

Do you think he's going to start asking me for shipping contracts?

No. Even if his family shipping line needed 'em, he wouldn't ask. And they don't need 'em, I've had our commercial-intelligence division keeping an eye open.

My very own guardian angel. You're wonderful, Grandpa.

You'll find him one day, Juliet. I'll be a great-grandfather yet.

Don't hold your breath, not the way I'm going.

I watched that Coleman woman this morning.

I don't want to talk about it! She reached for a comb and began to pull it through the knots. The face in the mirror was scowling petulantly.

I don't like you being ridiculed like that, Juliet. Let me tell you, my girl, it would never have happened in my day. People should have more bloody respect. You ought to blacklist that channel, no adverts, and pass the word around to everyone Event Horizon does business with. That frigid Coleman cow would soon get the message.

It was the second time temptation had been put in front of her that morning. She considered it, something like envy coloring every thought. *No, Grandpa. If I started using my power like that, where would it end?*

Use it or lose it, girl. I've told you before.

That is misuse, as you well know. I get into enough trouble using it where it's beneficial.

Ah, Juliet, a little bit of self-indulgence occasionally never hurt.

Don't you worry about me, Grandpa. I'll get that Jakki Coleman, you'll see.

My girl.

She put the comb down, the worst of the knots out. It would be safe to ask her maid Adelia to wash and set it now. Adelia always got mighty prickly if she was faced with a big untangling job every morning.

I've been thinking about Karl Hildebrandt, she said.

Oh, yeah? I don't think he'd be a suitable replacement for Patrick.

Behave! I meant his wanting me to take Greg off the Kitchener case. There's something very funny about that.

Well . . . it was a very high-profile appointment, Juliet. Bloody mar-

velous it is, girl, the first time in four years the company hasn't had an ulterior motive in twisting Marchant's arm and everyone starts banging on about undue influence. We just can't win.

Karl is a front for Diessenburg Mercantile, Grandpa, first, last, and always, even in these circumstances. He was too quick off the mark, and too insistent asking to see me just to be offering sociable advice. He was ordered to do it.

Conceded, it is a bit odd. Do you think it's important?

Yes. Why would Diessenburg Mercantile have any interest in a ghoulish murder in the middle of the English countryside?

Beats me, girl.

Well, find out.

Oh, yes, bloody abracadabra. Here you are.

Don't get stroppy, Grandpa. It's simple. Run down a list of Diessenburg Mercantile's other investments for me and see if any of them come into conflict with the work Kitchener was doing.

What, a stardrive?

She went to the basin and ran the cold tap, splashing some of the water on her face. It did sound pretty unlikely now she had spelled it out. *Yes, I know it sounds totally wonky, Grandpa. But there has to be a reason.*

I suppose so, girl. You've got to remember all this nonsense about actually building flying saucers sounds pretty bloody impossible to a relic like me. Listen, when I was a lad, the Daleks were the wildest piece of imagination ever to hit England. I was terrified of them. One time when the Doctor was caught in some caves by—

Yah. If you could get that data correlated in time for the conference this afternoon, I'd be grateful.

Bloody hell, Juliet, you've got a heart of ice. Black ice.

I wonder who I inherited that from?

All right, I'll get on to it.

Thanks, Grandpa. I really am super busy this morning. I've got a video-bite opportunity with the national swimming squad; then there's the Nottingham councillors' delegation, and the meeting for the Home Counties region managerial report.

You should complain to the union steward, they're working you too hard.

If I ever get the chance, I'll tell him.

Cancel Channel To NN Core.

She called Adelia on the housephone and asked her to be ready in half an hour. There was just time for a quick bath, wash off last night's tussle.

Hot water gushed out of the wide tap nozzle, kicking up clouds of steam. She stood in the middle of the bath as it twisted around her, reviewing what clothes to wear for meeting the swimming team. Event Horizon sponsored the England squad, so it was mainly a PR event, but she took a genuine interest in the team's performance. Swimming had been her sport at school.

She sat down when the water reached her knees and switched on the spa. Water jets and bubbles pummeled her skin, easing the tension out of her muscles.

It was no good, she couldn't think what to wear.

Access Dictionary File. Define: Fallal.

Fallal, the memory node reported. *Gaudy or vulgar, in reference to jewelery, or clothing, or ornament, etc.*

Bitch!

13

THE ORIGINAL BUILDINGS OF HMP Stocken Hall were still virtually intact, a regimented complex of stolid cell blocks squatting behind the five-meter perimeter fence topped with razor wire. Solar panels had been added to the south-facing walls, although they came up only to the bottom of the second-story windows, leaving a band of ginger brickwork free. The tall, concrete-segment chimney of the old utility building was swathed in dark ivy, abandoned now, the machinery it served rusted beyond repair. Solar water heaters had been set up on the flat roofs, like giant silver flowers with long tubular midnight-black stamens.

Greg could see work parties tending the vegetable plots inside the fence, men in gray one-piece uniforms lethargically scratching at the waterlogged soil with rakes and holes. Prisons were officially responsible for producing fifty percent of their own foodstuff, though the actual figure was often much higher. Grow it, or go hungry. A concept that the PSP had introduced and the New Conservatives saw no need to alter. Dismay at the idea of prisoners sitting unproductively in their cells for twenty-two hours a day was something both sides of the political divide shared, especially when Treasury funds were scarce.

He drove past the first set of large gates in the fence. The land around was rumpled with low, rolling hillocks and gentle dells, meadows, and beanfields cluttered with the spindly gray sentries of dead trees that marked the line of old hedgerows. A couple of largish woods to the north had that verdant shine that betrayed the new vine species establishing themselves on the bones of the past.

Stocken Hall itself straddled a rise east of the A1 just north of Stretton village, a fifteen-minute drive from Hambleton. He had taken the Jaguar; the car had been a present from Julia two Christmases ago. It was a powerful, streamlined vehicle that looked as if it had been milled from a single block of olive-green metal. He always felt incredibly self-conscious driving it, and Eleanor was no better, which was why it stayed in the barn eleven months of the year. But he had to admit that in this instance, the image of professional respectability it fostered was probably going to be useful.

The second gate was the one he wanted: two red-and-white pole barriers, with metal one-way flaps in the concrete. There was a big steel-blue sign outside that read:

HMP Stocken Hall
Clinical Detention Center

He stopped in front of the barrier, lowering the window to show his card to the white sensor pillar at the side of the road.

"Entry authorization confirmed, Mr. Mandel," the pillar's construct voice said. "Please park in slot seven. Thank you." The barrier in front of him lifted.

If anything, Stocken's new annex was even drabber than its older counterparts. The building was a three-story hexagon, fifty meters to a side, with a broad central well; a metal skeleton overlaid with gunmetal-gray composite panels, three rings of silvered glass spaced equidistantly up its frontage. Modular, factory-built, easy to assemble, cheap, and twice as strong as the traditional brick-and-cement structures.

He hadn't been expecting such a sophisticated set-up; like most government ministries, the Home Office—and therefore its subsidiary, the prison service—was currently cash-starved. And even in pre-Warming times, improving prison conditions had never rated highly in MPs' priority lists. Constituents didn't appreciate their tax money being spent on giving criminals a cushy number.

As he drove around to the car park outside the Center's main entrance, he saw another prison party at work in the dead forest at the back of the perimeter fence. Trunks were being felled, then trimmed before they were hauled off to a sawmill set up under a green canvas awning. It was hard work, rain had turned the ground to a quagmire, but even so, he was surprised that the inmates were allowed chain saws. Stocken was a category-A prison.

He hurried over the band of granite chips that encircled the building, discomfort trickling into his veins, as tangible as a gland secretion. Too many of his mates from the Trinities had wound up being sent to places like Stocken in the PSP years, and not all of them had survived transit.

There was another sensor pillar outside the big glass entrance doors. Greg showed his card again. The reception hall had a semicircular desk on one side and a row of plastic chairs lined up opposite. Walls and ceiling were all composite, powder-blue in color; the linoleum was a marble swirl of gray and cream. Biolum panels were set along the walls, below tracks of boxy service conduits. The place had the same kind of utilitarian layout as a warship interior.

That military image was reinforced by the two guards sitting behind the desk; they both wore crisp blue uniforms with peaked caps. One of them took Greg's proffered card and showed it to a terminal. An ID badge burped out of a slot.

"Please wear it on your lapel at all times, sir," he said as he handed it over along with the card.

Greg was fixing the badge on when one of the doors at the far end of the reception hall opened. The woman who came through was in her late thirties, dark hair cut short without much attempt at styling. Her face had pale skin, slender winged eyebrows, a long nose, and strong lips. She wore a white coat of some shiny material, there was no hint of what clothes might be worn underneath. Her shoes were sensible black leather with a small buckle, flat heels. A cybofax was gripped in her left hand.

"Mr. Mandel?" She stuck out her hand.

"Greg, please."

"I'm Stephanie Rowe, Dr. MacLennan's assistant. I'll take you to him."

The corridors were windowless, running through the center of the building. They passed several warders, all in the neat navy-blue uniforms, and always walking in pairs or larger groups. On two occasions they were escorting prisoners. The men had shaved heads, wore loose-fitting yellow overalls; white plastic neural-jammer collars were clamped firmly around their necks.

Greg frowned at the retreating back of the second prisoner. "Are all the prisoners fitted with neural jammers?"

"Yes, all the ones in the Center. We house some of the country's most ruthless criminals here. I don't mean the gang lords or syntho barons. These are the violence and sex oriented offenders: killers, rapists, and child molesters."

"Right. Do many of them try to escape?"

"No. There were only two attempts in the last twelve months. The collar's incapacitation ability is demonstrated to each inmate as he arrives. Besides, most of them are resigned when they get here, depressed, withdrawn. The kind of crimes they commit mean even their families have rejected them. They were loners on the outside; there is nowhere they can go, no organization that will hide and take care of them. It's our experience that a high percentage of them actually wanted to be caught."

"And do you think you can cure them?"

"The term we use now is behavioral reorientation. And yes, we've had some success. There's a lot of work still to be done, naturally."

"What about public acceptance?"

She grimaced in defeat. "Yes, we anticipate a major problem in that area. It would be politically difficult releasing them back into the community after the treatment is complete."

"Was Liam Bursken one of the two who tried to escape?" Greg asked.

"No."

"Has he ever tried?"

"Again, no. He's kept in solitary the whole time. Even by our standards, he's considered extremely dangerous. We cannot allow him to mix with the other inmates. It would cause too much trouble. Most of them would want to attack him simply for the kudos it would bring them."

"No honor amongst thieves anymore, eh?"

"These aren't thieves, Greg. They are very sick people."

"Are you a doctor?"

"A psychiatrist, yes."

They climbed a staircase to the second floor. Greg mulled over what she had said. A professional liberal, he decided; she had too much faith in people. Maybe too much faith in her profession as well if she believed therapy could effect complete cures. It couldn't; papering over the cracks was the best anyone could ever hope for, he knew. But then, the gland did give him an advantage, allowing him to glimpse the true workings of the mind.

"So why do you want to work here?" he asked as they started off down another corridor.

She gave him a brief grin. "I didn't know I was the one you wanted to question."

"You don't have to answer."

"I don't mind. I'm here because this is the cutting edge of behavioral research, Greg. And the money is good."

"I've never heard anyone say that about civil-service pay before."

"I don't work for the government. The Center was built by the Berkeley Company, they run it under license from the Home Office. And they also fund the behavioral reorientation research project, which is my field."

"That explains a lot. I didn't think the Home Office had the kind of resources to pay for a place like this."

Stephanie shrugged noncommittally and opened the door into the director's suite. There was a secretary in the outer office, busy with a terminal. She glanced up and keyed an intercom.

"Go straight through," she said.

The office was at odds with the rest of the Center. Wall units, desk, and conference table were all customized blackwood, ancient maps and several diplomas hung on the wall, louvred blinds stretched across the picture window, blocking the view. It was definitely a senior-management enclave, its occupier claiming every perk and entitlement allowed in the corporate rule book.

Dr. James MacLennan rose from behind his desk to greet Greg, a reassuring smile and a solid handshake. He was thirty-seven, shorter than Greg, with thick, dark hair, heavily tanned, with compact features. His Brazilian suit was a shiny gray-green.

"For the record, and before we say anything else, I'd like to state quite categorically that Liam Bursken did not slip out for a night, it simply isn't possible," MacLennan said.

His mannerisms were all a trifle too gushy and effusive for Greg to draw any confidence the way he was intended to. He guessed that Berkeley's directors were none too happy at suggestions that psychopaths like Bursken could come and go as they pleased. The method of Kitchener's murder hadn't been lost on the press.

"From what I've seen so far, I'd say the Center looks pretty secure," Greg said.

"Good, excellent." MacLennan gestured at a long settee.

Greg settled back into the bouncy cushioning. "I will have to ask Bursken himself."

"I understand completely. Stephanie will arrange your interview. Make as many checks as you like. I like to think our record is flawless."

"Thank you, I'm sure it is."

Stephanie leaned over the desk and muttered into the intercom, then came and sat at the table next to the settee.

"Right, so how can we help?" MacLennan crossed his legs and gave Greg his undivided attention.

"As you probably saw in the newscasts, I'm a gland psychic appointed to the Kitchener inquiry by the Home Office."

MacLennan rolled his eyes and grunted. "God, the press. Don't tell me about the press. I've had the lot of them clamoring on the door to interview Bursken, harassing the staff when they come off duty. You see them on the channel 'casts, these packs that follow politicians and royalty around, but I just never appreciated what it was like to be on the receiving end. And that kind of microscopic attention is precisely what we didn't want; Stocken is supposed to be a low-key operation."

"Suppose you fill me in on some background. What exactly is this behavioral reorientation work you're doing here?"

"You know what kind of inmates we hold?"

"Yeah. That's why I'm so interested in meeting Liam Bursken. I saw the holograms of Kitchener *in situ*. Tell you, it was plain butchery. I've seen atrocities in battle, and not just those committed by the other side. But the kind of mind that perpetrated that was way outside my experience. I want to know what it looks like."

MacLennan nodded sympathetically. "Well, the motivations behind their crimes are basically psychological, in all cases deep-rooted. None of the serial killers sell drugs, or steal, or commit fraud, any of the normal range of criminal activities. That sort of everyday crime is mostly a result of sociological conditioning; broadly speaking, solvable if they were given better housing, improved education, a good job, stable home environment, et cetera—it's a process for social workers and parole officers—whereas the Center's inmates probably had those advantages before they came in. They do tend to have reasonable IQs, steady jobs, sometimes even families."

"Do any of them have exceptional IQs?" Greg asked.

MacLennan flicked an inquiring glance at Stephanie Rowe. "Not that I'm aware of," he said. "Why do you ask?"

"Kitchener's students are all very bright people."

"Ah, I see, yes."

"No one here has anything above average intelligence," Stephanie announced; she was studying her cybofax. "Certainly we have no geniuses resident. Do you want me to request past case histories?"

"No, that's all right," Greg said.

"What we are trying to do at Stocken," MacLennan said, "is to alter their psychological profiles, eradicate that part of their nature that extracts gratification from performing these barbaric acts."

"Brainwashing?"

"Absolutely not."

"It sounds like it."

MacLennan gave him a narrow smile. "What you refer to as brainwashing is simply conditioned response. An example: strap your subject in a chair and show him a picture of an object, say a particular brand of whiskey. Each time the whiskey appears, you give him an electric shock. Repeated enough times, the subject will become averse to that brand. I have grossly oversimplified, of course. But that is the principle, installing a visually triggered compulsion. What you are doing in such cases is ingraining a new response to replace the one already in place. But it can only produce results on the most simplistic level. You cannot turn criminals into law-abiding citizens by aversion therapy, because criminality is their nature, derived subconsciously, not a single yes/no choice. And what we are dealing with in Stocken's inmates is a behavior pattern often formed in childhood. It has to be erased and then replaced."

"How?"

"Have you heard of educational laser paradigms?"

"No," Greg said dryly.

"It's an idea that goes back several decades. It was the subject of my doctoral thesis. I started off in high-density data-handling techniques but got sidetracked. Educational paradigms were so much more interesting. They are the biological equivalent of computer programs. You can literally load subject matter into the human brain as though you were squirting bytes into a memory core. Once perfected, there will be no need for schools or universities. You will be given all the knowledge you require in a single burst of light, sending the information through the optic nerve to imprint directly on the brain." MacLennan shrugged affably. "That's the theory, anyway. We are still a long way from achieving those kind of results."

"It sounds impressive," Greg said. "And you can use it to install new behavior patterns as well?"

"Behavior is rooted in memory, Mr. Mandel. Conditioning again. You fall into a pool when you are a young child, nearly drowning, and in adult life you are wary of water, a poor swimmer, nor do you have any enthusiasm to improve. It is these countless cumulative small events and incidents in your formative years that decide the composition of your psyche. You are a soldier, I believe, Mr. Mandel?"

"Was a soldier. I'm retired now."

"You volunteered for the army?"

"Yeah."

"And were you any good as a soldier?"

Greg shifted his weight on the settee's amorphous cushioning, conscious of Stephanie's stare. "I was mentioned in dispatches once or twice."

"And yet thousands, hundreds of thousands, of men your age were totally unsuitable for the military life you excelled in. Physically no different, but mentally, in outlook, your exact opposite. The respective attitudes determined in the period between your fourth and sixteenth birthdays. We are what we are because of that time, the child being the father of the man. And that is the time we must alter in order to eradicate real-time psychoses. My aim is to substitute false paradigmatic memories for real recollections, thus effecting a radical change of temperament."

"Have you had any success?"

"Limited, but most promising given we have been here only two years. We have already succeeded in assembling some highly realistic synthetic memories. There is one, a walk through a forest." He closed his eyes and the eagerness and tension that had built up as he

spoke drained out of his face, leaving him strangely peaceful. Almost
the same expression as a synthohead, Greg thought.

"I can see the trees," MacLennan said, his voice reduced to a placid
lilt. "They are large, tall as well as broad, in full leaf, oaks and elms.
This is pre-Warming, midsummer, with sunbeams breaking through
the overhead branches. I can see a squirrel, a red one; he's racing up
an oak, round and round the trunk. I'm standing below watching
him, touching the bark. It's rough, crinkled, dusted with a powdery
green algae. The grass is ankle-high, dewy, wetting my shoes. There
are foxgloves everywhere, and weasel-snout; I can smell honey-
suckle."

"Lasers can imprint a smell?" Greg asked skeptically.

"The memory of a smell," Stephanie said pedantically. "We
adapted the paradigm from a high-definition virtual reality simulation, then added tactile and olfactory senses, as well as emotional responses."

"Emotional responses?"

"Yes. Interpretation is a strong part of memory. If you see a particularly beautiful flower in the forest, you feel good about it; tread
in a dog turd on the path and you're disgusted."

Greg thought about it. He couldn't fault the logic, it was just that
the whole concept seemed somewhat fanciful. But someone on the
Berkeley board obviously had enough faith to invest in it. Quite
heavily, judging by the facilities the Center offered.

"Have you received this memory as well?" he asked her.

"Yes. It's very realistic. It feels like I was actually *in* that forest.
James forgot to mention the birdsong. The thrushes are warbling the
whole time."

Greg turned back to MacLennan, who was watching him levelly.

"How does this help to cure ax murderers?" Greg asked.

"Imagine when you were young if you took that same walk through
a tranquil forest for half an hour instead of having to endure your
drunken father beating you. If you had that walk, or played football,
every evening he came home drunk; if you could remember your
mother giving him a kiss instead of crying and screaming for mercy,
I think you'd find your outlook on life would be very different."

"Yeah, and is it going to be possible?"

"I believe so. Once we have solved the problem of how to erase, or at the very least weaken, old memories. This is the area of research that requires the most effort in order for the project to succeed. Neurology and psychology to date have concentrated on memory recovery, helping amnesic victims, developing hypnotic recall techniques for vital witnesses, even preserving memories in the face of encroaching senility. The only comparable work in the opposing direction is with drugs that induce a form of transient amnesia, like scopolamine. These are no use to us, as they only prevent memories from being retained while the drug is in effect. What we need is something that will go into a subject's mind and hunt down the original poisonous memories."

"Sounds like a job for a psychic," Greg said.

"It's an option we've considered. In fact, it was one reason I was particularly delighted when I was informed you would be coming today. I wanted to quiz you on the parameters of psi. The Home Office said you were one of the best ESP-oriented psychics to emerge from the Mindstar project. Are you able to interpret individual memories?"

"No. Sorry, I'm strictly an empath."

"I see." He clasped his hands together and rested his chin on the knuckles. "Do you know of any psychic who can do that?"

"There were a couple in Mindstar who had the kind of ability you're talking about. They used to be able to lift faces and locations out of a suspect's thoughts." He almost said prisoner, but with Stephanie leaning forward in her seat, hanging on to every word, that would never do. He wanted her wholehearted cooperation. "I don't think they could perform anything like the deep-ranging exploration you require."

"That's a pity," MacLennan said. "I might apply for a license to practice with a themed neurohormone if one could be developed along those lines."

"Are you completely stonewalled without psychic analysis?"

"No. There are several avenues we can pursue. Paradigms could be structured to wipe selected memories. A sort of anti-memory, if you like. The major trouble is again one of identification. We need to know a memory in order to wipe it—the nature of it, the section of the brain where it is stored."

"A real-time brain scan might just tell us," Stephanie said. "If the subject recounts a particularly traumatic incident, it may be possible to locate the specific neurons that house it. The erasure paradigm could then be targeted directly at them. Magic photons, we call it, after the magic bullet; like cancer treatments that kill tumor cells without harming the ordinary cells around it."

"You would need some very sophisticated sensors to scan a brain that accurately," Greg pointed out. "Not to mention processing capacity. Part of my psi-assessment tests involved a SQUID scan, but there was no way you could get the focus fine enough to resolve individual neuron cells."

"Berkeley has allocated us considerable resources," MacLennan said. His chirpy everything-under-control smile had returned. "We have one SQUID brain scanner already installed here at the Center. Although admittedly its resolution does fall some way short of the requirement Stephanie envisages for the magic-photons concept to function. But it is a modest first step. And several medical-equipment companies are working on models that offer a higher resolution. I have high hopes for the project."

"This paradigm research is an expensive venture," Greg said. "The Board must have a lot of faith in you."

"They do. I didn't promise them instant results and success. They fully understand that it is a medium-term project; commercial viability will not be realized for at least another seven to ten years. But they agreed to back it because of the potential. You see, if paradigm-based treatment does work, it will revolutionize the entire penal system. We would have to rebuild our institutions from the ground up. The only people who will actually require detention are petty criminals; everyone else will be reformed in medical facilities."

"Yeah, I see." He showed Stephanie a sardonic grin. "I still say you'll have trouble convincing people to let them out again."

She shrugged.

"Have you actually tried implanting any of these alternative memories in an inmate?" he asked.

"Indeed we have," MacLennan said. "Nothing dramatic. It's early days yet. We are in the process of acquiring baseline data on how well the paradigms are absorbed." He might have been talking about lab rats for all the emotion in his tone. "The older the subject, the more difficult it becomes, naturally."

"What about Liam Bursken? Has he been given any synthetic memories?"

"No. He was unwilling to cooperate. At the moment, it remains a purely voluntary program, although we do reward participants with extra privileges."

"So essentially he is the same person now as he was when he arrived."

"Yes."

"Great." Greg stood up. "I'd like to see him. He should be able to offer me a few insights."

"As you wish," MacLennan said. "Stephanie will take you down."

"Do you have records of the correspondence he's received?" Greg asked.

MacLennan glanced inquiringly at Stephanie.

"Yes," she said. "It's not much, mostly death threats."

"I'd like copies, please."

"I'll assemble a data package," MacLennan said. "It'll be ready for you when you leave."

"Thanks." There was always the possibility someone had admired Bursken enough to copy the murder technique. Pretty tenuous, though.

"How has Bursken reacted to the Kitchener murder?" Greg asked Stephanie when they had left MacLennan's office.

"He's shown a lot of interest," she said. "He believes it is a vindication of his own crimes."

"Oh?"

"According to Bursken, he is one of God's chosen agents of vengeance in a sinful world. Therefore someone murdering in the same way is proof that God is now instructing others. Therefore, God was instructing him in the first place. QED."

"What's he like? I mean, what sort of formative years did he have that could push him into that?"

She hesitated as they walked into the stairwell, her companion-ability glitched momentarily. Greg was actually allowed to see worry and even confusion.

"The honest truth, Greg, is I haven't got a clue. We did some research into his background, for all the good it did us. He had a perfectly ordinary childhood. There was some bullying at school, nothing excessive. We could find no evidence of any sexual or mental abuse, no deprivation. Yet even by the standards of this Center's inmates, he is completely insane. There is no rational explanation for why he went haywire. We have studied him, naturally; his brain function shows no abnormality, there are no chemical imbalances. Currently we're trying to determine the actual trigger mechanism of his psychosis, whether there is a single cause to send him off on his killing sprees. MacLennan thought that if we could just gain one insight into how Bursken functions, we might eventually be able to understand his mentality. That's why he's prepared to devote time and money on such a hopeless case. By studying the real deviants, we gain more knowledge of the ordinary. But the results have been very patchy, and completely inconclusive. I doubt we ever will understand. I simply thank God that Bursken is a rogue, very rare."

"You mean, even your laser paradigm couldn't cure him?"

"I shouldn't think so. You see, as far as we can tell, there is no evil memory sequence to replace, no trauma to eradicate. Maybe he did hear voices, who knows?"

The Center's interview room was slightly more hospitable than the one at Oakham police station. Greg imagined it had been patterned from a conference room at a two-star hotel, cheap but well-meaning. The table was a cream-colored oval with five comfortable sandy-red chairs around it, almost like a dining room arrangement; certainly the confrontational element was absent. It was on the ground floor and a picture window ran the length of one wall, looking out on the patio garden that filled the building's central well. Conifers and heathers were growing in raised-brick borders, tended by a working party of inmates under the watchful eyes of warders; there were several wooden park benches with inmates sitting and reading, or just soaking up the unexpected bonus of sunlight. They all had a blue stripe on their uniform sleeve.

Two guards brought Liam Bursken in. He wasn't a particularly tall man, five or six centimeters shorter than Greg, but powerfully built, with broad, sloping shoulders; his shaved skull had a slightly bluish sheen from the stubble, giving the impression of a long, gaunt face.

The neural-jammer collar was tight enough to pinch his skin; Greg could see it was rubbing red around the edges. Sober, almost mournful, emerald eyes found Greg and regarded him intently. There was a red stripe on his yellow uniform sleeve.

He sat down slowly, his joints moving with the kind of stiffness Greg associated with the elderly. The guards remained standing behind him, one with his hand in his pocket. Fingering the collar activator, Greg guessed.

He ordered a secretion from his gland. The four minds in the room slithered across his expanding perception boundary, their thought currents forming a constellation of surreal moire-patterns. Both guards were nervous, while Stephanie Rowe by contrast displayed a cool, detached interest. Liam Bursken's thoughts were more enigmatic. Greg had been expecting the ragged fractures of dysfunction, like a junkie who simply cannot rationalize, but instead, there was only calmness, a conviction of supreme righteousness. Bursken's self-assurance touched on megalomania. And there was no sense of humor. None. Bursken had been robbed of that most basic human trait. It was what unnerved people about him, Greg realized; they could all sense it at a subconscious level. He wondered if he should tell Stephanie, help her understand the man.

He put his cybofax on the table and keyed in the file of questions he'd prepared. "My name is Greg Mandel."

"Psychic," Liam Bursken said. "Ex of the Mindstar Brigade. Adviser to Oakham CID in the murder of Edward Kitchener. Strongly suspected to have been appointed at the insistence of Julia Evans."

"Yeah, that's right. Though you can't believe everything you see on the channels. So, Liam, Stephanie here tells me you've been following the Kitchener case with some interest."

"Yes."

Greg realized Bursken was neither being deliberately rude nor trying to irritate him. Facts, that was all the man was concerned with. There would be no garrulous ingratiation here, none of the usual rapport. Stephanie had been right, Bursken was utterly insane; Greg wasn't entirely sure he could be labeled human.

"I would like to ask you some questions, do you mind?"

"Any objection would be irrelevant. You would simply take your answers."

"Then I'll ask them, shall I?"

There was no response. Greg began to wonder if he could spot a lie in a mind as eerily distorted as the one facing him.

"How old are you, Liam?"

"Forty-two."

"Where did you live while you carried out your murders?"

"Newark."

"How many people did you kill?"

"Eleven."

Greg let out a tiny breath of relief. Liam Bursken wasn't attempting to evade, giving his answers direct. That meant he would be able to spot any attempts to scramble around for fictitious answers. Even a total mental freak couldn't escape the good old Mandel thumbscrews. He wasn't sure whether to be pleased or not. To comprehend insanity, did you have to be a little insane yourself? But then, who in his right mind would have a gland implanted in the first place?

He noticed the wave of hatred washing through Bursken's mind and clamped down on his errant smile.

"Where were you when Edward Kitchener was killed, Liam?"

"Here."

True.

"Have you ever been out of Stocken?"

"No."

"Have you ever tried to get out?"

"No."

"Do you want to get out?"

Bursken demurred for a moment. Then: "I would like to leave."

"Do you think you deserve to leave?"

"Yes."

"Do you think you have done anything wrong?"

"I have done as I was bidden, no more."

"God told you to kill?"

"I was the instrument chosen by our Lord."

"To eliminate sin?"

"Yes."

"What sin did Sarah Inglis commit?" The personal profile his cybofax displayed said Sarah was eleven years old, snatched on her way home from school.

"Let he who has not sinned cast the first stone."

"She was a schoolgirl." It was unprofessional, he knew, but for once didn't care. Anything that could hurt Bursken, from inducing pangs of conscience to a knee in the balls, couldn't be all bad.

"Our Lord cannot be held accountable."

"Yeah, right. What do you know about Edward Kitchener?"

"Physicist. Double Nobel Laureate. Lived at Launde Abbey. Advances many controversial theories. Adulterer. Degenerate. Blasphemer."

"Why blasphemer?"

"Physicists seek to define the universe, to eliminate uncertainty and with it, spirituality. They seek to banish God. They say there is no room for God in their theories. That is the devil speaking."

"So that would qualify Kitchener as a legitimate victim for the justice you dispense?"

"Yes."

"If you had been allowed out of Stocken, would you have killed him?"

"I would have redeemed him with the sacrifice of life. He would have been blessed, and thanked me as he kneeled at our Lord's feet."

"Would this redemption involve mutilating him?"

"I would leave behind a sign for the Angels of the Lord to help with his ascension into heaven."

"What sign?"

"Given him the shape of an angel."

"It's the lungs," Stephanie said. "If you look down directly on the body, the lungs spread out on either side represent wings, like an angel. Liam did it to all his victims. The Vikings used to do something similar when they came over pillaging."

"I'm sure they did," Greg muttered. He keyed up the next series of questions on the cybofax.

"Okay, you know Kitchener lives at Launde Abbey, and you know there is a kitchen there. Would you take your own knife?"

"The Lord always provides."

"Does he provide from Launde's kitchen, or does he provide beforehand?"

"Beforehand," Bursken whispered thickly.

Stephanie leaned over to him, an apologetic smile on her lips. "What are you getting at?" she asked in a low voice.

"Assembling a profile of the mind involved. Whoever did it has to have something in common with Bursken here. It wasn't an ordinary tekmerc, even they would balk at performing that atrocity. It must be someone whose normal emotional responses have been eradicated, like Bursken. What I want to know is how rationally can they function under these circumstances. If they were following a plan, could they stick to it? Sheer revulsion would cause most ordinary minds to crack under the stress, mistakes could be made. So far this investigation hasn't uncovered a single one."

"I see." She flopped back in her chair again.

"Which would be more important to the Lord," Greg asked, "redeeming Kitchener or destroying the computer records of all his blasphemous work?"

"You mock me, Mandel. You speak of the Lord, yet you carry no reverence in your heart. You speak of blasphemy, and you revel in its execution."

"Which would you prefer to do, kill Kitchener or erase his work?"

"A computer is a tool, it can be used or misused. In itself, it is unimportant."

"Secondary then, but if knocking it out would be a good idea, you would try to do it?"

"Yes."

"Were you ever nervous when you murdered those people in Newark?"

Bursken's throat muscles tightened, his thought currents spasmed heavily, thrashing about like wrestling snakes. Loathing predominated.

Greg allowed a smile to play on his lips. "You were, weren't you? You were frightened, trembling like a leaf."

"Of being discovered," Bursken spat. "Of being stopped."

"Did you take precautions? Did you clean up afterward."

"The Lord is no fool."

"You followed his instructions?"

"Yes."

"To the letter? Right afterward, I mean the minute after you had spread those lungs, you would start cleaning up?"

"Yes."

"No hesitation? No gloating?"

"None."

"During, what about during? Did you take care then?"

"Yes."

"It was hard work, bloody work, and there was always the danger someone might stumble in on you. The fear. You're seriously telling me your concentration never wavered?"

"Never," Bursken said gleefully. "The Lord cleansed me of mortal weaknesses for my task. My thoughts remained pure."

"Every single time?"

"Every single time!"

"The police found some skin under Oliver Powell's fingernails. Your skin. You missed that, didn't you?"

"They lied. There was no skin. Powell was struck from behind. He cried out but once before I silenced him. A plea. In his heart he knew his sin, he did not attempt to thwart the Lord's justice."

Greg could read it from his mind, the supreme pride in what he had done. The glowing sense of accomplishment, a kind Greg had encountered before in sports tournament winners, someone receiving favorable exam results. Healthy dignity. "Jesus!" Stupefaction pushed Greg back in his chair. Staring in bewilderment at the creature opposite, it had flesh and blood and bone, but that wasn't enough to make it human, nowhere near. "He's not fucking real."

Stephanie exchanged an embarrassed glance with one of the guards and made a cutting motion across her throat.

"Was there anything else, Greg?" she asked.

Greg shut down his gland secretion. Defeated, soiled and shamed by having been privy to Bursken's thoughts. "No. Absolutely nothing."

The lunatic sneered contemptuously as the guards led him away.

14

JULIA'S ROLLS-ROYCE PASSED UNDER a broad stone arch, watched by a pair of silent moss-laden griffins perched on either side. The wrought-iron gates swung shut as the car sped down the long gravel drive.

Even with the new year's punishing weather, Wilholm's grounds were maintained in pristine condition. Formally arranged flowerbeds alternated with cherry trees along the side of the drive. Broad lawns dotted with dumpy cycads rolled away to a border of glossy shrubs; behind them a thick rank of Brazilian rosewoods completed the shield against prying eyes. The Nene was a couple of kilometers away to the southeast. In the summer she could look out of the manor's second-story windows and watch the little sailing boats cruising up and down the river, dreaming of the freedom they possessed. But this time of year always saw the valley floor flooded by the monsoon rains, the boats safe on dry land. The water was deeper each year as more and more soil was washed away by the powerful current. Farther down, between the A1 and the tail end of the Ferry Meadows estuary, it became a permanent salt marsh, fetid and inutile.

But the secluded Wilholm estate remained a passive refuge, protected from environmental ravages by a wall of her money, changeless apart from the spectacular cycle of flowers that varied from month to month. Philip Evans had bought it as soon as he returned to England, paying off the communal farmers who had occupied it under the PSP's auspices. Landscape teams had labored for months, returning it to its former splendor. Actually, it was probably a lot better than it used to be, she suspected, especially after she saw how much it had cost. Grandpa hadn't cared, he wanted elegance, and by God, that's what he got.

It was worthwhile, though. Wilholm was easy on the eye; time flowed just that fraction slower across its trim lawns and through the sumptuous interior. The fact that she never, but never, used it for business of any kind helped strengthen the sensation of relief she always experienced when she crossed that invisible, and ultra-secure, threshold. Wilholm was for parties and lovers and friends. Today counted as friends; the Kitchener case was too intriguing to be classed as work.

She pursed her lips in self-chastisement; calling the murder intriguing in front of Cormac Ranasfari would never do.

Royan Access Request.

Expedite, she told the nodes.

Hi, Snowy.

She grinned broadly. On the jump seat opposite, Rachel gave her an expectant look, then went back to the view across the lawn. A black-furred gene-tailored sentinel panther was just visible loping along the grass in front of the shrubs.

Royan was the only person to call her that. It was her middle name, Snowflower, bestowed by the American desert cult with which she had spent her childhood. She never used it, but there was no unit of data on the planet Royan couldn't access.

Hello to you, she answered. Talking to Royan was always a real opiate. He had taught her all sorts of programming tricks. Thanks to him, she could write better hotrod software than half of England's professional hackers. She wasn't sure what he got in return, probably just the satisfaction of having someone outside his concrete eyrie who would listen. That and the fact she was *the* Julia Evans. Whatever, they had been firm friends ever since Greg's first Event Horizon case. He was another of those rare people who was honest with her.

Eleanor has been to see me.

I don't know. All these girlfriends.

I like Eleanor.

All you men like Eleanor.

Jealous jealous jealous. Is what you are.

Certainly am, all I've got is money.

How is Patrick?

Fine, I suppose.

Oh, Snowy, you haven't finished with him already? You only met him five weeks ago.

Don't you start, I get quite enough of that from Grandpa and Morgan and Greg.

They care. I care, Snowy. It's nice to have people who care.

Yah.

I saw you on the channels this morning.

Did you now?

Yes yes yes. Would you like me to put out a snuff contract on Jakki Coleman?

I would truly love you to put out a snuff contract on that bitch.

Really?

The only trouble is, everyone would know I was behind it. Lord, I hope nothing does happen to her! I never thought of that before. The way conspiracy theories are flying around at the moment . . .

Guilty guilty guilty. Chuckle. Serves you right.

Yes. Well, you would spring me from jail, wouldn't you?

For a price.

Thanks a bunch, some friend you are.

Seriously, I could glitch her 'cast something chronic. How about superimposing a blue AV recording? Give the porno starlet her face.

Julia had to rub her hand over her mouth to stifle the laugh. Rachel didn't look this time, she had probably guessed what was going on.

Don't tempt me! Julia implored. *I'll get that Coleman slag one day. You see if I don't. It won't be public, but she'll know and I'll know. And that's what truly counts.*

Let me know if you need a hand.

Yes, I will. Thanks.

I've been going through the Launde Abbey security 'ware for Greg and Eleanor.

Yes, and . . . ?

You were really looking out for Kitchener, weren't you?

Not me, I didn't even know a thing about him until two days ago. Apparently Cormac Ranasfari insisted on upgrading the security at the Abbey. He's always been concerned that Kitchener didn't have adequate protection, and this was a perfect opportunity to insist.

Oh. Well, that security system your people installed is top grade. The guardian bytes are hot hot hot stuff.

You can't melt through?

Didn't say that. I could. And possibly another five or six people in the country could. But it's tough.

Oh, so that takes the tekmerc penetration mission out of the possible, and into the improbable.
Looks like it.
Thanks for telling me. Do you want to sit in on the conference?
Yes yes yes.

Wilholm itself was a splendid eighteenth-century manor house. A broad gray stone façade with pink and yellow roses clotting the sturdy trelliswork on either side of the overhanging portico; the long windows fitted with silvered glass against the heat. Julia saw a hundred tiny reflections of herself climbing out of the Rolls. Lucas, her butler, was walking down the steps to greet her.

There were a couple of other cars parked outside. Morgan's caramel-colored Rover and a cobalt-blue Ford that she guessed was Ranasfari's.

"A pleasant morning, ma'am?" Lucas asked. He was in his mid-sixties, wearing a tailcoat with bright brass buttons, wonderfully dignified. The PSP had kept him on the dole for ten years, saying personal service was a humiliating anachronism and they'd find him proper employment. The day after Philip Evans bought Wilholm, Lucas had cycled out from Peterborough and asked for a job. The manor functioned so smoothly under his supervision, and he'd never attended corporate management-training courses.

She handed him her raincoat and boater. "Let's say I covered a lot of ground."

He inclined his head. "Yes, ma'am. Mr. and Mrs. Mandel have just passed the gatehouse, they will be here shortly."

"Great. Show them to the study as soon as they arrive." She raced up the steps and through the big double doors. Most of her major friends together, working on a problem and including her. It looked like a great afternoon.

The study was on the first floor. Julia took her deep-purple blazer off as she went up the curving staircase. She was still undoing her slim bow tie as she barged into the study. Morgan Walshaw and Cormac Ranasfari were waiting, along with Gabriel Thompson.

Gabriel was the only person Julia knew who was aging in reverse. The woman was another ex-Mindstar officer Greg had introduced her to. Her gland had been taken out two years ago, the precognition faculty it educed having brought too many psychological problems. Seeing into the future, Gabriel lived in perpetual fear of watching her own death drawing steadily closer. After leaving the army, she had gone to seed, badly.

Now, with the gland out, she was taking care of her appearance again; she watched her diet, kept up her health, and was beginning to expand her interests. After starting out as a dowdy spinster who looked about fifty-five, she had worked her way down to become a pleasant-faced forty-five-year-old with a pretty brisk attitude to life. Although Julia had detected some brittleness on more than one occasion.

Officially, Gabriel was acting as adviser to Event Horizon's security division while Morgan set up a team of psychics—Greg had refused the assignment point-blank. The two of them had moved into the same house eighteen months ago.

"Hello, Gabriel," Julia said brightly. She gave Morgan a quick peck on the cheek as she went past the long oak table that filled the center of the study. "Thank you for coming, Cormac."

Cormac had half risen from his own armchair; he ducked his head before reseating himself.

Julia plopped down in the hard chair at the head of the table and activated the terminal in front of her. "I asked Royan to attend, is that all right?" she asked Morgan. He didn't strictly approve of Royan.

"Certainly."

Her fingers pecked at the terminal's keyboard, loading the familiar code. Above the stone fireplace, the flatscreen she used for video-conferencing flickered dimly.

PLUGGED IN, it printed in bold orange letters.

Royan always refused to use a vocal synthesizer; the closest he came was the silent speech when her nodes were interfaced with the 'ware stacks in his room. Eleanor had described him to her once. Ever since, Julia had experienced a subtle guilt at her relief that she would never actually have to meet him. Although a bleak presence always seemed to float on the periphery of their electronic link, as if he was struggling to project himself through to her.

You're paranoid, girl, she told herself.

Another code and Grandpa was there, plugged into the study's systems. She talked banalities with her three guests as the first raindrops of the afternoon began to speckle the lead-framed windows. Sluggish gray clouds lumbered over the Nene valley, making the oak-paneled study seem funereal. Wall-mounted biolum globes came on, giant luminous pearls on curving tubular-brass arms.

Lucas's unmistakable soft knock sounded on the door. He ushered Greg and Eleanor in.

Julia listened to their resume of the case, trying to conceal a shudder when Greg ran through his interview with Liam Bursken. She could see he was still wound up about it, and it took a lot to affect Greg. Whenever she glanced at Cormac, he had the same politely attentive expression in place.

Can't fool me, Cormac, she thought, not anymore. His aloofness was a defense against the craziness and stupidity of the world, as much as his physical retreat into his laboratory complex. But now the world had pierced clean through and bitten him.

With some surprise, she realized she was actually feeling sorry for him.

After Eleanor finished talking, Julia asked Greg to squirt all the police files stored in his cybofax into the NN core. "Grandpa can run correlation exercises for us," she said.

"That's right, bloody skivvy I am," Philip muttered. "Nice to know why I was invited."

Greg smiled thinly and aimed his cybofax at her terminal. Eleanor added the bytes she'd built up.

"So it's definitely not one of the students," Gabriel said thoughtfully.

"Yes, I'm sure they didn't kill Kitchener," said Greg. "Although how my opinion would stand up in court, I'm not so certain about. But the physical evidence does tend to corroborate my interviews. Besides, none of them had a mind anything like Bursken's."

"Your opinion is good enough for me," Morgan said.

"Even your new friend Rosette Harding-Clarke is in the clear." Eleanor flashed Greg a spartan grin. "Her family is very rich, and according to Julia's legal office, the child wouldn't get a penny out of

Kitchener's estate. If the Harding-Clarkes were poor, Rosette might have been able to apply for a maintenance order against the estate. However, the question doesn't arise."

"Then it must have been a tekmerc snuff," Morgan said.

YOUR SECURITY GEAR PROTECTING LAUNDE ABBEY WAS THE BEST. NO ONE ON THE CIRCUIT HAS HEARD OF ANYBODY WANTING TO BUY THE KIND OF PROGRAMS THAT COULD BURN THROUGH.

Morgan turned his head to look at the flatscreen. "How reliable are your sources?"

VERY VERY VERY.

"Somebody got in."

"I still maintain it would be difficult for anyone to get in and out of the Chater valley that night," Greg said.

"Then who did do it?" Walshaw asked; his voice had risen a notch.

Gabriel caught his eye, a silent rebuke.

"Logically, it was a tekmerc snuff," Greg said unhappily. "Nobody else would have the know-how and operational expertise to get in and out without leaving a trace. That's what I find incredible. There wasn't a single trace, not one." He shook his head.

"We're missing method and motive at the moment," Eleanor said.

MOTIVE I HAVE PLENTY OF.

"What?" Julia asked.

ACCORDING TO THE CIRCUIT, KITCHENER WAS WORKING ON A BORON-PROTON REACTOR FOR YOU.

"Edward was doing no such thing," Cormac objected.

Philip chortled, the sound reverberating out of hidden speakers, directionless. "Ah, but it fits, m'boy. Doesn't it? Kitchener's speciality was atomic and molecular interaction. A successful boron-proton reaction would be almost as worthwhile as giga-conductor. Look at it from an economic point of view; a successful boron-proton fusion produces energized helium, that's all, no pollutants, no radioactive emission. It's a bloody marvel, or it would be if we could build one. Kitchener is just the kind of man to iron out the bugs involved in getting a smooth fusion process going."

"It would be a logical assumption," Morgan said grudgingly. "If someone was aware Kitchener was contracted to Event Horizon, was receiving money from us, they could well think it was for energy research. Especially if they knew it was coming from Cormac's office, the inventor of the giga-conductor."

Eleanor rapped a knuckle lightly on the table and tilted her head to look at Julia. "How are you going to power Prior's Fen?"

It took a second for her thoughts to jump between subjects. "I'm considering two options. The first is an ocean thermal-generator system, with floating platforms anchored out in the Atlantic and bringing the electricity ashore with superconductor cables. Second is to drill a couple of hundred deep bore holes across the Fens basin, then insert direct thermocouple cables down them, siphon energy right out of the mantle. The tower and the projected cyber precincts certainly can't be powered from existing mainland sources, the capacity simply doesn't exist. Costwise, direct coupling has the edge, naturally, since there are no moving parts to maintain once the holes have been sunk. In engineering terms, ocean thermal is a more mature technology. So at the moment, I'm just waiting to see if Cormac makes any significant progress on direct thermocoupling in the next ten months. We don't have to make the actual selection until the end of the year."

"I'd like it to be earlier," Philip muttered.

"Behave, Grandpa." She found the camera lens above the flatscreen and gave it a stern look.

"So it would make a lot of sense for you to be working on third, fourth, even fifth alternatives," Eleanor mused.

"Yes, absolutely. But we're not."

"What other embryonic technologies could supply the rise in industrial demand?" Greg asked. "And more important, who is working on them?"

"Grandpa?"

"Easy enough, m'girl. There are really only five viable candidates. Jetstream turbines, when you tether large vacuum bubbles twelve kilometers up and fit them out with giant rotor blades. The wind velocities up there are pretty impressive. Next, you've got cold fusion."

Cormac grunted disparagingly. But when Julia looked at him, he just moued and went back to gazing out of the window.

"Well, they might crack it," Philip said grumpily. "I'm just listing options."

"Go on, Grandpa."

"Microfusion reactors, which are sort of an advanced version of cold fusion, using molecular-scale compression techniques to fuse extremely small clusters of deuterium atoms in a gizmo the size of a processor chip. Something that small does away with the heat-sink problems you get in tokamaks, but you'd need to group a lot of reactors together to produce a decent output. Ocean current turbines. But there's a question mark over which currents. Gulf Stream, Mozambique current, the Kuro Shio, East Australian current, Cape Horn current; they're all possibles, but they're all remote from Europe. Then there's solar satellites. Cheap and practical, especially now we've got the *Clarke* spaceplane. But there isn't a government in the world that'll grant a license to site a receiver array. Too many environmental—or rather environmentalist—problems when it comes to beaming energy through the atmosphere."

"Who is researching them?" Greg asked.

"Apart from the powersats, just about every kombinate, plus dozens of universities under government contract. The whole world needs an energy source that won't add to the greenhouse effect."

Julia clasped her hands together, mind devouring the problem eagerly. She didn't even need to bring the nodes on line. "Grandpa, are there any research teams working on boron-proton fusion?"

"Yes, several."

"Okay, compile a list of the twenty-five most promising research-and-design teams for boron-proton reactors and each of the other projects you mentioned, then cross-reference them with Diessenburg Mercantile."

"Gotcha, girl."

"Isn't that one of our banks?" Morgan asked.

"Yes." She told them about the conversation with Karl Hildebrandt.

"Interesting," Greg said. "I wish I'd been there."

"Got one, Juliet," Philip said. He sounded slightly apprehensive, which was unusual. "The Randon Company. They have a loan package of eight hundred and fifty million Eurofrancs with Diessenburg Mercantile, two hundred million New Sterling. Two-thirds of it was spent constructing a laboratory complex outside Reims, which is dedicated to investigating microfusion techniques."

"Has to be," Morgan said quietly.

"Randon also sponsors Nicholas Beswick," Philip said flatly.

Greg sat up straight, staring at the terminal at the head of the table.

"No such thing as coincidence," Gabriel said. It came out almost as a challenge.

Greg glanced at her fleetingly. "No," he said firmly.

"Oh, come on, Greg. Psi isn't perfect."

"Tell you, if it had been any one of the others, I would have said maybe. But Beswick, no chance."

"If you say so." She looked away, uninterested.

"This is all based on very spurious assumptions," Cormac said.

"Yeah, maybe," Greg said. He sounded troubled. "Royan, this rumor about Kitchener working on boron-proton fusion, did it exist before he was snuffed?"

YES YES YES. HEAVY-DUTY SPECULATION AS SOON AS EVENT HORIZON PAYMENTS WERE MADE TO HIS BANK ACCOUNT.

"For Christ's sake," Morgan said tightly.

SORRY, BUT PEOPLE LIKE KITCHENER ARE ALWAYS BEING SCANNED BY HOTRODS. HIS WORK IS INTERESTING, NOT TO MENTION COMMERCIAL.

"But nobody knew for certain what he was doing, right?" Greg persisted.

RIGHT. THE LIGHTWARE CRUNCHER AT LAUNDE WASN'T PLUGGED INTO ANY DATANETS. KITCHENER PROBABLY DIDN'T WANT TO RISK HAVING DATASNATCHES RUN AGAINST HIM. SMART MAN. THAT'S WHY THERE WAS THE INTEREST IN HIM.

The lines on Greg's face deepened; he looked down at the table, lost in contemplation. Eleanor gave him a concerned glance.

Julia found the level of almost unconscious devotion between them utterly enchanting. Chiding herself for peeking.

"It couldn't be Nicholas Beswick," Eleanor said, "because he knew Kitchener *wasn't* working on boron-proton fusion for Event Horizon. So he wouldn't have wiped the Bendix, would he?"

Greg let out a relieved-sounding sigh and smiled at her. "I think I'll put a bonus in your wage packet."

She grinned back.

"Exactly what was Kitchener working on for you?" Gabriel asked.

"Wormhole physics." Cormac started to explain.

Julia was moderately surprised Morgan hadn't told Gabriel about the research contract. He must take need-to-know far more seriously than she'd ever imagined. She didn't know whether to be amused at the notion or not.

"A stardrive!" Gabriel said incredulously when Ranasfari finished. She looked at Julia for confirmation.

"Yes, 'fraid so." Schoolday discipline rescued her once again. But Gabriel's expression did look so funny, probably the same as hers when Cormac had first confronted her about having the murder solved.

"Royan," Greg said slowly. "Was there *any* hint of that on the circuit?"

NO NO NO. NO! WOW. A STARDRIVE, ULTRA EXCLAMATION MARK. HOW FAR HAD HE GOT?

"There was no prospect of his ever developing a stardrive mechanism," Cormac Ranasfari said, distaste at the idea showing on his compact face. "Edward was simply working on the physics that could open the opportunity for theoretical instantaneous transit."

"Did this research involve neurohormones at all?" Greg asked.

"Most certainly. Edward was attempting to formulate a themed neurohormone that would enable him to investigate the possibility of CTCs existing. He and I considered that to be the most promising route to verification."

"CTCs?" Greg clicked his fingers. "Nicholas Beswick mentioned them. What is one?"

Cormac maintained a blankly impassive expression. Julia knew he was disappointed, having to explain concepts that were so *obvious*.

"A Closed Timelike Curve is a loop through space-time."

"No messing?" Greg appeared so innocently interested.

"It has been postulated that they exist on a sub-microscopic scale, foaming space-time; approximately ten to the minus power thirty-five meters wide and stretching back ten to the minus power forty-two seconds. Theoretically, you could use one to travel into the past."

"What about creating a paradox?" Gabriel asked; there was bright interest in her eyes. "Killing your own grandfather?"

"If you killed him ten to the minus forty-two of a second ago instead of right here in the present, how would you know?" Morgan asked mildly. "I don't think you'd notice a vast difference."

She waved him down irritably, concentrating on Cormac.

"Yes, the classic question," Cormac said politely. "Traveling back to kill your grandfather before your father was born, thus creating a paradox. If your grandfather was killed, how could you have been born to travel back to kill him? This is a null question, because quantum cosmology allows for multiple parallel universes, an infinite stack of space-times with identical physical parameters, except each one has a different history—Hitler triumphant, J. F. Kennedy never killed, the PSP remaining in power. If CTCs do exist, the multiple histories will interconnect, effectively integrating the parallel universes into a unified family and facilitating travel between them. In this instance, quantum mechanics permits the establishment of as many connected universes as there are variant outcomes of the time traveler's actions. So you *can* travel back in time to kill your grandfather, because in another universe, the one you traveled from, your grandfather will remain alive to conceive your father."

"Yes." Gabriel sucked in her cheeks. "Whenever I looked into the future, I saw multiple probabilities; the farther into the future, the more probabilities there were and the wilder they became."

"Wilder?" Julia asked, fascinated.

"Improbable. Mammoths roaming round in Siberia, the greenhouse effect suddenly reversing, obscure politicians becoming statesmen, weird religions taking hold. I never looked too far," she added contritely.

Because death haunted those extremes, Julia completed privately.

"Had you looked back in time, you would have seen that same multiplication of alternatives," Cormac said. "That is what Edward hoped to see."

"What?" Gabriel asked sharply.

"To look in the past."

"You said Kitchener was developing a neurohormone to perceive CTCs, not to look into the past," Greg said.

Cormac's smile was wintry. "But don't you see, that's the same thing. Edward theorized that CTCs are the basis of psychic ability."

Greg and Gabriel exchanged a glance bordering on pained anxiety. "What made him think that?" Greg asked.

"These microscopic holes through space-time are too small for physical objects to pass through, so he suggested that they facilitate the exchange of pure data. Your mind, Mr. Mandel, is quite literally connected with billions, trillions, of other minds, a vast repository of visual images, smells, tastes, and memories. This so-called psychic trait in certain humans is no more than a superior interpretation ability; you can make sense of our cosmological heritage, filter out the scream of the white noise jumble, pick over the bones."

"If that's true, then how could I reach as far as I can? You said these CTCs are microscopic."

"Indeed, but there are so many of them. If you go down one of these wormholes, back in time for that fraction of a second, move an infinitesimal distance, you will be able to find another CTC at its terminus, perhaps several, and that connection will allow you to extend another increment farther outward. You understand? It is like a chain, appallingly convoluted, that accounts for the limits in range you experience, but a clear link nonetheless, stretching across infinity and up and down eternity."

"But I could see into the future," Gabriel said. "How could these CTCs produce that effect? You said they go back in time."

"They do. But the *now* we are in is the past of the futures you perceived."

"Yes," said Gabriel, though she sounded unconvinced.

"However, by itself, looking into the future isn't sufficient to prove the existence of CTCs. Psychic is such a prejudicial term, you see; people have always laid claim to the power of foresight. But if CTCs exist, then the past should be available on an equal basis. Edward hoped that by producing a neurohormone capable of opening up the past in the way that precognition opens up the future, he would make a case for microscopic CTCs that would be irrefutable. There could be very few alternative explanations."

"Julia?" Greg's voice was dead, devoid of all inflection. Everyone looked at him. "What was the result of the analysis on those ampoules Eleanor gave you?"

She had some trouble forming the words; her throat had dried up as soon as she started thinking about the implications. "The laboratory said it was a themed neurohormone, sharing some characteristics with the standard precognition formula. But it's not a type they were familiar with."

"Edward succeeded in formulating a retrospection neurohormone?" Cormac asked with a feverish note of hope.

"Looks that way, doesn't it?" Greg was staring at Gabriel. Julia saw she had gone quite white, her hands were trembling slightly.

"No," Morgan said. He didn't use a loud voice, but the authority he conveyed was final. He took hold of Gabriel's hand. "You're not infusing it."

"Who else can?" she answered. "My temporal ability is a proven one."

"You are proposing to use it?" Cormac asked; he blinked owlishly at Gabriel. "Why? We don't even know if it works, all Edward's records were erased."

Julia cursed under her breath. It was a perpetual mystery to her how someone as smart as Cormac could be so oblivious to the problems of life itself. "If it enables us to look into the past, we can use it to see who killed Kitchener," she told him, using the strained tone reserved for making company division managers wish they'd never been born.

Cormac opened his mouth to speak, then glanced at Gabriel, blushing furiously. "I . . . I'm sorry. I wasn't thinking. This whole series of events has been extremely stressful . . ." He trailed off.

"I'll infuse it," Eleanor said.

"No bloody chance!" Greg snapped.

"Why not? These themed neurohormones are designed to amplify single psi traits. Anyone with even a faintly psionic ability should be able to infuse one. And you always say I'm sensitive."

Greg's face darkened. "That's hardly a qualified, objective opinion."

"What have we got to lose? If it doesn't work, there's no disaster; we simply carry on the investigation as before. If it does work, we find out who the murderer is."

It was quite peculiar; Julia was watching Greg gather himself for a tirade, desperately trying to think of some way she could defuse the situation before it degenerated into a vicious personal row. She knew from past experience just how forceful Greg could get when he was really upset. And Eleanor was just as bad. Both of them complete stubborn-heads. But something happened, because Greg suddenly gave Eleanor a perplexed, almost awestruck, stare and sat back limply in his seat, his anger visibly draining away.

"What is it?" Eleanor asked. She was frowning at his behavior.

"Nothing."

Which Julia didn't believe for a second.

"You mean you don't object?" Eleanor said, suspicion charging her voice.

He gave her a lame grin. "No."

"Oh."

Julia looked at Morgan for guidance, but all he could manage was a confused grimace. She couldn't think what had made Greg change his mind so abruptly. The mood swing had struck him so swiftly she was tempted to call it a revelation.

"If Gabriel's precognition is any example, we'll need to do this at Launde Abbey itself," Greg said. "You'll have a job trying to focus on the temporal displacement of a location outside your immediate area. Right, Gabriel?"

"Right."

"Okay, two points. Well, three actually. I'll use my empathic ability to monitor your attempt, or at least try to. I want you fitted with a somnolence inducer; that way, if anything does go wrong, I'll sense it and simply send you off to sleep until the neurohormone wears off."

"Good idea," Eleanor said. She seemed relieved that Greg was taking it seriously.

"Gabriel, I'd like you there as an adviser. You too, Doctor, if it's no trouble."

"I will be happy to attend," Cormac Ranasfari said stiffly.

"Finally, we can't really exclude Vernon Langley or his team; I suggest we don't try. But I want him to bring Nicholas Beswick with him."

"Why?" Julia asked.

"You'll see tomorrow. Or at least I think you will."

15

AN AGITATED FLEECE OF CLOUD was stretched over the Chater valley the next morning, an easterly wind scattering meager curtains of drizzle across the slopes of Launde Park. The water flowing over the bridge was down to a couple of centimeters when the EMC Ranger splashed over it. Greg drove up past the series of lakes, hopeful that this time he might remember. Disappointed once more.

Maybe Vernon would have pulled something out of the police records by now.

Eleanor sat in the passenger seat, gazing out at the desultory stone-gray drizzle. She had been silent for most of the journey, his espersense revealing the pensive timbre of her thoughts, although she was careful to keep a neutral expression on her face.

He turned off down the loop of drive toward the Abbey.

"You know exactly what I'm thinking," he said. "Which means there's no point in my saying it. So, I'll say it anyway. I didn't really want you to do this, and if you want to pull out, I won't stop you."

She leaned over and gave him the briefest of kisses. "So why the dramatic about-face yesterday?"

"Because . . . well, you'll see in a minute."

"Sounds intriguing. Is it going to make me change my mind?"

"No. Quite the opposite, actually."

She gave him another of her penetrating stares, then turned back to the window.

One thing, he was going to be bloody glad when this was over, and no messing. When the snap of intuition had hit him in Julia's study yesterday, it was tough not to simply say it out loud. Then this morning he had lain on the bed with belly muscles cold and hard in anticipation as he watched her getting dressed.

She had gone through the big chest of drawers taking out a couple of blouses along with her underwear; then she'd started rummaging around the racks in the wardrobe. Two skirts were removed, and she went through the usual procedure of comparing them in the thin light coming through the window. He'd never noticed before how long it all seemed to take. In the end, she had slipped into a lime-green blouse and a full-length cotton flower-print skirt, with a walnut-colored fleece-lined sweat jacket that came down over her hips.

"Good enough for you?" she had asked tartly when she zipped up the front of the jacket.

"Sure." He hadn't realized how obvious his stare had been.

The two white vans belonging to the forensic team were parked in their usual places outside the Abbey; three police cars from Oakham and a blue Ford that had brought Gabriel and Ranasfari were drawn up alongside. They were the last to arrive, as he'd intended.

Eleanor pulled her jacket hood up and allowed him to take her arm as they walked to the front door. The roses along the Abbey's façade looked very scraggly now, sodden and beginning to rot. A uniformed bobby standing in the porch gave a quick salute as they hurried in out of the damp.

There were a lot of people milling around in the hall, the familiar figures of the CID team, Gabriel and Ranasfari standing together along with Ranasfari's bodyguard. The physicist was in earnest conversation with Denzil Osborne. A couple of uniformed bobbies made up the complement.

Greg spotted Nicholas Beswick standing at the foot of the stairs, hands shoved into the pockets of his jeans, his elbows sticking out at awkward angles, avoiding eye contact, trying to go unnoticed amid the hubbub of small-talk. The affection he felt at the sight of the boy was spontaneous; he wanted to go over and put a hand on his shoulder, reassure him everything was going to be all right. There was something oddly appealing about someone so timid.

He watched Nicholas very closely as Eleanor greeted the others in the hall. The boy turned around to see what was going on, full of reluctance. Then he caught sight of Eleanor. His brooding expression twisted into shock, then outright fright. Both hands lurched upward, almost as though he was warding off a punch. "You!" It came out as a mangled yell. He took an instinctive pace backward and tripped on the bottom step, sitting down jarringly.

Everyone in the hall froze, staring at him. Color began to rush into his cheeks.

Greg went over and offered him a sympathetic arm. "She was your ghost, wasn't she?" he asked gently.

Nicholas struggled to his feet, still staring thunderstruck at Eleanor. "Yes, but look, she's real now. She's alive."

"No messing. Allow me to introduce you; this is Eleanor, my wife."

Nicholas gave him a wild, trapped look. "Wife?"

"Let me explain," he said kindly.

"About time," Eleanor grumbled in his ear.

"You knew all along," Eleanor said, hovering between anger and bemusement. Undecided.

"I guessed all along," Greg temporized. And Lord preserve us if she decides on anger.

They were sitting on the circular bed in Nicholas's room. All the furniture was still in place, but swathed in plastic sheeting, embargoed by the forensic team, although there had been no need for the wholesale dismantling exercise that had occurred in Kitchener's room.

Nicholas had claimed the chair behind the desk, the translucent plastic rustling at each tiny movement. He had shrugged off his reticence as Greg explained his hunch about the ghost and the retrospection neurohormone. Asking questions, making observations. Almost behaving like a regular person.

Ranasfari was sitting on the window-seat in a virtual trance state. One hand stroked the stonework absently. Greg wondered what ghosts Launde had conjured up for him.

Gabriel had listened to him explain with a smile blinking on and off. She had assumed that knowing air of elder-sister tolerance he remembered so well.

Vernon, Amanda, and Denzil were grouped together in mutual confusion, attentive but saying little, swapping moody, baffled glances.

"You are saying this looking-back notion has already worked?" Amanda asked.

"No," Greg said. "Just that the retrospection neurohormone will work. I had some reservations at first, you see."

Eleanor's hand squeezed his leg playfully. "You wait till I get you home, Gregory."

"But . . . oh, I don't know." Amanda's arms flapped in expressive dismay. "You really think this drug is going to let you look back and see who murdered Kitchener?"

"She has pervaded the correct tau coordinates," Nicholas said. "I saw her. Dressed exactly as she is now."

Amanda's eyebrows shot up.

Probably never heard him speak unless he's been spoken to before, Greg thought.

"So what would happen if Eleanor doesn't take the neurohormone?" Gabriel asked. Her whole attitude was pure wickedness. "We know it works, so why don't we give it to someone else? Vernon here, he's a likely lad and it is his investigation."

"Behave," Greg said. The others wouldn't be able to tell how serious she was. Gabriel took some getting used to. He'd known her for close on sixteen years, through the good times and the bad, and he wasn't sure he really understood her. Made for interesting company, though.

"Perfectly legitimate question." She affected injured innocence. "Nicholas says he saw her, so what would happen if she doesn't go?"

"You and your paradoxes," Eleanor muttered.

"Nothing would happen," Ranasfari said. "As I explained yesterday, quantum mechanics eradicate any inconsistency. The ghost that Nicholas witnessed originates from a universe in which Eleanor will infuse the neurohormone. There are others in which she does not."

"Another me," Eleanor said wonderingly.

"This version does me fine," Greg said. But there was an image in his mind he couldn't shake free: a million Eleanors saying yes and infusing the neurohormone, another million pandering to Gabriel's whim, and refusing. Universes torn asunder. And never the twain shall meet.

Eleanor smiled at him, hand gripping tighter.

"Well, what's it going to be, then?" he asked.

"Oh, I'll infuse it, of course." She looked at Nicholas, her smile turning impish. "I'm sorry I'm going to startle you last Thursday night."

"That's all right." His eyes shone adoringly.

Greg had the uncomfortable thought that Eleanor and Nicholas were actually both the same age. Only chronologically though, an evil voice said inside his mind.

Eleanor lay down on the bed and let Denzil fit the somnolence-induction loop round her head. A pearl-white tiara with a coil of cable connecting it to a slim, oblong box of blue plastic. It reminded Greg of the neural-jammer collars at Stocken. The technology was the same.

"You should be able to reach down the landing into Kitchener's bedroom without any trouble," Gabriel said. "I could tell what was going to happen to a general area about a kilometer across. Or if I fixated on a person, I could track him three or four days into the future even if he went to Australia."

"She used to fixate on a lot of men," Greg told the room at large. Nicholas started to giggle.

"Bugger you, Mandel."

"I'll be happy if I can just manage to find the Abbey last Thursday," Eleanor said.

"You did," Nicholas said. "Or you do, I don't know which."

"Shall we just get on with it?" Eleanor said.

Greg could feel the nerves building in her belly. "Okay." He sat beside her, plumping up a pillow, then took her hand. Her grip was strong, in search of reassurance, of a rock of stability.

Denzil handed him the somnolence-induction box. There were three buttons and a small liquid-crystal display on the front. A column of black numbers changed occasionally below a row of symbols he didn't recognize.

"I've preset it," Denzil said. "Press this button and she should be under in five seconds."

"Right." He rested his forefinger lightly over the button, hoping to God he wouldn't have to use it.

Gabriel held up an infuser tube. "You want me to do this?"

"Please," said Eleanor.

Gabriel bent over her, face sober and professional, and pressed the tube to her neck, just over the carotid.

"Keep your eyes closed," Gabriel instructed. "You'll be seeing enough visions without trying to untangle optical images as well."

Eleanor's eyes closed and she clamped her jaw shut, facial muscles hard as stone. Greg ordered a secretion—gland thudding away like a second heartbeat—and joined her in the country of the mind.

Eyes closed, blockading the sleet of photons into the brain's reception center, a tide of starless night engulfed him. Eleanor's mind rose silently into the void, a gas-giant as seen from one of its innermost moons. Vast and heavy. Thought currents swirled, individual strands showing pink, white, and ochre-red, like meandering stormbands, curling round each other to produce complex interlocking vortices. Stains of trepidation bled up out of the deeper psyche, dissolving into the surface thoughts, quickening the rhythm.

Relax, he told her.

The mind's superficies quaked in surprise, sending out distortion ripples.

Greg?

Yeah. Why, who did you think?

Just remember this is all new to me.

I haven't experienced this sort of affinity many times myself.

Oh. Greg? I think I can see the bedroom. My eyes are still shut, aren't they?

He snatched a fast look. *Yeah, they're shut.* He let his own mind relax into passivity, a pure receiver. That eerie phosphorescent cloud-scape lost cohesion, filming over with watery streaks of alien color. When he studied them closer, they resolved into walls, furniture, people, himself. He was still sitting on the side of the bed. Gabriel was stuck in a ridiculous posture; mouth open, hands captured in mid-gesture.

You are smiling, Eleanor said.

I've just seen me as you see me. It's interesting.

The room is all still, like a hologram.

Yeah. Now, what I want you to do, very slowly, is hunt round for a watch, and just imagine yourself sliding toward it. Got that?

No problem.

The perception focus shifted, curved out and upward an eagle in flight, heading for Gabriel's wrist. Her watch was a plain silver band with dry scarlet numbers flush with the surface, as if they were floating on a lake of mercury.

Nine forty-seven, Greg read. *About eight minutes ago. Okay, now can you see anything around the fringes of the room?*

Like what?

A lack of definition, something like the blurred multiple you get right at the edge of a mirror.

No. Nothing like that.

Okay. Pull back from the room, the opposite of when you zoomed in on the watch.

Ah, yes.

The image flowed, rushing past so fast he thought he could feel the wind of its passage. Yet the walls, the furniture, the fittings, they all stayed in the same place. Darkness fell, siphoning out every shade of color. In the night sky outside the window, stars traced sparkling arcs across the heavens, flickering in and out of existence as blankets of cloud churned past at supersonic speed.

Very good, he told her dryly, *but can you stop?*

The vertiginous motion slowed. Halted. It was dusk, a paltry smattering of rain leaking from bleak clouds. The room was deserted, its frost of plastic sheets glimmering a dirty indigo.

Bloody hell, said Eleanor. There was a dazed quality to her thoughts, almost like giddiness. *I did it, Greg. The past!*

Yeah. Yesterday evening, I think. How are you standing up?

Okay. There's this feeling of pressure. Inside, you know? Like I'm pushing against something.

If it ever gets to be an effort, then stop. Right away, Eleanor. Don't try to tough it out.

Okay.

Any sign of alternatives yet?

God, no, Greg. This is bad enough.

Just asking. Now let's go back to the night of the murder. One week, Thursday night, midnight, or as close as we can get.

All right.

The room surged around him again.

They stopped a few times, watching Denzil or Nicolette come in and run hand-held sensors over the furniture and carpet. Sometimes they would bag an item up and take it out.

Last Friday was a blur of activity, with as many as seven or eight people crowding in at once, whizzing around. The sheets of plastic crumpled up, shrinking, vanishing, leaving the chairs and tables exposed again.

Night closed in.

Here we go, Eleanor said.

He could sense the tension, and the effort, in her mind, thoughts stretched as taut as an athlete's sinew.

Nicholas Beswick was sitting at the desk, absorbed with the dense sapphire graphics slithering through his terminal's cube. Erratic moonbeams were raking the parkland outside.

You were right about Nicholas, Eleanor said. *He does need looking after, doesn't he?*

Yeah. I like him.

Me too.

This ought to be about the time when Rosette and Isabel traipse off to see Kitchener. Move in to the bedside cabinet, we'll have a look at the clock.

The perception point drifted downward until it was level with Nicholas's head. Surprise scrawled across his face, eyes widening.

He can see me!

Greg could sense her startled thoughts as Nicholas opened his mouth to emit what must have been a gasp. There was no sound. Perturbed, Eleanor started to pull away, the image slowing. Graphics in the cube moved with increasing sluggishness until they finally froze.

This is what we came for, he reminded her.

Sorry.

She had moved directly above Nicholas when animation returned to the scene. Nicholas jerked round frantically in his chair, searching about. After a moment, the tension seemed to evaporate from him; he rubbed his hands over his eyes and typed a code into the terminal. Then he stiffened, his head turning slowly until he was looking at the door.

This is it, Greg said. *I want you to try to follow Rosette and Isabel down to Kitchener's bedroom, okay?*

Do my best.

Nicholas had walked over to the door. Greg watched him gathering up the courage to turn the handle.

As soon as the door opened, Eleanor glided through it, staying near the ceiling and looking down. Rosette was wearing a green silk kimono. Isabel was just in her bra and jeans; her raw sexuality was devastating.

Rosette said a few words to Nicholas, then both girls left him behind as they walked down the gloomy corridor. Greg didn't like the stricken expression on Nicholas's face, not one bit. The boy was far too young to have his heart broken so cruelly. But then, when is a good age?

That poor boy, Eleanor said.

No messing.

The two girls exchanged furtive whispers as they headed for Kitchener's room. Both of them looked guilty.

Hope you choke on it, Greg wished them silently.

Kitchener was wearing white cotton pajamas. He greeted both girls with an effusive smile. The old man gestured a lot, Greg saw, arms constantly on the move. Rosette and Isabel were both kissed exuberantly. Some of their chirpiness had returned.

The first thing Rosette did was to go over to a bedside cabinet and take out an infuser tube. It was gold-plated, the size of her middle finger. She applied it expertly to Isabel's neck.

Wants to get her cloudsailing before she says anything about Nicholas to Kitchener, Greg thought.

Isabel wriggled sinuously out of her tight jeans as Kitchener sat himself down in a big armchair beside the bed. His eyes never left her; Isabel moved into Rosette's embrace, where her hair was stroked, cheeks caressed. More than anything, it looked like she was being soothed, calmed like a skittish animal.

Tell me, Gregory, exactly how much of this do you envision watching?

He sensed she wanted to make a joke of it, but the mental tone fell terribly short. In a body a long way away, anticipation was building like a static charge along his spine. He had said he couldn't envision what kind of man would commit such barbarism; now he was going to be shown the atrocity in its entirety.

A naked Isabel stood at the side of the bed facing Kitchener, her head tipped back slightly, eyelids fluttering, hands rubbing insistently up and down the outside curve of her hips. The old man's eyes traced over her figure as he sipped a glass of port. Rosette began to kiss her throat with provocative tenderness, tongue licking at the curves and hollows of flesh. She descended along the cleft between Isabel's conical breasts, on to the flat expanse of belly, hungry now, her hands clasping the smaller girl's buttocks. Isabel's mouth parted to sigh, her eyes and soul shining by the light of syntho's icy fire.

Take us ahead to when they leave, Greg said.

Isabel lay back on the sheets, spreading her limbs wide, torso flexing sensually. Rosette dropped her robe and climbed onto the bed, slowly lowering herself onto Isabel.

Eleanor's focal shift accelerated the two squirming figures into hazy smears. The third figure rose from the chair and joined them. In combination, the trio had that same rarefied blur as a dragonfly wing.

The girls left at twenty-seven minutes to three. They were leaning against each other, Rosette with her arm thrown protectively around Isabel. The smaller girl was drowsy, a lifeless smile of satisfaction on her lips. Kitchener snoozed on the bed, white hair askew.

How are you coping? Greg asked.

That feeling of being squeezed, it's much tighter now.

Okay, let's shift forward a little then.

The door opened at eighteen minutes past four. Nicholas Beswick walked in.

"Greg!" The voice encompassed anguish and dread, finishing with a tiny whimper.

He heard it, actually heard it, the force breaking through the neurohormone's isolation.

No no no, her mind cried.

Stay with it. Keep centered, Eleanor. You must keep your mind centered here.

But Greg!

I know. It might not be him. Just a few minutes more, that's all, please.

He'd said it, but he didn't believe it.

Nicholas was wearing a brown apron, naked underneath except for a pair of underpants. His right hand gripped a thirty-centimeter-long carving knife.

Through a clammy chill of disbelief, Greg watched the boy walk over to the bed. He put the knife down on the cabinet and picked up one of the pillows. Kitchener stirred briefly. Nicholas lowered the pillow onto the old man's face.

Greg, oh Greg, stop him.

I can't, darling. I can't.

Kitchener woke at the very end, scrawny limbs thrashing about. Nicholas's teeth were bared in a feral smile, biceps standing proud as he kept the pillow in place. The feeble scrabbling stopped after less than half a minute. Nicholas didn't lift the pillow for another ninety seconds. After that, he put it back with the others at the head of the bed, smoothing out the wrinkles with the edge of his hand.

He looked down at Kitchener, head bowed almost reverently, then crossed himself. It took him two minutes to methodically unbutton and remove the old man's pajamas, folding them neatly and placing them on the armchair. When he was finished, he straddled the corpse across its hips. The tip of the knife was brought to rest just above the belly button, dullness of the well-worn metal contrasting against the now etiolate skin.

Nicholas leaned forward, pressing down with all his weight. The knife penetrated smoothly, almost up to the handle, and he began to move it forward, up the chest, in a rough sawing motion.

16

IT WAS TRULY A CELL now. The door remained locked, even when Nicholas knocked on it. Meals, interviews, and his lawyer; that was all it opened for. And the trip to the magistrates' court.

The police had taken him there on Friday morning, twenty-four hours after Eleanor Mandel had tossed about on the bed in his room at the Abbey, opening her eyes to reveal abject revulsion, and rolling over to throw up on the glossy polythene sheet covering the carpet. It was the look she had given him that wounded him the most, the absolute horror, as if his very presence could contaminate her soul. And she'd been so nice to him before, so friendly, not seeming to notice his embarrassment at the shock her appearance had triggered. Girls didn't normally treat him like that; he was either nonexistent or an object of pity, sometimes of scorn. He was secretly a little bit in love with Eleanor; she seemed so forthright, able to cope with life. She was also staggeringly pretty, even though thinking that was disloyal to Isabel.

The words had come stammering out of her mouth as she gagged, Greg hugging her shoulders, protective and concerned. "He did it. Jesus, he didn't even blink." She sucked down some air, wiping a sticky thread of vomit from her lips. "What are you?"

That was when her mad eyes found him, their stare an almost tangible force tightening round his throat.

Something shivered inside him then, enervating his legs. The cold, terrible certainty that she must mean him. She was accusing him!

"Who?" It was spoken by half the people in the room. He may even have joined in. He couldn't remember.

But she said nothing. Just glared, her ragged breathing the only sound. Then Greg's stare was added to hers, calm and hateful, and Nicholas felt his face reddening even as the clamor of bewilderment inside his skull made him blurt: "What? What? What have I done?"

"He did it," Greg told the detectives. His voice had gone husky, saddened more than anything.

Langley had looked at Nicholas, then at Greg, then back again. "Him?" he asked incredulously. "Beswick?"

"For Christ's sake, put some handcuffs on him," Eleanor rasped. "If you'd only seen what he did . . ."

Greg's arm tightened around her. She had started to tremble.

"But you interviewed him," Vernon Langley said. "You cleared him."

"I told you when we started that I'd never seen that kind of mind before, didn't know what to look for. Well, now I do. He's completely cracked, won't even admit it to himself. Jesus, he was fucking inhuman back there."

"No," Nicholas said. But nobody appeared to have heard him. "No. I didn't. I didn't do that."

"Are you sure?" Langley asked Greg reluctantly.

"Yeah. It was him."

"No," Nicholas said. "No."

Amanda Paterson and Jon Nevin had somehow moved to stand on either side of his chair. He glanced up at them, face pleading. "I didn't."

"Is there any proof; solid proof, I mean?" Langley asked. "Can we test the clothes he was wearing?"

"I can do you one better than that," Greg said. "I can show you where he left the knife."

"I didn't do it!" Why wouldn't anyone *listen?*

"It's downstairs, in the kitchen," Greg said.

"We checked the kitchen," Amanda retorted indignantly.

"Not all of it."

"You two"—Langley signaled his colleagues—"bring him with us, and keep an eye on him. I don't want any sudden sprints across the park."

"I'll stay up here," Eleanor said shakily.

"Me too," Gabriel said.

"Okay," Greg said. He patted Eleanor's shoulder. "I'll be back straightaway."

She nodded weakly, hunching in on herself as though she were freezing.

Nicholas felt Jon Nevin's hand on his forearm. He didn't protest.

His strangely leaden limbs needed all the help they could get to rise out of the chair. Gabriel had gone to sit beside Eleanor, the two of them with their heads together, murmuring quietly.

In the kitchen, Greg walked straight over to the iron range. "It's in here." He pointed to the copper bedwarmer hanging on the wall. "He hid it when he was burning the apron."

"Don't touch it," Denzil said. He and Nicolette cleared the kitchen table, covering it with a broad sheet of polythene. They put on thin yellow gloves and gingerly took the bedwarmer off its hook. The three detectives crowded round as Denzil opened it; Nicholas couldn't see.

Langley turned around, his face struggling against an expression of loathing. "Nicholas Beswick, I am arresting you on suspicion of the murder of one Edward Kitchener."

"No!"

There was a long knife in the bedwarmer, its blade snapped off at the base so that it could be wedged into the tarnished copper basin. The handle was rolling loose in the bottom. Both were stained black with dried blood.

"You do not have to say anything at this time, but anything you do say will be taken down and may be used as evidence against you in a court of law."

His hands were jerked behind him. Rings of cold metal constricting his wrists. The *snick* of the locks.

"I didn't do it."

They were deaf, immune to any words he said. They also detested him. He had never known that before. People so rarely paid him any attention at all. In the first few days after the murder, the Oakham police had treated him with a slightly puzzled indulgence, as if he was some kind of foreign animal that they didn't know how to feed properly.

But after Nevin brought him back from the Abbey, it had been different. The word had gone out in advance. Off-duty officers had stood in doorways as he was marched through the station corridors to his cell. He'd cringed from the way they regarded him, the naked revulsion, expecting to be set upon and beaten. There had been no violence. The cuffs had been tight though, his hands swelling and swelling until he thought they would burst. They had left them on for ages, long after his fingers had gone numb, dragging out the booking procedure.

He had caught one glimpse of Isabel just as he was being put into the cell. Nevin was finally taking off his cuffs in the corridor outside when she emerged from the cell she'd been sleeping in. He cried out her name and she turned. That was when he saw her face was like all the others.

"I didn't do it."

Her head tipped to one side, faintly nonplussed, at one remove from the world, like the times he'd seen her performing a difficult equation. There was virtually no sign of recognition.

"*Please*, Isabel. I didn't."

Her bottom lip turned down, as if it was all of no consequence, trivia. She was still utterly beautiful.

A shove between his shoulder blades sent him stumbling into the cell as blood and feeling shot violently back into his hands. The door slammed shut, lock whirring.

He had thought the night was bad, alone with near-suicidal confusion, the memories of the allegations. Eleanor's desolated face, the knife with its awful scale of black flakes. Nobody would talk to him; the sergeant who brought his evening meal simply slammed the molded tray down on the table, mute.

Somehow, somewhere, there had been a terrible mistake. He had waited and waited for them to find out where they had gone wrong, to come back and set him free. He didn't want an apology, he just wanted to be allowed to go.

Gnats and small ochre moths emerged from the dead air-conditioning grille, fluttering silenty around the biolum panel. The light stayed on all night. Nicholas huddled into a corner of the cell below the high window, drawing his knees up against his chest, a blanket around his shoulders, waiting, waiting—

Friday morning was worse, thrusting him from the extreme of his solitude into the bedlam of the media madhouse.

Oakham magistrates' court sat in the castle hall. It was a short drive around the park from the police station. Nicholas spent the whole time in the car with a blanket over his head.

He felt the car judder to a halt. The door was opened. Shouts were flung at him.

"Did you do it?"

"What was your motive, Nick?"

"Were you on drugs?"

He tried to screw himself into the car seat. A hand like steel clamped onto his arm, pulling him out.

"Come on, son, this way, keep looking at your feet, there's no step."

The questions merged into a single protracted yowl. He could see tarmac below his trainers, then pale yellow stone. The light changed. He was inside.

The blanket was pulled off.

He was in a short passage with whitewashed walls, narrow and cramped. Lisa Collier was standing in front of him, the two of them at the center of a jostling circle of police.

"I didn't do it," he told the lawyer frantically. "Please, Mrs. Collier. You have to believe me."

She ran a hand back through her hair, giving him a flustered glance. "Nicholas, we'll get all that sorted out later. Do you know why you're here?"

"Where are we?"

She groaned, shooting Langley an evil stare. "Christ. All right now, this is the magistrates' court, Nicholas. They've convened a special sitting. The police want you remanded in their custody for seventy-two hours so they can question you. You haven't officially been charged with anything yet, all right? There is no basis for me opposing the application. Do you understand?"

"I didn't do it."

"Nicholas! Pay attention. We're not entering pleas today. They'll just remand you in custody and take you back to the station. There will be a lawyer present at every interview. Now do you want me to continue as your lawyer?"

"Yes, yes please."

"All right, now look, we're going right in. You won't have to say anything, just confirm your name when the clerk of the court asks. Got that?"

"Yes. My name."

"Fine. Now look, there's no way I could have the press excluded, so it's a bit of a circus in there. But they're not allowed to take pictures in an English court, thank God. Do your best just to ignore them." She looked him up and down, then rounded on Langley. "There's no bloody excuse for him turning up in this state. It amounts to intimidation in my book."

Langley tweaked his tie. He was wearing a neat gray suit. "Sorry, we were a bit rushed for time back there. Won't happen again."

"You're damn right it won't," she said in disgust.

The ancient hall was so bizarre that Nicholas was convinced he'd fallen into some *Alice in Wonderland* nightmare. There were six thick stone pillars supporting a high-vaulted ceiling; each whitewashed wall was covered in horseshoes of all sizes, ranging from the genuine article up to elaborate gilded arches a meter and a half high. Most of them had crowns on top, all were inscribed with the names of the nobles, dignitaries, and royalty who had presented them to the county.

The court itself only took up the front half of the hall, an enclosure of tacky wooden pew benches painted a light gray, a defendant's box at the back. Behind that was an open space about twenty meters square.

When he walked out of a small door in the front wall, handcuffed to Jon Nevin, he nearly faltered. There were about a hundred reporters packed onto the rear floorspace. Every one of them was staring at him.

He was led to the box facing the magistrates' bench, ever conscious of those greedy eyes boring into the back of his neck. The proceedings were short, formularized. He remembered to acknowledge the clerk; then all he had to do was listen to the police lawyer read his request from a cybofax. Flowery legal language, grotesquely arcane. Why did the world stick to these rituals?

His lawyer was on her feet, saying something. Nicholas could hear the shuffling feet behind him, smothered coughs, gentle persistent clicking of fingers on cybofax keys. He could feel the curiosity they radiated, a silent demand to know, as though they had more right than the police and the lawyers.

"Granted," said the chief magistrate, a middle-aged woman from the same stout mold as Lisa Collier.

The officials on the pew benches were standing up, talking together in low tones.

"Come on," Nevin said.

Nicholas got to his feet, and halted. The reporters held still, collectively silent, expectant. Nevin was tugging insistently at his arm, equally uncomfortable at being in the limelight.

"I didn't do it," Nicholas said. They would listen, at least. Nobody else did. "I didn't."

There was no answer.

He was frogmarched out by Nevin and two uniformed constables.

The ignominious blanket, the car ride. He could hear rain pounding on the streets.

The cell. Confinement, keeping the monster behind bars, protecting the public from his savagery. Old men could sleep safer in their beds now. This time the walls were closer together, the ceiling lower. At night they closed around his body, embedding him in cold black marble.

Rosette was a natural channel star, the graceful curves of her face bewitching the camera, promoting her regality, betraying no sign of her contumacy. She was standing on the pavement outside the Oakham police station, beside a long, modern navy-blue Aston Martin driven by a chauffeur. The front passenger door was open and she held herself poised to enter, doing the reporters a big favor by indulging them. The sunlight caught her fair hair to perfection as it fell on the shoulders of her leaf-green jacket.

"The baby is due in seven months," she said. "I expect to have it in a London clinic. But it will definitely be born in England, Edward would have wanted that. He was a great nationalist."

The baby was news to Nicholas. He accepted the fact numbly. There ought to have been some tiny part of him that was glad, but he couldn't find it. Was that the kind of cyborg mind that enabled people to butcher their murder victims? But if he was so insensitive, why had he fallen in love with Isabel? It was most puzzling, his mind.

"How long had you and Kitchener been having an affair?" a reporter asked.

"I think I fell in love with Edward when I was eight years old. I remember seeing him on a channel science 'cast. He was so impassioned about his subject, and yet he always allowed his sense of humor to shine through. He was so much more alive than any other person. It was after that I concentrated on science subjects at school. He remained in my thoughts, an unsung mentor, an inspiration. Being invited to study at Launde Abbey was a lifetime ambition."

"He was a lot older than you, did that pose any difficulty, some tension?"

"His mind was fresher than anybody's on this planet."

"Do you know what he was working on when he was killed?"

"A stardrive, darling. A faster-than-light stardrive. Edward was going to give us the galaxy. He believed in human destiny, you see. It was to be his gift to all the peoples of the world, so none of us would ever be restricted and oppressed again. We could spread our wings and truly blossom amid the splendor of the night."

"It wasn't a stardrive," Nicholas said to the cell's flatscreen. Typical of Rosette to go for theatrical effect.

"A working stardrive?" Even the reporter was skeptical.

"Oh, yes. He was studying the loopholes allowed for in general relativity. With his genius and Event Horizon's money, I genuinely believe a starship could have been built. Now, though, who knows?" Her face was haunted by poignancy. "I have a dream that one day our child will take up the banner of his father's work and bring us that liberation Edward sought. Perhaps it is only a small hope, but I believe, after all this, that it is a hope to which I am entitled."

"How do you feel about the murder?"

"Grief, nothing but unending black grief. The other students have been tremendously kind and supportive; we've cried together, and we've laughed about the good times Edward gave us. You see, darling, he would have scolded us terribly if we hadn't laughed. It's the way he was. So alive, a celebration of life."

"And what about Nicholas Beswick?"

Rosette came right out of the flatscreen to stand in the cell beside him. A tall, glorious Venus; a goddess wronged and brutally vengeful. "I hope he is raped by every demon in hell."

Nicholas turned over, shuddering, and buried his head under the blanket.

He must have fallen asleep, because Lisa Collier was shaking him, her face anxious. "Are you all right?"

He blinked against the pink-white light of the biolum panel directly overhead. "Yes. Fine, thank you."

"Good. I brought you some clothes." She dropped his maroon shoulder bag on the floor by his cot. "Vernon Langley is going to start the interviews this afternoon. At least you can turn up looking respectable on the AV recording."

"Oh." Nicholas's mood damped down.

She shifted her skirt about and sat at the foot of the cot. "Now then, Nicholas, the idea of a police interview is to keep recapping the same ground until you start becoming inconsistent. That can happen only if you don't tell the truth in the first place. Which brings us to the murder and what happened that night."

"I didn't do it."

"Nicholas, please; just hear me out. If you choose to tell the police you are guilty, we can enter a plea of temporarily diminished responsibility. Kitchener was a tetchy old man, inflicting verbal abuse for several months; you'd just found out your girlfriend was sleeping with him. You certainly had enough cause to lash out, a judge would probably be sympathetic with that, although I have to say the actual nature of the crime would probably eradicate any possibility of a light sentence."

Nicholas took a deep breath. "Mrs. Collier, why will nobody listen to me? I didn't do it."

Her watery eyes were placid. The sort of gaze his mother used to rebuke him with when he was small. "Nicholas, there is a vast amount of evidence amassed against you, there is both motive and opportunity. And, Nicholas, your fingerprints were all over the knife. On top of that, we have the evidence from the Mandels. I might be able to nullify their testimony, or at least blunt it slightly; the courts are still pretty hazy on interpreting psychic visions. But at the moment, it adds up to a very convincing case in the prosecution's favor. I have to tell you, the way it stands, the jury is going to find you guilty."

He sat perfectly still, turning the novel concept over in his mind.

They, Mrs. Collier, the police, the reporters, Rosette, all truly genuinely believed him guilty. Against all logic and reason, he was going to have to accept that.

"Rational discrimination," Kitchener had said once, "that's the dividing line between savagery and civilization. We've thought ourselves up to where we are today, out of the caves and into the skyscrapers. Bodies never have mattered a toss, you are your mind."

So if you're smart, Nicholas told himself, think your way out of this, prove your innocence. Images of that night cluttered his vision again. He'd seen the girls, he'd cried on the bed, he'd heard the screaming. And that was it, the total. There was nothing new, no key out of the logic box. If he could just show he had been in his room sleeping, force them to accept that. But how?

"Will you still be my lawyer if I plead not guilty?" he asked cautiously.

The cybofax she held in her lap bobbed up and down as her hands twitched unconsciously. "Yes, Nicholas," she said slowly. "I'll still be your lawyer."

"Thank you. I want to plead not guilty."

"Nicholas, I will still be your lawyer if you admit you did it. A lot of people say they are innocent because they are too ashamed even to acknowledge their crime to their lawyer. It works against them in the long run."

"I understand. I didn't kill Edward Kitchener."

"Right." She unfolded the cybofax and touched the power stud. "Nothing like an uphill struggle."

It was the first frivolous thing he'd ever heard her say. He almost asked if she believed him, but fright that she might say no held him back. "I suppose I need an alibi," he said.

Her right eyebrow arched. "Yes. Have you got one you didn't want to mention before? We know Uri and Liz were together in his room all night. Were you with one of the other girls secretly, Isabel or Rosette? You said Rosette did make a pass once."

"No."

"Now, don't get me wrong, I have to ask. Cecil Cameron?"

The Nicholas of yesterday wouldn't have understood the question. Today he thought it was simply a logical thing to ask. "No."

"How about a channel program, were you watching one?"

"No."

"The other students, is there a likely candidate who would frame you?"

"No. Look, I know it's not much, but Greg Mandel said I didn't do it. At least that's what he thought after he interviewed me. Doesn't that count for something?"

"Hmm." She paused, her expression distant. "I can probably use any vacillation of opinion on his part to call his psychic ability into question. But that really isn't anything like good enough to get you off. It's the knife, you see. Have you any idea how your fingerprints did get on that knife?"

"No." And now he thought about it, really thought; the fingerprints were impossible to explain away. The murderer creeping into his room and wrapping his hand round the handle as he slept? Unlikely; he didn't sleep that deep. Drugged? But the police had taken a blood sample.

The first stirring of panic began to creep over his body, like immersion in a cold lake. Suppose he couldn't prove it? Suppose a jury did find him guilty?

There was a state he could sometimes reach, one where the external world became a fable, irrelevant, leaving his mind free to concentrate on problems. Like yoga, he always imagined, except yoga was for contemplating spiritually. He dealt with hard facts, that was all he knew.

"I didn't do it," he said. "Therefore somebody else did. That somebody also framed me. And framed me in a spectacularly clever fashion. He even has me doubting. So in order to prove my innocence, we have to find him."

He knew Lisa Collier thought he was crazy. Mood changes, from retarded child to punctilious cyborg. Who wouldn't think it of him? It didn't matter, because she could never get him out, not by herself. But she was a lawyer, she had to abide by the rules.

"Yes, Nicholas," she said. "But how are you going to find him?"

"I'm not. I'm not good enough, I admit that. We need a professional detective."

"Who?"

"The best." It was so simple, sneaky, perhaps even underhanded, but practical. And the last thing he could afford right now was scruples. At the back of his mind, the manes of Edward Kitchener nodded approvingly. He relished the endorsement. Nicholas Beswick finally twigging human emotions, what made people tick. How about that? "And I know how to get him." He gave Lisa Collier a rapturous grin and pointed at her cybofax. "Am I allowed a phone call?"

THERE WAS A CRESCENT OF dun-colored fur partially obscured by
the tall spires of grass on the edge of the orange grove. The picture
dominated Greg's optical nerves, fed to him by his Heckler and Koch
hunting rifle's targeting imager. A fan of nearly invisible pink laser
light swept across his vision from left to right, producing minute
sparkles when it touched the dewdrops clinging to the grass. A grid
of red neon materialized in its wake. The discrimination program cut
in, analyzing the shape behind the tussock from the tenuous laser return, and the grid began to fold, shrink-wrapping around the rabbit.
Cartoon-blue target circles materialized and Greg shifted the rifle
slightly, his finger on the trigger.

The infrared laser pulse drilled the rabbit straight through its cra-
nium. A tiny wisp of blue smoke curled up from the five-millimeter
circle of singed fur. It rolled over without any fuss.

I hope it fucking hurt, you fur-clad locust bastard.

Eleanor hadn't slept much for the last few nights. Snuggled up in
his arms, quiet face shaded by sporadic glints of moonlight. She
wouldn't voice her fear, so he kept his peace and let her hold onto
him for the reassurance she needed.

Even he, hardened by Turkey and the inevitable propensity toward
murderous fury by some squaddies, had found Nicholas Beswick's
profanity difficult to exorcise.

A rabbit was squatting on its haunches at the base of an orange
sapling, wet nose sniffing the air, whiskers vibrating eagerly. Thanks
to the target imager's enhancement, its melancholic liquid eye was
thirty centimeters across. The laser speared the shitty little vermin
straight through its pupil.

How his espersense could miss such an abominable maelstrom of
insanity in the boy's unruly thoughts was impossible to comprehend. He *knew* minds, from the sad and pathetic to the most dangerous brooding psychotic. He could tell, instantly. Engaging Liam
Bursken's mind had been a horrendous feat—there had not, could

never be, any common ground with such a demented personality. But Nicholas Beswick, he was so appealing; with his timidity and rashness, a humorous reminder of Greg's own adolescent shortcomings, an amplification of all the angst and fervor so wonderfully endemic to that age group.

I *liked* him.

To be so wrong, so blind, was to invite a fundamental disbelief in his entire empathic ability. But there had been nothing, no hint.

Two rabbits were frolicking together, a big old buck and a frisky doe. He took the buck first, then cooked the doe's brain as she quivered in confused distress.

Fifteen down, a thousand lucky charms to go.

Ranasfari had been badly upset. Shocked that a fellow Launde acolyte could do such a thing to his old mentor. Hiding his grief behind a flimsy gruffness, saying he was perturbed that there had been no alternates in the past. It didn't fit the theories. Gabriel had taken him home, for once subdued and sympathetic herself.

The alternative-universe notion was something Greg had clung to for a brief hopeful moment. Suppose Eleanor, untutored, on her first neurohormone infusion, had wandered sideways into one of those timelines where Hitler's grandchildren governed the world from a gleaming Berlin metropolis, where their Nicholas Beswick was certifiably deranged. That would give him the out he needed, that would mean he could carry on liking the boy.

But, as always, there was the knife. Here, in real time, real history. And so many peripheral details: the timing of the shower, Isabel, a possible complicity with the Randon Company, the implausibility of a tekmerc penetration mission.

Only his ineptitude had failed to spot the psychopath. And intuition. It couldn't be him, not that boy.

He slammed the rifle over to rapid fire and sent a barrage of laser pulses streaking into the long grass. Rabbits toppled over, small flashes of orange flame mushroomed from the dead undergrowth. The entire warren began to flee, bounding through the grass. Half the ground seemed to be on the move.

Fucking vegan rodents.

"Greg."

It was Eleanor's voice.

He plucked the target imager's monocle from his face, a ring of skin around his eye tingling as the glass peeled free. He had been leaning against the wooden fence around the grove for some support. Now he saw it had left smears of damp algae across the front of his jeans and black sweatshirt. He made a half-hearted attempt to brush it off, holding the rifle in one hand.

There were three people with Eleanor, walking toward him from the farmyard. A middle-aged couple and a young girl. The woman had a heavily drawn face, sun-ripened and lined; her curly brown hair flecked with lighter strands, not yet gray, but on the verge. Her ankle-length dress was a dun brown, a decade-old Sunday best, smart but fading slightly, the hem and neck fraying. Her husband—they were so obviously married—was as tall as Greg but leaner, arms and legs sinuous, large laborer's hands mottled with blue veins. He was in a suit, trousers with a multitude of iron creases down the front, never quite managing to fold down the same line, his gray shirt open at the neck, showing a vee of tanned skin. The color of his thinning sandy red hair was unpleasantly familiar. Greg felt his churlish anger at the rabbits fading out, opening up a dark void inside.

Eleanor gave him a soulful look, her hands gripped in front of her, fingers knotting in agitation. "Greg, this is Derek and Maria Beswick." She gave the girl a hesitant smile. "And it's Emma, isn't it?"

The girl nodded shyly, her eyes wide, staring at Greg's hunting rifle in trepidation. She was about thirteen, holding her mother's hand. Not a pretty girl, nor destined ever to be one, Greg thought; her cheeks were too plump, a bulge of cellulite already building up under her weak chin. Her blouse and skirt looked handmade, a green-and-blue print, with a generous cut.

Back when Mindstar was starting up, the specialists and generals had talked of educing a teleport faculty in some recruits. Flipping around the world, from country to country, over oceans, in zero time; just think of a location and *zip*, you were there. Like all the rest of Mindstar's brochure promises, it had come to nothing. Which was a great pity, because right now Greg wanted to be anywhere else on the planet—a dungeon in Teheran, an African republic police cell.

"We've come about our boy, Mr. Mandel," Derek said. There was a lot of strain in his voice. Derek Beswick was a proud man, not used to entreating strangers.

"I'm sorry," Greg said miserably. "It's all out of our hands now." Shit, and he'd called Nicholas a wimp.

"He didn't do it, Mr. Mandel," Maria said. "Not my son. Not those terrible things the channels are saying. I don't care how upset he was over a girl. Nicholas would not do something so awful."

Greg wanted to shout: I saw him, I watched him do it! But he couldn't do it, not to a woman like Maria Beswick.

"I don't understand the things Nicholas talks about, Mr. Mandel," Derek said. "The physics and the cosmic phenomena things in deep space. He tries to tell us when he comes home, but it goes over our heads. We're sheep farmers, that's all. But I was so proud of that boy, my boy, when he got to university, a scholarship . . . he was going to better himself. He wouldn't have to get up at five every morning, like me. He could make something of his life. And when he left home, it was about the worst year anyone could go to university, with all the troubles and everything. But he struggled through. Then he got asked to go to Launde. Blimey, even I'd heard of Dr. Kitchener. Nicholas worshiped that old man. He didn't kill him."

"There is a lot of evidence."

"Nicholas told us you were a detective," Maria said. "That you were the best detective in England. He said that at the start you didn't think he did it. Is that right?"

"It . . ." It's not that simple! "Yeah."

The Beswicks exchanged a pathetically hopeful glance.

"Please, Mr. Mandel," Derek said. "We can see you've got the farm to tend and everything, and we're not nearly as important as Julia Evans, but could you just keep investigating the case for us? Just one more day would help, something might turn up, something that might exonerate him. Jail would kill Nicholas as sure as a death penalty. He's a gentle boy."

Your gentle son stuck a knife into the belly of a sixty-seven-year-old man and ripped him in two.

"We'll look into it for you," Eleanor said. Greg gaped at her.

"Do you mean that?" Emma asked. She was looking up at Eleanor, chubby face filled with apprehension. "Really mean it?"

"Yes, I mean it. There are one or two ambiguities that need clarifying in any case."

Derek and Maria consulted each other silently.

"Anything," Derek said. "Anything you can turn up would help. That lawyer woman, Collier, she seems to think Nicholas is guilty."

"It's been a good year for us so far," Maria said. "Really, very good. There are a lot of our ewes pregnant, the lambs should fetch a good price in the spring. So could we possibly pay you in instalments, please?"

Greg just wanted to curl up and die. "There's no fee," he managed to say.

Maria's face stiffened. "We're not asking for charity, Mr. Mandel."

"It isn't charity," Eleanor said quickly. "We can't accept a fee, not legally. You see, we're still on the Home Office payroll for the Kitchener case, and we remain on it until the trial is complete. How we run the investigation is entirely at our discretion; that's in the contract we signed."

Maria looked as though she was about to protest, but Derek took her hand, squeezing a warning.

"Where are you staying?" Eleanor asked.

"I have to get home," Derek said. "With the sheep, and all. But Maria's got a room in a bed-and-breakfast house in Northgate Street, not far from the police station."

"Okay, we'll be in touch."

"What did you go and tell them that for? I can't believe you said that!"

"Calm down," Eleanor said.

"Calm down? That boy is a psychopathic killer, and you tell his parents we're going to get him off?"

"You don't think that."

"Don't think what?"

"That he did it," she said patiently.

"I saw him fucking do it! And so did you!"

"That's not what I said, Gregory. I said you don't think he did it."

"I . . ." He covered his face with his hands, massaging his temple. She was right. Eleanor was always bloody right, especially when it came to what went on in his mind. Bloody unfair, that was.

He gave her a reproachful smile. "How do you do that?"

"I had a good teacher."

"What ambiguities were you talking about?"

"The fact that your espersense didn't catch the guilt."

"Psi isn't perfect," he said automatically.

Eleanor just looked at him.

"Yeah, all right. I couldn't miss something that obvious. But we saw him do it, though."

"We, or rather I, had a vision that he did it. That's all."

"A vision that was backed up by finding the knife, complete with fingerprints."

"If Nicholas was framed, then of course physical evidence would be planted to corroborate the vision."

"So how did you come to have the vision if it wasn't what actually happenened?"

"I don't know. Another type of psychic who can make the images seem real? A fantasyscape artist? You tell me. You're the expert."

"I never heard of any psi ability remotely like that back in Mindstar, not even rumors. The nearest would be eidolonics, but no eidopath could work up an image like that."

"You hadn't heard of a retrospection neurohormone until last Wednesday."

"No, Eleanor. I just don't believe it. It's too complicated. The killer tried to obliterate all trace of the retrospection neurohormone, remember? He never intended for anyone to use it. So there was no way he would have some psychic on permanent standby in case we infused it to see what happened that night. Besides, I would have sensed another psychic operating at Launde, and don't forget Nicholas saw you. That's the real clincher. He actually confirms you went back there to witness the murder. And every event we observed that night matches the statements that the students gave."

"Everything except the murder."

"If everything else was kosher, why should the murder be any different?"

"So you do think Nicholas killed Kitchener?"

Greg thought about it, all the doubts and internal tension that had been twisting him up for the last few days. His intuition was the root, strong enough to keep goading against all logic; like a rash developing in his synapses, an itch you just couldn't scratch. Superstition, people called it. So what it boiled down to was, did he believe in his ability? In himself? "Oh, *shit*." He took a breath. "No, I don't think

Nicholas did it. I know he didn't. But how the actual murderer pulled that stunt with him and the knife . . ."

"Come on, Gregory, never mind the details; start thinking. Assume you are right and Nicholas is innocent, what do we do next?"

"Prove he was framed. Find the real killer."

"See? Simple."

"Thank you. Do you have any equally impressive suggestions for how we go about it?"

She gave him a pensive look, tapping a forefinger on her teeth. "The first thing to do is find out if someone else had a motive to kill Kitchener. Once we know who, we can start to work out how he pulled it off. What does your intuition say?"

"Good question."

He ordered a small neurohormone secretion and reached inward, down into that pool of silent solitude at the core of his mind, rooting around for convictions. The only time his intuition had tweaked him during the case was when he saw the three little fish lakes at Launde. Which he had then gone on to conveniently forget about once Eleanor had infused the retrospection neurohormone. The lakes, they were the reason he doubted Nicholas's guilt.

But why?

Greg switched the flatscreen in the lounge to phone function as he relaxed back into the settee. He flicked through the notes stored in his cybofax until he found the number for Stocken Hall and squirted it at the flatscreen's 'ware. A secretary answered and tried to fob him off when he asked for James MacLennan, so he did his conjuring trick with his cover-all Home Office authority again.

"You're getting to be a real bully with that," Eleanor observed. She was sitting in a chair opposite the settee, out of the flatscreen camera's pickup field.

"Yeah; feels pretty good, too." He spread his arms out along the back of the settee with a gratuitous sigh.

She gave him a derisory sneer in return.

Stocken Hall's director appeared on the flatscreen, sitting behind his desk, wearing a smart blue suit. The picture-window's blinds were closed, as before.

"Mr. Mandel, I believe congratulations are in order." A warm smile displayed perfect teeth.

"The police have a suspect in custody, yeah."

"Excellent news. Perhaps the media will now leave us all alone."

"Don't bet your life on it."

"No. Quite. How may I help you? My secretary said you were calling on urgent Home Office business."

"Tell you, I need some information on the way the human brain works, specifically in your field: memories. That suspect, Nicholas Beswick, he actually managed to fool me. Now he's the very first person ever to have done that. As you can imagine, that makes me a little nervous."

"Indeed. By fooling you, do you mean your empathic sense?"

"Yeah. He said he didn't do it and I believed him. You see, there was no evasion, no duplicity. Any mention of that murder should have triggered his memory of the event, and with it all the usual associated feelings of guilt and remorse. But I didn't sense a single suggestion of iniquity or deception. His mind appeared utterly normal, nothing at all like that cracked monster Liam Bursken."

"I see. It does seem somewhat strange."

"What I want to know was: is it possible he could deliberately make himself forget? I mean, even subconsciously; just wipe the murder from his brain? Beswick is still claiming he hasn't done it, even though the evidence is pretty conclusive. I remembered you mentioned some kind of drug that would cause forgetfulness."

MacLennan's smile downgraded to serious concern. "Scopolamine. Yes. It's a common-enough substance, extracted from plants. Normally it's employed as a mild sedative, and for travel sickness. And it has been used for ritual purposes for several centuries. But large doses can be used to induce what amounts to a trance state. There have been many cases of scopolamine intoxication identified, especially in Latin America. It was quite a problem with criminal gangs around the turn of the century. If you mix it with a tranquilizer, it can be used to render someone completely docile. And it can be administered with a simple spray. Under its influence, people would hand over their valuables, even empty their bank accounts from cash dispensers and then have no recollection of ever doing so. It went out of fashion when the cashless society became firmly established, of course. Money transfers can be traced too easily these days."

"Jesus." The idea was unnerving: muggers armed with aerosols instead of knives and you knew nothing about it until hours later when you returned to reality in a daze. He didn't like that at all—maybe it had happened to him already, how could he tell?—but then, drugs always left him cold. "Could Beswick have taken scopolamine to forget the murder?"

"Oh, no. It doesn't work that way. Besides, I'm sure the police would have found traces of it in his blood."

"Yeah." But would they have checked for it? He loaded a note in his cybofax to ask. "Is there any other method you can think of?"

MacLennan gazed inward for a moment. "As I told you, memory is perhaps the least explored facet of the human brain. However, there are two types of natural amnesia that I would offer as possibly applicable in this case."

"Two?"

"Indeed. A condition called transient global amnesia allows its victims to perform their usual jobs and maintain their standard behavior pattern. But at the end of the day, they cannot remember any event that occurred. An example: you could hold a long and intricate conversation with them, to which they would respond entirely within character; yet if you asked them about it the next day, they would have no recollection of ever having talked to you."

"Is there any way of telling if someone suffers from it?"

"The person concerned will often realize for himself—especially if the condition is acute. It's not very common, but a doctor would certainly be able to recognize the symptoms from what the patient was describing."

"Right, thank you." Greg made another series of notes on his cybofax. "What is the second condition?"

"Trauma erasure, which is even rarer; but there have been recorded and verified instances where it has occurred."

"Such as?"

"A certain type of event, often violent or terrifying. Something literally so horrible that the mind simply rejects it. A particularly bloody road accident, for instance. People have witnessed them and then failed even to remember they were present when questioned afterward. Police often have to deal with mugging victims who cannot remember what their attacker looked like even though they were in close proximity for several minutes. But it would have to be an extraordinarily potent event to trigger such a radical neural mechanism."

"An event like a grisly murder?"

"Yes, indeed. If Beswick acted in a fit of rage, he may not have been able to accept what he had done once that rage wore off. Under those circumstances, trauma erasure may have been enacted. I offer no guarantees, of course; I am merely generalizing."

"I understand. If Beswick is suffering from one of these types of amnesia, would a psychiatrist be able to coax the memory out?"

"I don't know. It depends on how deeply it is buried. You say it is beyond even subconscious recall?"

"Yes."

"Hypnosis may give us access. But from what you've said, I wouldn't hold out much hope. In any case, it would definitely be a long-term project. There would be a lot of counseling required first, he would have to want to recover the memories."

"I see. Well, thank you for your time."

"Not at all."

"We're not exactly helping our cause, are we?" Eleanor said after MacLennan's mechanical smile vanished from the flatscreen.

"Not a lot, no. But at least we know it is theoretically possible for Beswick to forget he murdered Kitchener. It explains why my interview with him was such a dud."

"It might help rebuild your confidence in your psi ability, but it's also a terrific bonus for the prosecution," she said indignantly.

"Hey, you were the one that told his parents we'd continue the investigation."

"Yes, I know." She folded her arms like a rebuked child, giving the carpet a moody stare.

He squirted another number at the flatscreen. Amanda Paterson answered, and once more the Home Office authorization was deployed like a blunt weapon.

"I know what I'd tell you to do with it," Eleanor murmured airily, her gaze switching to the ceiling.

The flatscreen showed a slightly out-of-focus view of the Oakham CID office, a couple of detectives working at their desks, the situation screen on the back wall still displaying a map of the town and surrounding countryside. Vernon Langley's face slid across the picture as he sat down facing the camera. "I was interviewing Nicholas Beswick," the detective admonished.

"How's it going?" Greg asked.

"Would you believe the little cretin still says he didn't do it? We've even shown him the report on the knife, confirming the fingerprints on the handle are his. He claims he was framed. Christ, and they all said he was the smartest of the bunch. Makes me wonder what the thick one must be like."

"Yeah, it's a real poser, isn't it?" Greg had felt like this once before, demob happy. When it didn't matter what he said to the brass, they couldn't do a thing about it. This time it was the sheer audacity of going up against ridiculous odds, confounding authority, that was producing an anarchistic glee.

"What did you want?" Vernon asked suspiciously.

"Several things. First, I'm following you up on the search program. You haven't squirted over the results yet."

"What search program?"

"For previous incidents at Launde Abbey."

"But the investigation is over."

Eleanor's hands traced an imaginary bulge over her belly; she grinned broadly.

"It ain't over till the fat lady sings," Greg said cheerfully.

"Hell, Greg, we're busy."

"Did you run the search program?"

"I think so. Hang on." Vernon started typing on a terminal keyboard, his face resentful.

Like old times, Greg thought.

"We ran it; there is no record of any previous police call-out to Launde Abbey. Satisfied?"

Greg closed his eyes, considering options. "How far back do those records go?"

"Four years. The station 'ware was infected with a virus when the PSP fell, the memories were wiped. A lot of stations had the same problem; they were all plugged into the Ministry of Public Order mainframe when the circuit hotrods crashed it. The fallout was pretty severe, they did a lot of damage. And of course the People's Constables weren't exactly sticklers for procedure. There was very little in the way of back-up memories. One of the reasons the New Conservatives formed the Inquisitors is because so many records from that time were lost."

"And you were transferred to Oakham after the PSP fell, weren't you?"

"Yes."

"Okay, I want you to check with everyone who was stationed at Oakham during the PSP decade and ask them if they remember anything about Launde Abbey."

"I see," Vernon said in a voice that was excessively polite.

"Good. I shall be coming into town to interview Beswick again this afternoon. You can tell me what you found then." He referred to his cybofax. "There is also Beswick's blood sample."

"What about it?"

"All my file says is that it doesn't contain any syntho. There are no tabulated results."

"So?"

"Did you run any other drug tests?"

Vernon started his laborious typing again. "There were some traces of alcohol, that's all."

"Call the lab. I want to know if they checked for anything else, and if so, what they found. And even if they did check, I want a full-spectrum analysis run again on both the urine and blood samples today. Tell them to look for scopolamine."

"Scopolamine?"

"Yeah."

"Anything else?" The irony hung poised like a scalpel.

"I need to look at Beswick's medical records. If you could have them ready when I come in, please."

"Is this official, Greg?"

"Very."

"In connection with the Kitchener murder?"

"What else?"

"All right, I'll phone the lab." The image blanked out.

"The first thing he's going to do is phone the Home Office," Eleanor said. "Find out if you're still authorized to shove him around like that."

"Yeah," Greg mumbled. He patted the settee and she came over.

"Second thoughts?" she asked. She sat with her legs up on the arm-rest cushions, back resting against his shoulder.

"Not just yet." He put his arm around her. "You do realize we are basing all this on my one tenuous belief that there was some incident in Launde's past. If it does turn out nothing happened, then all we've done is to bury Nicholas even farther."

"You really can't remember what it was?"

"No. I'm even starting to question if I did remember anything. It seems so fragile. Maybe it's me who's suffering from transient global amnesia."

"Not you, my love."

"Thanks." He tapped out a number on the cybofax and squirted it at the flatscreen.

"Who are you calling now?"

"Julia. I want to make sure my Home Office authorization isn't withdrawn. And then she can request a search through all the national and international commercial news libraries for me, going back, say, fifteen years just to be on the safe side. See if we can find out what happened at Launde that way."

Eleanor giggled. "A search through fifteen years' worth of every library's news files?"

"No messing. She ain't broke."

"She will be after that."

18

J ULIA KNEW SHE SHOULDN'T BE feeling so exultant, it wasn't gracious, but to hell with that for one long, sweet moment. Things were coming together just dandy. Maybe people were right when they called her a manipulator.

She was sitting at the head of the table in Wilholm's study. It was a wonderfully sunny Monday outside. For once, the windows were wide open, letting her hear the sound of querulous birdsong, a muggy breeze stirring the loose ends of her hair. She wore a sleeveless champagne-cotton blouse and a short aquamarine skirt, dangling her leather sandals right on the end of her toes.

There were twelve memox AV crystals lying on the glossy tabletop around her terminal, recordings of Jakki Coleman's show going back six months. Event Horizon's media research office had compiled them for her.

Caroline Rothman had delivered them that morning when she brought the usual stack of legal papers that required a signature. She hadn't said anything as she put them down on the table, but she must have known what they contained. Julia guessed the entire headquarters building was chittering with delight over Jakki Coleman's audacity, waiting for the inevitable counterstroke. This time they were going to be disappointed. It was too personal for threats of sanctions and financial blackmail screamed down the phone to the channel editor. This time she was going to be adult and subtle. But in the end, there was going to be just as much blood spilled, and it wasn't going to be hers. What better way to start the week?

Glowing with a strong amber hue in the middle of her terminal's cube was Jakki Coleman's bank statement. She could thank Royan for that; his patient tutoring had enabled her to worm her way around Lloyds-Tashoko's guardian programs last night, splitting their memory cores wide open. Of course it wasn't every hacker who had exclusive access to top-grade Event Horizon lightware crunchers to assist in decrypting financial security algorithms. To each their own . . .

She hadn't emptied the account, though; that was far too easy. Besides, Lloyds-Tashoko would know it was a hotrod burn as soon as Jakki complained; the money would be refunded, another point added way down the decimals on everyone's insurance premium. All she wanted was to look.

The figures burned with cold brilliance. The high-flying finances of a channel superstar laid bare.

Except we're not quite *so* valuable to the channel after all, are we, Jakki darling? Not if that's all they're paying you.

Beside each transaction was the creditor's code. A standard finance-directory search would take care of that. Julia set it up and watched identities wink into existence alongside the columns. She knew some of them: big-name companies, department stores, travel agencies, hotels. The rest, the unknowns, she plugged into another search program.

It was interesting to see what was there, and even more interesting to see what wasn't. Jakki Coleman didn't buy any clothes, not one single item in the last three years.

Julia clapped her hands in delight and slotted the first memox AV into the player deck beside her terminal. Jakki Coleman, six months younger, but looking just as antique, smiled out of the flatscreen above the fireplace. She was wearing a black two-piece suit with a bold mauve-and-green jungle-print blouse.

"For that fuller figure," Julia said to the flatscreen. She studied the style intently—the suit was either a Perain or a Halishan—and loaded a note into a node file, coded Jakki-Death. She moved on to the next show.

The last show the media office had recorded was the previous Friday's. There was Jakki in a black-and-white classical suit with an oversize side-tie. And herself, in her purple blazer and her long white skirt and her straw boater, with her hair pleated into a long rope, walking along a line of fit young men in dark-red swimming trunks, the team coach introducing her to each of them in turn. And afterward, sitting at the side of the pool while the squad went through its training routine for her.

"Dear Julia seems to have regressed to her school uniform today," Jakki said. "Now I remember why I was so eager to get out of mine after finishing lessons every afternoon."

"To get on your back and earn some money?" Julia asked the image sweetly. She flicked the AV player deck off and studied the results of JakkiDeath as they floated through her mind. She hadn't been able to identify all the makes of course, but approximately one-third of all the clothes Jakki wore on her show were by Esquiline. A lot of them even had the trim little gold intersecting-ellipses emblem showing, a lapel pin, or the buttons.

Product placement. Jakki's agent had done a deal with Esquiline.

She pulled a summary of the company from Event Horizon's commercial-intelligence division's memory core. Esquiline was a relatively new style house, aiming to follow in the footsteps of Gucci, Armani, and Chanel, with shops in every major English city—two in Peterborough—and just starting to expand onto the Continent.

Julia got Caroline to place a call to Lavinia Mayer, Esquiline's managing director, for her. *My office calling your office* was snooty enough to grab attention, and then there was the added weight of her name as well.

Lavinia Mayer was in her forties, wearing a lime-green jacket over a ruff-collar snow-white blouse. Her blonde hair was cut stylishly short. The office behind her was vaguely reminiscent of art deco, white-and-blue marble walls, building-block furniture. Impersonal, Julia thought.

"Miss Evans, I'm very honored to have you call us."

Julia decided on the idiot-rich-girl routine, wishing she had some bubble gum to chew just to complete the picture. "Yah, well, I hope this isn't an inconvenient time."

"No, not at all."

"Oh, good, you see one of my friends was wearing this truly super dress the other day, and she said it was one of yours. So I was thinking, you're a style house, do you by any chance supply whole wardrobes?"

Lavinia Mayer wasn't the complete airhead her image suggested, there was no overt eagerness; oversell was always a tactical error. She did become very still, though. "We can certainly coordinate a client's appearance for her, yes."

"Ah, great. Well, I'll tell you what I want. You'll probably think it's really silly, someone in my position, but I've been so busy this winter I really haven't had much chance to plan ahead for spring."

"That's perfectly understandable. I watched the roll out of your spaceplane myself. It's an inspirational machine. The amount of effort you must have put in is awesome."

"Yah, it is, not that I ever get any thanks. Everyone thinks it's the designers and engineers who do all the work."

"How preposterous."

"Yah, well anyway, the thing is, I've got about eighty or ninety engagements coming up in the next four months or so, and I need something to wear for all of them. It would be such a relief to dump the load off onto someone else, preferably a professional. I have so little free time, you see; this way, I might just scrabble a little more. It would mean a lot to me."

The corners of Lavinia Mayer's mouth elevated a fraction, the smile a talented undertaker would give a corpse. "Eighty or ninety?"

"Yah. Problem?"

"No." Her voice was very faint.

"Oh, I'm so glad." She pushed a twang of excitement into her voice. "Would Esquiline take me on as a client, then?"

"I will attend to you personally, Miss Evans."

"Oh, please, Julia to my friends."

She listened to Lavinia Mayer babble on about organizing a select Esquiline team to cater for her, when would it be convenient for them to call, what sort of engagements, did she have a particular look in mind? After a couple of minutes, she palmed her off onto Caroline to finalize details and sat back in the chair, rolling one of the memox AVs in her hands.

It would be interesting to see just how smart Lavinia Mayer was. The woman would never have clawed her way up to managing director without having some intelligence. An exclusive contract to clothe Julia Evans ought to be a prize worth killing for; the channel exposure time alone would cost millions if it had to be bought; then there were the socialite wannabes who would slavishly follow her.

If Jakki Coleman hadn't been dumped or brought to heel inside of two days, Lavinia Mayer was going to have her dream of world domination torn to shreds right under her pointy, over-powdered nose. To be rejected publicly—and it would be very public indeed—by Julia Evans would kill their fledgling reputation stone-dead.

Jakki would probably try to go somewhere else; after all, she couldn't afford to buy the *haute couture* her assumed lifestyle required. Julia would follow her, setting up checkmate after checkmate right across the board.

There was a subdued knock on the study door. Lucas came in. "Your guest has arrived, ma'am."

A warm buzz invaded her belly. "I'll be right down." Yes, this was one day where things were truly going right.

Robin Harvey's hands traced an intrigued line down the side of her ribcage before coming to rest lightly on her hips. "Try to hold your back straighter as your fingers touch the water," he instructed. "And stand so that you're balancing more off your heels."

"Like this?" Julia leaned back into him. Right out on the threshold of sensitivity, she could detect a minute tremor in his fingertips.

"Not quite that much." He let go abruptly.

Julia dived into the water, breaking the surface cleanly.

Her pool was a large oval affair at the rear of the house, equipped with high boards and a convoluted slide. There was a plentiful supply of colorful beach balls and lilos, a wave machine. The surrounding patio had a bar-and-barbecue area. It was all designed with fun in mind.

She surfaced and pushed her hair back. Robin Harvey smiled down at her.

She had noticed him on Wednesday in the England swimming squad line-up, a strong broad face, wiry blond hair, on edge at the prospect of meeting her. His powerful build, youthfulness—he was eighteen, a year younger than she—and that touch of awkward modesty made for an engaging combination. He was so much more natural than Patrick.

She had made a point of chatting to him during the training session. His stroke was the butterfly, and he enjoyed diving, though he claimed he wasn't up to a professional standard.

"Oh, gosh, I've always wanted to do that," she said guilelessly. "It looks so thrilling on the sportscasts, like ballet in the air. I don't suppose you could teach me some of the easier ones, could you?" She let a tone of hopefulness creep into her voice at the end. The lonely, precious princess not allowed a moment's enjoyment.

Turning down such a plaintive request from the team's sponsor wasn't a serious option.

"That was very good," Robin said as she climbed up the stairs. "You're a fast learner."

I was the Berne under-fifteen school's amateur diving champion. "That's because I have such a good teacher."

His grin was a genuine one. Julia liked it. She was going to enjoy Robin, she decided. At least with swimmers she had the perfect excuse to get ninety percent of their clothes off right away. That remaining ten percent ought to provide her with a great deal of fun.

She skipped off the top step and breathed in deeply. Robin's gaze slithered helplessly down to the swell of her breasts under the slippery-wet scarlet fabric of her backless one-piece costume. Bikinis always gave too much away, she thought; the male imagination was such a powerful weapon, you just had to know how to turn it against its owner.

"I'd like to try a back flip," she said.

"Uh, sure."

After they finished swimming, she showed him around the big conservatory that jutted out from the end of Wilholm's east wing. The glass annex had undergone a complete role reversal from its original function. Tinted glass now turned away a lot of the harsh sun's power, air conditioner units whirred constantly, maintaining the air at a cool two degrees Celsius. The team contracted to renovate the manor had sunk thermal shields into the earth around the outside, preventing any inward heat seepage. It was a segment cut out of time, immune to the warm years flowing past on the other side of the condensation-lined glass, home to a few rare examples of England's aboriginal foliage.

She led him along a flagstone path between two borders. Young deciduous trees grew out of the rich black soil on either side, their highest branches scratching the sloping glass roof. Streaky traces of hoarfrost lingered around their roots.

Both of them were in thick polo-neck sweaters, although Julia still felt the cold pinching her fingers. She rubbed her arms, shaping her mouth into an O and blowing steadily. Her breath formed a thin white ribbon in the air.

Robin stared at it, fascinated. Then he started blowing.

"Polar-bear breath," she said and smiled at him. He looked gorgeous with his face all lit up in delight.

"I've never seen that before," he said.

"You must remember some winters, surely?"

"No. They finished a couple of years before I was born. My parents told me about them, though. How about you?"

"I grew up in Arizona. But I saw some snow when I was at school in Switzerland. We took a bus trip up into the Alps one day."

"Lumps of ice falling out of the sky." He shook his head in bemusement. "Weird."

"It's not solid, and it's fun to play in."

"I'll take your word for it." He tapped one of the trees. "What's this one?"

"A laburnum. It has a lovely yellow flower at the start of summer, they hang in cascades. The seeds are poisonous, though."

"Why do you keep this place going? It must cost a fortune."

"I can't get into fine art; it always seems ridiculous paying so much money for a square meter of turgid canvas. And of course that whole art scene is riddled with the most pretentious oafs on the planet. I'll take my beauty neat, thank you." She pointed at a clump of snowdrops that were pushing up around a cherry tree. "What artist could ever come close to that?"

The conservatory always affected her this way, inducing a bout of melancholia. It was the timelessness of the trees, especially the oaks and ash; they were all so much more stately than the current usurpers. They made her cares seem lighter somehow. She was afraid she might be showing too much of her real self to Robin.

He was gazing at her again, quite unabashedly this time, thick hair almost occluding his eyes. "You're nothing . . ." His arms jerked out from his sides, inarticulate bafflement. "You're not what I expected, Julia."

"What did you expect?" she teased.

"I dunno. You come over all mechanical on the 'casts, like everything you do is choreographed by experts, every move, every word. Absolute perfection."

"Whereas in the flesh, I'm a sadly blemished disappointment."

"No!" He bent down and picked one of the snowdrops. "You should get rid of your PR team, let everyone see you as you are, without pretense. Show people how much you care about the small things in life. That'd stop all those critics dead in their tracks." He broke off and gave the flower a doleful look. "I don't suppose it'll happen like that."

" 'Fraid not. Nothing is ever that easy."

He tucked the snowdrop behind her ear, looking pleased with himself.

When she kissed him, he was eager enough, but he didn't seem to know what was expected. Her mouth was open to him for a long time before his tongue ventured in.

She was struck with the thrilling thought that he'd never had a girl before. After all, it took a lot of training and devotion to reach his level of swimming performance, a dedication that cost him every spare minute.

Her arms stayed around him as he gave her a delighted boyish grin. He had exactly seven days left to court her, then she'd have him. And this time she would be in charge in bed, so it would be a considerable improvement on the way it was with Patrick.

They rubbed noses Maori-style, then kissed again. This time he wasn't nearly so reticent.

The conservatory door was opened with a suspiciously loud rattle.

"Julia?" Caroline Rothman called.

Robin disentangled himself, looking extraordinarily guilty as Caroline walked around the end of the border.

"Sorry, Julia," Caroline said. "Phone call."

She wanted to stomp her foot in frustration. "Who?" Whoever, they were already dead.

"Greg. He said it was urgent."

She sat down at the head of the study table and jabbed a forefinger down on the phone button. The call was scrambled, she noticed, coming through the company's own secure satellite link. Greg and Eleanor materialized on the flatscreen. They were on the settee in their lounge, Eleanor at right angles to Greg, leaning against him, his arm around her. Perfectly content with each other.

The sight simply deepened Julia's scowl. She never shared such a homely scene with any of her boys. Not that she wanted to be stuck in all evening being boring, she told herself swiftly.

"This had better be truly astonishingly important," she told the two of them loftily. "I'm very busy."

They looked at each other, eyebrows raised, and looked back at the camera. "Doing what?"

They were so in tune, she thought despairingly, it wasn't fair. "Financial reviews," she said with a straight face.

"Sure," Eleanor crooned.

"What did you want?"

"Couple of things," Greg said. "First, I want my Home Office authority reconfirmed."

"What? Why?"

He gave an awkward grimace, which made her take notice. Something that could faze Greg was always going to be interesting.

"There are some aspects of the Kitchener case that I need to review, and what I don't need is a whole load of flak from Oakham CID right now."

"What aspects? Nicholas Beswick did it."

"It would appear so."

"You saw him. Both of you. You went back in time and saw him!"

"Yeah. Well. Tell you, my intuition is playing up about this."

"Oh." Greg placed a great deal of weight on his intuition. A foresight equal to everyone else's hindsight, he always said. She wasn't about to question that. Greg didn't act on idle whims. But— "Just a minute, there was the knife as well."

"Yeah. That's what makes this all so embarrassing."

"Julia, Beswick's parents came to see us this morning," Eleanor said.

"Oh dear Lord, that must have been awful."

"No messing," Greg said. "Look, Julia, just humor me."

She listened to him explain his hunch about an earlier incident at Launde and MacLennan's idea that some form of amnesia might be responsible for shielding any guilt in Nicholas Beswick's mind.

Julia requested a logic matrix from her nodes, her mind condensing what she was hearing into discrete data packages, loading them in. The matrix parameters were easy to define: assign all the case information to the two suppositions, that Beswick had committed the crime and forgotten it, and that some previous incident was involved. See what fits, what supports either notion.

"If it turns out there isn't anything to this incident of mine, then it was probably amnesia all along," Greg concluded glumly. "Which brings us to the second point. I'd like you to run a search program through every national and international news library to see if you can find a reference to Launde Abbey at any time during the last fifteen years."

"Oh, is that all?" Which was letting him off lightly; she could just imagine what Grandpa would say.

"Julia Evans, you yanked both of us into this investigation," Eleanor said. "We only did it for you. Just because it isn't working out all neat and tidy doesn't mean you're allowed to back out. You started it, you damn well see it through to the end."

Why was it all suddenly her fault? She wished she'd never heard of bloody Dr. Edward Kitchener. "I wasn't backing out," she muttered.

Eleanor nudged Greg. "You ought to ask Ranasfari if he can remember anything happening at Launde."

"Good idea," he said.

"Cormac was there over twenty years ago," Julia said.

"Yeah, but he kept in touch with Kitchener."

"Not through the PSP decade. He was working on the gigaconductor in our Austrian laboratory. Grandpa didn't want him mixing with the opposition. He was quite agreeable to the security regimen. You know what he's like, no personal or private life."

"Yeah, but I'll ask him anyway."

"Sure." The matrix run ended. Its results waited for her, not seen, simply present in the null-space that was the axon interface. There was no solution in connection with a possible past incident, insufficient data. But the matrix had thrown up one query though, an anomaly. "Greg, this idea that Beswick murdered Kitchener because he was so enraged about the old man seducing Isabel Spalvas, and then blanked it out later, how does Karl Hildebrandt and the Randon Company connection fit in?"

Greg and Eleanor exchanged another glance, puzzled this time.

"No idea," he said.

"We don't know for certain that Diessenburg Mercantile was involved," Eleanor said. "It might have been a coincidence."

When Greg opened his mouth, she laid a finger across his lips. "Coincidences do happen occasionally, you know."

"Yeah," he said unhappily.

"No," Julia said with conviction. "You don't know Karl like I do. He was anxious to talk with me, all to give me that one piece of advice: take you off the case. It was most deliberate."

"Does he have any financial or corporate interests outside the Diessenburg Mercantile bank?" Greg asked.

"No." She caught herself and pouted; it had been a reflex answer, she'd been scolded about that enough times by her teachers. "That is, I don't know. He's never mentioned any."

"Now I really wish I'd been there," Greg said. "Can you arrange a meeting, some kind of party?"

"I suppose I could invite some people around for dinner," she sighed. "But it's very short notice, he might suspect something, especially if you start quizzing him."

"Tough."

"I'll get on to it," Julia said. "Greg, do you really think there's a chance Beswick didn't do it?"

"There's something wrong, Julia, that's all I know."

"Good enough for me," she said lightly.

He winked.

She stared at the blank flatscreen for a long moment after the call ended. If nothing else, Eleanor had been right. She had dragged them into it, she had to see it through. Money and power always came with the price tag of obligation.

She pressed the intercom button. "Caroline, cancel everything for this afternoon. We've got work to do."

19

For once, the afternoon remained sunny. Eleanor could actually hear the Jaguar's air conditioner humming away as it battled the humidity. Greg had taken the EMC Ranger to scoot down to the Oakham police station, claiming the Jaguar would only antagonize the detectives further. Good excuse, she acknowledged a little enviously.

She actually enjoyed driving the big car: it really was disgracefully decadent, but like Greg, she always managed to feel guilty about it. There were still too many people on the breadline right now. She thought England in the nineteen-twenties must have been similar, when the barrier between the aristocracy and the workers was cast in iron and guarded by money.

A thriving giga-conductor-based economy should break down the polarization, like the internal combustion engine before it. Funny how the cycle of achievement and decay was almost exactly a century long. Though she doubted it would happen again. Surely this time we learned enough from our mistakes?

The A606 into Stamford was one of the better roads, but when she reached the town and turned off on Roman Bank, a street that ran down the slope toward the Welland, she heard the familiar bass grumble as the Jag's broad tires fought the mushy potholes. This part of the town was strictly residential, two-story houses with large gardens. Thick ebony stumps of horse chestnuts jutted up from the unkempt verge, wearing skirts of cheese-orange fungi. New acmopyle trees had been planted to replace them, already four or five meters high, silver-gray leaves casting long, black shadows.

At the foot of the slope she turned left, heading toward the town center.

Rutland Terrace was a solid row of three-story houses, two hundred meters long, perched strategically halfway up the side of the Welland valley to give the occupants an unencumbered view out across the storm-swollen river and the southern slope beyond. Tiny individual first-floor balconies sported overhanging canvas sun-canopies, striped in primary colors, providing a meager dapple of shade for the recumbent residents taking advantage of the weather.

She parked in front of Morgan Walshaw's house, halfway down the row. Despite a sleeveless dress chosen for its airiness, she started perspiring as soon as she climbed out of the car. The river's humidity lay over the town, pressing down like a leaden rainbow.

The small front garden could have been laid out by a geometrician, bushes and bedding plants standing rigidly to attention. A clematis had been trained up the front wall, producing a curtain of mauve dinner-plate flowers, broken only by the arched doorway and ground-floor window.

The black front door was opened by a security hardliner. Eleanor had encountered the type at Wilholm often enough now to recognize it: a young man in a light suit, attentive eyes, not a gram of spare flesh.

He showed her to the first-floor lounge. The air inside the house was still and relaxing, a coolness that came from the thickness of the old stone walls rather than modern air conditioners.

Gabriel came in from the balcony to greet her, wearing a simple silky blue-and-white top and skirt. Eleanor could never quite bring herself to accept that the woman was the same age as Greg. Even after all the counseling, the diets, and the fitness routines of the last two years, Gabriel remained stubbornly middle-aged. And prickly with it.

"What brings you to town?" Gabriel asked.

"Couldn't it just be to see you?"

"This trip isn't, no. And you ought to know better than trying to fool a psychic by now, even an ex like me."

They walked out onto the balcony and sat on the deck chairs Gabriel had set out. The fringe of the green-and-yellow awning flapped quietly overhead.

"I'm here because of the Kitchener inquiry," Eleanor said bluntly.

Gabriel's mask of politeness fell. "Bugger, now what?"

"Greg's intuition." She told Gabriel about the Beswicks' visit that morning.

Gabriel folded her arms across her chest, slipping down the curve of the chair's nylon. "If it was just the boy's parents protesting about how sweet and harmless he is, I'd be inclined to forget the whole thing, and ignore how excruciating it is. But Greg getting all worked up, that's different. There's a lot of people walking around today who would have been left behind in Turkey if it hadn't been for that cranky intuition of his." She opened one eye fully and gave Eleanor a close look. "Mindstar brass actually put an order in writing that he wasn't to use his intuition when he was assembling mission strategies. It wasn't a recognized psi faculty." The eye closed again, but her smile remained. "Dickheads!"

"Greg's sure this incident he remembers is tied in to Beswick and the murder somehow. Do you remember anything happening out at Launde Abbey in the PSP years? I can't, but then, we were kept carefully closeted away from the real world in the kibbutz."

"No, nothing. I was too busy trying to shut life out back then, remember?" She took a long sip from a glass of orange juice, staring out across the valley. Gabriel never, but never, touched alcohol these days, not even to be sociable.

"I also wanted to ask you about the past," Eleanor said. "I saw only one. There were none of these multiples that Ranasfari talked about."

"Ha! I wouldn't go around putting too much store in crap artists like Ranasfari and Kitchener if I were you. They don't know half as much about the universe as they make out they do."

"You don't believe in the microscopic wormholes, then?"

"I'm not qualified to give an opinion on the physics involved. But I think they're both wrong to try to provide rational explanations for psychic powers."

"You used to see multiple universes."

"No, I used to see decreasing probabilities. Tau lines, we call them; right out in the far future there were millions of them, wild and outrageous; then you start to come closer to the present and they begin to merge, probabilities become more likely, taming down. The closer you come to the present, the more likely they get, and the fewer. Then you reach the now and there's only one tau line left; it's not probability anymore, it has become certainty. That's why I'm not surprised you saw only one past, because there is only one now."

"Alternative futures, but no alternative past," Eleanor said, tasting the idea.

"The future isn't a place, don't make that mistake," Gabriel said sternly. "It's a concept. I've steered people away from hazards often enough to know. The future is a speculative nebula, the past is solid and irrefutable. Taken from the psychic viewpoint, anyway," she finished glumily.

"Then we really are in trouble, because Greg and I definitely saw Nicholas Beswick do it. I'd been hoping that I had somehow slipped sideways and seen an alternative past. That way, we would only have to explain away the knife. And it could have been a plant, a very sophisticated frame-up; those students do have high IQs, after all."

"Even if it had been an alternative past you saw, how could you explain finding the knife where you did unless Beswick put it there?"

"Because another student used the retrospective neurohormone and saw where the alternative Beswick put it. Does that make any sense?"

"Not much. If alternative pasts existed, why would you always see just that one?"

Eleanor let out a long breath. "Haven't got a clue."

"Now do you see why they stopped fitting people with glands?" Gabriel asked evilly. She poured some more orange juice out of a jug, filling a second glass and handing it to Eleanor.

"Yes. Thanks." Ice cubes bobbed about as she took a gulp. "I'm going down to the local newspaper office. It's the one that is most likely to have a record of anything happening at Launde Abbey. So we thought it would be best to give our search request the old personal touch just to make sure it's done properly. Do you want to come?"

Gabriel swirled the juice and slush around the bottom of her glass, staring at it morosely. "Yes. Morgan won't be home for hours."

Eleanor got to her feet and stood with her hands resting on the wrought-iron railing. The Welland was a vast, light-brown torrent obliterating the floor of the gentle valley, almost five hundred meters wide. Cobweb ribbons of dirty foam swirling across the surface showed her how fast the current was flowing. It couldn't even be said to have burst its banks; there were no banks, not anymore. The floodwater had swept them away years ago, as it had Stamford's ancient stone bridge and all of the town's riverside buildings. During the summer, the Welland died down to a slim silver contrail, and the mudflats on either side turned as hard as steel. The kids used it as the world's greatest skateboard park.

"You get on well with Morgan, don't you?" There had been a time when she thought Gabriel wanted Greg. It was only after she met Teddy that she realized all the ex-military people shared a strange kind of bond, almost a brotherhood.

"We fit well," Gabriel said. "He's hopeless around the house of course, so I'm needed here as well as in my advisory capacity to Event Horizon's security division."

Which was as close as Gabriel would ever come to voicing real feelings. "I'm glad."

"How about you and Greg? When are we going to see some little Mandels?"

"The farmhouse is more or less in order, and we've got all the groves planted now. It'll mean a long summer with nothing much to do."

"Greg did all right with you, better than most of us anyway."

Eleanor turned. Gabriel was staring moodily into the bottom of her glass.

"Thank you."

Gabriel grunted and swallowed the last of her drink.

The hardliner insisted on walking into town with them. His name was Joey Foulkes, and Gabriel treated him as if he were a small, anxious puppy. He accepted it affably enough, grinning at Eleanor when Gabriel's back was turned.

The *Stamford and Rutland Mercury* office was a five-minute walk from the house, situated in one of the older sections of the town, Sheepmarket Square, a small cobbled square just above the river. The offices must back onto the concrete-reinforced flood embankment, Eleanor realized; on one side of the building a narrow road ran right down a slope into the surging water. A fragile-looking red plastic fence had been thrown along the top, with a couple of council warning signs pinned to it. Four kids had ignored them to stand a meter above the river, chucking bottles and rocks into the water.

The building was made from pale ochre stone, like all the others in the heart of the town. The frontage was newer, a wall of copper-tinted glass showing misty outlines of an open-plan reception area behind. None of the furniture had been changed for years, and sunlight had bleached and cracked the wood varnish; the peacock-blue carpet was threadbare.

Eleanor got an *I know you* look from the girl behind the desk. Her name alone was enough to get them shown directly into the deputy editor's office.

Barry Simms was in his early forties, an obvious full-time data shuffler. Flesh was building up on his neck and cheeks, ginger hair had been arranged in an elaborate, but doomed, attempt to disguise its thinness. He had a quiet, almost weary, voice as he introduced himself.

Eleanor put that down to ingrained resignation. At his age, if he hadn't already made it out of a provincial news office, he wasn't likely to now.

"It's not about our coverage, is it?" he asked Eleanor. "I mean, you have to expect some interest if your husband is appointed to head the investigation over the heads of the local police."

"Detective Langley is, and remains, the investigating officer. Greg was never put in over him."

"Makes good copy though," Gabriel said smartly.

"There is the media ombudsman if you wish to complain," Simms said reproachfully. "I am obliged to provide you with his address. But I hardly think we were intrusive, certainly not after the pressure we were put under. Both our bank and the satellite company that handles our datatext transmission called us up to complain about unethical behavior. They said we shouldn't hound you. I don't like having editorial policy dictated to me like that, Mrs. Mandel."

"I think you and I are getting off on the wrong foot," Eleanor said.

"Guilty conscience," Gabriel muttered.

Eleanor gave her a hard stare. She rolled her eyes in defeat and folded her arms.

"I don't wish to complain," Eleanor said. "I would like the *Mercury*'s assistance in a peripheral matter."

Simms perked up. "Is this official?"

"I'm a private citizen."

"So I can report what you say? Without any hassle?"

"I'll do you a deal, Mr. Simms. You help me, and if it turns out to have any bearing on the Kitchener case, I will brief you ahead of any police statement. Interested?"

He stared at her for a moment, reporter's desire to know warring against having restrictions imposed. "All right," he said. "I thought it was all finished anyway. Nicholas Beswick did it."

"It looks pretty certain, yes."

"So what do you want from me?"

"A search through the newspaper's files. I want to know if there have been any other newsworthy incidents at Launde Abbey, specifically in the period between four and fifteen years ago."

Simms looked thoroughly disgruntled. "Typical of my luck. Mrs. Mandel, if you had come in here asking for anything else, we could have obliged. But that is out. Sorry."

"Your files can't be that confidential," she said. "I only want to see what was previously reported."

"It's not a problem with confidentiality. You don't understand. I want to help, but . . ." He waved a hand at the Marconi terminal on his desk. "We no longer have that data in our memory core."

"That seems very odd."

"Not really, just unfortunate. Look, we were an actual newspaper until 2005, black ink on real paper; then we switched to broadcasting on the local datatext channel, same as all the other regional newspapers. We leave features running for forty-eight hours, but the news items are updated every three hours if need be. It's a good system, any cybofax can receive it. We can turn over a lot of data, cover anything from stories like Edward Kitchener's murder to the results of village flower shows and never have to worry about capacity the way they did with paper. Any conceivable piece of information that local people would be interested in is available. Naturally, with that volume of data, everything was stored in a lightware memory." His jaw tightened. "Then some bastard hotrod went and crashed it all when the PSP fell. They actually went and left a message that said it had been done because we were part of the Party's propaganda effort. Jesus, if they knew what we went through to get stuff past the PSP's editorial approval officer. We might not have been out there physically fighting the People's Constables, Mrs. Mandel, but we did our bit. It's not bloody fair! Who the hell are they to sit in judgment?"

"So there's no local record of the PSP years at all?" Eleanor asked.

"No. We've got a complete microfiche library of newspaper issues from 2005 dating back to about 1750; some copies go back even farther than that, would you believe? And we now have a triplicated lightware memory of the last four years. But there's a thirty-five-year gap between the two, and no way on earth of plugging it. It's bloody disgusting. That's our local history they killed."

Eleanor consulted Gabriel, who was frowning thoughtfully. "I only knew about the hotrods crashing the Ministry of Public Order mainframe," she said.

"How about you, Mr. Simms?" Eleanor asked. "You covered the area in that time. Do you remember anything happening out at Launde Abbey?"

"I was in Birmingham when the PSP rule started. I didn't come back here until seven years ago. But no, I can't remember anything. Kitchener himself got the occasional mention, of course. Some of the scientific papers he published were contested by other scientists. Frankly, there were more important issues at the time. We didn't give him a lot of coverage. What type of incident were you looking for?"

"I don't know." She rose to leave. "By the way, our deal stands."

"Thanks."

"So as a final favor, could you tell me if there is anywhere else we could go that might have records of that period?"

"It pains me to say it, but you might try our rivals, the *Rutland Times,* or the *Melton Times,* possibly even the *Leicester Mercury.*"

20

JON NEVIN SHOWED HIS CARD to the lock, and the bolts clicked back.

"Thanks," Greg said as he walked into the cell. There was no response.

Back to square one, he thought. He pretended he wasn't bothered by the detective's attitude.

Nicholas Beswick was sitting cross-legged in the middle of his cot. He opened his eyes as Greg came in but made no attempt to move.

The boy had undergone a profound change in the last three days; there was no sign of the angst-burdened student Greg had interviewed at the start of the inquiry. He ordered a secretion from his gland and examined the smooth cadence of Nicholas's thought currents. Again there was virtually no trace of the old jittery mind.

Maybe it was a good thing; that earlier Nicholas would have been crucified under cross-examination by a professional prosecutor. But Greg couldn't help thinking that if the boy had changed so drastically once . . .

"I don't know who is the most unpopular at this station right now," he said, "you or me."

Nicholas favored him with a sly smile, a welcome from one conspirator to another. "It's me. You only irritate them. I disgust them."

"Yeah. What you did this morning was a bit over the top, wasn't it? Sending your sister as well as your parents. You upset Eleanor, you know."

"Exactly how many qualms should a condemned man own? I need you, very badly. There is nothing I wouldn't do to reach you."

"Jesus."

"I know what you're thinking. He's changed so much, attitudewise. If he's done it once, could he do it twice? That's right, isn't it?"

Greg grinned and pulled the single wooden chair into the middle of the cell, straddling it saloon-style, his elbows resting on its back. "You really have got a brain in that head of yours, haven't you?"

"Not good enough to think me out of here."

"That's a fact, and no messing."

"But you're going to work on the case again, aren't you? Mum said you were. She came back at lunchtime, she and Emma. I didn't know my parents were going to bring Emma with them. She's a lovely girl, we get on really well. Can you think how they're going to treat her at school after this? God!"

Just for a moment, the old Nicholas peeped through, insecure and desperate.

"Yeah. I'm still on the case. There are a couple of ambiguities that are bothering me. But, Nicholas, if I clear them up and you still look guilty, an army of weeping relatives isn't going to bring me back."

"I understand. I'm grateful, really. You're the only hope I've got. Lisa Collier is just going through the motions."

"Okay. Tell you, the way it is, Vernon Langley and the prosecutor are going to nail you with that knife we found. Everything else is circumstantial, and I'm sure Lisa Collier will do her utmost to crush any testimony Eleanor and I provide for the prosecution. But that knife . . . I'm still not entirely convinced you didn't do it. I saw you."

Nicholas brightened. "I had one idea: a *doppelgänger*, a tekmerc who underwent a total *plastique* reworking to look like me. If one of the others had seen him walking about in that guise, they wouldn't have thought anything of it. And I never used to say much, so they wouldn't expect him to talk to them. Just blush and walk on, that's what I normally did."

"Yeah, plausible. Except Eleanor and I watched you go back to your room after you hid the knife and burned the apron."

"Oh."

"I want to ask you some more questions. Do you want to get Lisa Collier to sit in?"

"No. I don't think I can dig myself in any deeper, can I?"

"There is that. Okay, first: did Kitchener ever mention an incident that happened a few years ago?"

"What incident?"

"That's my problem. I remember seeing some news item about Launde maybe ten or so years back, but I can't remember what it was."

"No, nothing comes to mind. Kitchener always had so many complaints about the past, people he knew, politicians he'd argued with, the other professors back at Cambridge, that kind of thing. His entire life was one giant collection of incidents, really."

"Yeah, I suppose it was. Well, keep thinking about it; if anything does spring to mind, get Lisa Collier to contact me at once. Okay?"

"Yes."

"Right. Now, you're sponsored by the Randon Company, aren't you?"

"Yes, they pay me an allowance, more like a salary actually, eight thousand New Sterling a year for the whole time I'm at Launde. Can you believe that much money? I sent two thousand back to Mum and Dad; they really struggled to help when I was at Cambridge, and I don't spend much at the Abbey, you see. Then there's a fund for any equipment I need for projects. Within reason, of course. But I never used any of that; most of my research was data simulations. The Abbey's lightware cruncher was enough."

"Did Randon ever ask you what Kitchener was working on?"

"No."

"So they didn't know about the wormhole research he was performing for Event Horizon?"

"No."

"What about anyone else? You obviously knew about it."

"Not very much, just that he was looking into it. Wormholes would plug very neatly into his cosmos theory."

"What is that?"

"He called it the Godslayer."

"The what?"

"Well, religion killer. Kitchener was hoping to put together a structural theory that went beyond Grand Unification. It would explain every phenomenon in the universe, from psi to gravity. He said he could use it to prove that there was no such thing as God, that the universe was completely natural, and therefore explainable. Provided you had the math to understand it."

Greg tried to imagine what Goldfinch, the Trinities' fundamentalist preacher, would make of that, and failed. It would have been interesting to watch a meeting between the priest and the physicist though—from a distance. "Kitchener genuinely didn't care about other people's sensibilities, did he?"

"Yes, he did," Nicholas said, a shade defensively. "You never met him; he was kind to me, really encouraging. But he hated religion. He said we'd all be better off without it, that it caused too much trouble and too many wars. He said people called him the Newton of the age, but he'd rather be the Galileo."

"And you didn't mind all this talk?" He observed the boy's thought currents boil with surprise.

"No. Why should I?"

"I take it that means you're not religious."

"Never really thought about it. Mum and Dad sometimes go to the Harvest Festival service, if they're not too busy. And I can remember going to the Christmas-carol service a couple of times when I was young. But that's it."

"What about the other students? Did any of them consider this Godslayer concept to be sacrilegious?"

"Nobody ever said anything, no."

"Okay. Was Kitchener working on any kind of energy-generating system, like microfusion, or proton-boron fusion, something new, something radical?"

Nicholas screwed up his face. "Nothing like that. He gave me a magnetosphere induction problem to solve, though."

"What's that?"

"Well, it's hardly new, but if you place a length of wire in orbit, its motion as it moves through the Earth's magnetosphere will generate an electric current. It's a simple induction principle, like a generator."

"How big a current?"

"That depends on the size of the cable, obviously."

"Yeah, right." Maybe the boy wasn't so different after all. "What I need to know, Nicholas is, are you talking about something that can power an AV player, or a city?"

"Oh. A city, definitely, or maybe a medium-sized town. Kitchener was very insistent about that. He said that we had to learn to concentrate on the practical applications of physics; abstract theory was all very well but it doesn't pay the bills. He was right of course, he was always right. He called it his ninety-ten law. He let us study abstract theories for ninety percent of the time, but we had to spend at least ten percent of each week working on practical ideas. He used to set us two projects simultaneously, one of each."

"How far had you gone with this magnetosphere project?"

"I hadn't done much work on it at all, I was spending most of my time on the dark-mass project. But I did confirm its basic validity. I designed a cobweb array, about two hundred and fifty kilometers across. The beauty of that is, if you give it a slight spin, it will retain its shape without any additional structural material, you only need the cables themselves. I was going to work on the strength of materials limits next. But—"

"I thought beaming power down from space was ecologically unsound."

Nicholas smiled vacantly. "I was going to use a superconductor cable, tethered between the equator and geostationary orbit. That's a perfectly practical solution; the orbital tower is an idea even older than magnetosphere induction. It was originally suggested that you build it with magnetic rails and run lift capsules up and down; that way, you'd never need any sort of spaceplane to get into orbit. My version was a lot simpler and cheaper, just a single strand fixed to a station that could receive power beamed to it from the induction webs, a bigger version of the communication platforms that are up there now. The superconductor would have to be held up by a monolattice filament of course, it couldn't possibly support its own weight. It was Kitchener who suggested it as an alternative method of bringing the power down. He joked about it; he said he'd be as rich as Julia Evans if it was ever built. He gets a royalty from monolattice filament, you see. It's only a fraction of a percent, but for a cable thirty-six thousand kilometers long, it would be a hell of a lot of money. He was really keen to see how the figures came out."

"Nicholas, how advanced is this project? I mean, could it actually be built with today's technology?"

"I don't know. It was really just a thought experiment; Kitchener tailored them to match our fields of expertise. The equations were interesting, I had to juggle so many factors, but it did look like it would come out pretty expensive. That's why I was excited about Event Horizon's new spaceplane, the way it's going to bring launch costs down. I was going to include those figures in my analysis."

"But you never got around to it?"

"No."

"Was the project stored in the Abbey's Bendix?"

"Yes, but I kept a back-up file in my terminal. It should still be there."

"Did you ever tell Randon that you were working on this idea?"

"Oh, no, I never discussed it with anybody else apart from the other students."

"So the company never really showed much interest in what you were doing at Launde?"

"They offered me the sponsorship money and a guaranteed research position, that's all. Kitchener's students have this reputation, you see. It's a bit snobby, but a lot of them have turned out to be real high achievers."

"Yeah." Greg couldn't help thinking about Ranasfari. You couldn't get any farther apart than he and Kitchener, the cold aesthetic and the glorious old debauchee. The chemistry must have been there though; Ranasfari clearly revered his mentor. And Kitchener had spotted the potential, just like he had with Nicholas.

"It was all arranged through an agency in Cambridge," Nicholas said. "They specialize in placing graduates. I've never actually met anyone from the company itself. I was looking forward to working in France."

"Do you speak French?"

"Not very well. I've got one of those teach-yourself courses on an audio memox. I'll speak it properly by the time . . . I mean, I would have spoken it properly by the time I finished my second year at Launde. There's only a vocabulary and syntax to memorize; that's not much of a problem for me."

"Interesting. You have a lot of confidence in your memory, don't you?"

"Yes, my recall is virtually perfect. I wasn't trying to boast," he added contritely.

"I didn't say you were."

"Kitchener said I should be proud of it. He said it was better than his."

"Have you ever had days that you can't remember? Events that are lost to you?"

Nicholas regarded him with a tinge of suspicion. "You mean like transient global amnesia?"

Greg was suddenly glad his thoughts weren't available for Nicholas to read. But he really should have known better than to try to creep up on a topic with Nicholas, especially anything remotely connected with science. "Yeah, transient global amnesia, or even trauma erasure."

"You think that's why your psi faculty didn't spot any guilt, isn't it? That I did murder Kitchener and I just blanked it out."

"It's a possibility, Nicholas, and you know it is."

The swift heat of belligerence faded from the boy. "Yes," he said softly. "But I don't have blackouts. And I've never forgotten a day or an hour in my life."

"Okay."

"I was telling the truth then, wasn't I?"

"Yes, Nicholas. You've never suffered from memory loss." He rose to his feet, still as undecided as when he'd walked in. "I'll let you know what happens."

"Mr. Mandel. Thanks."

"You're not out of it yet."

The CID office had been deluged with another wave of entropy. There were more folders and memox crystals littering the desks. Crumpled fast-food wrappers bubbled up out of the bin, waxed cardboard trays with congealed smears of sweet-and-sour sauce.

The detectives formed their usual closed-ranks knot around one of the desks beside the situation screen. Greg was given some dark, speculative looks as he came in. Only Amanda acknowledged him with anything approaching a smile. Vernon Langley broke away from the group, another man following him.

"Did he admit anything?" he asked.

"No."

"Christ, that kid is a smooth one. What about your ESP, did you pick up any guilt waves this time?"

"No," Greg said curtly.

"Shame about that."

"Yeah."

Vernon held up his police-issue cybofax. "I asked the lab to re-run tests on the samples Beswick supplied."

"And?"

"No trace of scopolamine or any other drug. The boy's blood chemistry is perfectly balanced."

"Okay, it was just a thought."

"I asked the lab people about scopolamine. You think Beswick made himself forget the murder?"

"It's one option, because he certainly doesn't remember. There must be a reason. What about his medical records?"

Vernon handed over the cybofax. Greg skipped down the datasheet it was displaying. There wasn't much: the usual childhood illnesses, chicken pox, mumps; a bad dose of flu when he was five; a sprained ankle at eleven. The last entry was a routine health check when he started university, again perfectly clean. Nicholas Beswick was a healthy, ordinary young man.

"Bugger," Greg mumbled.

"Anything there throw any light on the problem?" Vernon asked.

"No, not a bloody thing."

"Didn't think there was." He beckoned. "This is Sergeant Keith Willet," he said as his companion came forward. "Been at Oakham quite a while now."

Greg shook hands comfortably. The sergeant was wearing white shirtsleeves and shorts, regulation black tie in a tiny knot. He was in his early fifties, with the kind of hardened patience that said he'd just about seen it all. If he'd been in the army, he would have been perfect sergeant-major material.

"You were here during the PSP years?" Greg asked.

"Yes, sir," he said. "Twenty years' service in Oakham now."

"You might have been right about Launde," Vernon told Greg. "Though I still don't see how this fits in with Kitchener's murder."

Greg looked at Willet. "You remembered something about the Abbey?"

"Yes, sir. There was a girl drowned in one of the lakes in Launde Park."

"Shit, yeah!" *Now* he remembered. It had been on a local datatext channel, quite a few years ago. The report had gone on to say that the police were questioning the Abbey's other residents about the accident. At the time, he had assumed it was the start of a PSP campaign against Edward Kitchener. Anything like that had interested him in those days; someone as prominent as Kitchener would have made a tremendous addition to the underground opposition. But nothing had ever come of it.

The detectives had all turned to stare at his exclamation.

Greg ignored them. "Can you remember her name?" he asked.

"Clarissa Wynne," Willet said. "She was one of Dr. Kitchener's students."

The name didn't mean anything. "When was this?"

"About ten years ago, sir. Can't say exactly."

"Do you remember anything about the case?"

Willet glanced at Langley. He nodded, albeit with a trace of reluctance. Greg wondered what had been said before he arrived.

"Yes, sir, I'm afraid I do. We were ordered to shut it down straight-away, enter a verdict of accidental death. It came direct from the Ministry of Public Order."

"Jesus, the PSP wanted it kept quiet? Why?"

"I've no idea, sir."

"Was it an accidental death?"

Willet took his time answering. Greg sensed the disquiet in his mind, a real conflict raging. It was almost as though he was confessing a sin, relieved and shamed at the same time.

"The detective in charge was unhappy about the order. The girl had been drinking, but he thought it was more than student high-jinks that had gone wrong. But there was nothing he could do, certainly not launch an investigation. London said frog, and we all hopped. That was all we ever did in those days."

"Who was the detective?"

Willet gazed straight at him. "Maurice Knebel, sir."

"Ah," said Greg. Maurice Knebel was the major reason Oakham's police force had such poor relations with the local community. In the last two years of the PSP decade, when it was obvious to everyone else that the Party was faltering, Maurice Knebel had done his best to maintain their authority in Rutland, sending out the People's Constables at the smallest provocation. He epitomized the petty-minded *apparatchik*, blindly following the Party line, the kind who had inflicted almost as much damage on President Armstrong as had the urban predators themselves. He was on the Inquisitor's top-fifty wanted list. Notoriety of sorts. Nobody had seen him since the night the PSP fell. He had escaped the station minutes before the mob arrived, high on the deadly scent of freedom and vengeance. Not all the People's Constables had been so lucky.

"I didn't even know he was a genuine detective," Greg said.

"Yes, sir, started out a regular officer. He didn't go bad until later."

"How much later?"

"Sir?"

"You said he was upset about being ordered to close the book on the drowned girl. Was he a Party member then?"

"I think so. But he wasn't fanatical back in those days. He saw joining the Party as a way to promotion. It was the last three years, after he was appointed as the station's political officer, that's when the real trouble began."

"Okay, fine, I appreciate your help."

"Sir." He left the CID office, visibly relieved.

"Well?" Langley asked.

The detectives were still watching him, waiting for the verdict. The psychic's pronouncement.

"Why on earth would the PSP want to hush up a girl-student's death? Kitchener wasn't exactly one of their own."

"You think Kitchener killed her?" Langley asked.

He thought of that white-haired old man watching Isabel undress; the picture he'd built up from all the students, Ranasfari, the worship they awarded him. A larger-than-life character, capable of both disgraceful roguishness and unselfish charity. "No, I don't. Let's have a look at the coroner's report. I suppose it'll be a whitewash, but there may be something in it."

Langley rubbed awkwardly at his chin. The detectives were all abruptly occupied at their work again.

"Sorry, Greg, we can't do that."

"I thought my Home Office authorization is still valid."

"It is," he said dryly. "But the local coroner's office has the same problem we do. The hotrods crashed their memory core when Armstrong was ousted. There are no records left for the PSP years."

"They crashed a coroner's office? What the hell for? Coroners hadn't anything to do with the PSP."

"I've no idea. Perhaps they regarded all officialdom as the same."

That familiar cold electric charge compressed his spine. And the gland was barely active. He almost smiled, despite the worry. "No, I don't think so."

"Why not?"

"Intuition." He turned to the group of detectives. "Amanda, would you run a check through the Home Office for me? I want to know how many other coroner's offices were burned by the hotrods when the PSP fell."

She nodded and sat behind one of the desks, activating its terminal.

"Look, Greg"—Langley was trying for the reasonable approach—"I really appreciate your help in finding the knife. But Clarissa Wynne's death is hardly relevant."

"Two deaths in the same community, the first one questionable, the second one bizarre. They're connected, no messing."

"How? They're ten years apart."

"If I knew more about Clarissa Wynne, I might be able to tell you."

"I can hardly expand the Kitchener case to cover her death. For a start, there isn't a single byte on her remaining. We don't even know what she looked like."

"Yeah." He let instinct drive him. Important, the girl's death was important. "Tell you, we're going to have to rectify that."

"Not after ten years, we're not. The only person who could have told you anything was Kitchener."

"Wrong. There's Kitchener, the other five students who were at Launde with her, and Maurice Knebel. And out of all of them, good old Maurice has everything about the case I need to know."

"Knebel? You can't be serious! For Christ's sake, we don't even know if he's still alive."

"I'll find out."

He threw his hands in the air. "Sure you will. I mean, the Inquisitors have only been looking for four years, and their methods don't exactly go by the book. They wouldn't know what a warrant looked like if it pissed on their boot."

"Nobody can run from Mindstar, not forever, not even close." Greg said it with a deliberate bite of menace, enjoying the way it halted Langley's bumptiousness in midflight.

"Greg?" Amanda waved at him from behind her desk. He could see the cube had filled with datasheets, fuzzy green script with a perceptible Y-axis instability.

"What have you got?"

"There were five other coroner's offices in England that had their records destroyed in the two months either side of the PSP's fall. Two were due to firebomb attacks, the other three were hotrod burns."

"Where were the ones that got burned by the hotrods?"

She ran a finger down the cube. "Gloucester, Canterbury, and Hexham."

"Well spread around," he mused.

"What are you saying?" Langley asked.

"That it's convenient; four offices in the whole of the country and one of them is Oakham's, when we know that a dodgy report was loaded into its memory core."

"You can't be serious."

Greg clapped him on the shoulder, drawing a startled look. He knew Langley would never believe in a connection. The man was too good a policeman. Facts, facts, and more facts. That's what he needed.

It's also what you need to get Nicholas off, Greg reminded himself soberly.

"You keep plugging away at Nicholas," he said. "I'll need to borrow Sergeant Willet for the rest of the afternoon."

"All right." Langley seemed relieved that was all he was being asked for. "Why do you want him?"

"I told you: to find Maurice Knebel."

21

THE LIGHT WAS ALREADY BEGINNING to fade as Eleanor drove out of Oakham along the B668, up the hill toward Burley. An advance guard of dark copper-gold clouds probing out of the north had reached the zenith of the opal sky. She wasn't in much of a mood to appreciate sunsets.

The *Rutland Times* hadn't been able to help. Hotrods had crashed their memory core. They had suffered an even worse data loss than the *Stamford and Rutland Mercury*; all of their past issues had been transferred to the core from earlier microfiche records.

She hadn't known the hotrods were so active when the PSP fell. Royan had let slip a few hints that he had been part of the pack that had crashed the Ministry of Public Order mainframe. But as a general rule, the PSP had suffered remarkably little electronic sabotage during its decade in power. Maybe the hotrods had been saving themselves for the final assault. Although she found that hard to credit. They were too independent, preserving their anonymity through the faceless circuit. You could call them through the link they had infiltrated into English Telecom's datanet, but you never knew who you'd reached.

The Ministry of Public Order mainframe was an obvious target for them, one final shove to a government that was already toppling. It had happened within an hour of the bomb blast that annihilated Downing Street. People had talked about a link between the hotrod circuit and the urban predators; she thought that was pure tabloid, a subconscious public desire to juggle facts into a unified conspiracy theory. The mainframe burn wouldn't have required much forward planning, the viruses already existed, but newspapers were a different proposition. To be burned on ideological grounds, their output would have to be monitored continually, victims selected. That required organization, commitment. A cabal within a cabal. There had certainly never been any word of that. Perhaps Royan could tell her.

Forewarned by her failure at the *Rutland Times* office, she had returned to the parked Jaguar and simply phoned the *Melton Times*.

"I'm very sorry, madam," the secretary had told her. "But our records of that period were erased by hackers."

"There is no such thing as coincidence," Gabriel had said quietly as Eleanor swore at the cybofax.

"What do you mean?"

But Gabriel simply shrugged cryptically.

Then Greg had called and asked her to drive up to Colin Mellor in Cottesmore, saying, "I'll meet you up there."

The Jaguar's wheels scattered a volley of loose chippings into the lush verge as they reached the top of the vale, rattling the big scarlet geraniums that had infiltrated the old hedgerows. Four hundred meters to her right she could see the ruins of Burley House casting a stark, jagged outline against the rising velvet penumbra. A few fires were burning in the camp of New Age travelers parked in the embrace of its long, curving colonnade wings, pink-and-blue glow of charcoal cooking grills spilling distorted pools of tangerine light. The travelers had been there for as long as Eleanor could remember, ever since the public petrol supply ran out, the wheels of their antique buses and vans rooting in the earth, tires perished. Not that the ancient combustion engines would work now anyway.

They had raided the stately home for stones, constructing crude lean-tos against some of the rusting vehicles. A hundred meters from the road, they had tried to build a replica of Stonehenge. Still were trying, by all accounts; it changed minutely every time she went past. Not getting any bigger, but the configuration altered, as if they were still searching for the ideal pattern of astrological harmony.

Keeps them off the streets, she thought wryly. God alone knows where they were supposed to fit into the promised land of New Conservative regeneration policies. After fifteen years of doing nothing but picking and eating magic mushrooms, their brains must look like lumps of gangrenous sponge.

There was an estate of late-twentieth-century brick houses on the edge of Cottesmore, ornamental gardens given over to intensely cultivated vegetable plots.

As they moved into the heart of the picturesque village, she leaned forward, peering over the steering wheel. She'd never been to Colin Mellor's house before.

"Further on," Gabriel said.

"Right." She hadn't actually expected Gabriel to come with her to the *Rutland Times* office. Conversation was always so difficult with Gabriel, and this time, with Joey Foulkes tagging along loyally, it was virtually impossible.

The main street had a blanket preservation order slapped on it. All the buildings had stone walls, roofs were either gray slate or Colly-weston stone. Half of them used to be thatch, which had to be stripped off when the Warming started and the fire hazard became too great. Three staked goats were grazing on a wide grass verge in front of a row of cottages. Several men were sitting with their pint pots at bench tables outside the Sun, thin rings of foam marking their progress.

"Here we go." Gabriel pointed to a wooden gate in a long, ivy-clad wall opposite the pub.

Eleanor indicated and turned off. Greg was standing on the other side of the gate. He grinned and tugged at the bolt.

The house was a big converted barn, L-shaped, with a steep gray-slate roof. Dull silver windows reflected the sun falling behind the pub. She drew up next to the EMC Ranger on the gravel park outside the front door. There was a long meadow at the rear; she saw three or four horses at the far end, dark coats merging into the twilight.

A police sergeant she didn't recognize was climbing out of the EMC Ranger, screwing his cap ceremoniously into place.

"We only just got here," said Greg. He introduced the sergeant as Keith Willet.

The house's iron-bound front door opened. Colin Mellor stood inside, leaning on a wooden walking stick: a seventy-two-year-old with bushy white hair, wearing baggy green corduroy trousers and a mauve cardigan. A huge Alsatian nosed around his legs, staring at the visitors. Eleanor shuddered slightly at the sight of the animal. It was a gene-tailored guard hound, gray-furred, muscles sculpted for speed, supposedly owner-obedient. That was a trait which the geneticists didn't always succeed in splicing together correctly. Greg had told her that when the original military combat hounds were taken into the field, some of them had turned on their handlers.

And she'd seen firsthand what the modified beasts could do to people. It had been a gene-tailored sentinel panther that attacked Suzi.

"It's friends, look, Sparky," Colin said, patting the dog's head. "They're all friends." The dog gazed around at them with big cat-iris eyes and blinked lazily. It looked back up at Colin. Reluctantly, Eleanor thought. She could see Joey Foulkes all tensed up, hand hovering near the giveaway bulge under his suit jacket.

"Well, come in," said Colin. The stick was shaken vigorously for emphasis. "Sparky's sniffed you all now. He likes you." He backed into the hall, shooing the dog out of the way.

Eleanor found Greg's hand and held it tightly as they went inside.

Colin led them into his lounge. It was on the ground floor, furnished in plain teak, the upholstery a light green; big french windows gave him a view out across the meadow. Biolum globes in smoked-glass pendant shades cast a strong light. There were pictures of battle scenes on every wall: the army from the Napoleonic wars right up to Turkey.

"Before anything else," Eleanor said to Greg, "I've got some bad news for you. The *Stamford and Rutland Mercury,* the *Rutland Times,* and the *Melton Times* all had their memory cores crashed by the hotrods. The circuit said they were too sympathetic to the PSP. So there's no record of any incident at Launde Abbey."

Greg clamped a hand on each forearm and kissed her warmly. "The hotrods crashed the coroner's office as well," he said. The pleased tone confused her momentarily.

Colin eased himself delicately into a manor wing chair. Eleanor hadn't seen him since the wedding last year, and even then she'd had only a few words. She thought he looked a lot frailer.

"Now then, Greg," Colin said. "What's all this about?"

Eleanor listened to Greg summarizing the case. Somehow she couldn't draw much comfort from the enigma surrounding Clarissa Wynne's death. Greg's intuition had been right. As usual. But the entire sequence of events was becoming equivocal, shaded in a formless gray murk seeping out of the hinterlands, eroding facts before her eyes. It was sadly depressing.

Greg was in his element, of course. And Gabriel, although to a lesser degree.

Right at the center of her mind was a tired little girl who wanted to say: "I saw Nicholas do it. That's an end. Let's leave it. Why do adults always have to be so bloody noble and resolute?"

"Someone has gone to a lot of trouble to erase every trace of Clarissa Wynne," Greg said. "Not to mention expense. Hotrods don't come cheap, and they've burned three newspapers plus a coroner's office; maybe the Oakham police station was part of it, maybe not. But the fact remains, every last hard byte on the girl has gone. All we're left with is personal memories. And precious few of them."

"What about the international news libraries?" Colin asked.

"I checked with Julia," Greg said. "They all have files on Kitchener, of course. None of them mention Clarissa Wynne. It was a local matter, and as far as anyone knew, an accidental death. Not important enough. Although Globecast's Pan-Europe news and current-affairs office think there might have been some kind of hotrod burn against their memory cores. Several file codes relating to that period were scrambled. But they can't actually find anything missing, so there's no way of proving it."

"I doubt they could help anyway," Eleanor said. "If there had been any suspicion that Kitchener was implicated in that girl's death, it would have been headline news the world over. I'd say the PSP's cover-up worked pretty well."

"Yeah," Greg admitted.

"Which is where I come in," Colin said. There was a cheerful smile on his pale face.

Eleanor had the notion he was terribly grateful to be asked. Eager to show he could still pull his weight, not let the side down. Except it was so painfully obvious his health was decaying rapidly. His heart, she guessed.

"If you could," Greg said. He flashed her a shamefaced look. "There's no better tracker."

"Certainly can," Colin said proudly. "The map room's down the corridor." He pressed both hands against the chair, struggling to rise. Joey Foulkes came forward to help him, but he shook off the young hardliner with exaggerated self-reliance.

*　*　*

The map room was a plain white cube, three meters to a side, windowless. It put Eleanor in mind of Kitchener's computer room. Sparky wasn't allowed in.

The biolum panels came on to show a circular flatscreen mounted on one wall. There was a single 'ware module on the floor in a corner.

Colin gave a voice command to the 'ware, and a map of England appeared on the flatscreen. He stood in front of it, both hands pressed on the bulb of his stick, and looked the outline up and down, nodding in satisfaction. "It's there, Greg. I can still do it, by God!" His voice was a weak growl.

"That's why I came," Greg said. "Nobody else in your class."

She could detect a tremor in his voice. When she looked, his eyes were dark with pain. She fumbled for his hand.

"Talk to me, young Keith," Colin said.

Willet twitched uncomfortably. "What about, sir?"

"This dreadful Maurice Knebel chap, of course. I need your mind's image of him to work on."

"Sir?"

"Tell us about an incident you remember," Greg said. "A station cricket match where he got caught out. What did he wear? Bad habits, good habits. What sort of food did he eat? Who were his friends?"

"Yes, sir. Well, there was one suit that he always wore; this would be around the time of the Wynne girl's death, I suppose. Brown-and-gray check, it was. Used to get some ribbing about it."

Eleanor filtered out what the sergeant was saying. It was almost unfair to make someone so stolid and reliable relate trivial tales from the past.

Colin had become preternaturally still. His stare had developed that distance of all gland users, seeing at ninety degrees to the real universe.

The old man had been a major in an English army infantry regiment at the time the Mindstar Brigade was being formed. He was fifty-five and due for imminent retirement when the blanket service psi-assessment tests gave him the excuse he needed to extend his beloved commission. Mindstar hadn't intended to take anyone his age, but his farsight rating was one of the highest they recorded. Fortunately, his ESP faculty had almost developed as it was intended.

Willet was droning on about Maurice Knebel and his fondness for Indian food when Colin leaned forward and deftly pressed his open palm against the flatscreen. The map image shifted instantly, expanding the area around his hand. It was centered on Peterborough, she noticed with a start. The vivid featureless turquoise of the Fens Basin had bitten into a third of the screen.

Willet had stopped talking.

"Keep going," Colin instructed.

"Sir. Curries were his favorite . . ."

Eleanor could see a lone yellow dot in the basin, just east of Peterborough. Prior's Fen, she realized. Colin must keep the map scrupulously updated. He had spent most of the PSP years in France, charging kombinates a small fortune for his services. "Too old to join the fight against Armstrong," he had told her bitterly.

He touched the map again. This time, Peterborough jumped up to occupy half of the flatscreen, leaving a ten-kilometer band of countryside visible around the outside.

Willet flashed Greg a despairing glance. Greg gave him a fast gesture: *Carry on.*

"The woman he was living with left him when he was appointed station political officer. There was talk of him and one of the *apparatchik* women on the town's PSP committee . . ."

"Here," Colin said. His forefinger touched the map in a positive jab. A district turned a shade lighter, its scarlet boundary line flashing insistently. He stood right up against the screen, face coated in a backwash of artificial blue-and-yellow radiance, deepening the folds of flesh. "That's where he is. I can't get any more precise than that. Not from this distance."

Eleanor could feel a groan of dismay building in her gullet. She was afraid to let it out in case it sounded too much like a whimper.

"Figures," Greg said. "He's PSP, where else would he be perfectly safe right now?"

Colin's forefinger was pointing at Walton.

22

GREG'S EXISTENCE HAD COLLAPSED TO a flimsy universe five meters in diameter. Nighttime flying was always bad. But nighttime and fog, that was shit awful.

He was hanging in a nylon web harness below a Westland ghost wing, gossamer blade propeller humming efficiently behind him. The photon amp band across his eyes bestowed an alien blue tinge to every surface, the glow of electron orbits in decay. A column of neat chrome-yellow figures shone on the right-hand side of his vision field: time, grid reference, altitude, direction of flight, power levels, airspeed. The guido 'ware placed him eight hundred meters high, two kilometers out from Peterborough above the Fens basin.

Prior's Fen, and the Event Horizon security-division tilt-fan that had ferried him and Teddy out there, was twenty minutes behind, isolated by treacherously fluctuating walls of stone-gray vapor. The loneliness that had insinuated itself into his thoughts in that time was total, tricking his brain into finding shapes among the gray-blue desolation, the grinning specters of nightmare clamoring in on an unwary mind.

He used to be able to put his feelings on hold for missions, concentrate on details and their application to the immediate. It was the army way; training and discipline could overcome every human frailty, given time. But he'd lost it. Leaking slowly out of his psyche during endless sunny days beside the reservoir, smoothed away by Eleanor's kisses.

Now he could feel the unfamiliar and enervating stirrings of panic as the wing membrane murmured to itself in the squally air. His sole link to reality was a slim microwave beam punching up through the cloying seaborne mist to strike Event Horizon's private communication satellite in geosync orbit. Directional, scrambled, ultra-secure.

"You there, Teddy?" The modulated question slicing upward, hitting the satellite's phased-array antenna, splitting like a laser fired at a fractured mirror, bounced straight back down. Two beams: one received at the Event Horizon headquarters building in Westwood, the second targeted on another ephemeral five-meter bubble somewhere in the vast emptiness behind him.

"Where the fuck else?" Teddy's gruffness carried a trace of anxiety that Greg was learning to recognize from his own voice.

"Hey, you remember when we used to get paid for this?"

"Yeah. Nothing fucking changes. Weren't no fun in them days, neither."

"True. Okay, I'm one and a half klicks from the east shore now, starting to descend. Morgan? Any air traffic yet?"

"Negative, Greg," Morgan said, his voice sounding muffled in Greg's earpiece. "There's some tilt-fan activity in New Eastfield, but the fog has shut down ninety percent of the city's usual movements."

That was one sliver of joy; he didn't have to worry about colliding with low-flying planes. "Roger. Going down." He shifted his weight slightly, feeling the angle of the slipstream change. The fog density remained the same. According to Event Horizon's Earth Resource platforms, it was a belt ninety kilometers wide, extending westward almost all the way to Leicester. They had watched it boil up out of the North Sea through most of the afternoon. Perfect cover.

The mission had taken a day to set up. Naturally, Julia had wanted to send the police in, all legal and aboveboard. She hadn't quite grasped what they were up against. Someone—some organization?—methodical enough to guard against the remotest chance of a query being raised about the death of a girl ten years in the past. Paranoia or desperation—either way, they had it in massive quantities. And they didn't shy away from positive action to eliminate threats.

Even with the channels working themselves into hysterics over the Scottish reunion question, a police operation on a scale large enough to successfully arrest a single man in Walton would attract wide newscast coverage. The Blackshirts would resist the police incursion; there would be riots, sniper fire, a lot of people hurt. After that, leaks would be inevitable, and Julia's name would be foremost among them.

His way was much quieter, safer. Reducing the risk until it focused on just two people.

He would have been happier if Eleanor had shouted at him, put her foot down, told him he was being macho stupid. At least he would have been able to shout back, or argue, vent a bit of feeling. Instead, she had stuck to being silent and sorrowful. Which made it harder. Which put him on edge. Which wasn't good.

Gabriel had been reassuringly scathing, but that had taken on the quality of a ritual; she trusted his intuition almost more than he did. Morgan was frankly skeptical about the whole notion. And Greg had to admit even he was having trouble seeing how Clarissa Wynne's vaguely suspicious drowning could be connected to Kitchener's murder.

With the cocoon of fog acting like a mild form of sensory deprivation, his thoughts were free to roam through wilder realms of possibility, fantasy equivalents of Gabriel's tau lines. But even among the more fanciful possibilities he conjured up, there really was no getting around that memory of Nicholas walking so calmly into Kitchener's bedroom. Maybe the ambiguity he felt so strongly was focused on the boy's motive? Everyone assumed Nicholas had murdered Kitchener because he was overwrought over Isabel. But there was the question of the method. Maybe Launde harbored some dark secret instead?

Yeah, sure. Ghosts and ghoulies and bumps in the night, he told himself mockingly. Secret monsters would be too easy. Somebody wiped all those cores. Three and a half years before Nicholas Beswick ever set eyes on Launde Abbey.

He gave up, pushing the load into the future and squarely on Maurice Knebel's shoulders. Alarmed at just how much he was coming to depend on the absconded detective to provide him with answers when they finally came face-to-face.

One thing, there was no going back. There never bloody was; his character flaw.

His guido put him seven hundred meters out from the city's easterly shore, height one hundred and fifty meters. Closing fast. Fog split around the leading edge of the wing, re-forming instantly behind the trailing edge. A slick coating of minute droplets was deposited on the leathery membrane, streaming backward and shaking free in a horizontal rain.

The photon amp was boosted up to its highest resolution. He still couldn't see anything.

"Virtual overlay," he told the guido 'ware. Translucent green and blue and red petals flipped up into the retinal feed from the photon amp. He looked out across a city built from frozen laserlight.

Morgan's people had built the virtual simulation up from the afternoon's satellite passes. Accurate to ten centimeters, more comprehensive than any memory in the city council's planning-office data cores.

A flood of neutral pixels darkened and hardened below him, resolving into a solid black plane. He felt the illusion of space opening up around him again. Tremendously reassuring.

He just prayed that the simulation's alignment was correct.

The shoreline buildings of the Gunthorpe district formed a flat abrupt wall of dimensionless green dead ahead. It was the only eastern district to expand since the Warming; a quirk of fate had placed it alongside a low triangular promontory jutting a couple of kilometers out into the basin. The fields and pastures that had survived the deluge had been swiftly covered in blocks of flats.

Two hundred meters off the promontory's tip was a patch of spiky indigo waveforms, as though an iceberg had endured the Warming and sought shelter in the basin. It was Eye, a village still in the process of being subsumed by the sluggish currents of the mire, reduced to an erratic formation of mud dunes and crumbling brick walls.

The guido 'ware printed a trajectory graphic for him. A tunnel of slender orange rings snaking away from him, around the north side of the urbanized promontory and curving down to touch Walton.

Greg swung himself to one side, lining up the ghost wing in the center of the tunnel. Orange rings flashed past silently.

Morgan had wanted to send one of his security-division hardliners along on the penetration mission. Greg turned him down politely, hoping he wouldn't make an issue of it. They were tough and well-trained, but there was a world of difference between corporate clashes and all-out combat. He needed someone he could rely on totally.

Back in Turkey, Greg had been in charge of a tactical raider squad when they were cut off and pinned down in a mountain village by Legion fire. Half of the men had wanted to make a break for it, but Greg made them stay put. Teddy was in charge of the back-up team.

He had spent the next three hours cowering under a dusty sky as bullets thudded into the sandstone walls of dilapidated hovels and mortar rounds fell all around. Time had stretched out excruciatingly, but he never let go of that tenuous trust in his huge sergeant.

Teddy had eventually turned up in their aging Belgian Air Force Black Hawk support helicopter, flown by a shaken, terrified pilot. Greg didn't learn until much later how Teddy persuaded the man to fly into the heart of a grade-three fire zone. There would have been a court martial, except the pilot refused to testify.

Eleanor's right, I do dwell on Turkey too much.

But he was bloody glad it was Teddy in the second ghost wing.

The orange circles took him around the north of Gunthorpe. Here the basin mud had surged along a slight depression between Walton and Werrington, engulfing roads and buildings. It was only a meter deep, but the relentless pressure eroded bricks and concrete, exploiting every crack and crevice. Foundations were eaten away, day by day, year by year, cement pulverized, reinforcement prongs corroded, bricks sucked out. Roofs had collapsed, the abraded walls sagged, then fell. Even now the piles of rubble were still being assaulted from below, dragged down by the unstable alluvial substratum, a pressure that wouldn't end until the entire zone was leveled. Weeds and reeds choked the rolling mounds in a moldy mat of entwined tendrils. The satellite image had shown the whole area crisscrossed by paths worn by adventurous children, glimmers of metal detritus peeking through the limp foliage.

The virtual simulation had shaded it in as a lightly rucked pink desert.

One hundred meters in altitude and five hundred meters up ahead, the tunnel of rings had dipped down at a steep angle, narrowing like a whirlwind to touch the apex of an old factory warehouse.

Greg dimmed the simulation, reducing it to a geometric lithograph. He banked the Westland to starboard, preparing to overfly the warehouse roof. The tunnel twisted into an impossible helix. He throttled back the propeller speed to idle and glided in.

At last he thought he saw something through the scudding fog. Down below, a pale blur, broken by dark, irregular smudges. According to the simulation, he ought to be over the factory's yard. Big squares of cracked concrete with abandoned, gutted lorries, a scattered cluster of railway-van bogies in one corner.

With a bit of imagination, the dark smudges below could be rusted cabs.

The simulated green skeletal outline of the warehouse was upon him. If it corresponded with the actual structure, the Westland should take him six meters above the roof apex.

Solid surfaces suddenly materialized between the green lines, as if the building had been edged in neon tubes. Greg received a fast impression of breeze blocks smeared in rheumy ribbons of algae, and a corrugated roof, red oxide paint flaking away. He laughed as he twisted the throttle grip, shooting back up into the veil of fog.

"Morgan? Tell your programming team they've got a big drink coming. The guido virtual is perfect. I've just surveyed the landing site."

"Glad to hear it. Could you see anybody waiting?"

"No. It looks clear. I'm going around."

He made a leisurely turn and headed back toward the warehouse. This time, he came in lower. The orange tunnel stretched out ahead, perfectly level. It terminated halfway up the slope of the roof.

He saw the corrugated panels again, four seconds before he reached them. Legs running in midair. Then the rubber soles of his desert boots slapped down.

Every nerve was raw-edged with tension. If the panels couldn't take his weight, he was in deep shit and no messing. The satellite image interpreters swore they would hold.

The noise of his running feet sounded like a drumbeat after the graveyard silence of flight. He could feel the panels bending slightly under his heels. The apex was three meters ahead of him. Still, the panels held.

He yanked savagely at the throttle grip, reversing the propeller pitch. Tilting the wing back up as he fought to kill his forward momentum. The sudden backward impetus nearly toppled him.

"Shitfire! Tell you, next time we do as Julia says and send in the cavalry."

"Greg?" Teddy called. "You down, boy?"

He was crouched a meter short of the apex, balancing the wing precariously. Fog swirled beyond the guttering, cutting off any view of the yard below.

"Yeah. Wait one."

He killed the virtual-simulation overlay, then activated the Westland's retraction catch. There was a wet, slithering sound as the wing folded. The steering bar hinged up and back. He grappled with the frame, slapping the harness release. The ghost wing finished up as a fat damp cylinder three meters long, which he could just hold under one arm.

He scrambled up to the apex and walked down to the end. When he peered over, he could just make out the base of the wall, lined with tufts of grass and sickly dandelions. There was a monotonous dripping from the broken guttering. The roof would give them ample clearance for a swoop launch after they had completed the mission, a genuine running jump. Of course they had both been trained to launch from a much lower height, and a shallower slope. But those lessons had been an uncomfortably long time ago now.

"Okay, Teddy. The panels are solid, and our takeoff run is clear. I'm on the southern end of the roof. Come in when you're ready."

"Gotcha."

Greg unslung his pack and rifled through it, looking for the climbing gear. The propeller noise of Teddy's Westland was just audible as he overflew the warehouse on his guido check pass.

"Hell, Morgan, this 'ware is ultra-cool," Teddy exclaimed. "The virtual matches clean down the line."

"All Event Horizon gear works like that." Morgan sounded slightly indignant.

"Yeah? Man, I wish we'd had this in Turkey. Would've shown 'em Legion bastards."

Greg found the vibration knife, a slim black-plastic handle with a telescoping blade. He crouched down and pressed it against the breeze block just below the edge of the roof. Gray dust spurted out as the blade drove in, buzzing like an ireful wasp.

"Comin' round," Teddy said. "Here we go. Jesus Lord, protect your dumb-ass servant."

Greg shoved an expander crampon into the hole. It clicked solidly, locking into place.

Teddy's feet banged loudly on the roof, an elephant charging across sheet metal.

"Teddy!"

"Jeeze." Teddy was wheezing, an indistinct figure slouched over the apex. "Greg, I ain't no fucking bat."

"Yeah, right."

"Everything all right?" Morgan asked.

"We're down," Greg said. He clipped a climbing rope into the crampon's eye and let the coil fall down the side of the wall. Behind him he could hear Teddy folding his Westland ghost wing.

"Roger," said Morgan. "The security team is on alert."

"We'll shout if we want them," Greg said. Just knowing the hard-line crash-recovery team was waiting, that their tilt-fan could be with him in minutes if he hit any hazards, was a heady boost. Rule one: always sort out your escape route first.

He fed the rope through the clip attached to his belt, then swung himself out over the edge and rappelled down to the yard.

Teddy landed lightly on the rucked concrete and unclipped the rope. He was dressed in matte-black combat leathers, a tiny Trinities emblem on his epaulette, 'ware modules attached to his belt, the slim metallic-silver photon amp band around his eyes, navy-blue skull helmet. There was an AK carbine strapped tightly to his chest, an Uzi hand laser in a shoulder holster.

Greg was dressed the same, except he was carrying an Armscor stunshot instead of an AK. He wondered what the pair of them would look like to some poor unsuspecting sod who saw them emerge out of the fog.

He had considered wearing civilian clothes, but decided they were impractical; there was too much gear to carry. Besides which, the fog and the night should provide enough cover. The Blackshirts guarded their territory's boundaries tightly, but inside Walton, they could move about with a reasonable degree of freedom. And his espersense would warn him of any random patrols.

"Okay, Morgan, we're on the ground," Greg said. "Put Colin on, please."

Colin had insisted on being included, even though he really was too ill for an operation that required sustained gland use. But Greg didn't have it in him to say no, not to that brave, silently pleading face. More bloody guilt.

"I'm here, Greg." Colin's voice was reedy, anxious and eager.

He imagined them all in Morgan's ops room: Eleanor silently worried, Gabriel staring grimly at the communications console, Morgan keen-eyed and serious, Colin sitting in front of a flatscreen displaying the satellite image of Walton, technical support staff hovering around. The hardline security-team commander secretly hoping to be ordered into the fray.

"Where's our man?" Greg asked.

"He hasn't moved. It must be his house."

"Right, thanks, Colin." Greg requested the virtual simulation again. Featureless green toytown houses blinked in, marking the perimeter of the factory yard sixty meters away. He tilted the display to vertical and reduced it until it was a panoramic model of the whole district. The house where Colin had said Knebel was staying flashed a bright amber. It was seven hundred meters away, due south. A route graphic slid out from their warehouse, an orange serpent bending and twisting down the smaller streets and constricted alleys.

"Let's go," Greg said. The display reverted to its real-scale superimposition, the route a path of tangerine glass.

"I'll keep you updated," Colin said.

Greg saw Teddy's face turn toward him, blank band concealing his expression.

"No, Colin, just give us another scan when we're a hundred meters away to confirm he's still there."

"I can manage, Greg."

"Yeah, but if he starts to go walkabout, you're going to have to track him for us. I don't want you overstressed."

"Yes. Sorry, I wasn't thinking."

"Okay, call you when we're in place." He summoned up a secretion from his gland, then set off down the orange line, feet sinking into the placid current of photons up to the ankles.

The fog was sparser out on the streets, broken by walls and a light breeze coming off the basin. Visibility had increased to fifteen meters. Greg switched the virtual simulation back to outlines; the photon amp image shaded in the actual walls and roads a smoky gray and blue.

Spook town, and no messing.

There were no streetlights. Public utilities in Walton didn't receive much priority from the city council these days. Chinks of biolum light escaped from some houses, glimmers from shuttered windows. The amp showed them as near-solid blades probing out across the street.

Pro-PSP graffiti was splattered on every wall. They walked down one alley with an elaborate mural of People's Constables and socialist-stereotypical workers sprayed on the fence: bold, uplifted faces and stout poses; rotting wood had left vacant, jagged gashes, mocking the artist's vision.

Black bags like swollen pumpkins and cardboard boxes full of rubbish formed a humpbacked tide line along the pavements. The corrupt smell of putrefying vegetation was strong in the air, mingling with the brine from the basin. Greg saw rats crawling around the bags, gnawing at soggy tidbits. Tiny black glass eyes turned to watch him and Teddy pass, quite unafraid.

They had to sink back into the shadows and gaps between buildings several times as Greg perceived people walking toward them. Walton's residents invariably stuck to the center of the road, as if they were afraid of the buildings and what they contained. They never once heard or saw any kind of powered transport, though bicycles nearly caught them out a couple of times, rushing up silently from behind.

A street-corner pub produced the biggest obstacle. Bright fans of light shone out of its windows and open door, illuminating a broad section of the road. Men were lounging against its walls, drinking in small groups. Jukebox music reverberated oddly across the street: country rap, hoarse vocals booming against a background of a solitary steel guitar.

Greg halted on the fringe of the light field, consulting his virtual simulation. He pointed at the entry of a narrow alley on the other side of the road from the pub, and they edged off the street.

"Recognized some active Blackshirts back there," Teddy muttered.

"Mark it off for the future," Greg said.

"Sure."

One of the reasons Teddy agreed to accompany him was that the opportunity to scout around enemy territory was too great to pass up. Greg knew the detailed satellite images stored in the guido's memory would be handed over to Royan, who would integrate them with the Trinities' existing intelligence bytes. Lieutenants would pore over the resulting package, fine-tuning tactics for the final assault. Teddy hadn't said anything, but he knew the fight wasn't far away now.

The alleyway they had skipped down brought them out into a cul-de-sac. One side was a brick wall backing onto some gardens, the other was a row of garages, their metal swing-up doors either broken open or missing entirely. Walton's perpetual tide of rubbish had swollen to form a rancid mattress underfoot; bags rose like lumpy organic buttresses against the bricks. Rats scampered about everywhere.

Greg's espersense found the cluster of minds just as he heard the low, bubbling laughter up ahead. Something about the minds wasn't quite right; their thought currents wavered giddily, emotions burning fiercely. One of them was emitting a mental keening, gibbering with psychotic distress.

"Shit. Teddy, it's a bunch of synthoheads. And they're juiced up high."

"Where?"

"Ten meters. One of the garages." He drew his Armscor stunshot, a simple ash-gray pistol with a solid thirty-centimeter-long barrel. "I'll take them. Cover for any runaways."

"Gotcha."

The stunshot was accurate only up to twenty meters. If one of the synthoheads got away, Teddy would have to use the Uzi on him, providing the target laser worked in the fog. Tension clamped down hard; this was supposed to be a stealth infiltration. People being killed just for getting in his way wasn't part of the deal.

It was the third garage from the end of the cul-de-sac, a dim yellow glow spilling out onto the sludge of rubbish. Greg flattened himself against the wall, checked the stunshot, then spun around the corner.

There were five of them. Kids, still in their teens, two girls, three boys. Filthy, greasy jeans, frayed black-leather jackets, denim waist-coats with studs, long straggly hair. The garage walls were slick with condensation; junk furniture—broken settees and armchairs—lined up around the walls, and an oil lamp hung from the ceiling.

Greg's photon amp threw the whole scene into starkly etched focus. Two of the kids were screwing on the floor, grunting like pigs. Another two stood on either side, watching, giggling. The fifth was huddled in a corner, arms over his head, weeping quietly.

Greg shot the one closest to him. A girl, about seventeen, her neck freckled with dark infuser marks. The stunshot spat out a bullet-sized pulse of blue-white lightning. It hit her on the side of her ribcage. Her squeal was choked off as she reeled around. There was an im-possibly serene smile on her face as she crumpled onto the legs of the rutting couple.

Pulling the trigger was incredibly hard. They weren't innocent, not even close. Just profoundly ignorant, pitiable. He had to keep on re-minding himself the stunshot wasn't lethal, though God alone knew what it would do to a metabolism fucked up so badly by syntho.

He turned slightly. Aim and fire, nothing else mattered.

The second kid gurgled as the pulse hit him in the stomach, curl-ing up and falling forward. Aim and fire. The girl on the floor was struggling to get up as her partner collapsed on top of her. Aim and fire.

The boy in the corner was looking straight at Greg, face ecstatic, tears streaming down. "Thank you, oh thank you."

Aim and fire.

The kid slumped down again, head bowed.

"Lord, what a waste," Teddy said. "Someplace else, they could've been real people."

Greg stepped over the prone bodies and extinguished the oil lamp, letting the night claim its own. "You can get syntho anywhere."

"Not in Mucklands, you fucking couldn't. I look after my kids. Anyone tries peddling that shit near me an' they end up swinging by the balls. Blackshirts don't even look after their own."

"You're preaching to the converted. Come on."

According to the bright yellow coordinates the guido was flashing up, he was standing fifty meters from the target house. Its green template glowed lambently, the walls and roof remaining outside the photon amp's resolution.

"Colin, how are we doing?"

"He's still there, Greg."

"Okay, we're closing in now."

He trotted down the road, watching the house gaining substance. It was a large detached three-story affair, with bow windows on either side of the front door, built from a pale-yellow brick with blue-gray slates. Nothing fancy, virtually a cube. Diamond shapes made from blue bricks set between the first-floor windows were the only visible ornamentation. A tall chimney-stack was leaning at a worrying angle; a number of bricks from its top were missing. The chimney pots themselves ended in elaborate crowns, all of them playing host to tussocks of spindly weeds.

A meter-high wall enclosed a broad strip of garden at the front. Greg stopped just outside; it took him a moment to realize there were no solar panels. The house's residents must be right at the bottom of the human pile, and in Walton, the bottom was as far down as you could get. All the windows had their curtains drawn; the photon amp revealed vague splinters of light around the edges. There was no gate, its absence marked by rusty metal hinge pins protruding from the wall.

He walked down the algae-slimed path. Dog roses had run wild in the garden, reducing it to a thorny wilderness sprinkled with small, pale flowers. A panel with eight bell buttons was set into the wall at the side of the door. Very primitive; there was no camera lens as far as he could see. He took the sensor wand from its slot on his ECM 'ware module and ran it around the door frame. Apart from the lock system, it was clean.

"We're at the front door now," Greg said. He was surprised by the 'ware lock, a tiny glass lens flush with the wood. He already had the vibration knife in his hand, ready to cope with a mechanical lock.

"I can feel you," Colin said. "Yes, you're very close now. He's above you, Greg. Definitely higher up."

"Okay." He showed his card to the lock, using his little finger to activate it rather than the usual thumbprint. A Royan special was loaded in the card, a crash-wipe virus designed to flush lock circuitry clean. There was a subdued *snick* from the lock. He pushed the door open a crack and slipped the sensor wand in.

"It's clear," he told Teddy.

The hall went straight through to the back of the house. He saw a set of stairs halfway along. A candle was burning in a dish on a small table just inside the door. Its flame flickered madly until Teddy closed the door behind him. The lock refused to engage.

Greg let his espersense expand. There were four people on the ground floor, none of them showing any awareness that the front door had been opened.

They went up the stairs fast. The first-floor landing had five doors. One was open; he could just make out an ancient iron bath inside. His espersense picked out seven minds, two of them children. Murmurs of music from channel shows were coming through some of the doors.

"Which way, Colin?"

"Walk forward, Greg."

He took three paces down the worn ochre carpet. Teddy stayed at the top of the stairs, watching the other doors.

"Stop," Colin said. "He's on your left." The strain in his voice was quite clear, even through the satellite link.

"Thanks, Colin. Now you shut your gland down, right now, you hear?"

"Greg, my dear chap, there's no need to shout."

Greg let his espersense flow through the door. There were two people inside, one male, one female, sitting together. Judging by the relaxed timbre of their minds, he guessed they were watching a channel.

The door lock was mechanical, an old Yale. With Teddy standing behind him, he shoved the blade clean through the wood just above the keyhole and sliced out a semicircle.

Knebel's room was just as seedy as he had been expecting: damp wallpaper, cheap furniture, laminated chipboard table and sideboard, plain wooden chairs, a settee covered in woolly brown-and-gray fabric, its cushioning sagging and worn; thin blue carpet. The light was coming from some kind of salvaged lorry headlamp on the table, shining at the ceiling, powered from a cluster of spherical polymer batteries on the floor. An English Electric flatscreen, with shoddy color contrast, was showing a channel current-affairs 'cast.

Greg didn't know the woman, a blowzy thirty-year-old, flat washed-out face, straw hair, wearing a man's green shirt and a short red skirt.

Knebel had grown a pointed beard, but Greg would have recognized him anywhere. The *apparatchik* was wearing jeans and a thick mauve sweater, buckled sandals on bare feet. He had aged perceptibly; he was only forty, almost Greg's contemporary, but the flesh had wasted from his face, producing sunken cheeks, deep eyes, thin lips. Mouse-brown hair with a center parting hung lankly down to his ears.

The two of them were sitting on the settee, facing the flatscreen, heads turning at the clatter of the lock hitting the floor. Greg aimed the stunshot at the woman and fired. It sounded dreadfully loud in the confined space. The pulse caught her on the shoulder. She spasmed, nearly slewing off the settee. Her eyes rolled up as she emitted a strangled cry.

Greg shifted the stunshot fractionally.

Knebel stared at him, his mouth parted, jaw quivering softly. His startled thoughts reflected utter despair. He closed his eyes, screwing up his face wretchedly.

"One sound and you won't be dead, you will simply wish you were," Greg said. "Now turn the flatscreen off."

Teddy closed the door behind him.

Knebel opened his eyes, showing the frantic disbelief of a condemned man given a reprieve. A shaking hand pawed at the remote.

Greg ignored him, his espersense hovering around the other minds on the first floor. Two of them had heard the commotion. Curiosity rose, they waited for something else to happen. When nothing did, their attention wavered and they were drawn back into the mundane routine of the evening.

He waited another minute to make sure, then pulled the photon amp band from his eyes.

Knebel managed to crumple without actually moving. "Oh, my God. Greg Mandel, the Thunderchild himself."

It had been quite some time since Greg had heard anyone use his army callsign. Not since he left the Trinities, in fact. But of course the PSP had access to all the army's personnel files. "I'm flattered. I wasn't aware Oakham's Lord Protector had taken an interest in me."

"You were believed to be an active member of the Trinities, and you live in the Berrybut estate. No close family, no special woman as far as we knew. Very high ESP rating. Plenty of combat experience. I took notice all right."

"Lived. Lived in Berrybut. I've moved now."

"Of course," Knebel said with bitter irony. "Do excuse me, I haven't accessed your file lately. My mistake."

"If you knew all that, how come you never came hunting for me, you and your Constables?"

Knebel stroked the hair of the unconscious woman, gazing tenderly at her shivering face. "And if we'd missed? Which was more than likely with that freaky Thompson woman guarding your future. I had enough trouble keeping the ranks in order as it was. You were busy here in Peterborough. The last thing I needed was a fully trained, fully armed Mindstar monster gunning for us when we left the station to go home at night."

"Figures. You people never did try anything physical unless the odds were ten to one in your favor."

"Could you spare me this ritual of insults and just get it over with, please?"

Greg gave him a frigid grin. "Tell you, Knebel, this is the luckiest day of your entire shitty little life. I'm not here to snuff you."

Knebel's hand stopped. "What?"

"True. I only want some bytes you've got."

"An' you gonna give 'em to us, boy," Teddy growled.

Swellings of terror and hope disrupted the surface thoughts of Knebel's mind. "Are you serious? Just information?"

"Yeah."

He licked his upper lip, glancing nervously at Teddy. "What about afterward?"

"You join her in dreamland, we leave. And that's a fucking sight more than you deserve."

"God, you must be loving this, seeing what I've been brought down to." The eyes darkened with pain. "Yes, I'll plead with you for my life, I'll tell you anything you want, answer any question, I don't care. Dignity isn't something I have anymore, your kind broke that. But you gave me something in return; I've found there's a great deal of peace to be had once every pretension has been stripped out. Did you know that, Mandel, can you see it? I don't worry about the way things are anymore, I don't worry about the future. That's all up to you now. Your worries, your power politics. And you've wasted your time coming here, because I don't know anything about the Blackshirts' weapons stocks, they never tell me anything. I'm not a part of that."

"Not what we're here for."

"Speak for yourself," Teddy muttered.

"What then?" Knebel asked.

"Launde Abbey."

"What?" Knebel blurted loudly. He shrank back when Greg motioned with the stunshot. "Sorry. Really, I'm sorry. But . . . is that it? You came to ask me about Launde Abbey?"

"Yeah. Now, I've come a long way and gone to a lot of trouble to rap with you. So believe me, you don't want to piss me off. You know I'm empathic, so just answer the questions truthfully."

"All right. I saw you on the newscast the other night. You were appointed to the Kitchener murder, something to do with Julia Evans." His eyes lingered on the 'ware modules hanging from Greg's belt.

Greg switched in the communication module's external mike. "Tell me about Clarissa Wynne."

"Clarissa? God, that was years and years ago. I'd almost forgotten about her until the other day. That newscast brought a lot of memories back."

"Ten years ago. What can you remember?"

Knebel closed his eyes, slim eyebrows bunching up. "Ten? Are you sure? I thought it was eleven."

"It could have been."

"Well, what does it say in her file?"

"That is the reason I'm here, Knebel. Someone has erased every byte of Clarissa Wynne from Rutland's memory cores; police, council, local newspapers, you name it, the lot."

"God."

"Do you know who?"

"No."

"Right. You say you thought she died eleven years ago?"

"Yes, I'm sure it was eleven."

"Okay, what orders did you get from the Ministry of Public Order about her death?"

"To wrap it up immediately, make the coroner enter a verdict of accidental death, not to cause any ripples, especially not to antagonize Kitchener and the other students."

"Why not? Why was the PSP so anxious to hush the girl's death up? What made her so important?"

Knebel gave him a humorless smile. "Important? Clarissa Wynne wasn't important. God, the Ministry didn't even know her name. She was an embarrassment. You see, eleven years ago, the PSP was applying to the World Bank for a very large loan, billions. You remember that time, Mandel; the seas were reaching their peak, we'd got hundreds of thousands of refugees pouring inland from flooded coastal areas, we didn't have any food, we didn't have any industry, we didn't have any hard currency. It was a fucking great mess. We needed that loan to get the economy started again. And the Americans didn't want to help a bunch of Reds. No matter we were elected—"

Teddy growled dangerously. Greg held up a hand, sensing just how hostile Teddy's mind was.

"Okay. All right. I'm sorry," Knebel said. "No politics. But look, the point was, the PSP couldn't afford a human-rights issue. The Americans would have leaped on it as an excuse to block the loan, destabilize the Party. Kitchener, for all he was bloody obnoxious personally, was internationally renowned, someone whose name people knew all over the world. Can you see the disinformation campaign the Americans would have mounted if I'd started questioning the students and Kitchener thoroughly? Their friend and colleague has been tragically drowned, and all the PSP does is persecute them with inquiries and allegations. It would have been Sakharov all over again. We needed that money, Mandel, people were starting to starve. In England, for God's sake! Pensioners. Children. So I did what I was told, and I kept my mouth shut afterward. Because it was necessary. And to hell with you and your rich-bitch mistress. I don't care how wise after the event you are."

So much anger, Greg thought, and just from one question. Will we ever heal the rift? "Morgan? Did you hear all that?"

"Yes, Greg."

"Okay, check the date for that World Bank loan application, please. I'd like some verification."

"Right."

Knebel had cocked his head to one side, listening to Greg's side of the conversation intently. He still had his arms around the woman, cradling her. A ribbon of saliva was leaking from the corner of her mouth, eyelids fluttering erratically.

"Now," Greg said. "Why were you so upset about having to close down the inquiry? I was told Clarissa drowned in the lake after some sort of drinking session. Was it an accident?"

"I'm not sure. At the time, I didn't think so. You get an instinct, you know? After you've been on the job long enough, you can tell if something's not quite right. And I was a good detective back then. Before it all . . . I cared," he said defensively.

"Yeah. Keith Willet told me."

"Keith?" Knebel brightened for an instant. "God, is he still at Oakham? How is he?"

"Just get on with it, Knebel."

"All right." He shot Teddy another twitchy glance, then cleared his throat. "I wasn't happy with the circumstances around Clarissa Wynne's death. The students said they found her floating in the lake first thing in the morning, that she must have gone for a swim sometime in the night. Apparently the students always went swimming there."

"Still do," Greg said.

"Yes? Well, anyway, on the surface it was pretty clear-cut. She'd been drinking, she'd infused some syntho. That was the first time we'd ever come across the stuff at Oakham. She must have got into difficulty in the water. Those lakes aren't particularly deep, but you only need five centimeters to drown in."

"So what was wrong about it?"

Knebel sighed. "She hadn't drunk much that evening, a couple of glasses of wine. And the syntho, we couldn't be sure; we didn't know much about it back then, but it looked as though it was infused very close to the time she died. Almost as if she took it and dived straight in. Which I don't believe anybody would do, certainly not a bright girl like that. I was going to have the pathology samples sent to Cambridge for a more detailed examination, then the shut-down order came through."

"Suicide?" Greg suggested.

"Nope. First thing I thought of. We did get to ask the students and Kitchener a few preliminary questions. Clarissa Wynne was one happy girl. She enjoyed being at Launde. Her parents confirmed there were no family problems. In any case, there was some light bruising on the back of her neck." He shrugged limply. "It could have been caused by bumping into something in the water."

"Or it could have been caused by someone holding her under," Greg concluded.

"Yes. If the attacker had put her in a Nelson lock on the side of the lake, the bruising would have been consistent with her head being forced under the surface. Especially if she was conscious. She was young, strong; apparently she was in the women's hockey team at university, a sports type, she could have put up quite a struggle. The attacker would have had to use a lot of force."

"Any sign of a struggle?"

"No. The grass around the side of the lake was all beaten down. Like I said, the students used it each day."

A dire chill slithered through the combat leathers to prickle Greg's skin as he thought about Clarissa Wynne's death. She would have struggled that night eleven years ago, fighting her attacker under the silent, beautiful stars without any hope of success or help. Terribly alone as her head was shoved under the cold, muddy water. She would feel her body weakening, be conscious of the syntho breaking her mind apart. And all the while, the red ache in her lungs grew and grew.

No fucking wonder he'd been drawn to the lake. It was a focal node of horror and anguish.

Did her soul haunt it? Was that what I sensed?

But whatever the source of the misery, it still didn't explain how her death tied in with Nicholas Beswick.

"Who did you suspect?" he asked Knebel.

"God, I never had time to find a possible suspect. That Ministry order came through in less than a day."

"Well, start thinking about it now, Knebel. What about Kitchener himself? I mean, he was sleeping with his female students the night he died. Sixty-seven years old. Eleven years ago, he would have been even more capable sexually."

"No, I don't think so. He was reasonably fit, but not really what

I'd call physically powerful. And if Clarissa was held down, it was done by someone stronger than her."

"One of the other students, then?"

"Yes, possibly."

"Was there anyone else staying at the Abbey that night?"

"No. And Clarissa was still alive when the housekeeper and the maid left, we confirmed that."

"Okay, can you remember the names of the other students?"

"I think so. There were five of them. Let's see: Tumber, Donaldson, MacLennan, Spencer—"

"Wait! MacLennan? James MacLennan? Dr. James MacLennan?"

"Yes. That was his first name, James. I didn't know he was a doctor."

"Shitfire," Greg whispered.

23

JULIA COULD BARELY SEE THE far side of the rooftop landing pad. The fog was pressing in, turning the circle of close-spaced white lights around the perimeter of the pad into a hazy line of phosphorescence. The edge of the Event Horizon headquarters building was lost completely.

She was wearing a light nylon windcheater jacket over her plain amethyst-colored stretch-jersey dress. It was too warm to zip it up, but the fog was almost thick enough to be called a drizzle. Her hair was already hanging limply, sprinkled with a sugarcoating of droplets. Rachel stood at her side, suede jacket buttoned up, collar raised around her neck. The rest of the reception party—Eleanor, Gabriel, and Morgan, plus some security people—were huddled together a couple of meters away.

Eleanor's smile was blinking on and off, the outright relief on her face making Julia feel like an intruder just for looking at her.

Thirty seconds, Juliet. Can you hear it?

Not yet, Grandpa, she answered silently.

She saw Morgan raise a palm-size communication set to his face and listen for a moment. "They're coming in," he announced.

Now she heard it, the whine of the turbines, low-frequency hiss of air escaping from the fan nacelles. It grew louder and louder until the dove-gray security division tilt-fan was suddenly *there* above the landing pad. Landing gear unfolding, small red and green wingtip strobes flashing. Its fuselage was coated in water, shining dully.

In the end, she simply couldn't stay away. She didn't approve. She had made that quite clear. But ultimately, it was her responsibility. Greg was on the case only because she asked him. There was no way she could go out clubbing in New Eastfield while he was risking his neck on her behalf.

Another night lost to duty.

The tilt-fan's broad, low-pressure tires touched down, hydraulic struts pistoning upward as they absorbed the weight. The forward hatch hinged out and up, airstairs sliding down. The pilot cut the turbines. Micro-cyclones of steam poured out of the nacelles as the fans wound down.

Greg was first out, his black-leather combat jacket open to show a white T-shirt, his hair sweaty, clinging to his forehead. He had a stunshot with a shoulder strap riding at his elbow, 'ware modules clipped around his belt, skull helmet thrown back, photon amp band hanging over one shoulder. He looked so . . . dangerous.

She watched Eleanor walk over and embrace him, arms going around his waist, a brief kiss, then resting her head on his shoulder. He hugged her tightly. It was far more eloquent than whoops of joy and backslapping.

How she'd love someone to greet her like that. Not to be, though. Although perhaps Robin . . .

Teddy came down the airstairs, scowling around suspiciously.

"Hello, Teddy," she said brightly. "Thank you for going in with Greg. I'm really very grateful."

He grunted in disgust. "Goddamn fucking stupid thing to do, you ask me, gal. Still, we're back in one piece." He patted one of the 'ware modules on his belt. "An' these guido bytes gonna come in mighty useful sometime soon."

She smiled warmly. Teddy always used to intimidate the hell out of her, with his size and his menacing authority. Not anymore. He was a pushover. "Oh? Going to impress a lady friend with them?" She batted her eyelids.

"Je-zus wept!"

Then the security crash team started to emerge from the tilt-fan. They were wearing suits similar to Teddy's, all of them in their mid- to late twenties. They shouted a few boisterous greetings at her and she grinned back. She knew most of them by their first name; they treated her almost as though they were a rugby squad and she their mascot.

Morgan always kept one team on standby in case there was ever any attempt to kidnap her. She had watched them training a few times. Lord help any tekmerc who ever went up against them.

"Gabriel?" Greg was looking at her, one arm still around Eleanor. "Where's Colin?"

"One of my people drove him home," Morgan said.

"How was he?"

"Not too bad, considering," Gabriel said. "He'll need to rest for a week or so. Proper rest. I said I'd pop in tomorrow, make sure. You know what he's like."

"Yeah."

"Shall we go in?" Morgan said. "In light of what we learned from Maurice Knebel, I believe we have quite a bit to discuss."

"And no messing," Greg said gloomily.

Julia led them into the big executive conference room, her pumps treading soundlessly on the pile carpet. Biolums came on ahead of her, banishing shadows. Gray tongues of fog licked at the windows. Westwood could be in a different universe by now for all she could tell.

The conference room was empty with just the seven of them, no secretaries, no aides. She shrugged out of her windcheater and hung it on the back of her chair before she sat down. Freshets of cool air trickled across her bare arms, carrying away the perspiration.

Grandpa, bring Royan in on this. I imagine we'll need him. Besides, she wanted all her true friends together.

Plugging him in now, Juliet.

Teddy lowered himself gingerly into one of the padded chairs around the table, nodding approvingly. His combat leathers squeaked softly as he put his hands behind his head and sat back. "Man, now this is the life."

"Do you want anything to drink?" Julia asked.

"Hey, my kinda gal, you gotta beer?"

"I'll look," Rachel said. "Anybody else?" She sauntered over to the mirrored nineteen-twenties drinks cabinet.

Julia opaqued all the windows, cutting off the sight of that austere fog.

ON LINE, her recessed flatscreen printed. HI, SNOWY.

"Hi."

Morgan raised an eyebrow.

"I'm here as well," Philip's voice announced.

Julia enjoyed the startled look on Teddy's face, the way his eyes darted around. Greg had told her Teddy took his religion very seriously indeed. Grandpa was a little bit too much like reincarnation.

"Everybody's up to date?" Greg asked. "Julia? Royan?"

"Yah."

YES YES YES.

"Okay," Greg said. "We have a new player on the field, James MacLennan."

"I'm assembling a profile," Philip said. "Every byte I can find, public and private files, plus a financial rundown. Should be ready in a quarter of an hour."

"So what happened?" Julia asked. "Did MacLennan let Bursken out for the night?"

"I was thinking about that," Greg said. "We're faced with the same problem for Bursken as we were with a tekmerc penetration mission. How did he get in and out of Launde Abbey without leaving any trace?"

"Oh, yes." She felt silly for asking.

"And in any case, Eleanor and I saw Nicholas do it."

"It could have been an alternative past," Eleanor said; she sounded doubtful.

"No. If you ask me," Greg said slowly, "I think it was Nicholas Beswick who actually physically murdered Kitchener."

"Oh, Jesus," Eleanor murmured.

He patted her hand, receiving an exasperated glance.

"Physically, he did it. And that was what threw me the first time. Nicholas Beswick isn't the type. We all know that. He couldn't harm a fly, not ordinarily."

"Ah!" Gabriel slapped a hand against the table. "Now I get it, the laser paradigms."

"Right!" Greg said. "At some time during that Thursday, Nicholas Beswick was targeted by a laser that loaded a paradigm into his brain. One that ordered him to kill Kitchener. And I think I know what the paradigm was: Liam Bursken's memories, his personality."

"You told me the Stocken Hall team was constructing artificial memories from scratch," Julia said. "Like a perfect virtual-reality recording. How could they know what Bursken's memories consist of?"

Greg grinned. "Philip, you listening?"

"I'm still here, m'boy."

"Care to tell your granddaughter exactly what you are?"

"Oh," Julia groaned. "Of course."

"I'm not saying MacLennan copied every last thought from Bursken's brain," Greg said. "Just the basics would do. That unique psychotic behavioral trait. That's what he was after."

"If paradigms are that sophisticated, why didn't MacLennan simply load a straightforward kill order into Beswick?" Morgan asked.

"Because they're not that sophisticated, not yet," Greg said. "All the Stocken team have so far is a few ersatz sensorium experiences, nothing more. That's why MacLennan needed Bursken, as raw material. I told you Nicholas wasn't the type. If MacLennan had just given him something like an advanced version of a hypnotic order to kill Kitchener, he might have refused to do it when the moment actually arrived. Not everybody can kill; we can, you, me, and Teddy, because we've been trained to. In battlefield combat situations, it's pure reflex, we don't even think. In counterinsurgency or ambush situations, it becomes harder, you have time to think, to moralize; but if you hate your enemy enough, it's not much of a problem. That's why company commanders always had such trouble finding genuinely good snipers; it's not just marksmanship, it's a question of temperament. It's a rare person who can kill without any qualms.

"I kept asking myself all through this case, who could do such a thing? Coldblooded butchery on a sixty-seven-year-old. The only person I knew was Bursken. Out of all Stocken's inmates, he is the one who can kill without hesitation or remorse every time; he actually enjoyed it, he believed what he was doing was right.

"I'd say MacLennan recorded Liam Bursken's thoughts from a neuro coupling and then combined them with an order to kill Kitchener. Then after Nicholas Beswick committed the murder, the paradigm wiped itself from his mind, presumably along with his recollection of everything he did under its influence. The Stocken Hall research team has already developed a treatment they call magic photons, which can erase a memory, providing they know exactly what it is. And MacLennan certainly did, he made it."

"If MacLennan wanted a copy of Liam Bursken's memories, the only way he could obtain it would be through a cortical interface," Morgan said. "That means Bursken would have to undergo surgery."

"Good point," Greg said. "It's something we can look for, some solid, physical proof. Although if he underwent the surgery at

Stocken, you can bet your life there will turn out to be a legitimate reason for it. But there's no doubt in my mind." He turned to Eleanor. "Remember what Nicholas did right after he smothered Kitchener?"

She drew a breath, thinking back. "He crossed himself."

"Right. But Nicholas is virtually an atheist. Bursken, on the other hand, is a religious fruitcake; he believes he kills his victims because God tells him they're sinners. I'm telling you, it was Bursken's mentality in Nicholas's brain. A real live cyborg. I *knew* Nicholas was innocent." He looked pleased. More like relieved, Julia thought, studying him out of the corner of her eye.

"I know he's innocent, Greg," she said, hating herself for being such a pragmatist, for puncturing his mood. "We all do. But you still have the problem of proving it in a court of law."

"The prosecution still has the knife," Gabriel said. "Pretty strong evidence, especially when you'll be dealing with a jury that's going to be lost after the first ten minutes of specialist technical testimonies."

"Then we shall have to produce some counter-evidence," Eleanor said smartly. "Something that Inspector Langley can't ignore, something that'll mean Nicholas never gets into court. The paradigm itself." She looked at Julia. They both smiled. "Royan," they chorused.

Julia followed the burn's progress through her nodes. The others used the time to relax: Teddy trying to chat up Rachel over by the drinks cabinet; Greg, Eleanor, Morgan, and Gabriel all with their heads together, talking in low tones. Eleanor still hadn't let go of Greg, her hand gripping his, fingers entwined.

Royan, in hotrod mode, was awesome to watch. She had learned a lot about hacking techniques from him; modesty aside, she was good, she knew that. Good enough to crack Jakki Coleman's bank account—and Lloyds-Tashoko's guardian programs were the best corporate money could buy. But she watched Royan's infiltration of Stocken Hall's 'ware with something approaching envy; the speed of the penetration was incredible, and he didn't have lightware crunchers to back him up.

He didn't even bother trying to crack the authorized-user entry codes, he went straight for the management routines. A melt virus got him past the first-level guardian programs, opening up the prison's datanet. The structure unfolded in her mind, an origami molecule, individual terminals and 'ware cores linked by a spiderweb of databuses. She had access to menus of low-grade security files stored in the terminals, along with the Hall's day-today administration details and financial datawork. But the cell security and surveillance circuits were blocked, along with a vast series of memories in the cores.

Royan squirted a more complex virus at the second-level guardian programs, the ones governing access to restricted core memories.

Let's see what the medical department has on Bursken, Julia said, studying the menu. *At the least, his file should tell us whether or not he's got a cortical interface.*

Nice one, Snowy. It isn't on the restricted list. Here we go.

He pulled a Home Office identification code from the administration officer's terminal and used it to request a squirt from the records terminal in the medical division.

"This is Bursken's medical file," she said as the datasheets swarmed down the conference room's flatscreens. "Grandpa, review it for implants, please."

The datasheets flashed past, too fast to read. "Here we go, Juliet." The deluge of bytes halted. She was looking at some kind of official Home Office package. "Hell, girl, they really were wetting themselves over Bursken. This confinement order gives the director, MacLennan, permission to employ any method he sees fit to restrain Liam Bursken, including chemical suppression, or even remedial surgery such as a lobotomy."

"And who would ever complain?" Greg mused, not looking up from his flatscreen. "Even the human-rights lawyers wouldn't bother arguing in Bursken's favor. He's beyond the lowest of the low. You could do anything you wanted to him and no one would give a shit."

"I don't know about anything, boy," Philip said. "But a month ago, he was wheeled into surgery and given a cortical interface." A new datasheet slid into place. "It was ordered by MacLennan, part of a new mental-assessment project. According to this, it was supposed to provide data on his psychotic-state trigger stimulants. Follow-up results are restricted."

"I knew that . . ." Greg looked puzzled for a moment, then clicked his fingers. "Of course, it was Stephanie Rowe who filled me in on Bursken; MacLennan just sat there and let her recite facts to me. How stupid of me."

"You weren't interrogating them," Eleanor said.

"Thanks," he said.

Julia's nodes showed her the second-level guardian programs falling as the virus penetrated. Huge stacks of data materialized into the nodes' visualization, dense packages of colorless binary digits extending out to her mind's horizon. A batch of Royan's tracer programs slithered through them.

Bursken's surgical records vanished from the flatscreen in front of her. *PROBLEM,* it printed.

"What's the matter?" Greg asked.

I THINK I'VE FOUND THE PARADIGM FILE. IT IS LISTED AS BURSKEN'S CORTICAL INTERFACE FOLLOW-UP RESULTS, AND IT HAS A DIRECTOR-ONLY ACCESS CODE.

"So what's the problem?"

THEY WILL KNOW IF I ACCESS IT. A NOTIFICATION PROCEDURE IS HARDWIRED INTO THE CORES. ALL SQUIRTS ARE LOGGED AUTOMATICALLY.

"But the cores think we're the Home Office," Julia said. "Under that premise, we're entitled to access their data. Berkeley operates Stocken under government license."

IF WE ARE THE HOME OFFICE, HOW COME WE CAN ORDER A SQUIRT FOR A DIRECTOR-ONLY FILE? MACLENNAN WOULD HAVE TO BE AT THE HOME OFFICE TO AUTHORIZE THE SQUIRT.

"Okay, let's look at what we want to achieve," Greg said. "What we need is for Inspector Langley to go into Stocken first thing tomorrow morning, armed with a data warrant, and find that paradigm. So we have to be sure it's there before we send him in. Is there any chance this file will crash-wipe if you order a squirt?"

NO.

"Then I'd say do it. Morgan?"

"I can't see any objection. Even if you were to interrogate MacLennan, a lawyer might conceivably neutralize your testimony; there are still some legal queries over evidence obtained psychically. As Eleanor said, we need tangible proof. The evidence is piling up against

MacLennan; to my mind, he's guilty as hell. It has to be the killer paradigm in that file."

"Okay, squirt it over, Royan."

It came through the link, a large construct, taking half a second to transfer. In her terminal cube, it was nothing, a moiré patchwork of randomized data. In her mind—

She opened a secure file in one of her memory nodes and let the construct fill it. Analysis programs sifted through the bytes, trying to identify coherent segments. The patterns they formed were like nothing she had ever seen before; there were analog visual sequences, interlaced with data pulses that defied decryption. She accessed one at random.

Chiaroscuro images, black and scarlet, bloomed silently around her. She was standing on a rainswept street at night amid parallel rows of cheap terrace housing, their walls shimmering as sheets of water sluiced down over the bricks; it was almost as though they were melting. There were no stars above, only empty night. A solitary figure walked down the middle of the road, a man in a sodden greatcoat. Julia felt her heart ignite with exaltation.

She was stalking through woodland, the smooth boles of dead beech trees sliding past, a deep claret in color. Ribbons of black ivy were clawing their way up the crumbling bark; crisp, dry leaves like heart-shaped flakes of ash crunched underfoot. She circled a glade, the procession of boles eclipsing the sight of the two young lovers in its center. All she caught were fleeting glimpses; their bodies moved in a stop-motion sequence. And they were unmarried, profaning the gift of life with their casual coupling. Their skin was salmon-pink, their scattered clothes burgundy and ebony. A knife was heavy in her hand, its blade a glowing coral.

Her mind was alive with whispers, enticing dark promises. God's voice. His strength flooding through her limbs.

A face coalesced before her. An old man with bright, smiling eyes and wispy hair. Mocking eyes. Black eyes, light wells. The man stared into hell and laughed in joy at what he saw.

The whispers grew bolder, caressing her.

Exit.

The nodes shut off with an almost audible snap.

She took a deep gulp of air, shuddering violently.

"What is it?" Morgan asked sharply.

"I'm all right." She held up her hands, surprised to find them trembling. "I was accessing some of the paradigm's visual routines, that's all. Greg's right, it is made up from Bursken's memories." She stopped, remembering the confused montage. A smell of the street's sweet, fresh rain lingered in the executive conference room. And she *detested* the God-violator Edward Kitchener. Feeling a wild, primitive joy that he was dead dead dead. "Dear Lord, he's not human." She stared at Greg. "And you looked into his mind all the time you interviewed him?"

"Goes with the job."

"Yech!"

"So that settles it, then," Greg said. "Royan, do you understand the paradigm?"

MOST SECTIONS ARE ANALOG. BUT THERE IS ONE SEQUENCE THAT IS A DIGITAL COMPOSITION.

"Is it the instruction to kill Kitchener?"

GREEDY GREEDY GREEDY IS WHAT YOU ARE! THE DIGITAL SEQUENCE IS STRANGE. I WILL HAVE TO WRITE A DECRYPTION PROGRAM. TELL YOU TOMORROW.

"Okay," Greg said casually, as though he didn't care.

Liar! Julia thought.

Teddy walked back from the drinks cabinet to stand next to Greg, a dumpy German beer bottle in his hand, condensation mottling its silver-and-ice-blue label. "Hell, man, all this shit about paradigms turning the Beswick kid into a cyborg, it's kinda screwy, but I'll buy it. But you still ain't told us the *why* of it. How come this MacLennan guy wants to snuff his old teacher? He did all right 'cause of Kitchener. Christ, made it to the top in his field. Head of a premier-grade research institution, respected man, big bucks backing him. What's he wanna go and risk all that for?"

"Wrong question," Gabriel said. She was smiling faintly, head tilted back on her chair, staring at the ceiling. "What you ought to ask is, why did MacLennan kill Clarissa Wynne? That's the real question. After he murdered her, he had to get rid of Kitchener; it was inevitable. He was covering himself to protect that cushy number he's wound up with."

"The neurohormone!" Julia exclaimed, quietly pleased she could keep up with Gabriel.

WELL DONE, SNOWY.

Morgan flicked an ironic glance at the camera.

Gabriel suddenly leaned forward, resting her elbows on the table, fixing Teddy with an intent stare. "MacLennan must have been worried that once Kitchener perfected the retrospective neurohormone, he would look into the past and see him murdering Clarissa. That's why poor old Nicholas Beswick was also ordered to destroy the bioware that produced the neurohormone, and to wipe the Abbey's Bendix. To eliminate any possibility of anybody looking back. Lucky he missed those ampoules. I don't suppose MacLennan could think of every contingency."

"I couldn't have seen that far back," Eleanor said. "A week was a hell of an effort. Eleven years would have been utterly impossible."

"Yes," Gabriel said. "I never used to look more than a couple of days into the future when I had my gland. That was partly psychological, admittedly. But . . . well, with Kitchener working on it, who knows what might have been accomplished in the end?"

"I think I've found the reason she was murdered," Philip said.

"Yeah?" Greg perked up. "Go on."

"Ten years ago, there was a paper published on the possibilities of laser paradigms applied to education. The first of its kind. It was co-authored by James MacLennan and Clarissa Wynne."

"Ten years?" Morgan asked. "We confirmed that World Bank loan was eleven years ago."

"Published posthumously," Greg said. "That's why MacLennan killed her. I'll give you good odds that Clarissa did the real breakthrough work on paradigms while she was at Launde. And MacLennan was sharp enough to realize the possibilities. He was very keen to stress that when I talked to him. Once they are perfected, paradigms will be worth a fortune. He reckoned the entire penal system would have to be rebuilt from the ground up, and not just in this country. I suppose it would be the same for schools and universities as well; paradigms could replace lessons and lectures. And he's leading the project. He'll get all the fame and the glory, not to mention a share of the royalties. And it should have been her in charge of Berkeley's team."

"Ah!" Julia cried. She grinned at the curious faces. "Grandpa, that financial profile we assembled on Diessenburg Mercantile should still be in our finance-division memory core. Access it and run a check for me. See how much money Diessenburg Mercantile is loaning the Berkeley Company."

"You all hear that?" Philip's voice boomed. "Now that is a true Evans. Laser-sharp. My granddaughter."

There were times—like *now*—when she wished the NN core was loaded with only a simple Turing management program.

"Got it," Philip said. "The Berkeley Company has borrowed eight hundred million Eurofrancs from Diessenburg Mercantile. There are extension options covering another two and a half billion, but they're all subject to some kind of clause. Dunno what, it's classified, board members only."

"MacLennan succeeding with the laser paradigms?" Morgan suggested.

"Very probable," Philip agreed.

"Two and a half billion," Julia said, ruminating out loud. "That's more than Diessenburg loaned us before Prior's Fen."

"How much would it cost to build and operate an entire continent's educational and penal services?" Greg asked.

"A lot," she said. "And Karl Hildebrandt is on holiday. Unavailable for two months. I contacted his office yesterday after you said you wanted to meet him."

"We can't really blame the bank," Morgan said. "They were just protecting their investment. Natural corporate reflex."

Julia didn't approve of that attitude at all. "That doesn't take away the fact that MacLennan is a double murderer, or that an innocent man is in jail because of him."

"You'll have a terrible job trying to establish degrees of complicity," Morgan said. "I doubt Karl will ever reappear anywhere under English jurisdiction. The Diessenburg Mercantile directors will disclaim any knowledge of the affair. And if the bank does allow any of them to come into our courts to testify, you can be sure they will be genuinely ignorant so that Greg here won't be able to implicate them."

"Maybe," Greg said. "But at least we've got MacLennan nailed."

"Yes," Morgan said. "I'll get on to the Home Office, they'll have MacLennan arrested first thing tomorrow morning."

"I'd like the Oakham police to handle the actual arrest," Greg said. "They need the credit. I'll rap with Langley, explain what actually happened. And we'd better have a premier-grade programmer on hand to serve the data warrant. I'd hate for anything to happen to that paradigm now."

"Right." Morgan loaded a note into his cybofax.

Greg climbed to his feet, stretching laboriously.

Julia stood and tugged her windcheater jacket from the back of the chair. "Thanks again for helping, Teddy."

He took a last swig from his beer bottle and gave her a shrewd look. "No problem, gal. Does me good to get out and about, keep my hand in. But you leave off Greg once this case is over, hear me? He's a damn orange farmer now. Nothing else."

"I hear you, Teddy." She blew him a kiss.

24

IT WAS MIDNIGHT WHEN GREG and Eleanor reached the farm. Fog had given way to a steady rain, the darkness was total. Greg could hear the wind rustling the tops of the new saplings on either side of the driveway. The EMC Ranger's tires splashed through long trickles of water as Eleanor let the vehicle roll slowly down the slope.

Greg ran a hand through his greasy hair. What he wanted was a shower, a drink, and a bed. Worst of all, he wanted to go to bed to sleep. Arms and belly muscles were stiff and sore from hanging under the Westland ghost wing.

Surprisingly, given all the aches, plus a persistent post-mission edginess, he still felt easier than he had for a week. He grinned at his weak reflection in the side window. I knew Nicholas didn't do it.

"What's so funny?" Eleanor asked.

"Nothing. Tell you, I'm just glad it's over."

"Me too."

"Yeah. Thanks for understanding."

"Make the most of it. Next time, I'll stomp my foot and say no."

"Good," he said with feeling. "You'd better go see Mrs. Beswick tomorrow, give her the good news. I expect I'll be having quite a busy day. Christ, and Vernon was upset before about the murder being complicated."

"He'll survive. Like you said, they'll get a lot of credit for wrapping this up."

"Yeah." There's justice. But at least it will make life in Oakham more tolerable for everybody.

Beyond the window's reflection, Maurice Knebel's mirage rippled unsteadily on the edge of reality. Greg knew his last memory of the ex-detective would take a long time to dissipate. Knebel had closed his eyes tightly, teeth clamping down on his lower lip, whimpering softly as Greg aimed the stunshot at him. In the background, Teddy had muttered snidely about using the Uzi instead.

Then there was the trip back to the warehouse. Walton's minacious streets crowding in on him, plaguing him with the prospect of running into some kind of hazard now the mission was over—the oldest squaddie fear in the book.

The EMC Ranger's headlight beams tracked across the side of the barn, unnaturally bright under the cloud-blocked sky. They touched the house briefly, a flash of moth-gray stone.

Greg began searching around with his hand, lifting the stunshot from the back seat. He slung it over his shoulder. Bloody good thing Langley can't see me now, he thought. The man had always been dubious of Greg's real motivations, the underground politics behind his assignment to the case. Seeing him in full combat gear would confirm every black paranoid suspicion about Julia's undue influence.

Eleanor stopped the EMC Ranger in front of the door and the porch light came on automatically. They both climbed out, shoulders hunched against the rain. Eleanor blipped the lock, pulling her navy-blue jacket tighter across her sweatshirt.

Greg heard the lynch mob first. Footsteps crunching on the wet gravel behind the EMC Ranger. His gland gave a lurch, discharging the neurohormone into his brain. He grunted in shock as the five minds trespassed on his consciousness. They were all identical, possessed with unrelenting berserker arrogance, thought currents devoid of any rationality. A teratoid insanity. Recognition was instantaneous; he had encountered that mind once before: Liam Bursken.

They walked into the splash of light thrown by the porch light, a soft, dead smile on their lips: Frankie Owen, Mark Sutton, Les Hepburn, Andrew Foster, and Douglas Kellam.

Eleanor twisted around. "What—"

Mark Sutton raised a double-barreled shotgun, thoughts radiant with cool delight.

Greg's training took over. He fired the stunshot even as he was bringing it to bear. The pulse was dazzlingly bright to his night-acclimatized retinas. It missed Sutton, fizzling voraciously as it sliced through the rain. But it was enough.

Sutton jerked aside, complacency shattered. The shotgun went off, blowing out one of the EMC Ranger's rear windows. A lethal blast of crystalline splinters slammed into the stone wall to Greg's right. He felt stingers of pain jab down his chest where the combat jacket was open. Spots of blood bloomed on his white T-shirt.

He saw the other four men jump back into the concealing murk of rain and darkness that cloaked the rest of the farmyard, surprise and outrage rampant on their faces. Fury that their victim should dare to fight back, resist the Lord's will. His fumbling fingers found the stunshot's fire-selector catch and flicked it to continuous. A solid stream of glaring blue-white lightning speared out of the barrel as he tugged the trigger, illuminating the entire farmyard. Its end grew ragged over by the barn, flickering spasmodically as the close-packed pulses lost cohesion.

He swung the weapon down and around, not really aiming, simply chasing Sutton as the man scrambled for cover behind the EMC Ranger. The torrent of pulses caught him on the shoulder, spinning him around as if by a high-pressure water jet. The shotgun went flying off into the night as he whirled around, arms extended.

Greg let go of the trigger and Sutton collapsed into a bucking heap. To his left, he saw Frankie Owen making a grab for Eleanor, his normally sulky face snarled up in an expression of wrath. A flick knife gleamed as it slid out of his fist. Eleanor was blocking the stunshot's line of fire.

A narrow line of damp air in front of Greg suddenly fluoresced a vivid green. Raindrops scintillated with an uncanny beauty as they fell through it. Laser. He was being shot at! Overstressed nerves jerked him backward. He nearly lost his footing on the gravel as he dropped below the level of the EMC Ranger. He fought to regain balance. Judging by the angle of the beam, it was coming from the tangerine grove on the other side of the barn.

The beam swept along the farmhouse's stonework, across the door, toward the two figures thrashing about. It was too broad to be a rifle targeting-laser. Wrong color, anyway.

Realization struck like a spike of ice directly into his spine. The paradigm imprinter. MacLennan himself was out there, trying to zombie Eleanor.

"Down!" he screamed, and launched himself at the wrestling figures just as they broke apart. Eleanor was staggering backward. Green light stroked her torso. He caught her around the waist in a tackle that sent both of them crashing to the ground. Eleanor yelped in shock and pain as they hit the gravel. Somehow he managed to hold onto the stunshot; 'ware modules jabbed painfully into his side. Up above, the laser slashed furiously from side to side, producing a canopy of lurid green radiation between the EMC Ranger and the house, flecked with twinkling jade raindrops.

Frankie Owen groaned, his thought currents disfigured by supreme agony. Greg glanced up to see him curled up on the gravel just in front of them, hands clutching his groin, nursing crushed testicles. A mushy spurt of vomit sputtered out of his open mouth. His face was corpse-white, eyes red and wet.

Eleanor did that to him. Greg felt a crazy edge of glee. My Eleanor.

Out on the brink of his espersense, those remaining three joyless minds were congregating. Scattered thoughts refocusing on him.

"Are you all right?" he hissed.

"My arm's numb. Why did you pull me down?"

"Look up, that's the paradigm imprint laser."

"Oh, Jesus."

"Let's see if we can get inside."

He rolled over and rose to a crouch. Foster, Hepburn, and Kellam were moving apart again, fanning out around the EMC Ranger. It was four meters to the door; the laser painted a sharp green line two-thirds of the way up.

"I'll go first," he told her. "Start moving as soon as I reach it."

"Right."

He tensed his legs, then he was up and running. Fingers reaching for the brass door handle. The polished metal was slick in his palm. Turning slowly. His shoulder thudded into the wood and he was through, skating on the hall tiles.

Eleanor was racing past him less than a second later. He shoved the door shut with a burst of frantic strength. There was a quiet whine as the lock engaged. He aimed the stunshot at it and fired. The plastic covering melted with a flash of orange flame, droplets spraying out. The 'ware circuits inside flared briefly; sparks fountained, dying embers skittering over the cold tiles.

Someone outside smacked into the door. He saw it quiver in the frame. There was the sound of a fist hammering on the panels.

"Mandel." It was Les Hepburn's voice, but toneless, that same clipped precision Bursken used. "Come out, Mandel. You shall not escape the Lord's justice."

"Fuck off!" He grabbed Eleanor's hand. "Come on, they'll be inside in a minute." There was no light in the hall. He felt around for the photon amp band hooked on his shoulder tab and slapped it into place. The time-display and guido coordinates gleamed brightly. Walls, floor, and furniture shimmered out of nowhere, solidifying into their familiar places. He bled in the infrared. The photon amp's gray-and-blue world tinted into red, becoming fractionally brighter, losing some definition.

"I'll call the police," Eleanor said.

"No way," he said, leading her down to the study. "People like Keith Willet aren't going to be able to cope with a bunch of Liam Burskens, even if they believed us. In any case, it would take them too long to get here."

"Greg! We need help." She was battling panic.

"I know!" He switched on the communication 'ware and pulled his skull helmet into place. "Emergency!"

"What is it, boy?" Philip Evans asked.

"We've been ambushed at the farm. MacLennan is here with five people he's loaded with Bursken's paradigm. And this time, it's me they're after."

"Shit, boy; you all right?"

"For now. We need help, and fast."

"I'm launching the security crash team now. They'll be there in ten minutes."

Greg opened the study door. The room was supposed to be his den, but he still hadn't got it sorted out. There was a big desk over by the window, a settee; long planks were leaning against a wall, destined to be shelves when he got around to screwing them together. The floor was cluttered with cardboard boxes full of his accumulated junk. He could just make out the Berrybut estate through the window, pinprick glints of light from the chalets. The rain must have extinguished the bonfire hours ago; the photon amp's infrared function couldn't even pick up the dying cinders.

"Philip's launching the Event Horizon crash team," he told Eleanor.

"Right. Why are we in here?"

A dark, human silhouette moved across the window, eclipsing the chalets. The head glowed brightly in grades of red, hot blood highlighting the cheeks and nose; the eyes were cooler, darker. It contained the familiar thought currents of Liam Bursken.

"Shush." He gripped her hand tighter. Even with the infrared's ambiguous slant, he could recognize the features of the face pressed to the glass. Brendan Talbot, an engineer who lived in Hambleton. Christ, how many people had MacLennan loaded the paradigm into?

Greg's free hand closed around the stock of the Heckler and Koch rifle lying on the desk. A real weapon.

Ronnie Kay appeared next to Brendan Talbot and hurled a brick straight through the study window. Eleanor yelled in fright. A torch shone into the room with the force of a solar flare.

The photon amp filters responded immediately, reducing the glare until it was a manageable corona. Greg could see Talbot, his hand reaching through the jagged hole in the glass, scrabbling around for the catch.

"Face your judgment, Mandel," Kay shouted. "Embrace us. We will deliver you from sin."

Greg leveled the rifle at Talbot. And couldn't pull the trigger. It wasn't Talbot, only his body. Brendan had a wife, a six-year-old daughter.

"Shit!" he roared. In his army days, it wouldn't have made any difference. None. See a hostile and snuff him. Nothing else had ever been allowed to interfere with that maxim. It was simple survival. Life was so fucking *easy* in those days. Uncomplicated.

Brendan Talbot's fingers closed around the catch.

Greg yanked the stunshot around, strap cutting into his shoulder. Aim and fire. The pulse hit the glass and splattered, minute static tendrils writhing across the oblong pane. "Shit shit shit." Aim and fire. This time, the pulse struck Talbot's hand. There was a muffled grunt and he was flailing backward. His wrist caught the spikes of glass around the edge of the hole, skin tearing. There was a confused splash of heat.

The torch beam wavered about as Kay tried to catch him.

"Let's go," Greg said.

Runnels of Talbot's blood were seeping down the window below the hole, glowing like radioactive sludge.

"What's happening now, boy?" Philip asked anxiously.

"Trouble. Where's the crash team?"

"They're getting into the tilt-fan now."

"Jesus!"

Eleanor gave him a frightened glance as they charged back into the hall.

"The crash team is just taking off," he told her. "Philip, have they got stunshots with them?"

"Sure thing, boy."

"Tell them to use the stunshots wherever possible; remember, these people aren't responsible for what they're doing."

"I'll tell 'em."

"Upstairs," he said to Eleanor. They started to pound up the staircase.

There was an almighty crash of breaking glass from the lounge when they were halfway up.

Knocking the whole window out by the sound of it, Greg thought. He handed Eleanor the stunshot when they reached the landing. At least if she did have to shoot, she would never have the guilt of killing a complete innocent. He could always use the rifle to immobilize. If he had time, if the melee didn't become too confusing, if he could hang on to his scruples. They ran down the landing to the master bedroom.

"Philip, plug Royan in," Greg said.

"Right-oh, boy."

The landing's biolums came on just as they reached the bedroom door, three sets of wall globes shaped like lilies. Greg shot them out with the rifle. They disintegrated with loud popping sounds, showering the landing with radiant flakes that died as they bounced along the carpet.

From a tactical standpoint, there was little improvement; biolum light shone up from the hall, casting long, delusive shadows over the landing walls. He could hear people moving about below.

They went through into the bedroom. "Keep watching the stairs," Greg said. "Anyone comes up, shoot 'em."

"Right." Eleanor kneeled down beside the door, peering through the crack.

The photon amp's time numerals and guido coordinates blurred, then merged into a single wavery band of yellow light. There was a moment's pause, then the display printed: *I'M HERE, GREG.*

"Great. Listen, I've got about half a dozen people who think they're Liam Bursken coming at me. Now, there has got to be some way to flush that paradigm out of them. We know it erases itself after a set time. Access the recording you made and look for the magic-photons sequence, see if there's any way we can activate it prematurely."

GOT YOU. ACCESSING NOW.

"They're here, Greg," Eleanor called softly. She fired the stun-shot; ten or twelve pulses *zinged* along the landing, scorching long burn marks into the wallpaper, blistering the paint on the banister rail.

He was aware of the minds on the stairs. One of them ruptured in a flurry of pain, the thought currents fragmenting into comate insensibility. "You got one."

GREG, HAVE YOU GOT A LASER WITH YOU?

"Yeah, a Heckler and Koch hunting rifle."

TOO POWERFUL. HAS IT GOT A TARGETING IMAGER?

"Yeah."

GOOD GOOD GOOD. PLUG THE IMAGER INTO YOUR SUIT 'WARE.

"Right."

"The crash team has left," Philip said. "Be with you in eight minutes."

It was going to be too long, that was obvious.

Greg tugged the rifle's targeting imager monocle out of its recess and detached it from the fiber-optic cable. The interface was standard—thank Christ. He plugged the cable into a socket on the guido 'ware module. Blue target circles hardened in front of him, angling down toward the carpet, the same line as the rifle barrel was pointing.

"Come out, Mandel," Ronnie Kay shouted up from the hall, "or we will burn you out. Fire is always the great purifier. Your wife will die with you then. Come out."

"Don't you dare," Eleanor said.

"Royan?"

I'VE DECRYPTED IT. STRANGE. NOT LIKE SOFTWARE. NO SUB-

ROUTINES. EVERYTHING STRUNG TOGETHER, SIMILAR TO PIXEL CODES, MUCH HIGHER BIT RATE THOUGH.

"Have you found the magic-photons sequence?"

WORKING ON IT.

Greg went over to the window, standing beside it with his back to the wall, expanding his espersense outward. There were three minds below. He edged the rifle out past the curtains and activated the imager. The photon amp's picture of the bedroom faded away, replaced by a view of the garden below. Three men were standing on the lawn, waiting patiently. One of them held what looked like a shotgun, the other two were carrying clubs of some kind.

"Come out, Mandel."

Eleanor fired another barrage of stunshot pulses down the landing.

"We'll burn your flesh to ashes. Your last minutes will be the torment of hell. Repent."

THINK I'VE GOT IT.

"Thank Christ for that."

THERE ARE TWO SEPARATE SEQUENCES. BOTH BECOME ACTIVE AFTER A MEASURED INTERVAL FOLLOWING IMPRINT. TIMED BY HEARTBEATS. CLEVER THAT. THE FIRST SEQUENCE CONTAINS THE PARADIGM ITSELF AND THE INSTRUCTION TO KILL KITCHENER, ALONG WITH ADDITIONAL ORDERS TO DESTROY HIS RETRO-SPECTIVE NEUROHORMONE WORK. IT ACTIVATED ITSELF AFTER APPROXIMATELY NINE HOURS. THE SECOND SEQUENCE IS THE MAGIC PHOTONS, WHICH ACTIVATES TWO HOURS LATER.

Even now, Greg couldn't quite shake off his fascination with the case. Nicholas must have been hit before the storm, before the rising waters of the Chater closed the ramshackle bridge.

"Can you trigger the magic-photons sequence?"

YES. I'VE ISOLATED ITS ACTIVATION CODE FROM THE PARA-DIGM'S TIMER SECTION.

"Okay, there are three people we can try it on."

The target circles vanished as Royan took command of the rifle's 'ware. Greg watched the imager's laser send a fan of ruby light sweeping across the lawn. The grid emerged in its wake, splitting into three sections, folding around the waiting men.

HERE GOES.

The contoured lines around the central figure began to flash.

NOW.

Greg saw a single strobe-like flicker of pink douse the man's face. His espersense showed him the man's thought currents start to seethe furiously. A loud, destitute wailing penetrated the glass.

"What's happening?" Eleanor demanded.

"I'm not sure." Even as he spoke, he sensed the new tide of personality usurping Bursken's resolute thought currents. His empathy was caught by the backlash of petrified bewilderment raging inside the abused brain, feedback sending a quake of dismay shuddering along his own synapses. Then the man was dropping to his knees, curling into a fetal position, mind rushing headlong into welcome oblivion.

"Okay, we got him. Zap the other two, Royan."

Their grid outlines began to flash. The targeting laser fired twice.

"Flames, Mandel," Ronnie Kay shouted. "They will consume you. There will be no redemption."

"Wait," Greg shouted back. "I'm coming out."

"Greg!" Eleanor pleaded.

"Those crazies will torch the place if I don't. We have to clear them out."

"Let the crash team do it."

"That bastard MacLennan is still out there. He can load Bursken's mind into them as soon as they land. Then where will we be? They are armed and armored, Eleanor. At least the lynch mob only have shotguns."

"Come then, Mandel. Come to us."

She drew a sharp breath through her teeth. "God, you be careful, Gregory."

He knew exactly how much that cost her to say. "No messing."

They waited in the hall at the foot of the stairs. Five of them, a tight arrowhead, with Ronnie Kay at the front, two shotguns following him with mechanical precision. Their mouths were curved up in the same slight, vapid smile.

His espersense flowed around them, along the hall, through the empty rooms. They were the only ones inside. Right at the back of his head was the faint thrumming of pressure, the neurohormones stressing his synapses to their limit.

He held the rifle casually at his hip as he descended.

"Take the ones with the shotguns first," he whispered.

RIGHT.

The grid appeared again, peeling into five segments like cybernetic butterfly wings closing fluidly around their ignorant prey.

Ronnie Kay blinked, glancing distrustfully at the rifle. "Put it down, Mandel."

READY.

"Now!"

The laser lashed out, spiking each of them in turn. Elapsed time: seven-tenths of a second.

They wilted in unison, filling the air with a grotesque catlike puling. Arms and legs were infected with a life of their own, waving and flexing at random.

"Shitfire," Greg murmured.

DID WE GET THEM?

"Oh, yeah. We got 'em."

Eleanor was running along the landing, stunshot held ready, looking as if she was about to start a war.

"The crash team will be there in five minutes," Philip said.

Eleanor barged into Greg's side, hugging him tightly. She let out a gulping sob. "I'm sorry." She wiped her eyes.

His arm went around her, holding her roughly. He kissed the top of her forehead, damp hair rasping across his lips.

They went down the last few stairs, slowly, every step a great effort.

The front door had been forced open, the lock jimmied off. A draft of clammy air swirled in.

Greg used the rifle barrel to push the lounge door open. Shards of glass were heaped on the floor below the broken window. The curtains flapped feebly.

"It's clear," Greg said. "I'll go out here, through the window. MacLennan can see the front door." Eleanor's fingers clutched at him through the combat leathers. "I've got to finish this." And this time there would be no hesitation, no reluctance. MacLennan had come hunting him, broaching the sanctity of his home. Well, now it would be settled on those terms. One-on-one, zero rules.

"I know," Eleanor said.

He crouched down and scuttled over to the window. "Royan, kill the imager's camera feed. I don't want to be on the receiving end of that paradigm—" He stopped, intuition acting like a dose of wine, stealing warmly into his brain.

The gloomy image faded out, leaving him alone with the time-display and guido coordinates. He shoved the rifle through the shattered window.

"Give me the laser return."

The picture that built up was similar to the virtual simulation he had used to fly into Walton, photonic topology, except it was all red. The rickety fence was ten meters in front of him, saplings standing in long rows behind it, grass resolved as a fuzzy gauze mat.

"Okay, Royan, there's one last piece of reprogramming I need."

He poked the rifle around the corner of the house. The laser painted in the EMC Ranger, the barn, and the wall around the farmyard. Mark Sutton was lying where he'd fallen. Frankie Owen was crawling toward the driveway. It was like watching a time-lapse puppet in motion, the picture refreshing itself every second as the laser swept back and forth.

A grid tailored itself into a perfect fit around Frankie Owen.

"I'm here," Greg called out clearly.

Frankie twisted around. When he was looking straight at Greg, the laser fired the magic photon's activation code at him. There was a muffled gurgling, then he lay still. Greg sensed Bursken's thoughts routed by Frankie's usual dull anger and general life-resentment just before consciousness dwindled.

Not much of an improvement, really.

He pointed the rifle at the tangerine grove, where he thought MacLennan had fired the paradigm laser from.

"Focus shift, one hundred and fifty meters."

The grove filled his vision field. It lacked the sharp-edged clarity of anything close by, degraded by rain, almost like static interference. These saplings had been planted over a year ago, now two and a half meters high, starting to spread out at the top. They were covered with leaves and blossoms, which showed up like a layer of coarse ice crystals around the core of twigs and branches.

There was a vehicle parked in the middle of the grove, almost hidden by the saplings. A jeep of some kind.

Perfect for the terrain in the Chater valley, he thought.

LASER ACQUISITION, the photon amp display printed.

"Royan?"

THAT'S YOUR ECM DETECTOR WARNING. MACLENNAN IS FIRING THE PARADIGM IMPRINTER AT YOU. ONE MOMENT.

The image fluttered, then reappeared. A bright-red dot was flashing ten meters to the left of the jeep.

THAT'S THE EMISSION POINT.

"Right. Give me targeting mode."

The blue circles sprang up. Greg shifted the rifle until they were centered on the jeep. He pulled the trigger. Five shots into the bonnet, three into the front tire, another five into the bodywork.

MacLennan stopped firing the paradigm laser.

Greg pumped another ten shots into the rear of the jeep. He heard the unmistakable dull thud of an explosion. The back of the jeep rippled, opening up like a flower, jagged metal petals lunging jerkily for the blank sky.

"Cancel targeting mode." He started to jog toward the jeep. No way could he run; as it was, he had to try to remember what was immediately ahead at each footfall. The wall between him and the grove seemed to lurch toward him in two-meter increments.

A nimbus had engulfed the jeep, altering in size each time the picture updated, never the same shape twice. Flames, he guessed.

He reached the wall and clambered over, moss squelching below his gloves, ignoring the erratic images as the rifle shifted about, working by touch.

LASER ACQUISITION.

He landed on the spongy grass in the grove and automatically rolled to one side. Paratroop training. Furious flames from the jeep were making a loud crackling.

"MacLennan?" he bellowed. "It doesn't work on me, you shit!" He stood up, pointing the rifle ahead.

LASER ACQUISITION.

The red dot was flashing from behind some saplings away to his left, dancing about like a firefly caught in a hurricane. MacLennan was moving away from the jeep. Greg started to jog toward the dot, ducking under the low branches, swerving around the trunks.

"Greg?" It was Philip. "The crash team will be with you in two minutes."

"Keep them in the air until I give the all-clear."

"All right, boy, it's your show."

The laser picked out MacLennan running down a row of saplings, about eighty meters ahead. A clockwork humanoid, legs and arms pumping in a fractured rhythm. Slender grid lines chased after him, coiling around his limbs and torso.

DO YOU WANT TARGET MODE?

"Not yet. I have to be sure."

SURE SURE SURE? WHAT KIND OF BLOODY SURE? HE TRIED TO KILL YOU.

Greg ran out into a tractor lane, four meters wide, the branches arching overhead, not quite meeting. It made the going a lot easier; he risked increasing his pace. "Sure about Clarissa Wynne."

MacLennan vaulted over the fence at the bottom of the grove and sprinted over the field toward Hambleton Wood.

Gotcha, Greg thought. He arrived at the fence, scaling it quickly.

MacLennan reached the boundary of the wood and charged through the waist-high fringe of undergrowth. He suddenly fell forward, disappearing from sight below the nettles. Greg heard a distant curse.

The grass underfoot was awkward, tufty and slippery with rain. He had to slow down again, especially as he was cutting down the slope. There was that distinctive sound of brittle wood snapping up ahead as MacLennan thrashed about in the dead hawthorn bushes.

Christ, I hope it is MacLennan after all this! But his intuition was giving him a powerful high, as if he was just going through the motions. The outcome was already decided.

MacLennan's upper torso reappeared amid the bushes. He was flinging himself desperately at the knotted tangle of vines strung between the old trees. It wouldn't do him any good; you needed either a tank or a bulldozer to break into the wood. He jerked around, right arm coming up. Red dot.

LASER ACQUISITION.

Greg slowed to a halt thirty meters from the wood, raising the rifle to his shoulder. "Give me targeting mode and expand the magnification." He ordered his cortical node to increase the neurohormone secretion level.

ABOUT BLOODY TIME.

Blue circles clicked into place. The targeting-laser sweep contracted around MacLennan. It was as though he was standing two meters in front of Greg, the warped network of red lines bright enough to give off a faint coronal hue. An oversized pistol was gripped in his right hand, nozzle blazing.

Greg's espersense encountered the mind inside the reticulated head. It was MacLennan.

Greg aimed at the pistol and fired.

MacLennan howled, convulsing, right arm hugged to his chest. His pistol tumbling away. A hot throb of pain lanced into Greg's mind. Behind it came the raw malevolence, the near-frenzied fear, and the abhorrence.

"Hold it," Greg commanded as MacLennan began to look around his feet for the imprinter, the tendrils of desperation uncoiling in his gibbering mind. Greg walked forward until he came to the edge of the nettles. "Why did you come here, MacLennan? Why did you set them on me?"

"Because it was you!" MacLennan bawled. "You! Mindstar freak. You found the paradigm."

"How did you know that?"

"You were from the Home Office, you burned into the memory core. You! It was you. Freak fucker."

"Oh, shit." The rush of energy that had carried him out of the house and across the grove suddenly bled away. There was no determination left in him. No pride at completing the case, only weariness. He just wanted this over. Finished.

MacLennan started sobbing.

"Shut up!" Greg yelled.

"It hurts me! It hurts. You've burned my hand in half, you bastard. Get me to a hospital, for Christ's sake."

Every emotion reached rock bottom. Greg felt dangerously calm.

"It hurts, does it, MacLennan? How did Clarissa Wynne feel when you pushed her head under the water? Did she hurt, MacLennan?"

"Clarissa?" It came out like a whinny.

"You killed her. Didn't you? Eleven years ago, you shot her full of syntho and killed her."

"She was going to claim all the credit!"

"Even now you're lying! It was her work."

"Wasn't!"

Guilt corrupted every thought in MacLennan's head. And there was nothing left to say.

Greg took a labored breath. "Royan, shoot it over."

The grid snapped off for an instant as the targeting laser stabbed at MacLennan's eyes.

He heard the paradigm as it came surging through the communication link, a near-ultrasonic *wheee* in his earpiece, a blast of photons encapsulating the essence of Liam Bursken, accompanied by a monomaniac hatred for one man.

Poetic justice or intuitive inspiration; Greg didn't know which, only that it was right. It fit.

He pulled the photon amp strip from his face, twin circles of skin around his eyesockets pinching as it came free. The real world rushed back in on him, dark and dank, awash with human failings. The clean simplicity of the laser return virtual graphics was almost preferable. Somewhere behind him flames were soaring up into the night from the wreck of the jeep. Rain pattered down, beating the dusky vegetation toward the muddy ground.

MacLennan's prim face was contorted with pain, hair plastered down into a straggly cap. His jaw was working silently, as though he was choking.

"Do you know who you hate, Liam?" Greg asked quietly. "Do you?"

MacLennan stared back at him with insane eyes, mouth screwing into a joyous smile. "Yes. Me. It's me. Me!"

"That's right." Greg took the vibration knife from his belt, switched it on and dropped it at MacLennan's feet.

MacLennan snatched it up with his good hand. "Redemption. He has granted me redemption." He laughed rhapsodically as he shoved the blade into his stomach. Blood foamed out. He sank to his knees, teeth clenched with effort, cheeks bulging, and pulled the blade up toward his sternum. "Yes. Oh, yes, My Lord."

Greg turned and walked away. Back to the farmhouse and Eleanor, where he belonged.

High above the reservoir, the security team's tilt-fan dived out of the clouds, turbines shrieking with urgency.

25

JULIA FOUND HER HAND STRAYING toward Robin's hair. He was sleeping sprawled out on his belly in the middle of the bed, head fallen between two big fluffy pillows, mouth slightly agape. She stroked his hair softly, smoothing down the ruffled tufts. Seen in the lush morning light that was prizing its way around the edges of the curtains, he was even more handsome than the first time she had caught sight of him at the pool. And he was so terribly sweet. Tender, anxious, and eager all at once—excellent body, too. He lacked Patrick's ruthless dynamism, and this had made their sex far more sensual. She still wasn't quite sure if she was his first, but she was certainly near the front of the queue. A thought to treasure.

He stirred below her hand and she held her breath. She didn't want to wake him up just yet. The poor dear must be tired after last night.

She would have a cup of tea, skim through the breakfast 'casts, nip into the toilet; *then* it would be time for him to perform again.

NN Core Access Request.

No peace for the wicked. And last night she had been gloriously wicked.

Open Channel To NN Core.

Morning, Juliet.

Morning, Grandpa. We can't be having a crisis this early.

Not a crisis, no.

Thank heavens for that. What then?

I'm curious about something you did yesterday.

Spying on me again?

No. I was just reviewing some of your data traffic. Double-checking. That's what I'm here for, your safety net.

Yah, go on. She had a pretty good idea where this was leading.

You accessed one of our biochemical research labs yesterday. Using your executive code, no less. Mind telling me what for, girl?

No, I don't mind. She leaned over to the bedside cabinet and poured her tea from the silver service.

Juliet!

Oh, you wanted to know right now?

If I still had a body, I'd put you over my bloody knee, m'girl.

Grandpa, behave. Besides, I'm too big and too strong these days. And I don't fight fair, either.

You learned that from me, Juliet. Now, are you going to tell me?

She picked up her cup and saucer and settled back into the pillows. *Yah, all right. I wiped every record of the retrospective neurohormone from our memory cores: the analysis report, molecular structure, conclusions, everything. Then I sent Rachel over there and she tipped all the remaining ampoules into the toxic waste-disposal furnace. Happy now?*

Bloody hell, girl. Why?

The tea was too hot to drink. She blew across the top of her cup as she marshaled her thoughts. *Because I don't want something like that let loose in the world, Grandpa. It's bad enough having people like Gabriel being able to see what I might do in the future, or Greg knowing how badly I've been misbehaving just by looking at me. I don't want someone standing in this room ten years from now taking a simple infusion and being able to see what I did last night.*

Hardly a simple infusion, girl.

Exactly. The Home Office has slapped a restriction order on what really happened at Greg's farm and Launde Abbey. Admittedly, their main concern is the way MacLennan abused his paradigm project; if word got out that the New Conservatives had been allowing a company to research what amounts to a mind-control system, there would be hell to pay. Certainly it would cost them the next election. Marchant didn't need much prodding to include the neurohormone. And there are now only fifteen people in the world who know a retrospection neurohormone is even possible. With those numbers, we might just be able to keep it that way. Even if the news does eventually leak out, it would take an immense research effort to produce it again, if we ever could. Kitchener was a very clever man, not to mention idiosyncratic.

You can't fight progress, Juliet.

A retrospective neurohormone isn't progress, Grandpa. Quite the opposite. And there is already more than enough freely available technology in this world capable of being misapplied by tekmercs and oth-

ers. Corporations and kombinates are going to have to start becoming
responsible again. After all, we do fund ninety percent of all the signif-
icant scientific research these days.

Lord preserve us, a global citizen with a conscience.

Somebody has to be, Grandpa. There is more to Event Horizon than
making nifty household 'ware gadgets. Do you really want me to use
all that influence for the bad?

Juliet, you are beautiful. I'm so proud of you.

She knew her cheeks would be reddening. Didn't care. Not this
morning. *Thank you, Grandpa. I am what I am because I have the best*
teacher in the world.

I've said it before, I'll say it again. Seductress!

Yah. And proud of it.

Eat your breakfast in peace, Juliet. I've got plenty of datawork piled
up for you later.

Exit NN Core.

She took a sip of tea and fired the remote at the wall-mounted
flatscreen, keeping the volume low. It was the East England channel,
and she was on again. Yesterday's gala re-opening of the Stock Exchange. Another invitation impossible to refuse; half the companies
listed were heavily dependent on Event Horizon contracts. The exchange had been operating out of temporary quarters at Canary
Wharf ever since the PSP had fallen and trading became legal again.
Party activists had razed the old exchange a couple of months after
President Armstrong came to power. So a new purpose-built building had risen up out of the old site, one with plenty of spare data-
processing and communications capacity, ready for the challenge of
regeneration.

Very symbolic, she thought caustically.

She watched herself walking down the main hall with the exchange
officials, most of them male, and most over fifty. So boring, no conversation outside money. Esquiline had dressed her in a white dinner jacket made from a fabric that played clips of old black-and-white
films over its surface.

Superbly unconventional, and formal at the same time. Going to
Esquiline had turned into one of the best decisions she had made in
a long time—if for no other reason than Esquiline's fitting team was
a fantastic new source of gossip, opening up the underbelly of the

social scene. According to them, Lavinia Mayer didn't even need to intervene on her behalf with the Coleman cow. Apparently Jakki Coleman's agent had read her the riot act, effectively neutering her; it turned out he had a major contract with Esquiline to fit out several of his clients. And being thrown off an agent's books for being *difficult* was worse than death in the channel universe. At least if you were dead, cult status repeats boosted your ratings.

Jakki hadn't said a word against her for the last three days.

Julia on the flatscreen cut the ribbon to the trading floor as Charlie Chaplin waddled across her back, twirling his cane. All the jobbers cheered her enthusiastically.

Now they had been fun to talk to at the reception afterward. Most of them were under thirty.

She took another sip of tea as the scene changed back to East England's breakfast studio. The blond twenty-something female presenter in a tight sweater was lounging back on a deep settee.

"That was yesterday's opening ceremony," she gushed warmly. "And to review it, I have our fashion correspondent, Leonard Sharr."

The camera panned back to show the most effeminate man Julia had ever seen, sitting at the other end of the settee, dressed in leather jeans and a purple jacket with half-sleeves, topaz handkerchief hanging flamboyantly out of his breast pocket. She bit back on her giggles.

"Leonard, what did you think of Julia's clothes?"

"I found her choice so very, very appropriate. Tatty old design, showing tatty old films, at a tatty old function. It said simply nothing to me, except perhaps: look what a disaster I am, and I'm too rich to care. Really, this simply will not do for someone of her standing. She could be such a pretty little girl if she just made an effort and wore some nice frocks."

"Arsehole!" Julia completely forgot her cup was still half full. The tea went everywhere.

26

THE FORENSIC TEAM HAD CLEARED away all its polythene sheets and peeled the bar-code tags off the furniture; it had even returned the cacti to the table below the window, but somehow the room wasn't the same. Nicholas stood at the foot of the circular bed, surveying the place that had been home for a few short months. Coming here originally had been the pinnacle of his life. Now it left him totally unmoved. It wasn't that Launde Abbey was full of bad memories; rather, it didn't hold any memories for him at all, good or bad. Even the ghosts had departed—Kitchener, Eleanor . . .

He dropped his maroon shoulder bag at the foot of the bed and stared around in some perplexity. His rock band holoprints were missing. What had the forensic team wanted them for anyway?

He began opening drawers, and of course none of his clothes were where they should be. He settled for dumping everything on the bed to be sorted out later. The uniformed policeman who had driven him up to the Abbey wasn't going to hustle him along. Oakham police couldn't extend enough courtesies right now.

There had been a press conference to announce they were releasing him from custody, that he was in no way implicated in the murder of Edward Kitchener. The reporters had clamored for details; but apart from saying he was glad it was all over, and that he thought the police had done a good job under difficult circumstances, and no he wasn't going to sue for wrongful arrest, he didn't answer any questions. Amanda Paterson and Jon Nevin had stepped in to deflect any awkward shouted queries. And then amazingly the press had left him alone, no intrusion into his private life, no chasing after his parents or Emma, no big-money offers for exclusives. That was due to Julia Evans, he suspected. He was rather pleased he could assume that such underground pressures were being applied. The old Nicholas would have accepted their lack of interest without thought, never wondering about the fast maneuvering and horse-trading that must have gone on deep below the surface of public awareness.

He smiled. The old Nicholas, as if he'd emerged from a chrysalis, born again. But it was true enough. The world was exactly the same, only his perception of it had altered. Matured, rather. What did they call it? *Realpolitik.* And his first encounter with that phenomenon had come two days ago, the morning Vernon Langley had let him out of the cell, telling him he was free to go.

Greg Mandel had arrived at the station, looking grieved and tired, and told him what had actually happened. There was a secrecy order to sign and thumbprint, and it had been made very clear he wasn't to speak to anybody about paradigms or retrospective neurohormones ever again. Officially, MacLennan had let Liam Bursken out of Stocken Hall for the night, bringing him to Launde to murder Kitchener.

Bursken was permanently incommunicado, unable to protest his innocence, perhaps not even wanting to—let the sinners believe the Lord could reach out to them through bars of steel. MacLennan was dead. Suicide, Greg said. And looking at his stony, impassive face, even Nicholas's perpetual inquisitiveness had tacitly retreated.

As the price of being vindicated, adopting that particular masquerade was cheap indeed.

He emptied the last drawerful of socks onto the bed. It was raining quite heavily again, thick clouds darkening the morning sky. Roll on, April, and the start of England's long summer. When he walked over to the window, he could just make out the grubby gray strip of road running through the park.

Nighttime, when the rain had fallen like a biblical deluge. The Jeep crawling down the slope toward the river. The vivid flash he had thought was lightning.

He shuddered and turned away.

The cacti on the copper-topped table hadn't been watered for over a week; the soil in their pots was bone dry. And he never had seen them flower the way Kitchener had told him they would.

He decided to take a couple with him. There had to be something of the old man's that would stay with him, some tangible personal memento. And he doubted he would be welcome to visit Rosette and her baby. Although you never knew. Motherhood might soften her . . .

Nah. No chance.

Grinning, he picked up two of the cacti pots.

Someone knocked quietly on the door.

"Come in." He put the cacti down again, thinking it would be the uniformed policeman.

It was Isabel.

He stared dumbly at her, completely tongue-tied. The old Nicholas wasn't so distant after all.

She was wearing a lavender-colored dress, curly hair held back by a broad black-velvet band. As lovely as always. It was so painful just seeing her. Everything he ever wanted. Unreachable.

"Hello, Nick."

"Er, hello. I was just collecting my things." Nothing had changed; he still couldn't talk to her, say what he wanted. Pathetic!

"Me too. The executors are going to take over the running of the Abbey in a couple of days. Did you know they are going to open it as a sort of ashram for university science students?"

"Yes, I'd heard." He looked down at his socks on the bed.

"I'm sorry I didn't help you with the police." She clenched her hands in front of her, fingers twisting. "We all are, actually. It was so unfair to you. I don't know how I could have ever believed you were involved."

"That's all right."

"Hardly, Nick."

He risked a glance. She was looking out of the window, face composed, dispassionate.

"I did do it, you know," he said. "It was me."

"No. Your hands, but not you."

He considered that. If Isabel, someone so intimately involved with Kitchener, could accept his innocence, then maybe he was blameless after all. "Isabel?" he began.

She parted her lips in a small, knowing smile. "No, Nick, I didn't love him. That was just a part of Launde, the wonder and the craziness. I was swept along like all the others. I wanted to tell you. I was going to tell you the next morning."

He hung his head.

"And what about you?" she asked. "What are you going to do next?"

"Er, I've been offered a research post by Event Horizon, actually.

In Ranasfari's team at Cambridge. I think I detect the hand of Greg Mandel behind that. If Event Horizon is prepared to employ me, then I must be innocent. That's what people will think, anyway."

"Yes. That was nice of him."

"Greg's all right. Once you get around his having a gland."

"You've changed, Nick. You're stronger now. That's good."

Not enough. Not enough. I haven't! "What are you going to do?"

She smiled secretively. "I'm going to get my doctorate. At Cambridge, actually; I've been accepted by a college."

Nicholas turned bright red. He heard Kitchener's delighted, mocking laughter echoing out of . . . somewhere, and took a deep breath. "Isabel, I love you. And I know I'm not much—"

She kissed him softly, silencing him. His arms went around her. They fit just fine.